BLINDED AUTHORITY

BLINDED AUTHORITY

a novel

HOPE YOU ENJOY THE
READ. THANKS FOR THE
FRIENDSHIP.
IN CHRIST,

Chad Boles

Blinded Authority
Published by
Canary Media, LLC
Brookhaven, GA

The characters and events in this book are fictitious. Any similarity to characters, either living or dead, is completely coincidental and not intended by the author.

This work of fiction is not intended as an offer, or a solicitation of an offer, to buy or sell any investment or other specific product. The analysis contained herein does not constitute a personal recommendation or take into account the particular investment objectives, investment strategies, financial situation and needs of any specific recipient. It is based on numerous assumptions. Different assumptions could result in materially different results. I recommend that you obtain financial and/or tax advice as to the implications (including tax) of investing in the manner described or in any of the products mentioned herein. All information and opinions expressed in this document were obtained from sources believed to be reliable and in good faith, but no representation or warranty, expressed or implied, is made as to its accuracy or completeness. Opinions expressed herein may differ from or be contrary to those of other analysts in the municipal bond industry as a result of using different assumptions and/or criteria. At any time, my employer or one of its groups may have a long or short position, or deal as principal or agent, in relevant securities, or provide advisory or other services to the issuer of relevant securities or to a company connected with an issuer. Some investments may not be readily realizable, because the market in the securities is illiquid, and therefore valuing the investment and identifying the risk to which you are exposed may be difficult to quantify. Past performance of an investment is no guarantee for its future performance. Some investments may be subject to sudden and large falls in value.

ISBN 13: 9780692912881

Printed in the United States of America

ISBN: 0692912886

The United States has entered a recession roughly every six years since WWII. The average maturity of a high-yield municipal revenue bond is 25 years, and the average public retirement is 30.

CHAPTER 1

The Gulfstream tires chirped on the tarmac of the Orthus King Airport; call sign OSK. Patrick shook his head in his seat as Bob, the same Bob Drolland that had been twice elected Orthus County Commissioner, awoke from a boozy, opioid-induced coma. Stan, Superintendent of Orthus County Public Schools, and the flight attendant came out of the state room, the darkened glass wall barely containing their mutual attraction, while Patrick wondered if the flight attendant had any idea who Stan was. He imagined Bob, and Stan, had places to go when they disembarked, but he didn't. He'd probably drive up to the McDaniel Salvatore dealership he'd started ten years ago, hand-picked by Salvatore Motors North American president, Bretto Rossi, to open the Florida market. It'd been a long Easter weekend, and the five-hour flight back had felt longer, mainly because Bob vomited during takeoff.

Bob's sense of self-worth had been on display at every gaming table. Patrick knew Stan was disgusted by Bob, so that's probably why Stan had disappeared for the last twenty-four hours of the trip. *And to find some action*, Patrick thought.

Patrick was down, and assumed Stan and Bob were, too, but it didn't matter because they weren't losing their own money; it was Sterling Johnston's money to lose. Patrick had bet on sports in the gaming lounges surrounded by hundreds of TVs, pecking away at his phone to stay connected to his floundering car dealerships.

Keeping the Salvatore Motors North America Finance Department, and Sterling's attorneys, at bay had become a full-time job.

Stan was sprawled backward in the hand-stitched leather chair, exchanging phone numbers with the blonde, another special detail Sterling had added, probably through that asshole, Gene Dodd, Sterling's fixer.

The fifty-year-old scotch in Bob's lap had been in the plane when they'd boarded this morning. His peculiarities were limited to pie, pizza, and scotch. The things Bob had voted for, or done, to get his name on buildings, or property on the beach, baffled even the most strategic political thinker like Patrick.

Patrick's phone rang as they taxied into the hangar with Sterling's name registered on the phone screen. "Hey. We just landed."

"I know. That's why I called. Is Bob there?"

"He's here."

"I hope everyone had a good time."

"Uh huh, you lost a bundle..."

"Please come to my office for a visit before you go home. Jim Pinson's been asking questions that only we could answer. I need to speak with you both."

"Got it. I can ask. Can we wait until Monday to come in? Last night was especially eventful." Patrick laughed. "Stan might finally be a father."

Sterling's anger came through the phone over the whirring jet engines. "Get your asses in my office. I pay for these little junkets so I have complete access to you two."

"Yea, right. We're on the way." He turned to Bob in the seat next to him. "That was Sterling. Pinson is nosing around. He wants to know who you've been talking to."

Bob replied in his usual manner. "Fuck you, Patrick. I didn't tell anybody."

"You guys haven't even told me why I'm here," Stan said.

Patrick stared at Bob. "We've spent too much of Sterling's time and money on this deal. We lose this thing now, Bob, and you're going back to mortgage closings and small claims court."

"Patrick, don't be so sanctimonious. You're the development authority chair because I put you there. I'm going to make this deal happen and no one else."

"I need this, Bob. Sterling wants us in his office as soon as we leave the hangar."

Sterling had convinced Patrick of his vision to see the Bob Drolland, Sr. Interchange ferrying residents and customers to Johnston Limited Lofts, LLC, and Smithson Galleria. Funding approval for the interchange and Smithson Galleria would virtually save Patrick from financial collapse. Two years ago, he'd gained equity exposure in the North Orthus County real estate boom by partnering with Sterling on Johnston Limited Lofts, currently a slum next to a vacant construction site left by a bankrupt car manufacturer. Sterling had brainstormed with him about projects, like a multifamily mixed-use project, or "maybe something bigger," Sterling had said, but for now it was still the slum they'd purchased five years ago. The capital calls to pay the debt payments were draining cash flow from his dealerships, cash flow he needed to keep the car lot full. From his chair position on Progress Orthus, the Orthus County Development Authority, he'd supervised many income-generating benefits for himself and his friends, but Salvatore Motors-North America had plain language about bankruptcies in its dealership contracts, so Johnston Limited Lofts needed to pay off.

"Why are we here, anyway?" Stan asked, as he glanced away from the blonde. "I mean, not that I would turn down Vegas. My other Easter option was Paige's family in Atlanta. Are you two about to ask me to finance Smithson Galleria?"

Patrick glanced at Bob, out of Stan's view, turned back and said, "Flash, Sterling told me to continue inviting you as long as you can join us. Nothing more." Patrick needed him to remain accessible. "He's very thankful for your contribution to the MOTrail."

"MOTrail? What a disaster! I had to pay Mayor Tisdale's interest on the two hundred million last year. That's the last time I buy that bullshit line that the general fund isn't obligated to pay revenue bond debt. Governor Sikes almost fired my ass."

"Yep. You got hijacked on national news," Bob said. "How'd that feel, Dr. Jackson?"

"Shut up before I kick your ass off this plane," Stan barked. "The Orthus County School Teacher's pension fund is a billion short, and I've got to fill the gap, so don't come asking the School Board for any more money."

"You don't have to remind me, Flash," Bob said. "My employees get the same deal as yours. The unions won't budge."

"The unions were guaranteed their pensions long before we got here." Stan said. "By the way, I've three times the problems as you, because I got three times the budget, fat boy."

Bob laughed. "Not when you include all the debt financing I get from Patrick. When's the last time you built an airport, or a hospital, or a multi-family high rise in your neighborhood? I get free drinks in every downtown district in Orthus County. You built a trail for hippies, and what'd you get for it? One of Patrick's cars and an office. You're a joke."

The airtight jet door released with a hiss. Patrick moved his feet when Stan bounded for the open door and glided down the stairs with the agility of a wide receiver and the locker-room nickname to match. He strolled out of the hangar to the white Salvatore Motors Lux-edition sedan he'd given Stan at the request of City of Orlando Mayor, Brian Tisdale, who'd built Stan's new offices in the

Orlando Downtown District, in return for financing the MOTrail for Onward Orlando, the Orlando Development Authority.

"Thank God he's gone," Bob said. "We shouldn't even be talking to him. We can complete this thing without Stan Jackson, or his school board budget."

"I'm not so sure. Project Grand Slam is going to be huge. That's what Sterling wants to talk to us about. The governor's auditors are circling around your office, and Sterling wants Stan involved. I'm not sure why, but Sterling calls the shots," he said in an effort to keep Bob's ego in check.

"Patrick, I call the shots. Don't be so naïve. Why do you think Sterling wants Stan involved? It's not because of his big budget." Bob took a little longer getting out of the reclining jet chair; the last three days, and years, were beginning to take their toll. "I feel like shit."

"You look even worse. Are you ok?" Patrick said.

"I'll be alright, asshole. Just hand me that bottle of scotch for my roadie. I'm taking the whole thing since we have to walk over to Sterling's. I hope this doesn't take long. I need some sleep."

On the walk over, Patrick thought about the real estate legacy he'd spawned for generations from his own personal financing vessel.

CHAPTER 2

Sterling leased office space in OSK, having signed the lease documents after his first encounter with professional baseball team owner, Warren Sanderson, on the assumption they could benefit one another. OSK was a hub for private planes at a staggering cost to Orthus County, named for the county and for the largest citrus grower to leave for warmer weather, King Citrus. Landing at a small, private airport also eliminated the pedestrian requirement of traveling on MOTrax, Metro Orlando Transportation Authority's first commuter train. The suburban MOTrax stations on the North Line were blank canvases for the mass-transit experiments he'd trademarked as transit-oriented-developments, or TODs. The half-empty parking lots were underutilized because mass-transit ridership was shrinking, but only until Sterling's mini-cities could be constructed, at which point MOTrax would be reborn. His first TOD, Orlando Downtown District, was only the beginning and served as the central hub of a spoke-and-wheel mass-transit system with stations surrounded by TODs, encircled by a wheel-shaped metropolitan nature trail.

He thanked himself again for giving Bob and Patrick the idea to build OSK, because he could use it as his own private airport, avoid the public cattle call at Orlando International, and have office space next to his jet—although the jet fuel operator, Touch

Down, LLC, charged the highest prices in the southeast for fuel, but it was a boiler-plate kickback scheme Gene, his own personal Renfield, had set up dozens of times, and Bob and Patrick were simply plugged into place. Gene could get anything done with contract concessions and cash in a bag.

The only other drawback was that Esmeralda "Ezzy" King, the last remaining King Citrus heir in Orthus County, parked her jet at King Farms. He never got to see her at the airport, because she built her own, thanks to Bob and Patrick's airport services monopoly, but it was only a minor nuisance, as she didn't seem all that enthusiastic about his plans anyway. Having met her only a few times, Sterling was conscious of her prominence as Thomas, or more affectionately, "Papa T Sam" King's, only granddaughter. It was also immediately clear she was no fool.

While he waited on that imbecile Patrick and that walking walrus, Bob, he caught the refraction of light made by Gene's suit pants turning in a circle underneath the baseball stadium mock-up filling the floor-to-ceiling hangar space meant for an aircraft. He'd had his graphics teams work for weeks on a scaled-down version of a new stadium he'd been commissioned to design. Gene was currently standing underneath the object shaped like two stacked donuts, about where a clear glass turret opened to an inside view from the pitcher's mound. The lowest rim was elevated at head level with spaces to walk through so interested investors could get a three-dimensional perspective. Sterling watched his legs as he walked in a zigzag path to the far side of the hangar and then paused, probably to view the dugout and the scale models of restaurants crowded with baseball fans lining the perimeter of the imitation ballpark. Gene came back around from the back with his hands uncomfortably in his pockets, climbed up onto a stool next to the large studio table, hunched over, and began twiddling his thumbs.

As Sterling sat there trying not to wonder what made Gene tick, he thought about how the travel back and forth between the Johnston Limited corporate headquarters in San Francisco and Orlando, with stops in Dallas and New York, had become an almost monthly event for him, brought on by new public construction awash in loans from development authorities since the financial crisis. So many of his concepts were getting funded, and Metro Orlando was no different. Their traffic congestion, like every other city in America, was ripe for his ideas, but Sterling needed government partners to build the massive structures that his private enterprise partners wouldn't risk, and if they didn't get in his office in the next five minutes, he'd send Gene up the stairs of the jet to pull them out.

For Sterling, feeding the addictions of elected officials and small-time real estate players was a reality from Portland to Miami. All of them used their ability to loan money to extract perks and inside real estate information only he could provide, and he was going to use Progress Orthus to build the gold standard for skyscrapers and sports stadiums that were connected by mass transit systems. He wanted to connect communities from North Orthus County to South Orange County with mixed-used developments, not residential neighborhoods; sports mega complexes, not stand-alone event centers. He used pawns like Bob and Patrick as resources, like concrete and steel. "Do you think Jim Pinson knows anything?"

Gene stopped twiddling his thumbs and looked up. "No, that schmuck couldn't write a comic strip with someone feeding him jokes, much less decipher what we're up to. This deal's got more trap doors and fun-house mirrors than a Puerto Rican development bank. Enzo will get it done; don't worry about it."

Sterling's people met with Enzo Ruiz, Dunham Schauble's rainmaking municipal-bond banker, for lots of projects, which gave him some assurance it was just a coincidence Jim Pinson, editor of the *Orthus County Post,* had appeared at one of their meetings, but Sterling needed to plug any leaks pronto. Enzo weaved municipal financing webs from tax-allocation districts, enterprise zones, special-tax districts, bond-for-title-sale leasebacks, phantom bonds, and blind pools with a black widow's touch, which is why he'd introduced him to every metropolitan politician who wanted a building or a downtown district with their name on it. Offering them phantom bonds, the pea soup du jour of off-balance-sheet debt was just one more way Enzo had yielded oceans of dumb money that, yoked with his architectural genius, would cultivate his worldview. His Mediterranean good looks were a bonus of the financial connection. Sterling looked up when Patrick knocked on the door and opened it slightly. He yelled across the studio tables to the far hangar wall, made to close in a giant office space, "Come in, come in, hurry up."

Gene looked back down, started twiddling his thumbs again and said, "Speak of the devil."

Sterling picked his drawing pen up and put his glasses on, doodling while he waited on them. Patrick was first through the door, walking toward Sterling's large draft table in the center of the space large enough to hold a plane.

"Good afternoon, Sterling. Sunday back from Vegas is a rough day for a meeting," Patrick said.

Sterling stopped doodling and yanked his glasses off. "Patrick, what took you so long to get over here? Hurry up, Bob." He couldn't help but frown at Bob's untucked, rumpled button-down that fit like a tent as he slumped in behind Patrick, obviously still groggy from the trip. The crystal glass in his hand certainly came from Sterling's plane, filled with booze he'd bought to fill it.

"Why're we here?" Bob asked. "Molly and my kids haven't seen me since Wednesday. If they get back from St. Pete Beach and I'm not at home, you assholes will be the least of my problems."

Sterling's jaw muscles grimaced as he clinched his folded hands on the drafting table. He'd heard plenty about Bob's marriage of convenience. "Thank you for joining me, gentlemen. I have some concerns. Enzo Ruiz and my people were meeting over the weekend at First and Last. He was providing the outline for a blind pool of bond proceeds for both Smithson Galleria and our new project, when out of the shadows appears Jim Pinson." Sterling sat upright with his hands face down on the table. "He interjected himself into the conversation and asked if there was anything he needed to know. My people, of course, dismissed him for general rudeness. Apparently, as Mr. Pinson was walking away, he winked at my staff and asked, 'How much longer till the Coyotes bond matures?' Do either of you have any idea what he knows? And if you don't, you better find out."

Sterling heard Bob's stomach churning, and was glad his message was sinking in.

Patrick's voice quivered. "Look, Sterling."

Sterling interrupted him before he had a chance to make any ground, or whatever he was trying to do. "Mr. Johnston to you, McDaniel. Politicians, like you two, ruin too much with your inability to control what comes out of your mouth."

"Look, Mr. Johnston. Neither Bob nor I have told anyone. We have as much to lose as you."

Sterling pointed at Patrick across the wide table. "You've no idea what you're talking about. This project is going to be the capstone of my career. I'm going to prove to the world cities can be designed for the masses. Sports arenas will be multi-faceted facilities that create centers of populations. Cars are wasteful remnants of America's past, and if we don't plan now, traffic congestion will form the calendars of our lives. Smog will ruin the peace of our long-term vision. Humanity must migrate to frequent and scheduled mass transit. You? You'll lose a real estate deal that wouldn't afford the plane you rode in to Las Vegas, you ungrateful bastard. Do you have anything to add, Commissioner Drolland?"

Sterling watched as Bob put the dripping glass of half-melted ice and scotch on the drafting table, soiling a newly minted rendering for another project, shoved both his hands in his pockets, and seemed close to vomiting. "Look. Sterling," Bob said, and then paused and grabbed his stomach. "When, and if, I tell anyone about this deal, you'll be the second to know. The first will be my constituents. You want to build in my territory? You have to go through me. I'm the gatekeeper. I decide who gets what and when. If that prick, Jim Pinson, has any idea what's going on, it either came from your people or you. I don't know what you're up to, but I'm going home."

"Well, make sure it doesn't happen again."

"Thanks for the drinks," Bob said unceremoniously, and picked his glass up off the table, and took a swig. "Your plane's too big, but make sure you fill it up with gas before you leave."

Before they could get to the door, Sterling waved his hand and said, "You're both dismissed." He watched as Bob flipped him the bird on the way out, and told himself it was the cost of doing business.

Pinson knows something, Bob thought as Patrick headed away with a wave. *He always knows something.* Bob Drolland Jr. had mastered the craft of politics by watching his father. Although he had finished law school at the University of Florida in the middle of the pack, his name was Drolland, and that small inheritance paid handsomely in the political circles and bars of Orlando. The need to survive his father's legacy was his sole driver. He knew instinctively when developers were searching, and how to extract the most graft, but servant leadership had been his father's template for success: *"If you want to succeed in politics, you must always think of the voter first. It's not an easy job, and we don't get paid much. The underserved have no voice, but we can give them one. You and I have the ability to speak on behalf of the voiceless. That's servant-based leadership, Bob. That's loving one another."*

Although he'd gleaned something from his father's experience, Bob Sr. didn't have a bankrupt automobile manufacturer leaving a 150-acre hole next to the Smithson MOTrax station, and an even larger hole in the Orthus County budget, but he did watch his father endure King Citrus's exodus from Orthus County, and that gave him some perspective. Bob's reward for his service was going to be the kind of power only gained by financing nationally recognized large projects, projects his father never dreamed of. If only he could garner the kind of respect, and money, that came from being the hometown of a major American sports franchise, his service would finally be appreciated. The kind of respect and appreciation Mayor Tisdale was getting because he had two: the Orlando Ospreys and the Orlando Coyotes.

He threw his suitcase in the trunk of his SUV, pulled out the bottle of scotch, and refilled the glass: neat. He walked toward the driver's seat, when a miscalculated step bumped him into the corner of the truck before he climbed in and turned the key, sweat forming on his forehead from the early April heat. He'd managed to ignore the stock market dip lasting longer than anyone had forecasted, because a guaranteed government pension provided his security. Dropping property values, the sheriff's department's raise requests, interest payments on four billion in debt, and the county's payroll frayed the edges of his infrastructure, but his summer plans included more time at his St. Pete Beach condo and Vegas. Even though Governor Sikes's financial auditors had become a daily intrusion on his operating style, he couldn't get them to understand the revenue from his deals would support his dynasty for another fifteen years until the new Orthus County tax revenues from the projects he'd built could pull them out of the ditch, but then again, if he made it to the end of the year, it wouldn't matter anyway.

He drank from the crystal glass, and after a long tip, he settled the glass in the console, wincing when his throat contracted, and then wiped his palm across his forehead. Waiting on his Salvatore SUV to cool, he pressed the button on his steering wheel: "Call Molly." His wife's voice mail answered. "Hey Mol, just landed. As usual, the golf took a lot out of me. Patrick is a hammer off the tee box. I'm headed home to relieve the nanny. See you tomorrow if you get home after I've gone to bed. I'll order pizza when I get home." He hung up the phone, drove through the industrial buildings lining the streets like cubes in a corporate office, stopping at every intersection with a blinking traffic light. "When are they going to fix these street lights?" he muttered.

Bob knew Molly didn't buy the whole economic development routine, and her late arrival after he'd gone to bed would be another unspoken understanding of the empty agreement between them. Hopefully, she'd remember to stop and get the kids something to eat before she got home, because he could never keep himself from eating everything he ordered.

CHAPTER 3

Stan weaved his way through the Monday morning cars backed up in the parking deck of the Orlando Downtown District. Traffic in the streets was no better. The MOTrax train from Orlando International Airport sped north to the central hub about the time Stan reached the lobby, passing First Chance Last Chance, the building's restaurant bar. He saw Kate Brown, MOTrax Director, in the coffee shop as they headed upstairs to work. ODD was home to the new MOTrax executive offices, and the geographical center of the North and South Lines. Onward Orlando, the Orlando Development Authority, provided office space for the Orthus County School Board in return for Stan's help financing the MOTrail. In a move Stan had encouraged, MOTrax administration had moved its operations there as well.

The sudden, rippling boom deafened his senses. As he lowered his hands from his ears, plumes of dust bellowed from the MOTrax station entrance on the other side of the lobby. Sheets of falling debris landed on a mangled train lying on its side, exposed by the mass-transit station's wall of windows. People were screaming and running from the blast. Stan plodded around them and up the escalators to the train platform. Plain as day to him, the MOTrax train had crashed into the safety barriers protecting the riders standing on the arrival–departure platform. Sirens could be heard blaring in the distance, alerting him first responders were coming his way. The chaos worsened as people in shock emerged from the dust billowing through the cavernous boarding station.

He saw Kate trying to maneuver past the vagrant campsite at the MOTrax entrance, and frantically texting on her phone. Beggars, who'd made their daytime home at the central hub, scattered when the Orthus sheriff's deputies dismounted from their assault wagons. He'd suppressed the ironic comedy that MOTrax police never had the same effect on the vagrants.

The rudderless silence in the aftermath of the crash morphed into screams of pain coming as suddenly as if from a newborn as firefighters and medical technicians began pulling into the parking lot.

"Damn it. This can't be happening again," Kate whispered to herself as she finally made it to the top of the stairs where Stan was standing, surveying the wreckage surrounded by people using their suit jackets and torn shirtsleeves as makeshift bandages while trying to talk on their phones. Her ritualistic crisis management, in the face of mounting public inspection of her department's losses, was a dirty but necessary part of the job description. The fleeing mass of flesh bumped her to one side as she worked her way up the stair railing to Stan, her only immediate concern being that her text message went through.

Stan began to help people out of the train, while sheriff's deputies pulled crumpled guard rails off injured passengers, some who still weren't moving. One of the lifeless bodies had a pool of blood forming around his head as the officers left him for dead after performing triage, and moved on to the crying bodies lying around him. Bent support columns were perilously close to collapsing, when a suitcase-sized concrete block came crashing down next to him. "Stay over there, Kate. Don't come any closer. You should leave. It's too dangerous."

"Do you think it was a terrorist?"

"Don't say that. We don't know anything yet." People were running from the wrecked train, some of them stopping long enough to help each other off the platform. The Orthus County deputies were vacating people out of the MOTrax station and into the ODD lobby.

Kate returned back down the escalator and ran into Sheriff Bolek.

"Kate, are you ok? Do you know what happened?"

"I don't know, Sheriff. We'll provide you with all the camera recordings to seek out the perpetrator."

"The perpetrator? Do you think this was intentional?"

She shook the dust out of her hair to dodge a direct answer, and straightened her dress. "We can't rule anything out. Terrorists identify mass transit as soft targets."

"OK. I'll have my PIs get in touch with you. I've got to get up there. Jim Pinson with the *Orthus County Post* is out at the main entrance."

"Be careful and thanks for getting here so fast." *We need to figure this out on our own time,* she thought.

Sheriff Bolek yelled to her as she descended the stairs: "If MOTrax security was squared away, maybe MOTrax wouldn't be a soft target."

A man with a hand mounted camera was blocking her path as she headed to the parking deck.

"Miss Brown, Jim Pinson, *Orthus County Post.* Do you have any comment?" People were streaming by. Helicopters were flying overhead.

"MOTrax will begin an investigation immediately into possible criminal activity. Our first priority is getting people to safety."

"Is there any possibility the accident was caused by the driver or other causes?"

"We can't rule out any possibilities."

"What about claims of maintenance concerns and old tracks?"

"We have thorough and regular maintenance inspections, Mr. Pinson. To suggest this accident resulted from safety lapses is absurd. We're finished here." She turned, walked into the shell-shocked morning, diving back into her text messages to discover not only was her text received, but her request was also completed.

"Will you continue your charge toward real estate developments instead of your ongoing safety responsibilities?"

She was far enough away to ignore his question, and too relieved to care. After a couple of seconds, she turned back to see him racing up the escalators with the MOTrax first responders finally arriving to assist.

Jim reached the bottom of the escalators and saw Stan heading back down from the top. "Any comment, Dr. Jackson?" Stan kept hopping down the escalator, and disappeared behind him.

Sheriff Bolek met Jim at the top of the stairs. "Hey, Jim. Just in time as always."

"Hey, what happened?"

"Who knows? Follow me to the platform. I need to walk and talk."

A passenger groping for normalcy next to Jim turned to them, her business suit and face covered in dust. One of her sleeves was ripped. She was bleeding and seemed to be in shock. "We were flying up to the platform," she said, a certain numbness in her voice. "But we never braked. I don't know what happened."

"Did you hear any explosions?" Jim shouted above the commotion.

"Maybe, I don't know." She stood to the side and tried to brush the dust out of her hair. "We just came crashing into the barrier." The ODD lobby was filling up with the walking wounded.

Jim moved his camera from the path of an out-of-breath police officer lumbering toward Bill. His tag read Officer Bozeman, "Sheriff, we have a situation. There's a MOTrax engineer retrieving the black box. Should we assist?"

"Box? I thought there were two?" Bill turned to the lady. "Ma'am, please give your statement to Officer Bozeman." Jim could tell Bill was in field-general mode as he began to jog to the front of the mangled train. "This is where we split, Jim," Bill shouted back. "I need to assist the effort. Go get as much video as you can."

"You bet, Sheriff. I'll see you next week at the city council meeting."

"Not if I see you first."

Stan's cell phone rang as he stepped into his office. It was Paige. Stan answered. "Hey."

"Hey. Are you OK? I just heard."

"Yeah, babe. It was awful." Dust was still flying around the lobby and the parking deck. "Passengers are bleeding and screaming on the platform. The lobby is mobbed with police and paramedics."

"Please be careful. I know things haven't been good between us, but I love you."

"I know. I was almost hit with debris. When I saw what had happened, I thought about you. I got out of there."

"Good. Stay out of there."

"I need to go. I need to get my people out of the building until this thing is over."

"OK. See you tonight. Be careful."

When he arrived at his desk, his cell phone pinged. It was a text with a Las Vegas area code. Hey Flash. I miss you. I didn't know you were famous. After you left yesterday, one of my friends told me you played football.

He replied. Lose this number. What happens in Vegas stays in Vegas.

That's not nice, Stanley Jackson. I miss every part of you.

This wasn't Stan's first time. *If you just don't encourage them, they'll lose interest,* he thought.

CHAPTER 4

Paige Olmsted had been an energetic law student at Vanderbilt University Law School. She'd attended Auburn University on a volleyball scholarship and breezed through as an accounting undergraduate. She'd grown up in an upper-middle-class home in South Atlanta, but battled her emotions as a teenager because her hands and feet had outgrown her tall, slim body. She was on the math team because she loved the exacting accuracy, and the debate team because her father, Judge James Olmsted, required it. She'd complain in response to Judge's encouragement to pursue a law degree, "There are no compassionate pleas or negotiation with numbers. They're exact or they're wrong." He would lovingly reply, "What interest does our world have without compassionate pleas?" The routine became an instant family tradition and reminder of their love for one another.

In high school, she thought his nickname was corny. As college loneliness set in, "Judge" became a bright buoy in the darkness. Paige and her sister, Judith, loved James Olmsted even more than most daughters, because he took the place of two parents in every way that he could to support them. Paige's mother died of breast cancer when she and Judi were teenagers. Paige sought the constant approval of her parents, but Judi was just the opposite. They both remembered Judge at every one of life's special moments they shared as a family.

The debate team had been hard work, but she knew, like in volleyball, anything worth doing required practice. And no one could out-practice Paige Olmsted. She didn't date much in high school, because her size intimidated most smart kids and her brains intimidated most athletes. Her success on the volleyball court generated scholarship offers all over the Southeast, but she chose Auburn for its familiar feel. It was right where she belonged. She told her dad on their first visit, "Judge, this is it. I don't need to look anywhere else. Do you like it?" Judge reassured her, "If my princess likes it, I like it." She had been making Judge proud for years. This decision was no different.

Paige's inherited need to serve others, to be liked, to be loved inspired her law school desires. She applied to Ivy League law schools after nailing the LSAT, but hoped openly to legacy at Judge's alma mater, Vanderbilt School of Law. It was the next right decision. The gangly teenager had become a Milan runway replica but couldn't lose the feelings of emotional distance she'd felt as a teenager. Until she met Stanley "Flash" Jackson.

She leaned into service work as a first-year law student at Vanderbilt, and Paint Your Heart Out workdays were her favorite. Her short sleeves floating around her curved shoulders with every paint stroke, she bent down to fill her roller, and noticed a smile as electric as the Nashville nightlife. "Hey girl, I'm Flash. You're beautiful."

"I know who you are. My name isn't 'girl' and you've said that to every nursing school volunteer here. What makes you so special?"

"You know anyone else that scored on that field over there?"

"No, but I'm sure you do."

"I didn't mean it that way. Hey, yo', where you going? Look, I haven't said one thing to these nursing school, hell, whoever. I've been here keeping my nose clean painting houses for foreign students. Just like you."

"Was it court ordered?" She'd heard that one since she was a kid, when Judge would say it to Judi if she'd ever helped around the house.

Smiling, he wagged his finger at her and said, "That's a good one, girl, but, no, I like seeing the kids." As her heart melted, a young elementary-school-age boy came running around the corner yelling for him. "Flash Jackson is here, Flash Jackson is here."

Flash excelled in Nashville for the Vanderbilt Commodores in the bottom of the SEC. He begged coaches for playing time, caught anything high over the middle, and was the main receiver when the Commodores needed inches. Off the field, his moves attracted every co-ed on campus.

Paige began to love Stan, while she finished law school and he stepped to the next level. By her second year, her orated pleas had mesmerized her law class and earned her the top spot in the summer intern slots. When she first took Stan home to meet Judge, the introduction was awkward. There were two men, Paige, and no soothing motherly influence.

"Hello, Stanley. Are you ok?"

"Yes, Judge. Is it ok if I call you Judge? Or Judge Olmstead?"

"You can call me James. That's what my friends call me."

"No, it's not, Daddy. Everyone calls you Judge. You can call him James, Stan."

"Judge is fine. Just come on in."

The awkwardness slowly eased as Paige broke the ice by forcing their bond, instigating conversations about football, cooking food for them, and prompting Judge to tell golf stories that blossomed into Stan's introduction to the game. From the way Judge was laughing when they returned that afternoon, she surmised he'd enjoyed beating the SEC's leading wide receiver in front of his local foursome.

Stan walked back in from a shower in the shirt and pants she'd bought him before their visit, looking as adorable as they did on the mannequin, when her phone rang. It was Judi calling from Athens. Paige took the call and stepped out onto the porch, leaving Judge and Stan in the kitchen. The Judge's spaghetti was the family favorite whenever the girls brought new boyfriends home. Judge wanted them to see what manhood looked like. Paige could hear her father giving Stan the third degree, as she half-engaged in her conversation with Judi.

"How long have you two been going out, Flash?"

"Since we met at the volunteer day last fall."

"What's next after Vanderbilt?"

"I had a pretty good senior year. Do you watch SEC Football?"

"Who doesn't? Please don't think I ignore the on- and off-field antics of my first daughter's boyfriend whom she can't stop talking about. You didn't make it to Atlanta for the SEC Championship, though. Correct?"

"Well, no, but we did a whole lot better than South Carolina and Florida care to remember. Those games were good for me. I got some agents interested. I went to the professional football tryouts and did good."

"Did well, son. Did well."

"My performance got check marks with a few teams. My hometown team, the Ospreys, is interested, too. There aren't many wideouts in this year's draft, so I got a shot."

Judge turned the marinara off and poured the pot of boiling noodles into the colander in the sink. "Look, Stan. I know you have good prospects in football. I also know people at the law school in Vanderbilt. And they see you. I don't want to come on too strong.

Paige warned me, but let me be clear. Paige is my oldest daughter and most like her mother. She is gifted and strong, but do not misunderstand me. She is fragile. If you hurt her, it will hurt me. From all Paige tells me, you're good to her. Don't betray that loyalty she so rarely gives."

She'd heard enough to know Judge had given him more of an interview than he deserved, and walked back in.

Judge calmly averted his eyes back to the spaghetti, preparing their plates for dinner in the family dining room. They ate and then finished the evening watching basketball on television. The weekend ended uneventfully.

Stan and Paige continued to date through the winter. Stan's fearless style caught the eye of the Orlando Ospreys' coaching staff. He had flare and was durable. Check, check. The coaches thought that if he was willing to work hard for cheap, there was no risk. So they took a chance on him as their seventh-round pick.

Narrowing her intern applications to Orlando meant she would compete with a different crop of interns from the University of Florida and FSU. She beat out the best and brightest, and even some of the politically connected not-so-brightest. She clerked for the Orlando District Supreme Court, and Bob Drolland did not. The Orlando Supreme Court judge appreciated Bob Jr.'s pedigree but could not afford to miss the grooming of young Paige. She had a future. It was a quick decision. The Florida State Attorney's Office hired her the day after graduation.

Stan married Paige in the First Baptist Church of her childhood. The chapel was filled with their Nashville friends, as well as politicians and pro-football players. It was the event of a lifetime for the Olmstead family and Judge's local church friends. They were the perfect couple. The traditional wedding was only slightly marred by vague rumors of bachelor party shenanigans. One of Judi's high school boyfriends revealed to her, "I don't know what happened, but

I heard it was a professional shoe show. If you know what I mean?" Stan shifted any suspicion to his Osprey team mates and high school friends' activities.

Separated from family and friends, she felt them drifting in the early years, brought on by her intermittent self-doubt and Stan's occasional distance. He was finishing his degree, mostly online, but then he'd disappear to Nashville for a week or two for on-campus study to complete his doctoral thesis in early childhood education. Paige's mind-numbing ride to the top of the State Attorney's Office was a substitute for marital bliss. She had won several high-profile cases with national implications and the press to go with it. She and Stan both could sense the political handlers around her. Judgeships didn't interest her. Higher office seemed more competitive.

Sheriff Bill Bolek's Orthus County Sheriff's Department was devoted to her honest and fair-handed style. Paige reminded them at every step that she was someone they could entrust with their futures, with their careers.

Stan's pro-football career was like that of so many others. He dedicated his life to the Ospreys and made it into the starting line-up. If his star continued to shine, his next contract would set his family up for life. Then tragedy struck. Playing for all the marbles in a loser-go-home playoff game, "Flash" cut across the middle in heavy traffic. He paid the price. The collision went viral. Stanley Jackson was carted off the field with a career-ending shoulder injury. The last year of his contract with the Ospreys was his last year of football.

But that was just the beginning of his next story. His love for inner-city kids fueled him through the doctoral program at Peabody College. Fortunately for Stan, his passion for helping these kids coincided with the Orthus County School Board retirement-system scandal. The Orthus County School Board ceased funding the teacher retirement system during the last recession. The CFO of the pension board claimed it was only temporary. Years later, re-starting the contributions was still only a promise.

Inspiration and over-confidence were part of Stan's DNA. He couldn't persuade Orlando and Orthus County leaders to give him the top spot, but they needed his attributes. The Orthus County school system needed a good-news jolt. His celebrity persona coupled with hometown appeal came at the right time and the right place. Stan was selected as deputy superintendent.

His supporting role lasted only a few years while he got noticed doubling Orthus County School Board's fundraising efforts. He supported and managed the construction of a new high school and two middle schools in inner-city Orlando. He was a shining star on the rise. Being married to Paige Olmstead Jackson was a big plus, having provided him with a walking library of financial mechanics and political savvy.

He'd worked around the edges, kept his nose clean, and then he'd hit another lucky streak. After the retirement-system scandal settled, Stan's boss was implicated in a purchasing-card discrepancy—a petty, but common, infraction. Stan swooped in and preached a narrative of stability and legacy to the political leadership, and discovered they were in no mood for another scandal either. Stan quietly relayed his relationship with local union boss, Darrell Cross, to the decision makers, and lo and behold, Orthus County School Board Superintendent Dr. Stanley Jackson got his next and second call off the bench.

CHAPTER 5

Ezzy King was one of Progress Orthus's board members. Patrick McDaniel, board chairman, was another. King Citrus had the first irrigated groves in central Florida. Early irrigation technology locked in decades of profits. Pesticide treatments allowed the company to ship farther than the limited competition, and soon the operation grew from a small family farm to a nationwide organization branded in every grocery store. In fact, King Citrus grew faster than available capital in local banks. It bridged the shortfall by funding and operating banks throughout Orthus County's small cities. Controlling the boards of the bank ensured free-flowing capital.

Her raven hair, now dusted with shades of grey, embodied a Seminole princess as fierce and beautiful as her mother. T Sam's two sons, Jr. and Ezzy's father, Jep, ran the operations. She'd loved the people of King Citrus and they loved her. Ezzy learned the land business on the job. Jep's mechanic, Matt Pinson, had given her the nickname Ezzy working on orange pickers in her early summers. The Pinsons were her second family.

The family's realization that operations should move south coincided with Ezzy's post-graduate studies at Parsons in New York. It was abundantly clear from her freshman year that design was not her forte, but her shape and unique features were sought after by her fashion idols. Magazine covers framed her beauty, but she was most comfortable leading. New York's highest fashion couture wanted Ezzy before she graduated because her natural instincts were uncommon and hard to teach to the uninspired. She could bolster retailer acquisition, manage product launches, and be the face of the next generation. Bilger and Freese made the clothes she adored and offered the most responsibility. She would settle for nothing less than the best placement, most coverage, and highest ad expenditures for her lines.

She celebrated her new fashion buyer's apprenticeship by flying home for a weekend to witness two Thoroughbred mares giving birth. The new stables, experimental farms, and groves-turned-pasture awaited her arrival. King Farms sold land to support King Citrus R&D and put undeveloped land in conservation easements.

Ezzy had turned heads in her apprentice years by street brawling her way through the Fashion District. She made the final list of new partner candidates at Bilger and Freese, and they were making the final announcement in two weeks, when Jep called her one Saturday morning ten years ago.

"Morning, Daddy." She yawned. "What's got you up so early?"

"Morning, Ezzy. The day I sleep in till seven thirty is the day I quit riding tractors and picking oranges."

Ezzy laughed. She hadn't slept late in years. Last night was one of those howl-at-the-moon nights she used to enjoy out in the groves, except she'd been howling from a Manhattan skyscraper until about five hours ago. "Daddy, you'll never grow old. Is everything ok?"

"Oh yea, sure. I'm calling you about a family matter. The family got together last Saturday and had a meeting."

"Uh oh?"

"We've got all this land all over central Florida. Headquarters are way down in Fort Myers. All the groves are in the glades now."

"Yea, Daddy. I know."

"We miss you something crazy, Ezzy. King Farms has become too much for any of us to handle. We've got our hands full with all these new product lines. Sam wants to take us public. Your performance in New York got us thinking. We'd like to offer you the trusteeship of King Farms."

"Oh, Daddy, I don't know what to say."

"Really. You'd be the general partner. We'd be silent partners to meet certain legal obligations, but it would be your show. We'd give you advice, but we need you. We know you're making a home in New York. We always knew you'd do great wherever you went. Everything you touch is a success. Is King Farms something you'd come home for?"

Ezzy felt her cheeks cool with a rolling tear. "Of course, Daddy. I don't even have to think about it." She lied. Manhattan had become her home. Her fashion career was everything she'd ever dreamed. She would've been the youngest partner in Bilger and Freese's history. "I love Manhattan, but I'm just playing fashion. I can't design. They love me because I get their purses on shelves. They want me back on the runway anyway. That'll never do. Skinny models hopscotching across the globe? They should try tossing hay."

He laughed and said, "So you'll do it?"

Ezzy could hear the relief in his voice, which only made her tears flow faster. "Of course, I'll do it, Daddy."

Within Ezzy's first ten years, King Farms had become more than anyone could have imagined. Her first act was to file for a state charter school. After a year of politics with the Orthus County School Board and the teacher's union, King Christian Academy was opened. Every child of every King Citrus employee that stayed in Central Florida was accepted.

Ezzy represented the family in every way historical dynasties demanded. She was wealthy, a shrewd negotiator, and trustee of the largest tracts of land south of the Florida-Georgia line. Agricultural and equestrian operations had been her life-long experience. For fun, she would take the world's wealthiest suitors on bareback rides through gin-clear rivers and palmetto swamps. Her involvement with downtown district development and county industrial authorities provided a different challenge. The financial mechanics were repeating loops of liability indemnification. She knew from her upbringing that when something is bought, a bank usually provides financing. She learned quickly: the municipalities were acting as the bank.

If the little cities wanted a downtown district, they should buy King Bank buildings. If a county needed an airport or a hospital, they should be built on an old King Citrus grove. If Orthus County wanted a mass-transit system, it should naturally buy King Citrus distribution hubs along the railroad line. King Farm's role was to maintain racehorses, research and development, and political campaigns so King Citrus could fund OJ, frozen snacks, and vegetables operations.

CHAPTER 6

The Orthus County administrative offices were low slung with red brick and black glass. Five stories rambled around one corner with a diagonal back edge against a park. Ezzy dismounted from her four-wheel drive. Her feet barely touched the running board as her boots landed on the pavement. Big sunglasses hid her diamond-blue eyes. She walked with an early summer stride, dressed in the latest European outback wear. Confidence comes easy if you're the second-largest landowner in Orthus County and sit on the board of the first. Bob Drolland pulled up to the complex as she headed toward the building. She timed her arrival at his car to give them a long walk for a private discussion before the commission meeting.

"Hello, Bob. It's hot as seven hells out here, don't y'think?"

Bob took a labored breath. "May and already ninety. I've got to lose some weight. This traffic is awful." Rush-hour cars were gridlocked on the internal city streets.

Ezzy had learned to suppress sympathy for Bob. He complained about his own solvable problems every time they met. "Are you going to rezone the MOTrax parking lots, Bob?"

"You know we are. We've been talking about it for three months, but you're too busy to come to the meetings." He wiped the sweat off his forehead.

"I'd have to go to two meetings a week to keep up with your development agenda. Will you fund new park improvements for Sterling's new mass-transit experiment?" Cars were leaving the parking lot for home. One was pulling out of a space in front of them.

He hitched to one side and leaned on the trunk of a parked car. "We can consider that. Did you create proposals?"

Ezzy detected his sense of phony interest, not quite the authenticity to which she'd become accustomed, and looked at him in disbelief. "I sent you three along with the name of the park architect. Did you read any of them?" She knew Bob and Patrick's publicly financed projects were normally negotiated in the privacy of uninterested voters and silent board members, but she was too busy to stay as constantly engaged as they were. Ezzy had been the first Progress Orthus appointee to show any opposition over the last several months, and she'd begun to feel the cold shoulder of isolation. To get Bob and Patrick to understand her reasoned alternatives would require the effort of a second job, or maybe it was hopeless in the face of their bold, unrelenting real estate vision. She'd seen Bob reward citizen courage while at the podium explaining their grievance with his baffled ignorance, and now she was hearing it, too.

"My designs are complete, but I can put your designs on the agenda for fall."

Ezzy had had enough. "Maybe you'll remember who signs your campaign checks before we get in that room." Blackbirds lifted off a live oak into the afternoon skyline. "Improving the parks I gave the county is the right thing to do. If MOTrax needs you to rezone the land for high-density apartments, maybe they could pay for park improvements, too. And by improvements, I don't mean new stripes in the parking lots."

Bob rolled his lean from one hip to the other, enjoying the rest. "You gave us those parks. They're ours now. Where am I supposed to find money for park improvements? MOTrax isn't going to pay for that."

"I'm sure MOTrax is going to want tax breaks. I'm on the board of Progress Orthus. Remember? I have a vote. You need to pull your weight and stop acting like I don't know how political bargaining works." She pulled her sunglasses off and put them in her leather bag. She snapped the buckle and glared at him.

Bob's forward momentum brought him off the car, and at the top of the movement, he wiped his forehead with his handkerchief. "Ezzy, I've been doing this for almost ten years. MOTrax's developer can't afford to pay for neighboring parks. They don't have enough money for their sewer liability. They need federal grants, so they offer market-rate, subsidized housing. You think MOTrax is swimming in money? They lose five hundred million dollars every year. People don't ride their piss-stained train. The ODD hub is still a mess from the train wreck. They're lucky trains still run. Hell, they're lucky those drivers don't wreck more trains." She watched him waddle toward the main entrance, and lagged behind so as not to be perceived as sharing information with him.

She called forward to him, "Then why do you continue to support them?"

"If they build these apartments, it's one less empty parking lot people complain about. Transit-oriented developments are going to increase ridership in spite of the higher costs and generate a lot more tax revenue for Orthus County." She was beginning to discern he wasn't concerned with empty parking lots, or voter complaints, but the increased tax-digest storyline provided him cover for his own needs. Lately, she could recite Bob's answers before he gave them.

In her frustration, she blurted out, “Why do projects you and Patrick want get tax breaks from Progress Orthus, but taxpayer services like roads and schools go to the ballot box for financing?”

He stopped and turned back to her. “Ezzy, that’s just the way business is done.” She groaned as his jowl curled into a smirk.

She attempted one last time to break through to his sense of pragmatism. “Don’t you remember what Papa T Sam did to your dad as a political reminder?”

He rolled his big lazy eyes. The bags under them were sweating under the early May summer. “Who doesn’t, Ezzy?”

Bob Drolland, Sr. had threatened to remove all King Citrus tax abatements because the company didn’t train all the workers. King Citrus promised to train new workers, but only new workers, not all of their employees. Papa T Sam responded to Bob Sr.’s threat by paying all King Citrus employees for three months in two-dollar bills. Orthus County businesses were flooded. They turned up in grocery stores, gas stations, midnight poker cabins, and banks. The message was loud and clear: King Citrus greases the Orthus County economy. T Sam proved his point. As long as Bob Sr. was paving streets and protecting the public, King Citrus would support him.

With great effort, Bob swung his legs forward in a wide sweeping motion. She could tell he was speeding up to avoid her interrogation. “That’s right, Ezzy. Everyone knows the Kings are the job creators. You all stick around for the long haul. That is, until the oranges freeze or the tax breaks dry up. Then you move with the thermometer because your contracts are made to be broken. Good business ethics be damned.” He shouted loud enough for anyone in the entrance to hear.

“King Citrus has never broken a promise. Some parts of our business are out of our control. Add the parks’ expenditures around the MOTrax Stations or you’ve lost me.” She knew from her business associate contacts his real estate law practice was, at best, a loose affiliation with a normal workweek, and at worst, a vacant storefront, which made her suspicion that he was being compensated for his votes all the more logical. What she hadn't learned was that Bob was close to his original political goal: getting past the ten-year pension hurdle. If he finished this year, much less the term, he was entitled to the state employee pension: a lifetime of income.

When King Citrus moved in the 90s, hundreds of jobs moved with it. Matt Pinson, Jim's dad, didn't want to risk Jim's prospects by pulling him from the only life he knew. He kept working for King Farms and coaching football until he retired. He was determined to take care of his wife and one remaining son.

Jim moved south to Orlando from Lochloosa during college, where he excelled with his determination in class and on the school paper. Where wealth and power didn't exist, the Pinsons relied on their perseverance to get ahead. The Lochloosa High School principal sent Jim's editorials and current-event essays to the University of Central Florida, resulting in a full scholarship. Jim's work for the college paper won him recognition at the National Press Club.

He was a fearless journalist with the tech savvy to deliver the story to the most for the least. His website media presence had grown from nothing to one hundred thousand clicks per month. The *Orthus County Post* was his second job. By day, he crafted marketing campaigns for Fortune 500 companies, but no one covered Orthus County like the *Post.*

Enzo Ruiz didn't have a seat on stage, so he had to walk by Jim. "How's tricks, paperman?"

"Nice suit." Jim replied. "Do they all come in pinstripes? Or is prison a hard habit to break?"

"What did you say, cabron'?" Enzo turned his cut but aging physique toward Jim and walked around the last chair next to the wall before heading down the aisle without slowing down. His dark mane flowing to the top of his tailored collar eliminated any real physical threat.

"You're crippling my hometown, asshole. I'm reporting it all."

Enzo flipped him the bird out of sight of the scattered newcomers, and continued to walk toward the front of the room, glancing back in the way only a self-made Cuban-Italian can. His thin smile was ensconced on an olive canvas. Thick dark eyebrows shadowed dark green eyes. He tugged on his shirtsleeves, flashing the sterling silver Dunham Schauble cuff links. Jim nodded. *Keep it up, Big Money. Find out what kids learn early in the Lochloosa swamps.*

Jim came to all the Orthus County Commission meetings. They were bi-monthly affairs of scripted dialogue, predetermined votes, and municipal chatter. The passionate calls for more transparency were good theatre mixed in with the dull monotony of county operations. The stage for commissioners was high enough to create a judgmental effect on anyone at the speaker's podium. He wanted his stories to be self-evident, so he relied on the people in them to stand on their own. He kicked himself for not bringing more battery back-up, because tonight was going to be a long one, and eventful, too, given the full agenda of potential bombshells, but no one showed up until 7:00 PM. Jim reported the official start times in his stories, which cautioned people the first hour was always slated for Executive Session. Part of Bob Drolland's winning campaign strategy was the transparency promise: *"All, and I mean all, meetings of the public's business will be broadcast live. The* Orthus County Post *is always welcome in our chambers. Orthus County will double the effort by live streaming on our website."*

Jim chuckled every time he heard it, but to put any remaining confusion about closed-door meetings to rest, Bob began to communicate, "*Folks, we have to meet privately in Executive Session to discuss confidential matters of real estate or human resources. You wouldn't want your boss to have a conversation about your performance in public. Would you? The outside claims of secrecy are just more disinformation spread by the misinformed and cynical.*" Jim was a local at Orthus County offices, where he ate lunch with half the staff, and he knew no one had been fired in nine years.

Whispers had circulated through his media connections that Orthus County Regional Hospital was going to miss its bond payment. He'd started his newspapers with the stories about the bond market and Progress Orthus's place in it. His first story was about Progress Orthus's issuance of a fifteen-year bond eight years ago to fund a new wing, doubling the facility's size. Orthus Regional was good for gunshots and car accidents, but not much else. The hospital was understaffed and overwhelmed with people seeking Medicaid or indigent care. Hospital management reduced doctors and nurses as a first rule of cost cutting. Debt payments owed to Progress Orthus took priority over equipment needs and patients. Voicemail was the only option after 2:00 PM, because front-desk staff was considered non-essential.

The room was empty except for the Board of Commissioners, who came up on stage from the back room, Reverend Thomas, Enzo, three women, and himself. Jim hoped the presenters were ready. He'd seen Bob lecture on their misguided advocacy many times, while feeding his addiction to power with their deflated looks of the confused.

He lifted his head as Reverend Thomas finished the prayer, followed by Bob's rapping gavel. "Good evening, everyone. I'm Bob Drolland, your Orthus County Commission Chairman. Welcome to the June Orthus County Commission meeting. We are a government of the people to serve the people. The Orthus County motto is Forever Dream. Thanks for the invocation, Reverend Thomas.

I'd like to move we excuse ourselves for an Executive Session to discuss human resource matters." Jim had lost all doubt years ago that it was anything but a kangaroo court display when, after they all voted "Aye" in lockstep, one of the commissioners hadn't even sat down. All seven exited to the left and back into the room from where they'd entered. He never got used to Enzo's constant presence around county officials. He followed them in and had become a constant fixture in their meetings, like their own personal banker.

Jim taped Bob's opening and the unanimous vote every time. Tomorrow's *Orthus County Post* headline story would begin, as it did every second and fourth Tuesday of the month, with the vote and the county commissioners exiting into the secret meeting.

The three women left in the empty chamber looked around at each other in amazement. They must've been new or they wouldn't have been surprised. The preacher was walking out the main entrance to leave. One of them, tall and thin, put down her notes and yelled to Jim across the room. "Where did they go?"

"Executive Session."

"Huh? What the hell is that? We have to get home to relieve babysitters."

"They go into Executive Session to avoid camera exposure. They're discussing real estate deals. That usually means bond payments are coming due." The other two kept reviewing their presentation.

"How long will they be in there?"

"As long as they want or until you leave."

Her arms dropped to her sides as she turned to the others. "Well, that's just great. Ladies, better text your families. We could be here a while. We can't let all this work go to waste. If they vote this through unopposed, it would be our fault because we were ready and didn't say anything. Are you with me?"

They both nodded and pulled out their phones.

"Good for you. Probably won't be longer than an hour," Jim said as he looked up from his computer again. "There's a coffee shop next door."

The women whispered to one another, and when they arose, the leader turned to Jim. "We'll be back in a bit. Do you want anything?"

"No, thanks," Jim replied. "I'll be here when you get back." They were about to walk out the main entrance with their computer bags and purses when he saw them turn back. The others followed her to the podium and began to put their fingers on the buttons below the microphone. Jim yelled over to them, "You can lay pieces of paper on that table and the camera will project the picture or text on those TVs."

They all turned to him and smiled, practiced with a few pages, then turned and walked out. "Back in a little while."

Once the county commission was inside the Executive Session, Bob waded into the immediate problem. "Enzo tells me Orthus Regional Hospital has its biannual payment coming up next week. The CEO has mentioned the hospital could be short this time and in November. That raises a dilemma."

"What dilemma?" The Ocala Chamber of Commerce president asked him.

He watched her shovel the last of her catered sandwich and chips into her mouth. "Enzo, would you like to chime in?"

"Sure thing, Bob. Seven years ago, Progress Orthus issued a billion-dollar blind-pool bond to expand services for all of Orthus County's healthcare and transportation needs and to build the Orthus King Airport. Since then, the hospital has been losing money. Neither it nor the airport pays any property taxes.

Progress Orthus holds the title to both properties. The hospital bond requires forty million per year. The airport owes about fifty million per year. As far as we know, the airport is in no danger of missed payments or default. At maturity, Progress Orthus will sell both the hospital and the airport to the owners for ten dollars apiece."

Bob relaxed back in his chair with the ends of his fingers meeting at his belt buckle and listened to Enzo. His eyes met each of the commissioners that were trying to follow Enzo's audit trail, consoling them with a nod. They had acquiesced to Bob's demands because he had convinced them they would bring massive new tax revenues in the long run, and they would be politically shielded from any problems that might occur. "If there's ever a problem, the bond buyers will take the hit."

The alcohol alarm clock in his head began to ring, as his hands begin to quiver. He had tolerated almost all he could listen to as Enzo continued the advisory charade he was paid to deliver. "Because of the economic and public benefit to Orthus County, you approved Progress Orthus giving both projects tax breaks. There're two requirements for any tax abatement. First, unsecured debt, or a revenue bond, has to be issued. Second, Progress Orthus has to hold the title to the property, ergo bond-for-title. The bond is called a PILOT bond because the developer pays interest in lieu of taxes, or PILOT. The development authority takes the place of the bank. The developer takes advantage of low-interest loans it would never get at a bank, and eliminates the costly burden of taxes. It was a very reasonable accommodation to secure healthcare services and a world-class jet port for small aircraft and traffic helicopters."

Bob hated questions, but knew they were inevitable, and was proven right when the hotel owner from Sanford chimed in. "I heard at the golf club Orthus Regional denies private practice doctors operating room time even when there's space. What's that about? I thought the hospital needed revenue."

"What about the young doctors?" another asked. "I hear they're going to strike if Orthus Regional increases 'normal hours' to reduce overtime on the busy weekends."

He looked at Enzo for an answer, and when Enzo smiled back with a blank stare, Bob said, "Well?"

Enzo closed his leather binder. "Bob, I have no idea how the hospital runs its operation. I know if they miss a payment, you'll be given few options. The first is asking the airport to pay the missed payment. Both properties collateralize the same debt. The second is to allow the hospital to default on the bond. The third is funding the missed payment out of the Orthus County general fund or the tax-anticipation note you use as a one-year line of credit."

"We'd have to vote on a general fund bailout?" The hotel owner blurted out before Bob could say anything. "I'm not putting my name on that. Let's let the airport pay it. They do pretty good, right?"

Bob held his hands up in the air. "We'd use the tax-anticipation note first, not the general fund, but letting the airport pay for it is a good idea, too. I'm sure OSK could see their way to helping out."

The district commissioner from Orlando yelled at Bob, "The tax-anticipation note or the general fund? What's the difference? All that money has been spent on this year's budget." Bob watched him close his notebook, too. "Now listen here, Enzo. You told us point blank the taxpayer is not obligated to pay this debt. We tell our voters the exact same thing. Can we trust you or not?"

Bob was concerned he was losing the voice of wise counselor, until Enzo looked them all dead in the eyes as if they were fools and said, "I told you the truth then and I'm telling you now. You can let the hospital default on those bonds, but all of Orthus County will be downgraded by the credit-rating agencies. It is also very likely the airport will suffer." Bob eased back in his chair again as Enzo continued, "Please try to remember that both properties collateralize the bond. Your future interest rates would double as your ratings disintegrated. Imagine the same billion-dollar bond Progress Orthus issued for these two projects doubling in cost for a bridge or an interchange. If we issue a bond for the Bob Drolland Sr. Interchange, you'll need a high credit rating."

"Well, I guess we need to look hard at letting Progress Orthus default, because I don't give a damn about building the Bob Drolland Interchange just so Smithson Galleria has an off-ramp," the hotel owner said. The commissioners were beginning to grasp the dilemma brought on by their own actions. "Furthermore, Bob...and Enzo...I don't own a private airplane."

Bob leaned forward on the desk in front of him and said, "Oh no. We can't do that! Blame your local tell-all blogger out there in the Commission Hall. We should've set up different authorities for different projects. Then the separate entities would have reasonable amounts of land ownerships instead of it all being owned by Progress Orthus. Enzo here has always insisted we transfer the titles of the property to Progress Orthus, and now the collective beast is exposed just as I predicted." Bob glossed over the nuances of development-authority structure to disguise its trap doors, and the few banking terms he remembered were perfect word candy for his audience. With the passion of a roaming internal auditor, Bob said, "Thank God Progress Orthus doesn't have to post financial statements or reports."

Out of the corner of his eye, Bob could see Enzo grimmacing, which usually meant he'd said something inaccurate. He remembered all the times Enzo had told him, *"There is no other way to create a tax abatement without holding title to the property. You don't have to post financial statements, because you are a conduit, not an entity."* Bob grinned, having used the education of Enzo's constant lectures to keep the others in the dark, and continued, "We could then allow the separate authorities to default without a snowball of financial bullshit coming down on top of us."

The Orlando commissioner pointed his finger at Bob. "What the hell are you asking us to do on these MOTrax developments on the agenda tonight?"

"We're going to create a development wave that will sweep north through Orthus County all the way to Smithson."

"How much is that going to cost us? I've heard all this before, Bob."

"Nothing, yet. We're just rezoning the property tonight so MOTrax can issue another bond. It issued its own bonds years ago because it's a development authority, too. Sterling Johnston took the money and bought all those railroad distribution hubs from King Citrus and turned them into MOTrax stations. Then MOTrax used TREP to build all the stations and parking lots. Once we re-zone the empty parking lots, they'll build new apartments."

"Who?" The Ocala representative asked.

"Transportation Real Estate Partners," Bob said. "They build affordable housing and mass-transit projects all over the country. They specialize in government contracts because they know the price of doing business."

"But they're not going to build on all that park land next to the parking lots Ezzy gave us…are they?" The hotel owner asked.

"Of course not. Our green spaces are near and dear to all of us."

"So, what, Bob?" Bob began to think the Orlando commissioner wasn't going to let go. "We're not talking about the MOTrax bonds; we're talking about Progress Orthus bonds. Progress Orthus is the largest landowner in Orthus County because Enzo advised us to do it that way. We own the industrial parks, the downtown districts, the airport, the hospital, all of it. Then we just rent it to the developers."

"Why do we own all that land?" another asked.

"The county commission doesn't own it. Progress Orthus does," Bob said. "Like I told you all, Progress Orthus has taken the place of the bank. These transactions are like your mortgage. The bank owns your house until you pay it off." Bob threw his thumb up and back toward the door. "Jim's advocate friends forced us to keep all bond debt and economic development under one entity: Progress Orthus. Blame him."

He kept looking at them, noticing Enzo bowing his head at his chair. *He thinks I'm an idiot,* Bob thought.

The Orlando commissioner brought the conversation back to the immediate problem. "What are we supposed to do? What about all those missed tax dollars? When did you say the next payment is due from Orthus Regional?"

"The first half, next week, and the second half in November," Bob answered.

"We're in a box. Enzo, this is bullshit. Why in God's name didn't you describe this scenario to us earlier?" the hotel owner asked. He'd pulled a pen out and was tapping it on the table nervously.

Bob allowed Enzo to lay down the threat one more time. "Enzo, anything else?"

"You can allow the hospital to default or the airport can make the payments for them. You were armed with this information when you voted to approve Progress Orthus's bond issuance. How could I know a hospital would default on a bond?"

Bob turned to the hotel owner, who was looking back to the group from the window in disbelief. He said, "If Orthus Regional Hospital misses a bond payment, we're going to have to explain what happened."

Bob had already forgotten Jim quoted him using his own words: "risk-free development." He tried to force consensus in the stunned room. "So, we're clear. If the hospital misses another bond payment, we'll cover it from the general fund line of credit?"

"Never in all my life have I been backed into a corner like this," the Orlando commissioner said. "God help us all if we get stiffed by the hospital. If our economy stays in this recession, our property-tax revenues will fall off a cliff. Where will the money come from then?"

Bob stood up so he wasn't isolated and powerless at the table. "It will come from the buckets of money we're going to make on the MOTrax developments. We're not staying in this recession. We just came out of the last one. It's all going to be OK. So our line of credit avoids default?" He asked one last time. They all nodded, but no one spoke.

Bob led them out and didn't see the hotel owner in the back of the group talking to the Ocala Chamber of Commerce president. "It's too bad we can't get some of these deals for our city. Every time Progress Orthus gives a tax break to a new developer, my city's general fund gets shafted."

The chamber president nodded toward him, making sure Bob couldn't hear. "So does Ocala. We created a development authority to make our own deals. We're going to start cutting Bob out of the loop."

"Really? How?"

"At the very minimum, you should create a development authority. Next, get your citizens to vote for Redevelopment Powers. Then you can create tax-allocation districts. Call your development authority Sanford Synergy or Satisfy Sanford, whatever. The name will keep the voters in the dark.

"No kidding. That easy?"

"Yep."

CHAPTER 7

Jim looked up from the back bench when the main door opened. Sheriff Bill Bolek walked by the camera tripods, wearing the brown and gold uniform of the Orthus County Sheriff's Department. Ezzy was walking in front of him. She smiled. "Hey, Jim."

"Evening, Ezzy. You look spectacular as usual. Hey, Sheriff. The streets still safe out there?"

Jim put down his laptop to get up and say hello to Ezzy, when Bill stopped, too. "They are. As long as you're not on them. Hope you're OK."

"How are Matt and Beth?" Ezzy asked.

"They're good. Dad still runs the bait shop. Mom still grows the garden. She retires next spring. They both still go to Lochloosa football and baseball games."

"Are we any good this year? Remember when we won State three years in a row? Your dad is a football genius." Jim adored the way she connected with people, especially when it came to old friends.

Coach Pinson was a volunteer coach for all three teams while keeping the water flowing on King Citrus groves. Lochloosa was so far from anything that no one wanted the job. "We had the best running back in Florida and played in the smallest class. Hard not to win it, don't y'think?"

"Always so cynical, Jim?"

"Always so beautiful, Ezzy? Dad would say the same thing, by the way." Jim glanced at Bill only long enough to notice he was glancing back at him.

"I know he would. When are you going to ride with me again?"

"Ezzy King, you're dangerous and I'm married. I'll meet you anywhere in Orthus County when you want to hear King Citrus slogans, but you save those Thoroughbreds for your big-city boyfriends. I can ride bareback and your horses know it." He exchanged smiles with Ezzy like two stowaways on the ship of old memories. Jim noticed Bill's nervous laugh, and for a moment wondered if they were together.

Jim's older brother, John, and Ezzy had dated in high school. Lochloosa was a close-knit mosaic of cultures and families. Rich, poor, brown, or white, Jim's family and their friends had survived together under the oppressive, orange-colored heat.

After Ezzy and Sheriff Bolek had walked away and separated down different aisles to sit down, the room filled with the usual suspects; every-meeting attenders, hopeful citizen volunteers, and a few Boy Scouts. He flipped up his video camera lens when a small crowd seated in front of him began to buzz as the Orthus County Commission came back in the room and took their seats. Bob led the group of commissioners as they walked along the back wall to their seats at the panel kitted out with microphones at each of their places. The three ladies had returned with their coffee and presentation materials along with throngs of people. He cross-referenced his copy of the attendee list of city contractors, engineers, and lawyers for any conflicts of interest, as he watched them take their seats in different sections for privacy, while local citizens ended their day away from their families in jeans and khakis. Kate Brown walked past him in a business suit, with a much younger man in a tight navy-blue coat, slacks, and a bowtie. Jim caught her glance, but she looked away as their eyes connected, as if to avoid any possible questions he might have about the MOTrax accident. As loyal as the commissioners were to the process of secrecy, their faces couldn't hide their stress. Jim allowed himself an unkind snicker when Bob's chair listed to the left. The pedestal groaned under his weight every time he shifted in an effort to rebalance the tilt.

Jim's phone pinged and it reminded him, and everyone within hearing distance, to silence their phones. He snuck a last glance.

Please show Bill Lochloosa for me. Thanks.

The last time Ezzy had asked him to give a Lochloosa tour was ten years ago. Jim looked up. Bill had taken a seat near the front and center, and Ezzy was on the left and near the back. She turned around and smiled.

Jim started his recorder as Bob began. "Folks, we have a lot on the agenda. It could be a long night. If you think your particular matter could wait a month, we'd very much appreciate it for the sake of getting back to our families." Jim would always nod politely when first-timers passed him on their way out, inspired by Bob's readily provided justification to spend their evening somewhere more interesting. Jim knew those same attendees would then call to complain the next morning that Bob had voted on their issue anyway. He smiled at the veteran advocates remaining in the room, as they dismissed Bob's request as easily as they'd dismiss a request from him to "trust that we're making the right decisions for you."

The buttons of Bob's shirt were like coiled springs as his suit coat expanded across his heft. "First we'll hear from MOTrax representatives and the public about their parcel rezoning request for MOTrax station parking lots on the North Line. We'll also honor our first responders with a pay-raise discussion. Then we'll hear from the Orthus Regional Commission about the traffic study we funded last year. Finally, we'll hear from the property owners and developer surrounding a few minor land-use variances in unincorporated Orthus County. Again, thank you for participating in the democratic process. We're here to serve you."

One of the city staff on the front row leaned into the microphone. She announced the names of the public representatives speaking in opposition to the MOTrax parking-lot rezoning. Jim had been getting information from the neighborhood rezoning committees, some on the list of speakers, some not. They were there, prepared and ready to tell the commission that turning the parking lot into a TOD would have dire consequences for their neighborhood. Bob's last sentence had the sound of a prison warden: "Each person will receive three minutes with a total allotted time of ten minutes."

The three ladies from earlier had signed comment cards back-to-back. The three-minute timer lit up in the corner. Jim was gaining more confidence in their strategy when the first two women reached the podium in unison and leaned into the microphone. "We yield all of our time to Shannon."

Jim watched Shannon, the apparent leader, approach the podium with her presentation papers. She handed a packet to the city staff representative filled with presentation documents. She had no notes, but she was prepared with maps and drawings, which she placed on the table so the entire room could see them. The TV screens lit up with a presentation cover page.

"Mr. Drolland, I bought my property before MOTrax ever expanded north into our neighborhoods. Now we have drug dealers and criminals walking around all hours of the night. It takes Orthus County sheriffs an hour to come around after a car break-in," she said and flipped the page. "The MOTrax police almost never patrol the station. We have five break-ins a week. You can watch the criminals walk across the giant, empty parking lot toward our neighborhoods. Now they want to rezone the parking lots so they can add 700 new apartments on ten-acre lots and ruin my commute in the process. Every time it rains, the parking lot floods and our sewers overflow into the creek. Are you going to build a septic tank big enough for a giant apartment complex? Not in our neighborhood, you're not." She continued for the entire ten minutes, clicking through slides of brown water gushing through the tops of manhole lids, rudimentary traffic diagrams she made herself, and homeless people sleeping and living near the entrance to the station. Jim had a surreal admiration of Bob's ability to completely ignore a speaker standing right in front of him. "We need you all to do something about two-lane roads that won't accommodate fifteen hundred new cars every day. Hire more police officers. Fix our sewers. Deny this rezoning request. There're millions of people in Orthus County, but not one police officer around the MOTrax stations. When the MOTrax police do come, they don't leave their cars. Mr. Drolland, I knew your daddy. He would've stuck by us. This isn't a transit-oriented development. It's a traffic-oriented disaster."

Jim was writing her quotes into his story as she finished and reached over to turn off the podium link to the TVs. The crowd of after-work advocates clapped around him as he noticed Bob lift his head as if from a nap. The two women supporting Shannon gave her a nervous standing ovation, inspiring all but the consultants to do the same. He knew something was amiss when Ezzy didn't stand up but only glared at Bob. If the MOTrax parking-lot rezonings were going to be another railroaded vote Jim had seen time and time again, they probably had the votes to approve before the rezoning application asking for higher human density weeks ago. Jim had heard rumors Bob was advocating for Ezzy's donated park land to become additional MOTrax parking spaces in the secrecy of earlier work sessions.

Bob banged the gavel. "Thank you very much for those comments. Audience, please refrain from any clapping or other distractions and respect the decorum of our county government. Thank you." Jim waited for the second crack as Bob pounded the gavel again, probably for his own pleasure. "Now we'd like to hear from the applicant."

The city staff representative spoke abruptly into the microphone. "Kate Brown, MOTrax Director, will now have the full ten minutes plus any time added for a rebuttal period."

Kate cleared her throat and tucked her shoulder-length hair behind her ears before reading directly from a typed memo. "Mr. Chairman, county commissioners, I'm Kate Brown, MOTrax director. We've met with all the surrounding neighborhoods and heard their concerns. We've tried to integrate their responses into our plans. As you are aware, all of the parking lots surrounding the MOTrax stations north of downtown Orlando are half empty. We're asking Orthus County to rezone the parking lots so we can build vibrant new communities. The five existing stations will become hubs for commerce and increased ridership as we envision large, mixed-use developments." She wandered on ideologically, without addressing any of the advocates' concerns. "Our principles at MOTrax require all of our developments to include an affordable housing component. This will ensure a diverse group of residents of all socioeconomic backgrounds for a more livable community. We'll continue to work with our new neighbors in the area as we move forward. We're asking for additional shared parking in the parking lots of the public parks to meet our onerous parking-space requirements." Jim looked over to see Ezzy shaking her head no. "The neighbors should all be very happy we are expanding in their area. We're removing a blighted parking lot. Thank you again for your time and your wise decision to rezone these parking lots for a better Orthus County."

The designs on the monitor were no different than the ones submitted to Jim for the original story published months ago showing half-empty parking lots, created by MOTrax's overly ambitious ridership forecast, and replaced with renderings of new buildings. He'd reported on the hand-appointed committee of in-town urban planners to meet with MOTrax, completely excluding the surrounding neighborhood. The commenters on the *Post* saw the Citizen Review Board as a sock puppet for Bob. Casual knowledge Jim could gather led him to believe they were told to approve anything MOTrax wanted. If this deal went down like the rest of the stories Jim wrote, MOTrax would want tax abatements, too.

"Thank you very much for your public comments," Bob said. "MOTrax stations aren't meeting their full potential. The Metro Orlando Transportation Authority has submitted plans for all five parcels on tonight's agenda. As everyone knows, these parcels have been zoned industrial since the beginning of this nationally heralded mass-transit system." Jim did an exposé on MOTrax ridership the previous year outlining decreased MOTrax ridership for every year since it was hailed as the "Grand Experiment" decades ago. The annual rider surveys were a rite of passage for any new MOTrax director. The complaints Jim tabulated were consistent. The stations don't stop anywhere convenient, the bathrooms don't work, the vagrants use the elevators as makeshift living quarters while their panhandling verges on assault, and finally, the trains are never on time. After Jim reviewed their financial statements, he ceased wondering why the complaints were never addressed. MOTrax's unfunded pension liabilities eliminated any money to make MOTrax better. Pension obligation bonds were issued instead of new construction bonds.

"MOTrax needs our full support to reduce traffic around our city for all constituents, not just the privileged few," Bob barreled ahead. "The past three months have provided us with a clear understanding of the surrounding neighborhoods' opinions and suggestions."

Jim could never correlate the passionate pleas to increase ridership with apartment-complex construction. All of his data supported the theory that Orthus County residents loved their cars, cheap gas, and ride sharing. The only reason he could surmise for the rezonings was that MOTrax wanted to cash in on the cyclical, multifamily apartment-complex boom and improve the societal greater good, but without the pesky details of infrastructure improvements to support the increase. The TODs would increase affordable housing where it was eliminated on the MOTrail. Parks and neighborhood streets would minimize the need for costly parking decks.

MOTrax leadership had been preaching the new city gospel since Jim started his online media presence; *"People won't need cars. They'll be riding MOTrax."* What they didn't say is, *"We're going to make traffic so bad, you'll have to take the train."* Jim speculated what was in it for Bob. Maybe a new courthouse or county office space like Stan got?

Bob leaned forward to grab the microphone. "We need to do a better job educating our constituents on the possibilities these projects bring. The Orthus County Planning Commission and the Zoning Review Board have applied a recommendation to approve without any changes to their request. With that, I'd like to take a vote." Jim caught his eyes as Bob looked out at the audience. The votes were unanimous. "Motion passes. The MOTrax rezoning request is approved!" He rapped the gavel. MOTrax was one step closer to being in the real estate business. Jim looked around the room and felt the tension. He saw a big guy with a towing-company logo on his shirt stand up. He gave a passionate plea from his seat, but it was too late. Bob admonished him with a threat to be escorted from the room.

Jim time-stamped the vote in his notes as the county commission began Sheriff Bill Bolek's pay-raise request. Bob began with a somber tone. "We all know the Orthus County Sheriff's and Fire

Departments are a valuable part of our county," he said. "We also know they haven't received a raise in three years. Our budget is about a billion per year and we only receive about nine hundred million. As much as I'd like to pay our first responders what they deserve, which is more, we just can't afford it at this time. There will be no vote on the subject." Jim thought, *classic Drolland.* The Orthus County Commission would rather not vote than be excoriated in the press for voting down a police and firefighter pay raise. The crowd groaned and mumbled.

Jim checked his camera angle when Bill got up from his second-row seat and stormed up the aisle toward the exit. Jim leaned over as he passed, cameras rolling. "Sheriff Bolek," he whispered. "I have something you might like to see."

Bill halted and turned to him mid-stride. "I've got to get out of here. I knew he was going to do that. Call me tomorrow, OK? I have phone calls to make."

"Absolutely, Chief. Let's go shellcracker fishing after the next full moon."

"Roger that," Bill answered as he pushed through the doors.

He turned back to the stage when Bob rapped the gavel again for the room to come to order. "We have a lot to discuss tonight, people. I know these are some tough decisions, but we have a county to run. We can't please everybody all the time. Next up, we'll hear from the ORC."

Jim checked his internet feed as the consultants and engineers of the most powerful transportation committee in the state, the Orthus Regional Commission, huddled one last time before the speaker took the podium. Jim's agenda handout said they were asking for a tax increase. The state roads in Orthus County had long held the unspoken title of the worst in Florida, with expanding populations overburdening metro Orthus County highways and bridges. Jim noticed a couple of trucking and logistics lobbyists sitting with the ORC. After interviewing several of them, he got the feeling potholes in neighborhood streets were voter problems, whereas potholes on the edges of highways and lane closings were business problems. Orthus County had commissioned a traffic study the previous summer after a blistering rebuke from Governor Sikes. One of Jim's sources inside the county administration had told him Governor Sikes said, "You need to get those roads fixed, Bob. Tourism is Florida. Tourists drive through Orthus County. Fix it. The Orthus Regional Commission is going to give you some advice. Take it."

The bald man from ORC pulled his glasses from his shirt pocket and read from a prepared statement. "Mr. Chairman, county commissioners, we have completed the traffic studies for Metro Orthus you commissioned last year. Florida ranks among the best roads in the country. Revenue raised by the toll-road system is the life blood of maintenance and safe highways. Drivers and transport trucks find a different story once inside Metro Orthus. Lane expansions begun years ago idle with closed lanes and no construction. Tax revenues are funneled into your development authority and away from roads. The Orthus County population has increased thirty percent in recent years. Not a single infrastructure bond has been issued in that time. The state has decided any funding for Orthus County projects currently approved, but unfunded, will hinge on of one of two requirements. First, you can levy a special penny sales tax devoted to your county highway system. All increased sales revenues won't be diverted to the Orthus County general fund, but a special highway fund. Or second, Orthus County can issue a bond that is the equivalent of fifteen years of the special penny sales tax. Orthus County has several pending state projects approved by the Florida Highway Traffic and Safety Administration. That list includes the Bob Drolland Sr. Interchange. The funding for those projects will rest on your constituents' voter-approved tax increase or transportation bond issuance. Thank you for your time. We have delivered copies of our report to all interested parties including the governor's office. It is also loaded on our website for all to view. It has been our pleasure working together with your constituents and the Orthus County government on this commissioned project."

Jim could tell Bob was rankled when he rubbed the back of his neck and looked at the man without a response. The ORC representative returned to his seat, put his glasses back in his pocket, crossed his legs, and glared right back at Bob. Jim knew the voters wouldn't pass another sales tax, because Orthus County already had the highest sales taxes in the state. A bond issue was unthinkable given the analysis Jim had done. They were leveraged to the hilt with Wall Street bankers who bought all the muni bonds Enzo could issue. Bob smiled with professionalism toward the audience. "Thank you for the study. In every way, Orthus County will continue to be the best county in Florida for business and tourism. Our voters deserve highways, bridges, and roads befitting our economic productivity. Our parents are confident their children are on the safest streets going to and from work or school. We'll take your study very seriously and report back in a few months." No vote was taken that would have given the governor any satisfaction to his threat of shutting down Bob's namesake legacy.

Gauging by the participant attrition in the room, Jim could tell it was getting late. As usual, in the absence of naïve citizen plaintiffs who'd left earlier, Bob granted the building variance he'd implied he would postpone. Jim could tell what Bob was thinking: time for a drink at First and Last. "The May Orthus County Commission meeting is adjourned," Bob said and dismissed the room.

County commissioners began exiting the stage with some small talk. Jim positioned himself in the pathway of the county commissioners, between the stage exit and the door. He pointed the recorder in Bob's face. "Commissioner Drolland, sources say Orthus County Regional Hospital is on the brink of default. Will you bail them out with the General Fund?"

Bob scoffed. "That's a ridiculous question. Your sources are uninformed. I've heard of no such occurrence. Orthus County Regional Hospital has served, and will continue to serve, our county for years to come. Their finances are strong with a balanced source of revenue from both the private and public sector."

Jim kept the fastballs coming. "The same sources say Orthus Regional Hospital won't allow private practice physicians to utilize the operating rooms, further increasing the hospital's dependence on Medicaid patients. Would you like to comment?"

"Orthus County Regional Hospital operations are the purview of their director, not me. All I know is there've been some bumps in the road. And, well, everyone is still trying to manage through the last recession. We have a vested interest in seeing them succeed."

Jim moved to the side slightly to allow the other county commissioners to scurry by. "Is there any credibility to the rumors credit-rating agencies are currently auditing Orthus County quarterly financial statements to see if we can bail them out? Or if we have deeper financial problems?"

"We have asked the credit-rating agencies to come in voluntarily to pour over our books." Jim had asked because he observed their invasion daily, not quarterly. "We're asking for an increased credit rating because we've continued to meet our debt obligations in a very challenging environment. The recession hit Orthus County particularly hard because of our outsized residential market and dependence on tourism. Once the credit-rating agencies have finished their analysis, we will follow up with all of the local media outlets to distribute their results. And if that is all, it's been a long night and I need to get home to my family."

"One final question, Mr. Commissioner. The Orthus Regional Airport and the hospital were all issued via a blind pool or a phantom bond. Which is it? Aren't they connected?"

"How should I know what kind of bond it is?" Bob caught himself. "Don't print that."

Jim turned off the microphone and whispered to Bob, "First and Last 'Twofer' Tuesday' drink specials ends in twenty minutes. Better get a move on." But Bob had since shoved on by.

CHAPTER 8

Enzo was already zipping back to Tampa in his new Audi. The smooth, tight fit allowed him to shift effortlessly into fourth and up to 110 mph before reaching the end of the on-ramp. Flying around the only car lights he could see on the interstate, he raced ahead imagining he was driving the Dunham Schauble Le Mans Audi. Lately, he thought about it constantly, determined to get the Dunham Schauble brand on a car in the Grand Prix.

Enzo Ruiz based all his operations from Tampa, and he called South Florida home. His mother had rolled cigars in old Ybor City, and he'd inherited the soul of his childhood. His father was an Italian speed merchant on the summer road-course circuit, and raced the Rally circuit in the winter. Enzo worked his father's pit crew between soccer state championships. He mastered academics at Jesuit, but was lured there for his scoring ability.

History's most dominant college soccer team noticed. On his first campus visit to the University of San Francisco, Enzo strode around the facilities with accomplished bravado. European teams had already called before his visit, but European teams didn't pay for finance degrees and law school. The back alleys of Ybor City were an authentic community where he learned street-style negotiations. Enzo glanced around the head coach's office at the university: *"In both my mother and father's culture, a Don is the most important person in the room. I want to play soccer as a Don, but you'll pay for it."*

Dunham Schauble had grown from a regional firm to a publicly traded investment bank since Enzo's first interview thirty years ago. Dunham Schauble's market research drove the executive strategy into small second-tier cities in the beginning. Places like Tampa and Philadelphia had cheap office space. The risk-averse Germans began their municipal-bond business.

Enzo started within two weeks of coming home from college. Dunham Schauble got a bond salesman and a bond attorney in the same employee. Dunham Schauble worked in a small backwater of the global bond market in the beginning, so small that most municipal issues didn't require Securities and Exchange registration. His mind was awash with the possibilities of an unlimited upside.

The major difference between corporate debt and municipal debt is that the council member voting to issue municipal debt is not personally responsible. Conversely, CEOs faced immediate dismissal for bad decisions. Municipal borrowers don't have the ethical bright line of the corporate world.

Enzo was compensated with commissions, but early compensation afforded him large blocks of stock options in Dunham Schauble. He learned the municipal-bond business fast. There was a steady flow of municipalities needing debt. Dunham Schauble would offload the debt to junk-bond mutual fund managers or individual bond buyers. In many instances, the debt load would include overflows kept on the Dunham Schauble books. Overfunded bond requests coming from blind pools inflated the commissions. The excess debt could be used for Dunham Schauble operations. Dunham Schauble also became the biggest player in phantom bonds because of Enzo's innate talent for hiding off-balance-sheet financing.

The German's had huge checkbooks. Enzo was their gifted entertainer. After the Dunham Schauble Initial Public Offering, he was named National Sales Manager of the new publicly traded company. His knowledge of the law, and his ability to use it, put him in the center of development authority strategy decisions. It was the perfect process. He would tell municipalities how to ask for money. Then he would structure the deal, issue the bond, and charge for both. Enzo built financial frameworks like racetracks. Then he raced them over and over.

Traffic on the road back to Tampa was light. Cruising at ninety with an hour to go, he lit up a Cuban cigar and pushed the call button on the steering wheel. "Call Tim." Tim was the Midwest Regional Manager of Dunham Schauble.

"Hey. You busy?" Enzo had hired Tim right after the financial crisis. The municipal-bond business heated up during recessions. Developers need loans, and banks aren't lending. Enter the most reliable bank in the country, the local development authority.

"No, I'm good," Tim answered. "I'm at a Cubs game with the Chicago Pension Board and the mayor." Enzo could hear the echo of play-by-play announcers in the background. Tim was likely in the company's box at Wrigley Field. "We're about to close on three hundred million to fund the teachers' pension. My people are ripping all over up here. What's up with you? Driving around late, lonely, and old?"

"You know better than that, esé. Orthus County might let Progress Orthus default on the upcoming bond payment on Orthus Regional Hospital."

"What a bunch of assholes. Did you keep any of the bonds on the books?"

"Not many," Enzo lied. "The interest rates were so high we sold most of them on day one. Five and half percent tax free is hard to beat." Enzo's CFO agreed. The counter-party risks were worth the junk yields. Plus, Enzo was on the inside. He could sway the conversation if the pigeons tried to default. "You sound like you're having fun." Clinking glasses could be heard through the phone.

"I'm having a ball. I might get you up here to close the deal in a few months. So, why would Orthus let the hospital default?"

"If they pay the hospital debt, who will pay the pensions?"

"I thought pensions were just Chicago, New York, and Atlanta problems."

"My man, pensions are sinking all the boats. But, hey, as long as they borrow to fund them, me and you get paid. Comprende?"

"Yea, comprehend—O, slick!"

Enzo chuckled, downshifted, and pulled left around a long caravan of motorcycles. Halfway past, back into fifth gear, and the night riders disappeared into the rearview mirror.

"Do you think the airport can make its payment and the hospital's?" Tim asked.

"Probably. Nothing to worry about."

"Did they start whining about covering the bond payment out of the General Fund because they told all their voters it was an iron-clad, risk-free deal?"

"Yep, they all do." Enzo passed two cars like they were standing still in the night heat. "Bob is trying to talk the Board out of a default, but his sheriff is pissed they didn't get a raise. He stormed out when Bob didn't bring it up for a vote. The Orthus County Board acted like it was our fault in Executive Session."

"*...and that's the top of the 8th. Cubs lead two-zip,*" Enzo heard coming from the background. "Typical! Are you still talking to Flash Jackson? We need another bite of that apple. Does he know about Smithson Galleria yet?"

"Sort of. They're asking him tonight."

"Does he know the insurance companies aren't going to relocate there?"

"No. Sterling and Gene will test the waters tonight to see if his appetite is big enough to play ball."

"Does he know about Project Grand Slam?"

"Nope."

"Good Christ, Enzo. You're ice cold!"

Enzo pulled on the big cigar, and then downshifted around two tractor trailers. "All part of a good year…every year… esé!

"Use English, dipshit."

"Only when I have to."

They both laughed and hung up.

Enzo tapped the button on the steering wheel again. "Call office." It rang through.

"Hello, Dunham Schauble."

The Australian accent swirled in his mind like warm honey. "Kirsty?"

"Obviously. How did your meeting go?"

"As expected. And you're burning the midnight oil. You have the potential to be the next star at my firm."

"I'm doing everything I can to make this place better." Enzo never doubted she picked Dunham Schauble because of the upward mobility a small regional firm can offer, but he would be the arbiter of opportunity on his time schedule. "When you presented at the Harvard Australian Club, you gave me hope I could make a difference, too."

"If you continue developing in our organization, the sky's the limit. Our technology platform needs a miracle. We're outgrowing the system." He passed more cars.

"That's why I took the job. I'm your miracle because the system flaws you want corrected are easier said than done. It's going to cost you. They should've been updated when you went public, but it's not too late. Lucky for you I can program as well as I can surf. I can integrate all of the legacy systems into one functioning platform, but I'll need a team. Some of the redundant platforms are much better suited for the cloud. That'll free up overloaded storage that's slowing down our execution speed. Dunham Schauble needs a larger presence on the exchanges. We'll have bigger bandwidth to compete in the mega-debt issues across the country, or maybe even international sovereigns. You know? Really crank this bitch up."

"Build your team. You're my dream girl. Hiring you was the second-best thing I've done."

"What's the first?"

"I haven't done it yet. Can I buy you a drink this late?"

"I thought you'd never ask. Where?"

"Do you know how to get to St. Pete Beach?"

"I go every weekend."

"Meet me at Pass-A-Grille Marina near the entrance."

"Sounds like a moonlight cruise. Should I bring a bikini?"

"Don't leave home without it."

"I have three in my car. See you there."

He hung up, and tapped the steering wheel again. "Call Marina."

The dry dock master answered. "Good evening, Mr. Ruiz."

"Drop Touch Down in the water. I'm coming in tonight."

"Yes sir, Mr. Ruiz. Your boat will be ship-shape and cranked in twenty minutes. We'll leave the main cabin light on for you."

Enzo threw his car back into fifth and gripped the steering wheel as the back end set down close to the road, almost bottoming before the rear axle stabilized. The 430 horsepower Le Mans motor thrusted him forward toward his rendezvous.

CHAPTER 9

A high-rise office tower was the centerpiece of the sprawling Orlando Downtown District. First Chance Last Chance was the restaurant bar on the first floor. The entrance bar spanned the length of the first room. The mirror behind the chorus line of liquor bottles was filled with regular faces who looked up at TV screens molded in the corners. The business news squawked for the Tuesday night business crowd. Hopes for a second-quarter rebound faded with more corporate earnings losses on the top and bottom lines. The mess left by the train derailment slowed bar traffic to a crawl.

The development was built around the central MOTrax hub as the first TOD in Orlando. After Bob's concurrent approval tonight, five more were soon to begin on the North Line. Passionate, but impotent, opposition to the northernmost parking lot of Smithson Station was no match for the grinding wheels of progress. All the while, the recession resulted in rising vacancies and withering profits as young renters moved in together to save money.

Sterling sat at an outside table with Transportation Real Estate Partners president, Gene Dodd. The patio overlooked a giant lake. Sterling was thirty percent owner of TREP with complete architectural and design authority.

Sterling needed the benefit of development authority tax abatements to cut project costs. Development authorities issued public debt in order to finance his real estate projects. Johnston Limited could avoid banks' annual reviews and high interest rates. His real estate ventures could avoid paying taxes on the improved land for decades. He would be handpicked by local governments in a one-sided negotiation benefitting only Johnston Limited, but the politicians were paid not to care, because they, and Sterling, knew if things went wrong, he'd be long gone. Should Bob ever demand extra payments, taxes, or concessions, he would simply fold or bankrupt the project. Sterling structured a limited liability company for each project with the promise that the names of supportive politicians today would be on his buildings and bridges tomorrow.

He loathed Bob's presence and didn't hide it when Bob arrived at the table with a swirling glass of wine and a plate full of chicken wings. He must've finished his first inside, because he always took full advantage of twofer' Tuesdays. Sterling sat on the far side to avoid the stench of Bob's sweat-drenched linen, but he warmed up as he remembered why they were meeting. "Good evening, Bob. I received word all is well. The rezonings for the MOTrax TOD's went as planned."

"Damn, it's hot out here, Sterling." Bob wiped his forehead with a napkin. Sterling wondered how long it would take the first drops of alcohol to ease Bob's anxiety brought on by his table choice. "Why do you always sit outside?"

Sterling curled his mouth at the corners and said. "Because watching you sweat gives me great pleasure, Bob. Smelling you does not."

"Fuck you, Sterling," Bob said out of habit, winced, and threw his arms forward as if to relieve physical stress. "Hey, Gene. Flight in from Dallas ok? Did I leave enough liquor on Sterling's plane? If you had to drink out of plastic cups, it's because the crystal glasses are at my house."

"Hey, Bob," Gene responded. "It was fine. I'm pretty busy. Can we get this over with? Stan is coming downstairs from his office in thirty minutes."

"Sure. I was born ready." Sterling smiled and shook his head when Bob downed the wine and ordered two more from a waitress walking by. "It's time to get paid," he said as he set the empty wine glass on the table.

Gene said, "I'll be in the red sedan on the second floor of the parking deck." Then he got up and walked back inside the bar toward the main entrance.

Sterling picked up a few stray napkins and handed them to Bob, who was shoving another chicken wing into his mouth. He was relieved when Bob lifted himself out of the chair, threw the stained napkins on the ground, drank one of the wines that had arrived, and walked out.

Jim Pinson finalized the recordings from the interview and packed up his cameras. Editing text could wait until tomorrow morning before work. The meeting and interview would arrive on the *Post* first thing. A drink didn't sound all that bad. First and Last would be a great "last chance" for a story before going home. The streets outside ODD were jammed with on-street parking by the residents. He finally maneuvered up to the top deck of the parking garage next to the escalators, and saw Bob Drolland standing next to a car. *Is that Bob? Is that a wine glass in his hand? Don't make the news. Just report it,* he told himself.

He wheeled into a spot between two cars, and then climbed into the back seat with a perfect view out the back window. Bob was now leaning by the open window of a red sedan. The person in the car looked familiar but Jim couldn't place him. He handed Bob an envelope. *So cliché,* Jim thought. The two figures exchanged a few words and then the window rolled up. Jim checked his camera to make sure it was recording. Bob headed back toward the elevator. He put his wine glass down on a trash can lid next to the elevator door and pushed the button. His sausage fingers plumbed the bottom of the envelope and pulled out a stack of cash as a couple of the bills fell to the ground. When he bent over to pick them up, he bumped his head against the elevator door right before it opened. He stood up like a used-car-lot balloon man, and shoved the money back in the envelope. It took a couple of stabs at his coat pocket to conceal the deal as the elevator doors closed behind him.

Jim watched smoke drift out of the sedan window for five minutes before the second person exited the car. He still couldn't quite make out the face. Then it dawned on him like the last piece of a puzzle. Bob had pushed rezoning of parcels around MOTrax stations tonight. Jim watched the flight plans of Sterling's private plane on his OSK navigator app. It came in from Dallas this afternoon, but Sterling never left Orthus County. Jim had taken an interest in the comings and goings of all the major political players in Orthus County. TREP was located in Dallas. *That's it,* he thought. Bob was getting paid by the Transportation Real Estate Partners local representative, Gene Dodd. As Jim checked the camera one more time, he pushed the instant replay button, and verified the event would be reported.

As Bob walked back into the bar, First and Last owner Craig Walker met him at the door of the second room. "Hey, Bob. How's my favorite commish?" Bob indulged his bartender's long stories and bullying behavior in return for free drinks and cocaine. Any time after 9:00 PM, and sometimes before, he'd have to listen to drug-induced diatribes as part of the charade.

"What's up, Craig? You guys turn it up after nine?"

"It brings the ladies down from their lonely apartments. It brings the guys down after them." Bob felt his blood warm when Craig covertly tapped his nose and sniffed. "Want a bump?"

"I've been looking for you since I walked in." Bob followed Craig into the office behind the bar after he jostled open the jammed door, and waited as Craig tapped out two lines of blow on a tray and bladed it together. He leaned over the mirror, sniffing through the tightly wound dollar bill. The ridges of powder vanished as Craig took the bill from Bob and finished the second line.

"Whew! Alright! Now we can begin." Bob opened his eyes wide and looked out over the lake to Orthus Park, which could be seen through the back window of the office. He noticed the old black pistol on the desk. "Is that an antique?"

"It's protection." Craig cleared his throat. "Before you run off, the AB&T has been nosing around. I'm a little late on my liquor license payments. These kids come in here with their own bottles. It's taking a bite out of my cash register. The National Transportation Safety Board's yellow tape is not exactly the kind of decoration that says swingin' hot spot. Can you cut me some slack on the liquor license renewal?"

"I don't control those guys. They make the rules. If you don't stay current with that license, they'll come in here and start trouble you don't want. Any illegals working in the back? Got a concealed carry permit for that relic? Stashing any of this booger sugar in your office?"

"Yeah, yeah. They've already warned me. Orthus County's finest are always in here casing the place. If you can just help me out this once, I won't ask again."

"I'll see what I can do. I need to get back to my table." Bob wiped his nose and turned to walk out of the office without waiting on Craig.

"Sure. Sure, Bob. Thanks, man. Really! What a prince! I'll send some scotch out." Bob was already through the door headed back to Sterling's table. Gene Dodd was sitting at the table smoking a cigarette when Bob arrived. Sitting with Gene and Sterling was Stanley Jackson.

Bob didn't see Jim, who had followed Gene inside and kept a safe distance around the entrance area until Bob had cleared the main bar. Craig walked out of the back office after Bob had walked away, and saw Jim hovering. In a single motion, he grabbed a liquor bottle and filled a glass. Then he yelled at Jim without looking up. "You following politicians around tonight?"

"Just thirsty like everybody else." Jim seated himself inside at a table where he could peer outside to their table unnoticed.

Bob heard the friendly, confident roar of a football hero as he walked up to the table outside. Stan loosened his tie, flashed his thousand-watt smile, and said, "You got a little something on your nose. Might want to clean that up." Bob's heart sank. He jerked up his jacket sleeve and wiped his nose.

"I've been sitting here talking to your friends," Stan said. "You been over at the bar with Craig, I guess? How you doing, fat boy?"

Bob caught Sterling's smile that must have been stimulated by Stan's voice, because it was his reaction every time they sat next to one another. "Pretty good, Flash," he said. "Hotter than Key West spiced rum, but other than that just fine. I adjourned our county commission meeting not thirty minutes ago." He could feel his face glowing from three wine shots, a rail, and ten thousand dollars in his coat pocket.

"Join us, Bob." Gene said. "We'll get you another drink."

"That's OK. Craig is bringing out his private reserve scotch. He thinks I'm going to help him keep his liquor license."

"What? He having trouble?" Stan asked. "Bob, if he loses his liquor license, this place will float away. If you can help him, do it. This place is already a train wreck. Pun intended."

"I'll see if I can help him out if I get some time away from the important matters of governing." Bob reached for one of the glasses when the scotch arrived. "We wouldn't want your precious restaurant to disappear right underneath your new office."

"Just make sure this place gets what they need." Bob looked up at him behind his raised glass, but Stan turned away and said, "What did you want to discuss, Sterling?"

"Dr. Jackson, as you're aware, the old car plant in Smithson has been abandoned. It's an eyesore and an environmental problem. After the automobile manufacturer left, they filed for bankruptcy automatically releasing them from any liability with the cleanup. The new company that emerged from bankruptcy was kind enough to offer thirty million out of a sense of honorable responsibility. Our design teams have branded our proposed mixed-use development Smithson Galleria in deference to the unique history of the area. But to be sure, this is more than just a mixed-use development. It's located a few short blocks from the northernmost destination of MOTrax: Smithson Station. It's a parcel ripe for a walkable, livable development. Dr. Jackson, we're on the cusp of one of the largest developments of its kind ever envisioned or constructed. Masses of people will embrace diverse lifestyles inside twenty-five hundred new apartment units. Four high rises will tower above the east side.

Boutique shops will line wide sidewalks with bike lanes. Movie theaters and a farmer's market will provide entertainment and healthy lifestyles for a young and mobile workforce. A new downtown district, much like here, will connect the Smithson MOTrax Station to this new endeavor. Should the residents ever decide to leave their comfortable surroundings, they'll simply venture through the wide sidewalks of Downtown Smithson and hop aboard MOTrax. Smithson Galleria will integrate MOTrax and Downtown Smithson. The city of Smithson will be redeveloped with a new courthouse and police station inside the downtown district. A special precinct station will provide onsite public safety. It will be the safest, most holistic design I've ever created." Bob watched Stan's face for any hint of his thoughts. He allowed Sterling to weave the story of the development plan that had already changed to fit the evolving dynamics of the deal.

"That's a lot to take in, gentlemen," Stan said. "I'm assuming you're talking to me because you haven't purchased the land. Or have you?"

"We've been in contact with the Smithson City Council," Gene said. "They've introduced us to the bank and the bankruptcy trustee. The site sits scraped and vacant. The City of Smithson spent the environmental cleanup fund on remediation and the three-year comprehensive planning study. Our investment partnership, Smithson Galleria, LLC, has estimated the rough cost of completion at around four hundred and fifty million dollars. Our group consists of TREP, Johnston Limited, MOTrax, and an insurance company looking to relocate into the area. The insurance company will fill the office tower with their new global headquarters. Progress Orthus will be the conduit involved in abating taxes and providing the loan, much like Onward Orlando was the conduit on the MOTrail. This is where you come in."

"Thought so." Bob detected a frown on Stan's face as he asked, "What do you need from the Orthus County School Board?"

"We need you to issue a four-hundred-and-fifty-million-dollar bond to take on the commercial bank financing role," Gene answered.

Stan looked down, grabbed his glass and tipped it high. Bob steadied himself for his response. "Like the MOTrail? I don't think so, guys. Governor Sikes almost fired me over that one. Orthus County is done with scandals, bribes, and corruption. For Christ's sake, I'm going to issue another bond this year to cover the pension shortfalls." Bob took another drink, trying to keep his high going as long as possible while he watched them prod Stan for weakness. His jittery teeth began to relax. He picked up one of the cold chicken wings and stripped it clean.

"Stanley, this project will generate an additional twenty million dollars of tax revenue for the Orthus County School Board," Sterling said. "It will provide Orthus County with a showcase for the entire world to see."

"We won't see that additional tax revenue for twenty years."

"I need that additional tax revenue as much as you, Stan." Bob said, trying to persuade Stan to see the bigger picture.

"Pipe down, Bob. Progress Orthus is going to own the entire development with money borrowed on my credit. Your deal will abate my taxes for twenty years and give most of it to Progress Orthus." Bob felt the back of his neck prickle. "Patrick will use it for his staff and side deals. Don't start popping off about 'we all need tax revenues.' A four-hundred-and-fifty-million-dollar bond is a giant risk for twenty million per year that won't get paid until after we're all gone. The future tax revenues you're pitching are a drop in the bucket for what I need starting yesterday!"

Bob quietly envied Sterling's perseverance when he smiled again at Stan and said, "Stanley, how can we help you see this through?"

"Gene and Sterling, you both seem reasonable. This is going to take me a while to process."

"Of course," Sterling said. "We know this is a lot. But we needed to get your input to see where you stood. A toast to the future of Orthus County schools and Florida's future leaders."

Bob thought about the campaigns Sterling could finance, and if Stan was smart, he'd be thinking the same thing. They all finished their scotch.

"I have to get home to my lady," Stan said as he arose from the table. "I'm sure you guys know how it is." No one responded.

After Stan left the table, Bob turned his fading attention back to Gene and Sterling. "Patrick will take it from here at Progress Orthus on the TODs I rezoned tonight. I need you guys to set up a meeting with me, Patrick, and the MOTrax people."

Gene nodded. "I'll set it up. Will the city take care of all the traffic studies and intersection upgrades?"

"Sure. We've got all the traffic studies in some old files. You're golden," Bob slurred.

"Can we use on-street parking to complement our parking-space ratios?" Gene asked. "Then charge non-residents for parking in our garage?"

Bob picked up the last chicken wing on the plate. "Don't see why not. You do it on all the others." He shoved it in his mouth and pulled out the bone.

"And we can use the parks for parking?" Sterling asked.

Bob talked and chewed. "Yep. It was included in the application. Can you fund my campaign early? Now you have to cover Ezzy's donation, too. I've still got a year and half but might as well start now."

"You have a deal," Sterling answered.

"Great. Get that meeting set up." Bob stood and stumbled his way through the thumping jumble of youth. He saw Craig on the way to the door, and one decibel too loud he asked, "Hey buddy. How about another rail?"

"Easy, Bob. Damn it. Quiet down. Follow me." Bob obeyed and walked into the room behind the bar one more time. He leaned on the counter as Craig tapped out two more lines. "By the way, you know Jim Pinson has been watching your entire conversation. Right?"

Bob's arm slipped off the counter. "That son of a bitch. When did he get here?"

"Right after you walked in."

"Is he still here?"

"No. He walked out behind Flash. You OK?"

Bob could feel the sweat pooling at the small of his back when the stomach cramps kicked in. "I have to go."

"Sure, Bob." Craig's voice followed him out the revolving door. "Don't forget. You said you'd help me."

Out of Bob's sight, over on the other side of the parking deck, Stan was sitting in his cranked car, sending himself normal reminders. Think about Smithson Galleria. Get car washed.

As he started to set his phone down, it pinged with a text.

I'm pregnant.

CHAPTER 10

Jim was loading stories from the County Commission meeting onto the *Orthus County Post* website. The headlines read "Is Orthus Regional Hospital Default Imminent? Readers Want to Know" followed by "Orthus County Commission Denies Sheriff's Raises." The third story was an exclamation point to last night's horribly perfect storm. "Orthus County Approves MOTrax TODs - Residents Ignored." Jim's readership was unusually well educated because of all the community colleges and major universities in the area. Hard-working advocates needed a platform for their voice, and Jim obliged, his *Orthus County Post* being the natural answer. Approval requests for the Comments section were pinging Jim's phone as he responded, Approved, Approved, Approved, Approved. His phone rang. "Hello, this is Jim."

"Jim, this is Orlando Mayor Brian Tisdale. Do you have a minute?"

"Sure, Mayor. How can I help?" Jim's relationships with Orlando politicians were tentative at best, but like everywhere else in the world, politicians needed news outlets.

"I need to speak with you privately. Is there a place we can meet?"

"Uh, yea. How about the Lorna Doone entrance to the MOTrail? That's pretty close to City Hall. Parkside Café'? This afternoon after work?"

"Great. See you then?"

Jim saw the mayor, tall and slender in a pair of work slacks and dress shirt, as they met up and began walking together down the bike trail filled with runners and bikers. "Hey, Mayor." Jim's clothes ruffled when a group of riders whizzed past them both.

"Hey, Jim. Thanks for coming. And call me Brian. This place sure has changed. Ten years ago, we'd have had to have a police escort to walk this trail."

"Ten years ago, you wouldn't have found any police around here to help, mayor. And gentrifying the place hasn't guaranteed lower crime. Try walking two blocks off the MOTrail and into the neighborhoods."

Brian shook his head. "You still haven't learned, Jim. This place needed a boost. It was real estate ripe for development." A woman pushing a stroller jogged around them, while Jim tried to keep up with Brian's long strides. Brian hopped up the stairs and onto the patio of Parkside Café. The hostess stand was steps off the trail. "Miss, can we get a quiet table?" Brian asked.

Jim took the menu from the hostess as he sat down across from Brian and looked around the patio of the big, roomy deck. Giant wooden paddle fans hung from a thatched roof, offering them a breeze on an otherwise balmy evening. He flipped open the menu. "So, what did you want to see me about?"

Brian turned his attention back to Jim from the view on the trail. "I know this may seem out of character, Jim, but you've always been a pretty straight shooter." Jim heard a note of apprehension in Brian's voice. "Not coincidently, you creamed me on this trail when I missed last year's payment, but I probably deserved it. The optics weren't good, but we couldn't pay Stan because we just didn't have the money."

Jim looked back down at his menu. "It goes with the territory. You handled it pretty well, though. If you don't have the money, you have to use the courts, but that can't be why you wanted to meet me. That's old news." The waiter set water glasses on the table and took their orders. Brian waited for him to leave before continuing.

"Look. I shouldn't even be having this conversation with you. I'll just get to it. Word on the street is you know something about the Coyotes I don't."

"Like what?" He leaned back. "We have the worst record in the league. The ownership gutted the lineup last year, and they keep bitching about their stadium. That's all I know. What do you know?" They both laughed hard enough for the afternoon hostess to notice. Jim caught her smiling at them as she turned away, continuing to count tips.

"Yeah, Jim. That's all public information." Jim was glad Brian was loosening up. "That's not what I'm asking, though. Word on the street is you think they're moving."

Jim thought back to the afternoon in the bar when he ran into Enzo and a couple of Johnston Limited junior partners. "Oh, you heard I asked their bond salesman if the Coyotes were moving? I didn't think I was that loud. I saw them at First and Last about three weeks ago."

"Jim, this is my town. I get paid to know what's going on and make the tough decisions." He stopped when the waiter brought their beers, on the way to another table with food.

The sound of motorcycles roaring up from near the trail drowned out the young man's voice. Jim looked up to the waiter's rolling eyes and asked, "What's that?"

He put his empty hand on his hip, with the other holding a plate of food in the air and said, "It's those damn wheeley-poppers. Pardon my French, but they do it all day on the weekends. You'd think the cops could stop them. Anyway, I'll have your meal out for you in a few."

Brian tipped his beer, winced from the first sip and put the bottle back on the table. "What do you know, Jim?"

Jim's head was spinning as puzzle pieces came together. "I'm a sports fan like anybody else in a big city, but I don't have any help, so I cover government, sports, planning commissions, zoning, everything. I had to figure out finance and budgets to follow the conversation and report to my readers. Turns out sports teams move stadiums about every fifteen years, but lately, it's been almost automatic. Fifteen years is up; get a new stadium. Anyway, I noticed the teams asked for new stadiums when the tax abatement bonds matured. Isn't the Coyotes tax abatement up in four years?"

"Yea, the Ospreys are asking for a new stadium, too, right next to the one they're in now. They have to compete with all the other football teams for sports marketing and players just like the Coyotes." The "we have to compete" argument had never made sense to Jim since they had a monopoly in the town where they played, and the players came from a graduated-scale draft so the only competition should be on the field. "The Ospreys made the playoffs the last four years in a row," Brian continued. "The Championship appearance two years ago makes them one of professional football's most valuable franchises."

"Valuable? That game cost the city fifty million in tax revenue from tax-exempt ticket sales and event-space breaks."

A couple of female runners were seated two tables over. The early-evening fitness crowd swarmed onto the MOTrail as spring melted into the late sunsets of long summer days. Brian lowered his voice. "Jim, a football championship brings economic development like no other event, except maybe the Olympics. I'll give them anything they want."

Jim felt the breeze through the patio as young people moved about. A group of artists set up their easels in a meadow across from the patio entrance on the other side of the trail. He slowly turned to Brian. "Do you have proof of economic development? There's a growing consensus among economists that sports stadiums don't generate any, nor do rails-to-trails projects. Your financial statements only show liabilities. Nowhere do you show revenue that offsets the giveaways."

The waiter brought their food order and hustled over to the patrons beginning to get seated. "That's ridiculous. Look around you. This place is the definition of vibrant. By the way, those so-called economists don't run cities. They just pipe off from their ivory towers. There's no way we can collect city-wide fragmented data tallying all revenue generated from a sports championship game or the MOTrail." Jim expected the dodge, because, like every politician, Brian didn't have to produce economic development data, so he didn't. "But you're avoiding my question, Jim. Do you have specific information about the Coyotes?"

Jim paused, counting to five like his mother had taught him. "You know, Brian, we news people have a sixth sense. I was making a guess to see if I could stir the pot, so my entire theory is complete speculation, but the Coyotes lose their tax abatement in two years, the Osprey's is up in three. Johnston Limited, or, more specifically, Sterling Johnston and his investors, design and build stadium monstrosities all over the world. Their European soccer stadiums are all the rage."

"I know all that. Sterling's kids are on the MOTrail advisory board. He designed most of it," Brian said. Jim hoped the mayor was reading the *Orthus County Post*, because he had written broadly about Sterling's international pursuits, and his children's local philanthropic efforts including, but not limited to, the MOTrail.

Jim continued to describe what he liked to call his speculative method for following hunches. "His people were hanging around First and Last with Enzo Ruiz. I put two and two together and got five. I thought, What the hell? I tossed a grenade to see what would come out of the beaver dam."

"Man, you were pulling that out of your ass? That's more like a *sick* sense. Onward Orlando still has hundreds of millions in bonds outstanding for both stadiums. If the Coyotes leave, I'm stuck with an eighty-thousand-seat baseball stadium. It's not like another team will just decide to drop into Orlando because we have some free baseball space. Although if they didn't bitch and moan so much, and won a pennant every so often, I'd give them what they've been asking for. They can't go two months without asking for better parking facilities or why we haven't gentrified the neighborhood around the stadium yet."

Brian stopped abruptly when the waiter approached their table. "Anything else, gentlemen?"

"I'll have another beer. You, Jim?"

"Sure. Fine by me." The waiter headed back toward the bar. Jim began to suspect Brian had been thinking about the risk of losing one of the professional sports teams, too. "So now you know my instincts. What do you think they're going to do?"

"Who? The Ospreys or the Coyotes?"

"Either."

"This is all off the record, and the only reason I'm telling you is because I would appreciate you telling me anything you find out."

The idea of having the mayor of Orlando as a mutually beneficial source was music to his ears. "Off the record then."

"The Ospreys are solid, but we've been doing the usual negotiations with the Coyotes since last year. You're not the only one that sees these teams moving around every fifteen years. I just can't figure out where they'd go. Tampa already has a team. Jacksonville maybe. Miami won the Baseball Championship two years ago, so they're not going anywhere. North Florida doesn't have a market large enough."

"Why don't they issue their own bonds instead of borrowing from you?"

"Basic banking principal," Brian said. "National sports teams aren't publicly traded. Only publicly traded companies and governments issue bonds. Banks charge interest so they come to City Hall to avoid paying it. We just make them pay for the debt and eliminate their taxes."

The waiter brought two more beers over, condensation dripping off the glass in the afternoon heat. He put a bowl down. "Here's some chips you boys can munch on."

Brian reached for a couple of chips. "Jim, you have no idea, or maybe you do. Bob is having money troubles. How did he pay the Orthus Hospital miss?"

"He pulled it from his bank line of credit, and it doesn't look much better for the November payment." The roar of motorcycles and four-wheelers screamed back up the street as they returned to their home base. "Damn, that's loud, Brian."

"They're just kids. They come down the trail to City Hall and then turn onto the streets. No harm, no foul." Brian sipped his beer, set it down, and wiped off the sides of the glass with a napkin. "You think Bob will allow Orthus Regional Hospital to default?"

"I don't know. The last time the hospital got in trouble, a couple of billionaires bailed them out."

"Missed payments are happening all over the country, Jim. It's not just me. Our pension system is a wreck. We've got people that have no idea they can save their own money in the retirement plan, because we fund it, and their union bosses tell them we owe them more. I have to go along with it to keep the peace."

"Funny thing to threaten a strike for benefits no one can get in the public sector. Can't say I have that luxury at work. The irony of the recalcitrant always amazes me." Jim tipped his glass. "Don't you guys have the money for it? I thought you all had these huge budgets?"

"Drolland gets about a billion a year. Stan gets about three. I get about two. We have to pay for the pension underperformance out of our budgets. Their performance stinks. The rest of the money is left for police cars, roads, fire trucks, and sewer systems. We can't even afford decent parking lots at the public MOTrail entrances.

"I thought unpaved parking lots were part of the urban appeal of a rails-to-trails project." Jim chuckled and assumed Brian didn't get the joke, because he smiled, but not at him.

Brian stood up from the table and spoke across the patio toward the hostess stand. "Paige. Over here." Jim turned to see Paige Jackson standing on the steps across the deck. He followed suit and stood up, too. Paige arrived at the table and fell into a hug with Brian. "Hey Jim, you know Paige Jackson, right? She's been a great friend of the City of Orlando's benevolent efforts."

Jim extended his hand with a smile and said, "I sure do." His fingertips slipped across her smooth hands. "Hey, Paige."

She was still smiling when she said, "I'm meeting some friends here to run in a bit. Am I interrupting anything?"

"Nothing that can't be postponed to visit with you," Brian said. "We were just talking about how great this place is, and how much more money the City of Orlando could make if it didn't have to pay pensions, so we could finally begin MOTrail's phase two."

"First you need to figure out how to pay for the first phase, according to Jim's articles." Paige turned to Jim. "They're very enlightening. I look forward to reading the *Post* every morning."

"I'm sure your kitchen table conversations are very enlightening, too," Brian said.

The waiter was coming toward the table but reversed course when Paige waved him off. "Stan is having serious problems. His school teachers haven't been paid their contributions since the last administration was in control. He can't do anything about it because the money's not there, but he's cornered by politics, just as you are."

"How much of your budget goes to pensions, Brian?" Jim asked.

"Half," he answered, seemingly resigned to Paige's observation.

Jim looked at Paige. "Did you know that?"

Her elbows rested on the chair, her hands dangled over the side as if she would be as comfortable on an Olympic team as she reportedly was in a courtroom. "Because of the pension guarantees, every urban municipality in the country spends the same." She nodded at Brian. "Stan and Bob included."

Jim saw Brian's demeanor change when he leaned up to the table and grabbed his beer with both hands. He looked at Jim. "State law requires us to have balanced budgets. If we spend a billion and take in nine hundred million, we have to issue a hundred in debt. It doesn't matter if pensions are half the budget and getting bigger, our state charter says we have to balance the budget. We're kicking the can down a very long road, Jim."

"Well, then, 'balancing the budget' might be the most misunderstood term in the English language. How have you been able to sustain it for so long?"

"Economic development has to be part of the equation. You might not think so, and that's your prerogative, but we use revenue bonds to build sports stadiums, mixed-use developments like this one, and mass transit to increase tax revenues. They bring countless jobs, new businesses to serve the development, and higher taxes; we just have to wait fifteen to twenty years to get the money."

"My offer stands," Jim chuckled. "Get your staff to send me the economic development numbers, and I'll write the article."

Paige caught Jim off guard when she abruptly stood up. "That would be a worthwhile article, Brian. Then we'd know once and for all about the benefits of tax abatements. Nice to see you, Jim. My running club is beginning to show up, and we try to start at 6:00 sharp."

Jim glanced past her and saw several running enthusiasts stretching and hopping around on the trail. “Nice to see you, too, Paige.”

Paige shook both their hands before hurrying toward her group, which had already broken into a half-sprint down the trail.

Jim turned back to Brian. “Speaking of Johnston Limited, I did notice Bob, Sterling, and Stan in First and Last. That guy from TREP was there with them, too. Do you think they were meeting about the MOTrax TOD developments on the stations north of town?”

“Maybe,” Brian replied. “But now I think I get your sixth sense. If Stan was in the meeting, they need his school board money. Smithson Galleria is going to cost a bundle, and Orthus County is obviously up against their bond cap.”

“How can they be considering more development at Smithson if things are so bad?”

“Because everyone wants it,” Brian said. “The project is graded down to the parking lots. Now they just need money to get started. They’ve been through three developers already and none of them can make it work.”

Jim finished his beer. “Well, I’ve got to get out of here, too. Stories to write and all.” He threw a ten-dollar bill on the table and stood up. “Let me know if you hear anything about more Orthus Hospital trouble or Smithson Galleria.”

Brian followed suit, throwing down another ten as he stood. “Will do. Keep me posted on any Coyotes information you come across.”

As Jim walked toward his car, he gauged his timing for the video release, now knowing he had a friend in the Attorney General’s office.

CHAPTER 11

The young assistant pulled the large glass door open on its hidden hinges. Stan Jackson watched her move to the side as Darrell Cross walked in. He half expected Darrell, whom he'd nicknamed DC in high school, to put his arm around the girl's waist. Stan put his hand over the receiver and yelled, "Come on in here, DC. That girl's got work to do." When she pulled her hand away from the door, she slid it onto her hip, emphasizing her long fingernails. Stan caught the Grady High School Panther logo emblazoned on DC's golf shirt when he turned to watch her head back to her desk. "If you boys need anything else, be sure to let me know," she called out, her voice echoing down the marble hallway.

"I'm sure we will, miss. Thank you," DC yelled back. Stan waved him in as he continued his phone conversation.

His old football buddy walked past a conference table and toward the stainless steel and glass desk. Stan could tell he was checking out the office. Crystal, porcelain, and steel facades adorned the interior. Coffee and drink services were behind the conference table next to the full-length floor-to-ceiling window. The outside balcony was wrapped in glass, but Stanley rarely ventured out because of the imposing view of the parking lot below.

From anywhere in the room, Stan could see North Downtown Orlando and the interconnected squares of the government district. He heard the rumble of the afternoon MOTrax train as it barreled north and south through the center of town like a faded dream train of yesterday. The image was blurred by the stifling humidity of the Central Florida heat. Honking horns were his constant reminder that parallel white ribbons of buckled highway, and the surface streets below, choked on new in-town residents and tourists. Yet no workers ever appeared at the construction lanes marked by barriers and caution signs. Stan could see the small cityscapes that starved his school district where once-lush King Citrus groves used to feed the economy.

Stan nodded at DC with two fingers in the air. As if on cue, his friend went over to the side liquor cabinet, pulled out a bottle, and poured two gins. After he closed the cap on the bottle, he walked past a long black leather couch bookended by two matching chairs facing each other in the middle of the room. The African print rug could be seen through the coffee-table glass. Above the couch was a large picture of Martin Luther King Jr. on the Washington Mall. Stan hung his Vanderbilt diploma behind his desk in view of anyone who sat in his guest chairs. The TV in the corner was tuned to financial news. Stan frowned. "I'll get back to you," he said into the phone's receiver. "These things never work out the way you guys promise."

He hung up and took the drink from DC's outstretched hand as he sat down. Stan knew DC loved the office. It became obvious as he sat there, rubbing his hands over the leather armrests and looking around, after he drank from the clinking crystal glass. Stan had been to the teacher's lounge at Grady High School where DC taught, and it didn't compare. He lifted his shoes off the desk, brought them to the floor, and swiveled around to face him.

"Who was that?" DC asked.

Stan moaned. "Just another one of TREP's pocket politicians asking for more money. Orthus County is getting close to their bond limit. He was trying to get me to play ball on the Smithson Galleria project. He said, 'Uh, Dr. Jackson. Uh, you don't know me, but I've watched many a Commodore game where you caught long passes for touchdowns.' That asshole went to FSU. We never played the Seminoles. Then he says, 'Uh, what if we built you a high school in Smithson Galleria? We'd like to meet as soon as possible. The developer's spent all his money on excavation. The project will be the first of its kind in the country. It will generate tax revenues for the Orthus County School Board and Orthus County for decades to come. As you know, it doesn't create any now.' That's what they all say."

"Heh." DC thumbed his nose. "The last place they need a new high school is up in private-school territory. All you got are white boys and Latinos. White boys can't ball and Latinos don't vote." For a brief moment, Stan was jealous of DC's low-pressure job with so few responsibilities.

Out of site but on Stan's mind were the leaking roofs, broken lights, and cracked pavements of the North Orthus County schools. If track and field existed at all, the grass centers were barren deserts of brown. Stan had deferred action in the Latino neighborhoods because the kids were too grateful to care, and from what he'd read, it was better than the childhood they'd left behind. His office would take frantic calls from helicopter moms every time they witnessed private-school luxury during mixed sporting events. Explaining public schools would have to charge admission to experience that kind of luxury firsthand only seemed to raise their ire. "If the City of Orlando hadn't screwed me out of two years of MOTrail bond payments, I wouldn't need a promise from a senator. We could build our own new high school. How could Brian do that? We've been friends for years. The MOTrail people keep spouting off about property values going up. DC, two blocks off the trail they're going down. You know rich people don't want to live next to the hood. They put a couple of coffee shops and steakhouses on the trail and added some bike racks. Brian is watching too much of that lily white, bowtie news." He realized he was venting about a neighborhood he actually lived in and that DC couldn't afford, and stopped.

"Then why you always giving in, Flash?"

Stan crumpled up the phone-message note and tossed it into a trash can, imitating his best fade-away jumper. "Giving in? I did it for the City of Orlando, one time. What the hell are you talking about? Now a North Orthus County senator wants to build me a high school."

After he had finished Grady High School, he took the first ticket out of the inner city to Vanderbilt for a better life and a financial future. He thought back to the day of his last Ospreys paycheck, through the administrative appointment to school board superintendent, and ultimately, a campaign victory. He revealed to DC what had weighed on him since the day he left professional football and the moment he took the reins on the Orthus County School Board. "DC, how much you think I got paid playing ball?"

"Damn, Flash, the *Orlando Journal* said your first contract was three million for five years with a one-hundred-and-fifty-thousand-dollar signing bonus. That about right?"

"That's it. I got six hundred thousand per year as a seventh rounder. I make a quarter of that now."

"Damn shame when the Sharks busted you on that fourth down. They were doin' it to everybody, but nobody got fined. But you still makin' twice as much as me. Why you askin'?"

"Because Orthus County, Orthus Public Schools, and every state employee in the country has a better retirement plan than professional athletes—with respect to contributions and guarantees anyway. Don't get me wrong. It was a pleasant surprise to me, too." Stan got up from his seat and went over to look outside. The sun shone through the balcony and the glass in his hand. He shook the ice to scatter its reflection on the Martin Luther King painting across the room.

"Oh, bullshit," DC said. "You haven't made any contributions to our plan in years. That's why my people want to file a class-action lawsuit. Can't everybody catch touchdowns on Sunday."

"DC, you're not getting it. Our retirement has a guaranteed rate of return that's impossible to match. A one-hundred-percent stock market portfolio returns about nine percent." He walked over and turned off the financial news, not wanting to hear anything else about a real estate recession, but knowing that's how Brian had provided him with this office space. Then he walked back over to the balcony exit and looked over the city. "That means the Pension Board running our retirement money has no chance of meeting that goal. They are handcuffed by a fiduciary rule."

"A what? You startin' to sound like Paige more and more all the time. You the only one I know makin' more than two hundred." Stan watched DC's reflection in the glass door as he got up from his chair and paced around the room with his drink in his hand, but keeping his distance.

Stan turned around. "The Pension Board, by law, has to hold safer, lower-performing securities like Treasury bonds. They can't ever make the eight-percent guarantee over our work lives. When they don't, it comes out of the General Fund, y'know, money it takes to run a school system."

"Now you startin' to sound like that asshole Bob Drolland." DC raised his hands out to his sides in the middle of the room. "We don't get Social Security, man. We gave it up because all the new union people said we'd get a better deal if we did it ourselves." DC frowned when his hands came back down, tilted his head to one side, and thumbed his nose.

"I know, DC. I got the same deal you do and I spent all my football money." He walked back over to his chair and sat down. "If the teachers win a class-action lawsuit, half will go to the teachers and the other half will go to the lawyers. What could we do with that money? There's no way I'm shorting the kids. We'll issue more debt for all of it—court settlement, pension plan, and new schools."

"Now you're talkin'. You keep buildin' high schools and middle schools and you'll keep gettin' elected like we did last year." Stan raised his glass when DC walked toward the desk to toast their shared success as candidate and campaign manager. "Man, your campaign was almost as much fun as your bachelor party, but if you don't refund all that money you ain't paid, they will take your ass to court. My members get scared when you start talkin' about pension reform. They got a reason to be."

"Have you ever heard the term unfunded pension liabilities?"

"Yea, man. I know what it means." DC backed away from the desk and began pacing again. He put his drink down on a glass table and twisted his watch. "The Orthus Public School teacher is the only qualified adult that gives a damn about these kids. They work hard. Our schoolteachers didn't get a scholarship to Vanderbilt, but they stayed up nights at UCF. They battled the traffic jams and the MOTrax bullies. They take shit off fourteen-year-olds that get sent home to play video games for a week. They deserve what's comin'. Everyone deserves an honest retirement."

"You're right, but I'll throw you a curve ball. When your mom passed away, what happened to her teacher's pension?"

"It stopped. That's what they do."

"If that money would've been in a 403(b), you and your sisters would've received an inheritance. But because it's a pension, the school board keeps the remainder. They would keep the remainder if you retired and got run over by a bus the next day."

"Yeah, I know." Stan instantly felt sorry for making the comparison as he remembered back to the funeral and seeing DC cry twice in one year for losing a state championship and his mother. DC sipped his drink and put his hands on the back of the guest chair facing Stan.

"Orthus County kids are as bright as any in America, DC. They just need a chance to learn with new rooms, electronic devices that work, digital white boards, better teacher lounges, and sports facilities. Man, our kids are getting ripped off. An insurance company beholden to the state legislature runs our pension system. The fees they're charging every single teacher is more than any private sector retirement plan would ever get away with. Hell, it would be illegal."

Stan saw an opening when DC jerked his head up. "What fees?"

Stan leaned forward and looked up at DC. "The fees inside the pension plan investments. They don't work for free. When's the last time anyone from the pension gave you an answer you could understand?"

"They bring someone down here to talk in the lunch room in the summertime before school starts."

"Yeah, right. They could be speaking Russian and no one would know. Look in the teachers' eyes. That's if you can see them through their cell phones."

"I'm lookin' around alright." DC laughed, sat back down in the leather chair, and took another sip of his gin.

"Did you see our math teacher, Charlene, put them on the spot last year? She asked the guy, 'Does the state match occur at the beginning or end of the year?' The guy actually blinked. Then he tried to brush it off with, 'It's not really all that important because you'll get paid for life'." Stan used the opportunity to concede the teachers would win a lawsuit, but wanted to emphasize his leadership responsibility of maintaining teacher morale. "He was literally stunned when she asked if she could roll the funds into her IRA along with the money she planned on winning in court. I don't think any of these guys could pass one of Charlene's classes."

"I almost missed our state championship game because of Algebra, but she got me through it. Teachers like her are the reason I do this shitty union job. So, what do you have to do for the senator to get another high school built?"

Frustrated DC had moved away from pension negotiations, Stan leaned back in his chair and tried to explain. "Development authorities like Progress Orthus and Onward Orlando need taxpayer funds to finance big government projects like the MOTrail, MOTrax, and Smithson Galleria. They give away tax abatements we can't control. All those new developments being built never pay the promised increased property taxes, and now they want the Orthus County School system to loan them more money to build the Smithson Galleria project. The guy on the phone said he'd get funds appropriated to build a high school on an abandoned apartment complex next to the site if we did it. It's still not worth it, though. A ten-million-dollar school for a twenty-five-million-dollar tax abatement, and up to our asses in real estate risk? I don't think so."

DC leaned forward and put his elbows on his knees with the rim of the glass dangling from one hand. "You mean the last stop on MOTrax is getting a new mall?"

"Not just a mall, DC—an entire urban complex with movie theatres, shops, high rise towers, parking decks, and an apartment complex. They want me to lend them the money and forego twenty years of school board taxes."

"I thought Progress Orthus and Onward Orlando were private enterprises, or companies, or somethin' like that."

"That's what they'd like you to believe. That's what they want to be, too, but no. They're off-balance-sheet operations for politicians."

"So, they just take part of your tax revenue?"

"Yep."

"Damn, bro. That is messed up! Then why would you ever help them?"

"First of all, abating my tax revenue without my consent is legal, but with regard to loaning them money, I had to see it for myself first. Thanks to the MOTrail, once bitten, twice shy. See, all these developers are convinced their projects are so good the areas surrounding them will grow twice as fast with the new improvements. I've learned the hard way, not only is it bullshit, but development authority tax abatements also create government-subsidized segregation. Want proof?"

"I'm listening."

"Who lives in Section 8 housing right over there?" Stan pointed through the glass toward the MOTrail.

"The hood? That's easy. Guys like me and you. Brothas' and sistas'."

"What do you think the MOTrail is?"

"The MOTrail? Old train tracks turned into running and bicycle trails all inside Orlando's city limits. Pretty cool if you're single, rich, and you live there."

"To me and Paige, it's home, but it's not what it used to be. You've seen all the bars and restaurants going up everywhere? When's the last time you went over there to ride a bicycle?"

"I don't."

"Coincidentally, neither does the rest of car-driving America."

"Can you see me in one of those bicycle costumes?" DC laughed.

"Damn, DC. I can't un-see that." Stan smiled and took a drink. "Neither the bars nor the restaurants pay taxes. The Orthus County School Board funded the whole thing when we issued the two-hundred-million-dollar bond."

"I remember that. I didn't know what you were doin'. I thought it was just a deal with City of Orlando liberals or somethin'. Now I remember. They said, 'Orlando Public Schools will be the direct beneficiaries of increased taxes.' And you tellin' me they don't pay any."

"None."

"Well, sounds to me like you need to stop loaning them money."

He considered how peaceful DC's life must be without the tit-for-tat political negotiations required to fund any vision, or campaign. "I learned my lesson last summer when the mayor didn't make the MOTrail bond payment. I owed Enzo over at Dunham Schauble, and had to pull money from the general fund to cover it. Money that pays for our unsustainable pensions."

"There you go talkin' about pensions again. Now I mean it, Flash. Just cause you gettin' screwed by those development companies, or whatever, don't touch our pensions. The membership is houndin' me now about plans they've heard comin' out of your office. That's what started all this class-action-lawsuit talk. Somethin' they heard about fewer sick days and changes to the DROP program. I'm getting another drink." Stan thought about DC's staged opposition, recognizing he was simply being a standard-bearer until a better offer came along, but his current insolence was almost too much to bear as he watched him shake the ice in his glass and walk back over to the bar. "Paige ain't been tellin' you to cut the pensions, has she? She ain't got no business with our pensions, Flash."

"You know me better than that." He watched DC pour the drink, and decided his emotions wouldn't get the best of him, but DC needed a reminder of the chain of command. "Make me another one, too, and don't spill any on that rug. It's real zebra."

"She was sure barkin' orders the mornin' after your bachelor party. You best be glad I got those girls out of the room." DC chuckled. "So how is the City of Orlando goin' to make the next payment for the MOTrail if they can't make the last one?" he asked as he sat down again.

Stan reached over and took the drink off the table where DC had left it, and wondered if him leaving it there had been intentional. "Like every first rounder after a great rookie year, the mayor wants to renegotiate the contract. Move the payoff out so the payments are lower. What he doesn't want to hear is that those bond-market guys are ruthless. They want their money we said we'd pay. They don't see black, white, school kid, or orphan. Wall Street wants payment on time, every time. If we miss one payment, the credit-rating agencies will cut my bond rating and double my interest rates. The bond managers are on me all the damn time, DC. It never stops."

"I feel ya', bro."

Stan shook his head knowing DC had no idea what it meant to talk to institutional bond managers. His anger began to well up just as it had the day Brian had called to tell him he was going to miss the semi-annual payment. He made a final push to convince DC of what was going to happen. "I could have bought a new football stadium and a baseball field for Grady High School with the bond payments Orlando missed. The money is tight! You get it? We should raise teacher pay and scrap the pension. Their pension payments should be rolled into 403(b)s. It's the only way."

"If you're in bad business, that's your fault. Don't start bullshitting me about that pension plan again. You know that won't happen. I'm not goin' to a war I've already won. Keep it up and we'll finish the war in court."

Stan had internalized the union tactic of not giving an inch, and they had obviously coached DC on his position, but he would have his way with or without him so he conceded the afternoon to his high school friend. "I can't argue with that. I'm doing this 'shitty' job the same reason you are: the kids and the teachers. Speaking of kids, how's Grady going to be this year? Are we going to see you walking the sidelines again this fall, Coach DC?"

"You damn right you will. Grady's got all the pieces. They got a chance at State!" Stan watched him pour the last of his gin into his open mouth, swirl the piece of ice in the bottom of the glass, and then toss it back. He put the empty glass on Stan's desk as he got up still chewing the ice. He walked out and yelled back, "See you this summer."

You sure will, Stan thought.

Stan forwarded himself an email from his office, GET GAS. TEXT BLONDE FROM STERLING'S PLANE.

As he hit send on the email, his assistant forwarded a call from a local principal with a scheduling conflict. Summer workouts had barely begun, but Stan was already facilitating the annual ritual of scheduling football games at Grady High School. One of three high schools that shared the stadium had a Friday night conflict and needed a favor. The tragedy was not lost on Stan. He loved football and inner-city kids.

After Stan hung up from the conversation his phone pinged with a text. You going to call me? I'm having your baby.

CHAPTER 12

Jim was still wondering why Ezzy had asked him to invite Sheriff Bill Bolek up to Lochloosa, as the two men drove through the North Florida farmlands crawling south into shallow swamps and hyacinth-choked lakes, forested with live oaks and palmetto hammocks. Most of the arable highlands were owned by King Citrus Company. Jim's parents, Matt and Beth Pinson, owned the bait shop next to Estelle's BBQ. His mom was a schoolteacher at Lochloosa High School and was soon to retire after thirty years, plus five, in the DROP program. She taught summer school for kids who needed extra help in English, French, or Spanish, and he knew she finished before lunch and was expecting a visit from her son—but not before he stopped into Estelle's for breakfast, which is the only place he'd known Bill to visit in Lochloosa one hot, unfortunate night two years ago.

Estelle's was a central hub of North Orthus County at the crossroads of a multiracial melting pot. The gas pumps and BBQ counter were a mixture of legacy grove employees, University of Florida kids out for a road trip, and Florida wildlife rogues searching for cheap hunts and unwatched fishing equipment.

The door jingled as Jim and Bill walked in. "Hey, Jim Pinson! You think you can catch any fish today? You bring the sheriff to help you? Did you warn Big Mike you brought the law?"

"We couldn't risk him backing out," Bill said, as he pulled off his baseball cap and tossed it on one of the empty tables. "He might think I was out here to take him to jail again."

"Morning, Estelle. I never had a problem puttin' the whoop on shellcrackers, but I brought Bill just in case Big Mike's nose ain't workin', but if he calls before we leave here don't tell him."

Jim loved coming home to the heavy laughter that poured out from behind the chest-high counter. "Don't come up here talking that country nonsense to me. We know who you are!" Estelle was taking orders while the day cook was fast managing a large, commercial flat iron filled with bacon, country ham, and eggs. Jim remembered when his dad had installed the stainless-steel smoker embedded in the back wall. Smoked pork BBQ glistened on the racks.

"Two of the usuals?" Estelle yelled while she brought plates to the order counter.

Jim saw Bill reading the menu above and behind her. "I think I'll try…"

Jim was close enough to hear Estelle whisper, "Sheriff, order from this menu on the counter. If this is the only time you ever visit Estelle's—to eat—you need to know what we're good at."

"Uh, OK. I'll have the eggs over easy, pork BBQ, and biscuits."

"Good choice, Sheriff." She winked. "You won't be sorry."

"I get the feeling you're right."

Jim could tell business had only gotten better right along with Estelle's staying power as the door jingled with every customer that entered to buy gas, groceries, and breakfast. He was brought back to the moment, when Estelle reverted back to the trademark dialogue of loud. "Jim?"

"Why do I even bother? I'll have the same. It's been too long."

"It sure has. Full moon was Tuesday. Your daddy said they started to pick up yesterday afternoon. It should be good."

Estelle yelled past the coffee-service counter to where Bill had wandered, "You remembering where everything is, Sheriff?"

"Oh, yeah. I find the exits first and the coffee second." Bill poured a large cup of black mother's milk. "Want one, Jim?"

"Sure do. Thanks, Sheriff." Bill walked back and sat down at the table with Jim. They sat patiently at the small tables with the other early-risers reading the paper. Estelle moved in two constant motions from the front counter to the flat iron. The uneasy feeling of Bill's last trip out to Estelle's weighed on Jim's mind.

Two years ago, Big Mike, local fishing legend and Jim's childhood friend, found his stolen boat on a trailer outside Estelle's. Mike walked in where Jim and his father had been sitting eating dinner after fishing the night spawn and said, "Anybody know whose boat that is outside on the trailer?"

"What's going on, Mike?" Estelle had shouted from behind the counter as they were near closing time, and she was shutting the kitchen down.

Two men sat drinking beer by themselves when one stood up to tower above the room. "It's my boat. What's it to you?" He sneered at Mike and ignored the peace accorded by people sharing ignored poverty this far out in the countryside.

"It's my boat and I'm going to unhook it and take it home. If you got anything to say about it, I'll be outside." The big man had followed Mike out while Estelle was calling 911.

Jim walked out in time to see Big Mike crank the trailer stand down and witness the stranger hitting him across the back of the neck with a tire iron. It must have been a deafening thud, but Mike moved into the attack following only his rage. The stranger had pulled Mike's shirt over his head and was whaling on his face and ribs. Before it got any worse, Jim had reached the back of the stranger at the same time Mike had managed to pull out his pocketknife in the chaos. When Jim grabbed the stranger to pull him back, he fell limp as Mike yelled out, "Boy, you're hurt. You're hurt bad. You keep swingin' and I'll keep cuttin'."

"You cut me open. Oh, shit. I'm gonna' die." Subdued, the man stumbled backwards holding his blood-stained shirt as Jim guided him to the front-porch steps to sit down.

"We're done, right? I'll get you some rags so you don't bleed to death. Stealing my boat? I oughta' haul you out in the swamp. Damn it, why'd you make me do that?" Mike came back out with rags and gave them to Jim while he applied pressure to the wound. The Life Flight helicopter arrived soon after the police cars and landed in the large open sand parking lot in front of Pinson's Bait Shop. After he was loaded onto the helicopter, the engine whirred to a fever pitch as it ascended into the sky. The noise of the vanishing helicopter lights bled into the eerie quiet of the Central Florida Highway. Sheriff Bolek began his investigation under the streetlight high above the lone convenience store.

One of the locals sitting on the front porch yelled out, "Mike cut 'em from da' rooter to da' tooter, Sheriff, but he had it comin'. Steal a man's boat like dat'. He know betta' next time befo' he come stealin' boats agin'." His neighbor on the bench hollered, "Yea he will." They swiveled toward one another until their smiling, bloodshot eyes connected. They toasted their brown bags high in the air, swilled beer, and laughed at the darkness set in motion by the blinking four-way light.

"Pipe down, gentlemen. It's been a long night and you're drinking beer from open containers." Jim was standing next to the patrol car when Bill put the cuffs on Mike himself. "Damn it," Bill said. "You couldn't kick his ass without a knife? Why do all you shit kickers out here have to butcher each other?"

"Man needs to know his limitations, Sheriff. He's lucky I didn't shoot him."

"Well, you're going to jail, but you won't be there long. My guys are getting the video from the owner of the place. If it's like everyone says, I won't file any charges."

"Sheriff, we're the only law out here. People need to stay in line."

"I'm the law. I'll read you your rights on the way to Orlando. I'll get one of my guys to bring you back out here after we watch the video." He put his hand on top of Mike's head and guided him into the back of his SUV. "Lean over. I'll pull these cuffs off. It's going to be a long ride."

"Thanks, Sheriff."

After Bill came back out from getting Estelle's statement, he looked at Jim in the empty parking lot cleared out by all the sirens, and said, "I need to get going cause it's a long drive back."

Big Mike had the rural fearlessness of a man that lived for the Lochloosa wild. Estelle's security camera caught the whole thing on video. The boat was stolen. It was Mike's and he'd acted in self-defense.

Estelle put the two plates on the counter, wiped her hair out of her eyes, and yelled in Jim's direction. He'd been watching her with his chin in his hand as a boy would watch a favorite aunt make his favorite dessert. "Order up. Enjoy it fellas." Then she picked up the ticket book and took the next order.

"Breakfast never looked so good." Jim got up and grabbed both plates and sat back down with Bill. They finished, paid, and walked next door. Old four-wheel-drive trucks pulling small aluminum boats idled in front of Pinson's. The line reached out the driveway to the dirt road that intersected with the Central Florida Highway. The main entrance amounted to little more than a small wooden shed with a raised metal-seam roof and a dirt floor. Off behind the main bait shop was the yard garden next to the clapboard house Jim grew up in. A couple of stand-up kitchen freezers sat between

Pinson's pole-barn opening and the line of trucks. Jim had helped his father hand weld the BBQ grill sitting off to the right. Fish fryers stood in random areas around the front yard next to giant wooden cable spools sticking out of the ground. Matt had buried one side to create oversized bar tables, but right now, he darted back and forth to the line of trucks with the best bait in Central Florida.

"Morning, Jim. Watch out for those chickens. That rooster is ornery."

"Hey, Dad. You got plenty of bait?"

"Morning, Mr. Pinson. It's been a while."

"Morning, Sheriff. Glad you could make it out here to have some fun, instead of cleaning up after Big Mike's self-policing efforts." He turned to Jim and said, "Boy, you know I got the best baits for miles. Excuse me for a minute. Business is pickin' up." After filling orders for three waiting trucks, he moved with the erratic motion of a tightly compressed spring over to the garden. Jim and Bill were looking over the mid-summer squash, pole beans, and okra.

"Glad you came up, Sheriff. A few of your officers park right here in this parking lot at night and on the weekends. We appreciate the support way out here on the lonely Central Florida Highway. State Patrol and Orthus County deputies eat free at Estelle's every day, you know?"

"I just found out, Mr. Pinson. We appreciate the support."

"Call me Matt, Sheriff. They were bitin' on the north end yesterday morning. How much bait you need, Jim?"

Jim's dad worked for King Citrus in its heyday after his stint in the Marines. Jepson King, Ezzy's dad, hired Matt the day he got home from Vietnam. Matt flew helicopters picking up wounded. He fought his way through the back rooms of the Bangkok Thai Boxing Circuit for R&R.

Prospects weren't good for helicopter pilots coming back from Vietnam, but Matt would do anything. King Citrus operations afforded a helicopter budget and had just begun large-scale grove irrigation and needed industrial-strength minds. Jepson King asked Matt if he could build pipelines. "Twisting big wrenches and flying your Bell Helicopter is exactly what I'm looking for, Mr. King." He'd become a King Citrus employee and retired a decade ago.

Jepson hired John, Matt's oldest son and Jim's brother, right after he graduated from high school. Matt coached his two sons all the way through football and baseball. John and Ezzy dated through high school, and though they both knew the distance of different futures would eventually take its toll on the young romance, they didn't care. Ezzy was home from New York one weekend from college, and John had a pocketful of cash from his King Citrus maintenance job and a convertible. Jim remembered everyone that night at the Fish Camp next to Citrus Lake. The stars went on forever as John and Ezzy danced their last dance. On the way home, John's car spun off the road under the night sky and into the groves. Ezzy walked two miles back with a broken arm to get help. John's funeral became the event that would bond them all together forever.

"Two sacks should do it," Jim said. "Can I borrow the boat?"

"You bet. I gassed it up this morning and put new lines on the bait casters. They might bird-nest the first few casts, but once they get wet, they'll smooth out. The gears are greased and I put new eyes on the rods. Try Frogs around the banks and Beetlespins in the middle."

Matt's hunched, six-foot frame reached across the cage of singing crickets. He grabbed up a can and pushed a bag into the open end. Then he pulled out an old aquarium scoop, raked through the cage, and dropped the net over the bag. He leveled it off with his hand at the rim, then zipped the bag, and pulled it from the can. He recreated the same motion and tossed both bags to Jim. "You going to see your mom?"

Jim smiled. "Of course I am. The son of a schoolteacher knows better than to get out of line."

Matt cocked his head. "This is her last year, you know. If you don't start coming up more, she's coming to see you in Orlando. You don't want that, do you?"

"I know, Dad. I wish I could come home more often."

Bill dropped twenty bucks on the makeshift bait store table.

"Thanks, Sheriff. We'll put that in Beth's Lottie Moon can for church." Matt pulled a speckled blue coffee pot from a creaky shelf and dropped in the donation.

"You guys can come visit me anytime you want," Jim said.

"Jim, I said Beth might come see you. I ain't gettin' anywhere near Orlando. You guys go see your momma and then go catch 'em. It's gettin' late."

"Love ya, dad." Jim shooed the rooster away from their feet as they walked back to the truck.

"You too, Jim. Send me pictures with that phone if you can get it to work. If you manage to catch anything, we can fry 'em before you head back. The okra's ready, too." Jim hooked up the boat trailer and they rattled out of the sand parking lot.

CHAPTER 13

Jim and Bill pulled onto the seventy-year-old campus of Lochloosa High School. Jim pointed to the Bulldogs football team that was holding varsity-led practice in the outfield of the baseball diamond. The last-era, mold-stained concrete stadium stood in the background. Jim read aloud the sign below the miniature press box:

Lochloosa High School Bulldogs
Florida State Champs
The Pride of the Black and Gold

He looked at Bill and smiled. "Three strings of state, regional, and district championships are stenciled across the bottom. You know, in case you're wondering."

Bill answered in the language of a grid-iron veteran. "I'm from Thompson County. I know a little something about it."

The insulation was falling from the angle-iron roof structure over the bus loading area. The stucco exteriors on the top edge of the brick walls needed repair and paint. Old concrete sidewalks led students through a maze of earthen public areas ending at outdated school buildings and portable trailers. Jim saw his mom walking down the path toward them on her way to class. Students were parking bicycles or their old cars, and filing into class as they greeted her when they passed.

"Hey, mom," he called out as she got closer. "Are the kids getting any smarter?"

She hugged him close, kissed him on the cheek, and said, "Every year. We must try not to get in their way. Lead them to…" Jim joined in: "the truth and they will see it for themselves."

"Hello, I'm Elizabeth Pinson. I'm Jim's mom. It's a pleasure to meet you, Sheriff Bolek."

"Pleasure's all mine, Mrs. Pinson. Please call me Bill." He looked back and forth at Jim and Beth. Jim could tell Bill was discovering what everyone did. She looked half her age, and her youngest son looked just like her.

"Call me Beth."

"Jim tells me about this place all the time. Ezzy King tells me about it, too."

"What do you know about Ezzy?"

"Not much." Jim noticed Bill blushing under Beth's spotlight, and was glad he could avoid it for the moment. "We occasionally run into each other in Orlando."

"Bill, it will take someone very special to make Ezzy King happy. We all hope she finds him." Jim caught Bill's surprised look in his peripheral vision.

"Well, I don't want to keep you boys. Fish are bitin', and I need to get to class. I'll be at the bait shop after, making sure Matt doesn't spend all the profit at Estelle's."

"Thanks, Mom."

"Be safe out there, Jim. I love you, son. We're all so proud of you. See you this afternoon?"

"Yes, ma'am."

"Very nice to meet you, Beth."

"You, too, Bill. Good luck."

Jim and Bill pulled into the parking lot of the public boat launch. They passed Big Mike's early model Ford 4 X 4 with an empty boat trailer. "I always get nervous when I see Mike's boat trailer with no boat on it," Bill said.

"Heard that," Jim replied and shook his head.

Jim backed his trailer down the boat ramp to unload Matt's camouflage aluminum boat. Between the bench seat and the boat motor was an elevated seat on the stern. The driver sat on the bow with two one-armed bandits on each side of the seat: one to steer, one for throttle. It was stripped down with only the essentials for speed and ease. It took Jim's lifetime to learn all of Lake Lochloosa's shifting hyacinth islands, but having some local help was always an advantage.

A circling boat just off the end of the dock killed the motor. "You didn't tell me you were bringing the law." The words rolled off Big Mike's tongue like a family of sunning box turtles falling off a log.

Jim was about to cuss him out for good measure when Bill said, "If no one says anything, no one will know, Big Mike. I'm just out here taking in the sights." Jim thought those were good ground rules considering that's what authority figures do: set ground rules. He was also glad he didn't have to act as Mike's translator as so often happened when he brought his Orlando friends to the swamp. This was Bill's first invited trip to the best fishing in Florida since he'd been elected sheriff, and Jim didn't want it to be the last.

"Sheriff Bill, half the guys out here know you professionally. I'll try and keep us off the radar, but it won't be easy," he said.

Jim appreciated Mike trying to lighten the mood, as meetings between two fiercely independent alpha males can sometimes be uncomfortable.

"Just put us on the fish. We'll take care of the rest. Let's get it on."

"I'll do my best, Sheriff. You know I will."

Jim cranked the boat motor and drove from the bow with Bill reclining on the back bench. "Just follow me around the lake," Big Mike called out. "I found most of the beds yesterday. Cast up into the lily pads. I'll stop when I smell 'em. You guys start casting as soon as you can. We'll cast and move." Big Mike cranked his motor, circled, and got up on plane moments later. Jim followed through the early-morning pristine wilderness beauty. Alligators were motionless until the boats sped by. Then, with a thrush, they vanished into a whirlpool of small waves. Humidity blurred the horizon into the lake surface. Hyacinth islands were moving landmarks, but the heavy morning mist burned away with sunrise.

Big Mike waved and cut his motor. Jim was accustomed to the hit-and-move strategy for big lakes, which involved cruising large expanses and counting on first strikes at hidden holes. Big Mike was out of hearing distance and keeping them away from the other boaters. Bill and Jim both stood up and started casting.

"Why did Ezzy want me to see this, Jim?"

"That's a good question."

"I know she asked you. She showed me the text."

"Are you two a thing now?" Jim asked. His drag screamed and stopped. Line sliced through the water fifteen feet off the bow. "Hooked one. This might be a keeper. Damn sure! Look at the sides on that thing."

Bill put his rod down and picked up the net. "Bring it around here. I don't know if we're a thing or not. I saw her in the parking lot after one of those city meetings back in January and said hello. I know she's out of my league, but I haven't dated much since Abigail died." The fish went from the net into the live well. Jim slammed the lid shut. "I've never seen her with anybody, so I took a shot. She said hello back. We go to dinner sometimes, but I've only been out to King Farms once or twice."

"You've been to King Farms? Now *you're* hooked. She doesn't let any men out there. The last time she asked me to show someone Lochloosa was ten years ago."

"Who was that?"

"She was engaged to an investment banker she met in New York when she worked for Bilger and Freese. He was coming down to meet her parents, but his plane crashed in a summer pop-up storm. I never actually met the guy. Tragedy seems to follow Ezzy. It was the last time I saw her with anyone."

"So why did she want me to see Lochloosa with you? I just don't picture her doing any of this."

"What if I told you she taught Big Mike to fish?"

"I'd say she was lucky to make it out of the boat alive." They both winced at the realities of rural America. "Bam! There's another fish." The line whisked through the water. The drag screamed. Bill reeled, and his rod tip bent from the weight.

Jim grabbed the net. "Bill, she grew up with us. Her dad, her family, we're all part of King Citrus. She's hauled hay. She's delivered foals. Hell, she spent time with Big Mike after his dad checked out, because she couldn't stand to see a kid hurt so much by adults." Jim netted the fish one handed. As soon as he dropped it in the live well, Bill closed the lid to the muffled sound of splashing fish. "She's even driven tractor wagons filled with oranges she picked. Ezzy King might be the richest, classiest person we all know, but deep inside, she's one of us. I know you know the story of her and my brother. Those memories are burned into our collective conscience. I guess that's why she wanted you to see this."

"She told me about your brother." Jim was confused when he saw Bill crack a smile. "She said you and he were totally different, which gives me some relief," he teased. "On the one hand, he must have been good looking. On the other, he must have been smart. She goes for that type, you know?"

Jim's shoulders bounced with laughter as he casted far away. The bait landed right next to a lone lily pad, "Uh huh. Don't get a complex, Five-O."

When Jim was cranking the bait back in, he glanced back at Bill, who looked out over the horizon and casted. "I could get used to this. I grew up in North Florida doing the same thing. Orthus County politics wears thin. The political circus can't be like this everywhere."

"I don't know if it is or not, but truth around here is definitely stranger than fiction. What're you going to do about Bob denying the department's raises? Damn, there's another one." Jim set the hook.

"Bring it around here. I got it." Bill netted the fish. "Right now, I'm dealing with a tornado of anger. The police union, the fraternal order, the fire department, everyone is pissed off and wants to strike. Other counties are trying to pluck the top cops as we speak. Firefighters, too." Bill looked inside the live well for a moment before he closed the lid.

Jim reassured him. "Don't worry. The live well is big enough."

"It's hard to argue with the folks that want to strike, but we took an oath and it didn't come with a price tag. But it doesn't seem there's any other way. Negotiations with Bob all end the same way. We come in. He tells us how great we are. How crime is down and response times are lower, but the bond debt has to be paid. Bob says, 'We pay ten percent of our budget every year on interest payments.' So, what? I didn't issue that debt. I'm working with old, banged-up police cars and no raises."

"I shouldn't tell you this, because most of my stories all begin as hunches or speculation."

"Now you have to tell me." Bill chuckled, but Jim couldn't tell if he was serious or not. "Boom! Fish on! Now it's your turn to net fish."

"You know that bar, First and Last?" Jim asked with his arms raised in opposite directions above his head, net in one hand, rod in the other ready to net Bill's fish.

Bill worked the fish closer to the boat and answered, "Who doesn't? Onward Orlando built a giant party complex for singles. Then they added a bar, the Orthus County School Board offices, and MOTrax headquarters. To make my life harder, it's connected to a mass-transit system I have no control over while all my suspects disappear into thin air. That guy Craig Walker is treading on thin ice. He sells most of the blow in the apartment complex. He's also late resubmitting his liquor license. What do you know about it?"

Jim held the net and looked up at Bill, expecting the fish to come closer. "I'm in there occasionally. I get scoop once the truth serum starts flowing through the county commission and Progress Orthus. Just the other night I saw Stan, Bob, Sterling, and another guy there. Just having drinks, you know."

He stopped fishing abruptly while his fish languished on the end of the line. He turned to Jim. "No. I don't know. Were you with them?"

Jim felt Bill's ability to unnerve someone during an interrogation, but steadied himself. "Sheriff. Easy. I'm the press. We go lots of places. No, I wasn't 'with them.' You know Sterling Johnston?"

"I know of him. Ezzy said he's some big-time architect, know-it-all type. Didn't he design all those renderings for MOTrax in your articles? All those stations are going to look like a theme park. I think he's helping Bob push for the Smithson Galleria project. What a mess that thing is! Did you hear anything?"

"No. But I saw some stuff."

"Oh, yeah, Mr. Jim? Did you see something?" Bill turned and whipped the rod so hard the line careened off his rod tip, and into the last trace of morning mist, like bottle-rocket smoke over a pre-historic swamp, until the bait plunged into the water on the edge of a bonnet patch.

Jim sensed Bill losing interest in his story, and wasn't surprised since he'd probably dealt with cracked-out informants most of his career. He glanced ahead at Big Mike's boat as it faded away behind a floating hyacinth island. "I saw them trying to talk Stan into something. Then I saw them toast glasses."

"Yeah, so?"

"And I saw Bob Drolland take an envelope full of cash from the other guy visiting. That sound like something?"

Bill craned his head around toward Jim, but continued to crank the bait. "Now you have my attention." Two ospreys came diving down to the lake surface. One picked up a water moccasin in its talons, instinctively folding the snake's head over with its middle talon to pierce the fragile skull. It wriggled as the osprey headed back to the nest to feed. The second one swooped back high above the lake and continued to hunt. "But without evidence, it's just a story."

"I have it on video."

"Now you're talkin'. Did you get any audio?"

"Hell, no. They didn't even see me. They were up by the escalators in the parking deck where we walked during the MOTrax accident. I think it was the Smithson Galleria developer."

Bill had put down his rod after the bait was cranked in and looked at Jim, who continued to fish. "Does anyone else know? Did you show it to District Attorney Jackson yet? The First and Last is her jurisdiction."

"Not yet. I wanted to see what I was sitting on first. See what else pops up, y' know?"

"That's very useful information, Jim."

"Fish on!" Jim yanked the rod backwards. "You got some catching up to do. I'll show it to Paige when the time is right."

"Don't wait too long. My silent investigation is going to begin on Monday. I'll need that video sooner or later." Bill unhooked Jim's fish and tossed it in the live well. Big Mike came around the back side of the island, waved, cranked his motor, and they drove to the next spot.

After a good day on the water, Jim, Bill, and Big Mike scaled fish at Pinson's. Matt had fish-fryer grease on full roil. Beth dropped yesterday's bluegill into the grease from the tips of their tails, igniting the popping hot grease with the first drops of batter flour. Jim got his groove back on at the fish-cleaning table, and was scaling and cutting as fast as Big Mike within minutes. They went straight into an ice cooler for the ride home.

Big Mike tossed the last carcass into the bucket and asked Bill, "Now I'm gonna' put this knife in my truck, Sheriff, if that's ok with you?"

Bill said softly above the crackle of frying fish, "I guess one will be OK, but don't touch it unless you're cleaning fish."

"Keep sum bitches from stealing my boats and I'll keep my knives and guns in my pockets."

"Make sure you get carry permits for those guns. I'm pretty sure you don't have any now. I checked after the last time I was out here for your vigilante seminar."

"Hey, I filled out all those forms a year ago. I haven't heard anything since, so I just figured you all were ok with it."

"I know you did." Bill reached into his back pocket. "Here you go. I had to pull a few strings, but you've waited long enough." He handed Mike the hard copy of the approval.

"Well, I'll be damned. Thanks, Sheriff. Now I'm legal."

"Keep it that way."

"Yes, sir." Big Mike took the buckets of fish carcasses over to Matt's garden for fertilizer.

Jim dreamed about home as they talked and ate okra, cheese grits, and fried bluegill around the cable-spool tops between Pinson's and Estelle's. No-see-ums floated down from the live oak that shaded the big sandy spot. Their skin was thickened from a long day of bites and insect repellant.

"Bill, we've always been on the outskirts of larger society out here," Beth said. "We prefer the freedom of Lochloosa. Our closeness among neighbors here keeps us informed. Sometimes we feel overwhelmed with the changes in our society. Your patrolmen make us feel much safer."

"Thank you for the feedback. We need all we can get," he said.

"I'll be blunt, Bill," Beth said. "The only two patrolmen we see out here in unincorporated Orthus are the two patrolmen sitting at Estelle's. They're responsive as they can be, but we need more visibility."

"I'll see what I can do. I really will. I'll follow up with Jim on the changes you can expect. I know what it's like out here. You deserve more."

"Thanks," Matt said. "She says what she wants to say. I've learned to listen."

Beth hugged Jim and Bill before she headed back toward the house. "Do come back and see us soon, Jim. Bill, please tell Ezzy we said hello. We miss her very much."

"You bet I will." Jim hoped Bill would keep both his promises to his mother. The first would take more effort than the second. Matt unhooked the boat and loaded the iced coolers as Mike, Bill, and Jim walked over to Estelle's. Bill grabbed three tall beers from Estelle's wall cooler, as Estelle yelled out from behind the counter, "On the house, Sheriff. Make sure that third goes to Matt, and don't be a stranger."

"What about me?" Mike hollered.

"You're on your own, Big Mike. You still owe me from last week." She winked at him.

Jim grabbed a six-pack for Mike and paid for it while Bill strolled down the snack aisle past the early-evening crowd back to the entrance. "You all got my number if you get trouble."

"We do, indeed. Now scat. You're driving the customers away." Estelle's doorbells jingled when they walked out. Bill hopped in the passenger side of Jim's truck. Jim made final goodbyes with Big Mike and Matt. "Don't tell anyone we were here, Big Mike. No one. He's got a lot on his plate," Jim said.

"Got it." Big Mike threw his paw around Jim as he returned the embrace. "You weren't here. Sheriff Bill wasn't here. I wasn't here. But all those fish were. We put the whoop on 'em today, my friend."

"We surely did, Mike. See you in a few weeks," he said, and slung the bag of beer into Mike's hand.

Jim eased onto the four-lane highway. Matt waved as they drove away. The beers went down smooth with the Central Florida sunset coming through Bill's window as they drove south. They didn't pass one patrol car all the way in. Traffic started to slow as they entered Metro Orthus. The lane construction signs squeezed the cars together. No progress had been made in months.

CHAPTER 14

"Ms. Brown, your ten o'clock is here," the receptionist's voice came through the receiver. Randall, the train driver, and Antonio, the Transportation Union representative, had arrived for their pre-investigation hearing. MOTrax offices were above the Orthus County School Board's offices, with a fraction of the panache. Kate had to furnish MOTrax headquarters from her annual budget, whereas Stan's office décor was a gift from Sterling.

Through her office door, Kate could see the two men standing apart from one another, passing the moment looking at the empty shelves on the wall opposite Marsha's desk. Randall's leg was in a cast, and a neck brace restricted his movement as he glanced around the reception area.

Kate's experience suggested crash events needed story consolidation before a National Transportation Safety Board investigation took any wrong turns. She'd called them in for an informal interview before any official questioning was able to take place.

"Thanks, Marsha," Kate said. "Please send them in. And please bring me a cup of coffee." She nodded when Antonio and Randall walked through the door, and then looked back down at the papers on her desk, tapping a pencil. She'd filled the shelves behind her desk and next to the wall with mass-transit research reports, books, and small accolades from her last jobs in Philadelphia and Baltimore. The large round table in the corner was covered in plan layouts and construction drawings. The expansive window revealed clouds that moved through the sky as a downpour began. A blustery early summer wind howled against the window and whipped through the flag on the building next door and the palm trees visible on the street level below. Thunder rolled in the distance. "Good morning, Randall. How're you doing?"

"Horrible. My neck hurts all the time. The doctor says I'll walk with a cane the rest of my life."

"That's strange. You walked away from the accident just fine the morning I saw you. Good morning, Antonio. I hope you're OK." She was in no mood to waste time on evasive answers. Her progress couldn't be stopped by a low-level train driver with a drug problem.

"I'll be much better after the NTSB investigation is completed and Randall is compensated for his life-long loss of the use of his right leg." Antonio said.

She smirked and shook her head at the suggestion this was going to go well for Antonio's union client. "Please take your seats. Randall, have you been contacted by the NTSB?" Kate began, locking in on Randall as they all sat down.

Randall leaned his crutches against one of the chairs at the side table to avoid her glare, when Antonio answered for him. "They stopped harassing him after our attorneys sent them a cease and desist order. Kate, please understand that Randall has been through a lot. The lack of appropriate safety investments MOTrax refuses to make puts our union employees in grave danger."

She turned to Antonio, who she knew would persuade his client to settle, because they'd worked together on cases like this before. "Antonio, I appreciate your concern, but we're under considerable financial stress. Our operating budgets are stretched to the limit. If

Governor Sikes would fund Orlando's mass-transit system like every other state, we'd be able to keep up with the latest technology, but with that said," she turned to Randall, "we've recovered the voice and data recorders, and Randall's urine sample test results were returned last week. Would you like to know what we found out?"

Randall lowered his head and his eyes darted to Antonio. Kate sighed heavily at Randall's obstruction, leaned back in her chair, and started tapping her armrest with the pencil. Antonio answered for him once more. "Kate, you can direct all your questions to me. I represent Randall in this meeting."

She ignored Antonio's fake concern for his client, and tried once more to get under Randall's skin. "OK. Randall, you tested positive for alcohol. The forensic test proves you were drinking within five hours prior to the accident. Do you like to take a nip before coming to work?"

He twisted in his seat, and she got the confession she'd awaited. "I was at the Coyotes game the night before. We beat the hell out of the Barons. It was the Sunday night baseball TV special. Who wasn't drinking?"

"Randall, please don't speak again," Antonio said. "Unless you'd like to navigate the investigation that will point every finger at you, please allow me to represent you."

"Randall, Antonio is right. If you don't cooperate with me today, I'll make sure you're the scapegoat for the accident. I'll kill two birds with one stone. I'll make an example of you and lobby our state legislature to provide more funding to MOTrax." Marsha knocked on the door before she came in with the coffee. She smiled at Kate and put it on her desk. "Thank you, Marsha."

A gust of wind blew against the creaking expansive window frame, followed by flashes of lightning bouncing off the clouds in the distance from a singular bolt that connected the ground to the sky. The boom crashed off the window moments later. "They're calling for forty-mile-per-hour gusts by lunch," Marsha said, closing the door behind her as she left.

"What are you thinking about, Kate?" Antonio asked.

"You tested positive for cocaine, too, Randall." She sipped her coffee.

"I take cold medicine."

"Shut up, Randall," Antonio said. He turned back to Kate and smiled. "Kate, we all know how inconsistent drug-testing results are. Can we get to the point?"

She set her coffee down and flipped a couple of papers on her desk. "The voice recorder revealed Randall didn't return at least three requests for information one minute, one minute forty-two seconds, and two minutes thirteen seconds before impact. Randall was asleep at the wheel, and because of his lax attitude with regard to his responsibility to protect passengers, four people died."

Antonio stiffened his spine before speaking. "Because of the operational lapses of MOTrax and your management, four people died. We've been asking for new automated braking features for two years."

"And you've always argued any investment in automated technology eliminates the need for your union membership. You can't have it both ways, Antonio." A bright flash lit up the room. Moments later the crack exploded into a boom. "Damn it! I never get used to that. I had no idea it rained so much down here."

"We're trying to protect jobs as long as possible, Kate. MOTrax can't operate on machines alone."

"Yes, I know, and now we have another accident making national headlines and ruining the integrity of our mission of societal good."

"Your societal good is getting crushed by cheap ride-sharing services sweeping across the globe," Antonio said. "It's not our fault the stations drop off in the worst parts of town. Don't get me started on the buses. Now the ride-sharing services have these big fancy vans with TVs and rolling Wi-Fi. We can't compete with that."

Kate was uninterested in obstacles that detracted from high-density real estate models connected by mass transit, including fly-by-night technology apps and cheap oil. "But it's your union membership causing the problems we have," she said, while another loud gust of wind creaked against the frame.

"Kate, your operational problems are because of your real estate distractions." He waved at the table beside them filled with drawings of large apartment complexes and movie theaters. "You're trying to generate revenues from real estate because you lose twice as much every year as you take in. That's not our fault. We're labor. You're in charge of operations."

Kate forced a smile. This meeting was wasting time that could be spent getting projects permitted and tax abatements approved. She moved to the negotiation stage of her meeting. "So, it seems we're at an impasse. May I make some suggestions before the NTSB goes full bore into information collection?"

Antonio jumped on her comment. "That may be a good idea. What are they? Maybe we can find some common ground."

"First of all, Randall's ER bills are of his own making. Even if they aren't, his drug and alcohol tests will eliminate any shred of his credibility."

Randall looked up without bending his neck. "Ms. Brown, I'm hurt. My neck is really messed up. I can't turn it. That's no bullshit."

"The families of the victims are already preparing a class-action lawsuit. Randall's bills are a drop in the bucket compared to the coming legal settlement," Antonio said.

Kate sipped her coffee again. "Gentlemen, that's not my problem. A class-action lawsuit will be paid from our General Fund. You wrecked a train because you were in a drug-induced nap while driving twice the legal limit. Paying your medical bills doesn't help my narrative with Governor Sikes."

"May we get a copy of those drug-test results?" Antonio asked.

"Of course." She handed him a copy. "There are two, this one and the one in my file. I'll hang on to it just in case Randall decides to get drunk at a football game and tell his version of the story. The morning of the accident, I managed the process at the MOTrax medical laboratory contractor, purposefully requesting all paper documents so that we might come to some sort of compromise. Randall, I don't want you to be hurt financially, but you will be if you don't cooperate."

"I'll sue the hell out of you. You can't fire me," Randall said.

"Randall, please be quiet," Antonio said. "She can, but if you'll zip it, we can work something out." He turned back to Kate. "What do you need from us?"

"I need you to blame the crash on lacking state funds for updated safety technology, and have Randall sign this form releasing MOTrax from all liability regarding his," she cleared her throat, "injuries." Rain spattered against the window, blown by the driving wind.

"I ain't doing that. Orthus County Regional Hospital is billing the hell out of me already. My ER charge was twenty thousand dollars."

"Randall, you have the best health insurance available anywhere in the country. Your insurance plan will pay for everything. If you think you're going to sue us, I'll put the entire crash squarely where it belongs: on you."

"Randall, she's right. Let's make this thing go away quietly. Kate, do you have access to the voice and data recorders?"

"I do. But the NTSB has been notified the voice recorder was destroyed in the crash. The data recorder is right here under my desk. It recorded speed and time. Voice recordings are conveniently absent. I'm turning it over to the NTSB this afternoon."

Antonio paused. "Do we have your assurance the voice recorder will not be delivered to the NTSB?"

Antonio's suspicion of her motives aroused her deeper desire to fire him, but she held back in favor of reminding him of their shared risk. "You have the assurance of two allies with different goals but a common threat. You need to keep people employed, and I need to make up for substantial losses from our public's refusal to embrace an eco-centric transportation option. We both face the competition we've no control over. The voice recorder will never see the light of day. If the NTSB issues a subpoena for it, I'll have it destroyed, but they are normally very cooperative with delicate situations like this. As you're well aware, this isn't our first accident investigation together." Thunder rolled in the distance again, and Kate assumed the storm had passed. "I also need him to take another drug test at Orthus Regional Hospital. Call this number." She slid a card across the desk. "Do we have a deal?"

"Randall?" Antonio asked.

"Can I have a couple of days, y'know, to detox?"

"From an abundance of caution, I notified the person on the other end of that phone number you probably wouldn't be ready. It's worked out."

"Can I work in this office from now on instead of driving the train?"

Kate couldn't care less what happened to him, or where he worked. She'd have Marsha find an empty closet somewhere he could sit in, if he needed to come in at all. "I'm sure we could find you something to do with your new-found limited mobility. You certainly shouldn't be behind the wheel of a bus, or a train brake, ever again."

"Then we got a deal." Randall said.

"Good. Go get a clean drug test. The medical technician will backdate it. Antonio, would you please send me a draft of your press release so I can review it and make specific changes?" Another thunderbolt cracked in the distance as its electric fingers spread out across the Orlando skyline, the boom rattling the window. "Damn it! That was close. It's never over when you think it's over." She handed the clipboard holding the liability indemnification form across the desk to Antonio.

"Sure." Antonio held the form on the clipboard in front of Randall so he wouldn't have to get up. "Randall, sign the form."

Randall did as he was told, reached over to grab his crutches, and hopped up into his medical injury disguise.

Antonio set the clipboard on Kate's desk and shook hands with her. "Thanks for your time and your commitment to our employees, Kate."

"Of course, Antonio. Randall, see Marsha about something to do after your injuries have healed in the next few days. Please see yourself out." She watched them turn and walk out the door. As the sub-tropical storm churned outside, she was beginning to regret her decision to waste her talent on Orlando instead of the other lucrative offers in colder climates.

CHAPTER 15

The electronic gates of the Orthus King Airport opened and closed at the end of a long chain-link fence as Patrick McDaniel's Salvatore SUV drove through to pick up Ezzy at The Hangar, the airport restaurant. Her plane was having the annual inspection, and she'd asked to be picked up there. She came out of the restaurant, down the stairs, and over to the passenger side door he was holding open. "Thanks for joining me," he said as he climbed back in on his side.

"No problem," Ezzy replied. "I was up here anyway."

When Patrick exited the gate and turned north, one of his gas trucks was driving parallel to them on the tarmac on the other side of the fence toward a small private plane. "Second busiest airport in Florida and the most expensive gas," Ezzy said. Her observation sent chills through Patrick's shoulders with the fear she might know about his cut. It only worsened when she asked, "How could that be?"

He stuffed his paranoia back down in his gut. "Probably because the big suppliers don't want the hassle. At least, that's what I heard." He caught her rolling her eyes, but said nothing, preferring non-confrontational ignorance to explaining the nuances of municipal deal making. As they reached the end of the long fence marking the corner of the airfield, he said, "To think, all of that land used to be orange groves."

"And all the MOTrax stations were King loading docks, Orthus Park was a packing house, and the Smithson City Park was our fleet maintenance," she said and paused. "It wasn't so long ago, was it, Patrick?"

Patrick dodged her insolence in order to smooth his message's delivery. He came to a red light and looked across the seat at her. "It's amazing you didn't sell the land to the car company for their plant, too."

She sighed. "Well, you can't own everything."

They drove the next several miles in silence before an open space that looked like a giant, white parking lot appeared behind a fence. Patrick turned on his blinker and drove through the industrial-size construction entrance. The chain-link fence was high on both sides of the open gate, with a couple of private cars parked on the inside of the entrance next to trucks connected to heavy-equipment trailers. Off in the distance, a couple of motor-graders smoothed the surface as dust rolled off their tires, breaking up the stillness.

"We're here," Patrick said. He'd seen Central Florida thunderstorms wash gullies through the large white expanse, and knew it provided steady work for earthmovers. The bankruptcy court trustee had shared with Patrick the on-going maintenance costs when they'd discussed new ownership possibilities he might bring to the table. The enormous challenge of the Smithson Galleria development was worth every minute Patrick had invested in it and the adjacent property just past the crest of the horizon.

"My first truck was built here," Ezzy said while Patrick continued around the edge of the rim road. "Papa T Sam bought it for my sixteenth birthday. We watched it roll off the assembly line together. They made really good automobiles here. Just goes to show, you never know how good you have it until it's gone."

He was grateful to get a glimpse of her memory, but ignored the normal reverence given to conversations about her grandfather. "You mean he wouldn't buy his only granddaughter a Salvatore?"

She looked straight ahead and raised an eyebrow. "Patrick, every orange picker from here to Miami knows Salvatore Motors hasn't made a truck that could handle King Citrus swamps."

"Well, we do now, and I've got them in an array of colors: black and white." He caught himself, but not before she responded to his nervous slip up.

"Why would I want black or white? What is it I need to see out here?"

Patrick pulled to the side and parked. He got out and looked up to see she was joining him at the front of the truck.

"Look, Ezzy. You know Bob approved rezoning the MOTrax stations on the North Line for transit-oriented developments."

"Yes, I'm aware. I experienced his vote first hand."

"TODs are the coming wave of residential housing. People and hi-tech companies looking for temporary housing demand livable, walkable communities. That's urban-planner lingo for living next to a train station." He walked past her toward the edge of the road and looked out over the smooth-graded desert. His golf tan and gold chain were exposed when the wind blew through his open collar.

"Who's decided TODs are the coming wave? Won't your business be affected by a wave like that?" she asked, one hand on her hip and the other blocking the glaring sun from her blue eyes.

"Of course not," he lied. He ran his fingers through his hair, which was turning gray at the temples thanks to his real estate partnership with Sterling. All the emails from Sterling's work-out attorneys, the constant barrage of demand letters, and the harassing phone calls were making an old man of him. Coupled with Sterling's insistence on honoring the original partnership terms of the loan on the real estate just past the fence, and he was barely hanging by a thread. "People like me and you aren't riding mass transit. We like cars and trucks. I make my living selling the finest automobile in the world."

"How would you know my transportation preferences? I've many, but I lived in New York and love subway trains."

"I know, but kids just out of college don't want cars anymore. They want to live in these little microcosms. To them, an adventure is hopping on MOTrax and going to the development two stops south."

"For what?" Ezzy asked. "The only place MOTrax goes is Ospreys games. You have to take a train to a bus to Coyotes Stadium. Kids are buying cars and trucks and they aren't taking the train. The only thing slowing the automobile industry is this recession we've entered. You've been reading too many Southern California urban-planner studies." His neck hair bristled with her insinuation he was nothing more than a pawn of urbanist prophets, but he kept listening in order to keep her attention. "MOTrax ridership has been going down for years. I think it's correlated with cheap gasoline."

"Ezzy, I'd like to agree, but the facts don't support your argument. When all of the new TODs are finished, they'll be themed neighborhoods with different but unique attractions. Ridership will explode."

"My facts don't support my arguments?" She crossed her arms and turned to Patrick. "You have an interesting perspective. New York built the subway to serve the neighborhoods, not the other way around. New is new until you decide to have kids. Then you move to the suburbs with the good schools. Again, why am I here?"

Just as she spoke, the flight path of one of the private jets that had departed from OSK flew over them, stopping their conversation for the moment. When it'd passed, Patrick said, "As you can see, the future Smithson Downtown District and Smithson Galleria is massive...and vacant. The bankruptcy trustee spent all the EPA grants on environmental reclamation preparing it for the City of Smithson to buy it, with our help of course." He hoped he wasn't coming across as desperate, because that might alert her he had more than economic development in mind. "The City of Smithson is left with what you see here. The Smithson mayor has come to Progress Orthus as a willing partner to buy it out of bankruptcy. They need our help to exploit this opportunity for economic development."

"What help? I thought Orthus County was tapped out? Didn't Bob just pay a missed hospital bond with a tax-anticipation note?"

He bowed his head, and then looked back out at the heavy machinery rolling in the distance. "Yes, but that was a one-time-only event. Progress Orthus needs to provide financing for Smithson Galleria, but we don't need to burden Orthus County taxpayers as we normally do. We just need to play the role of conduit for Orthus County School Board financing, but we still must persuade Stan Jackson to issue the bond to buy it from the bankruptcy trustee. Progress Orthus will facilitate the tax abatement for the new project as usual."

"This site has never paid any property taxes. Has it? It didn't pay any when the car manufacturer was here, and it won't pay any if Smithson Galleria is built here either."

Patrick ignored her questions that only prolonged the inevitability of the coming construction, but watched while she dropped her arms and walked over to the edge of the road in her jeans and cowboy boots, put one hand on her hip, and propped her foot on a mound of earth. She raised her fingers above her eyes again. "Don't you mean projects? The Smithson Downtown District and Smithson Galleria sound like two projects. What is the City of Smithson asking of the school board?"

"If you include the new high school we're offering Stan, Smithson City Hall, and their new courthouse, about four-hundred-and-fifty-million dollars. New equity partners that Sterling is pulling together will make up the rest."

Ezzy shook her head. "All that debt for tiny little Smithson. How did the Smithson mayor come to the conclusion her three-million-dollar budget could swing this? They're living in a fantasy land."

People like her were always suspicious of his ideas and vision for progress. In his most condescending voice, he said, "Ezzy, I'll kindly remind you of all the Progress Orthus bonds that went to buy King Citrus land. Now the City of Smithson and Orthus County need your help." He leaned backed against the truck and crossed his arms.

"Patrick, I wasn't on the development authority then. You needed land, and I had it. I told the City of Smithson council they shouldn't get involved with an old automobile plant in bankruptcy court, but the mayor smelled money. Now they want to connect a bunch of high rises to the MOTrax station inside of a new Smithson downtown district. Smithson Galleria? Dear God. They should call it 'The Sterling Johnston Streets of Borrowed Gold.' Smithson wants Progress Orthus to build a new City Hall because they can't afford it. Sterling needs you to talk Stan into issuing the bond, because the bond markets don't take Sterling's calls anymore. He keeps manipulating them using their own contracts."

Patrick knew what that felt like, but hid his feelings. "The money will also pay for the new Bob Drolland Interchange that will exit off the interstate and right past the Smithson MOTrax station."

"What about all the businesses that have built their lives in this area?" she asked unexpectedly.

"What about them?" Patrick looked far off into the distance at the Johnston Lofts, LLC, run-down apartments on the edge of the vacant land. He had reminded his wife "all money is green" when she'd called him a slumlord. "You can plainly see this is a blighted area."

"Blighted?" She scoffed. "This big open wound of real estate might be blighted, but the business owners surrounding it will have to compete with your hand-selected businesses that won't have to pay property taxes. You and your Smithson buddies will pick whoever gives them the biggest kickbacks. Just because you think ethnic businesses are unbecoming neighbors doesn't mean they're blighted."

"Ezzy, nail salons, movie theaters, and restaurants are only a small portion of the businesses coming here. Two insurance companies are considering moving their headquarters to Smithson Galleria." That had been partially true, but since they'd already signified they weren't coming, Patrick had begun other development plans. He was determined not to let anyone know they'd backed out in order to hide the identity of the newly interested buyer. For good measure and secrecy, he'd nicknamed the new venture Project Grand Slam when discussing it with Bob and Sterling.

"Any new tenant contracts signed yet, Patrick?"

"Not yet, but they're all on board." He moved forward from leaning against the truck and walked toward Ezzy.

"Sure. All the apartment complexes surrounding this property, the movie theater you see over on the Southside, and the restaurants will go out of business because the businesses on this site will have the competitive advantage of lower fixed costs."

"If I recall, King Christian Academy was also the benefactor of tax abatements."

"You're being boorish. I donated twenty acres of prime real estate to Orthus County for parks. A tax abatement for a charter school was the least Progress Orthus could do. KCA has been audited three times in the last six years. It's all legal. Now Bob is going to turn the park land I donated into parking lots for MOTrax TOD projects. I didn't think your new residents drove cars, but apparently, they need parking lots. And besides, Orthus County School

Board doesn't pay property taxes either. You're better than that, Patrick."

"Those parking spaces are required by our outdated codes. We included the shared parking at the parks to satisfy a substandard requirement. The streets between the neighborhoods and the TODs will be used for parking as well, as if they'll need them. By the way, the KCA's tax abatement was a gift."

"Patrick, it was a phantom bond. Progress Orthus issued a piece of paper, not a bond. KCA pays Progress Orthus an administration fee. We don't pay the Orthus School Board anything. We cut our taxes in half because we gave the county park land. A bond was issued to meet all the legal requirements of the tax abatement. A transaction had to occur. I paid for the grounds, the buildings, the fields, and the courts out of my own pocket—all of it, Patrick. The campus is collateral on that piece of paper. When it's over, I'll rip up the paperwork and start paying both Orthus County and school board taxes."

"I know how tax abatements work, Ezzy."

"Poor kids in North Orthus are getting an education the Orthus County School Board can't provide. KCA has a higher graduation rate than any metro Florida high school. Sixty percent of our kids are going to college or a vocational school. Our students not only learn from the newest technology; they're inventing it." He'd heard her tell anyone who'd listen about King Christian Academy.

"But until the bond matures, Progress Orthus owns KCA. Remember?"

"Temporarily owns it. Progress Orthus holds the title at my pleasure, Patrick. The only reason they hold it is development authority law requires it. The only reason I'm on the development authority is to protect that title. If you continue to try my patience, I'll pay full taxes starting tomorrow if you think you have some power over KCA. Progress Orthus will cease getting the three hundred thousand dollars I pay every year for your office staff. This is not a negotiation, Patrick. I'll vote on any financing for Smithson Galleria based on the benefits, not deals we may, or may not, have made in the past. Besides, I provide a balanced approach to Progress Orthus. You and Bob offer these board members power they could never achieve on their own. They'll buy off on any deal you bring them."

The noose was tightening on his quest for Progress Orthus's unanimous approval of the Smithson Galleria tax abatement. Patrick saw his chance of selling his equity portion of Johnston Lofts, LLC, slipping away. If Progress Orthus didn't approve Smithson Galleria, he'd be handcuffed to Sterling as buyers for the boarded-up apartment complex waited on new development on the site they were standing on. "Turns out you know more than I thought." He crossed his arms as the breeze blew around his slacks.

She walked back toward him. "Patrick, your other partnerships aren't hidden, you know? The airport manager at OSK is a friend of mine." Her eyes softened. "Did you partner with the good Robert Drolland's son for exclusive rights to sell jet fuel at Orthus King Airport? Did you guys name your distribution company Touch Down, LLC? Are you kidding, Patrick? You two are like a couple of frat boys. Are there any others?"

Patrick's stomach sank. "All that may be true, but Orthus County needs this project." Patrick turned and looked back across the barren, blowing expanse toward the apartment complex. Did Ezzy know he owned it? "No one else can afford to build such a massive development on top of an environmental disaster without government assistance." He twisted his Rolex around his suntanned wrist.

"This deal is fragile, Patrick. I warned the Smithson mayor of costly delays if she didn't get letters of intent and hard contracts up front. No bank in the Southeast will touch this project, because the loan metrics don't work. You can't find a private equity partner to put up the money, and I'm betting your insurance companies know better. Your concept is based on studies not yet proven, but it's gospel in the minds of urban planners. It's the largest project of its kind in the nation. Now you're borrowing from the biggest bank in Orthus County, the Orthus County School Board. And all Stan Jackson gets is a new high school?"

"You just don't see it, Ezzy. This is going to provide additional tax revenue to the school board and Orthus County."

"Damn it, Patrick. I'm not fresh off the voter wagon. If those additional tax revenues happen, it won't be for another fifteen years. What's so confusing to me is why you all continue to take these huge risks for what is a drop in the bucket to both Orthus County revenues and the school board's. If your estimates hold true, they stand to increase their revenues by a tiny one percent. The risks far outweigh the gain."

"I'm sorry you see it that way, Ezzy. The new jobs, the influx of new capital from companies not yet here is enormous. It's almost unimaginable unless you allow yourself to see it." One of the motorgraders had gotten close enough Patrick could see the driver operating a row of levers attached to the long metal blade below the driver's cab, scraping the earth's edge with one hand and steering with the other. A trail of dust was blowing behind the machine and getting closer to them.

"You're blind, Patrick. I've seen enough. Take me back to OSK." She unfolded her arms and walked toward the truck. He walked behind her, hiding his disappointment. She could unlock doors with just her looks, but her money could close them in his face. They hopped in the truck and drove back to the entrance in silence. When they arrived back at the airport, Ezzy stepped out of the SUV, closed the door, and put her hand on the door's open window. "Patrick, I've only known you a few years. You seem like a bright guy. You have a bright future. Don't let greed get in the way."

He put his arm on the center console and leaned toward her. "Ezzy, we're doing this with or without you. I need you on board because people trust you. I want you on board because you're a force of nature. This is going to happen and it's going to work."

"Then it will all be on you. I'll see you in town in a few weeks." She lifted her hand off the door and walked back to her truck, leaving Patrick alone with his ringing telephone. He wanted to say something else, but his phone ID registered Gloria, his main dealership's receptionist.

He answered, "Hello."

"Hey, Patrick. It's Gloria. Sterling's attorney, Conner Jenson, wants me to patch him through to your cell. Should I?"

"No way. I'm in a meeting with Ezzy King. Tell him I'll call next week." He hung up the phone as quickly as he'd answered it, while his throat filled up with the angst of looming default and total loss.

CHAPTER 16

Paige pattered down the stairs into the kitchen. Stan had left her a note that he'd gone for a run and let her sleep in before she started yoga on the back porch. She tried to embrace their flexibility of never planning anything for July 4th because they didn't have kids, but it never seemed to register, especially with red, white, and blue flags hanging out of strollers up and down the MOTrail. She checked her phone for the text that came in as she dozed off the night before. 11:45 from Stan: At First and Last with Bob, Patrick and Sterling. Don't wait up. Home soon. Love you. On the kitchen table, next to his note, was the *Wall Street Journal* and the *Financial Times*. "At least he's reading my subscriptions," she murmured to herself, filling a bottle with water before heading to the back deck for a yoga workout.

After Paige was named Orlando DA, she and Stan had upgraded to a slender, three-story mission-style house one block from a trail entrance downtown. Stan liked to take long runs on the trail any chance he could. The constant influx of young professionals provided plenty of opportunities to see and be seen. The MOTrail cut through the gentrified neighborhood of her husband's youth, but it'd kept none of the nostalgia he talked about constantly. The old clapboard houses next to the tracks had transformed into a hotbed of upper-middle-income lofts and townhomes. Rotting old houses remained one block on each side of the new improvements. Her running routes meandered past high-end apartment complexes and shared restaurant spaces. Stan had convinced her it was a good move even though she had read how the concrete path had replaced the old railroad tracks, legalizing one of the largest tax-allocation districts in the country. Orthus County shared the second largest: Smithson Galleria.

She remembered reading urban planners pushing the MOTrail and other rails-to-trails projects as a one-way trolley or bus route while in her final years at Vanderbilt, but it finally got off the ground when Stan loaned them the money four years ago. After meeting Mayor Tisdale's appointed surrogates to Onward Orlando, the Orlando Development Authority, she knew they weren't going to waste prime real estate on trolley lanes. The first ten miles had renderings of multi-family apartment complexes awash in diversity, nightlife, and boutique retail. She immediately noticed the fragmentation between the old families giving way to the new community of young professionals. Onward Orlando used eminent domain to confiscate all the abandoned properties next to the tracks. The property was then leased to mixed-use developers, and the Orlando Tax Assessors office set artificially high property values on the remaining homes. She saw injustice foisted on the old neighbors who didn't know how to appeal higher property taxes, but knew they weren't wanted. She knew another family was leaving when she saw code-enforcement officers at the front door of an old home, with an elderly grandparent behind the screen door and an angry young man hitting the street out of the driveway on a motorcycle. Her senses were tested daily when she read the constant mantra of comprehensive plans in the *Orthus County Post.*

As early morning faded into day, Paige saw Stan's image through the privacy fence as he came around the house to the back porch.

He grabbed a towel off a linen rack and threw it around his neck, his muscles glistening in the sun. "Morning, baby."

"Good morning, Flash Jackson." She was just finishing her last downward dog with her hips high in the air. She thanked the heavens her flexibility was virtually unchanged from college.

"Paige, baby!" Almost in a whisper, "You should model sportswear."

She heaved erect and tall, then twirled toward him. "I hope you have something left in the tank, Mister. I've been working up a sweat. We're on vacation."

Stan wrapped his arm around her lower back, pulling her forward, their bodies barely touching, and whispered, "Baby, my tank is always full."

Paige looked up into his eyes. She felt his build completely around her. "Can a lady get a shower with her husband?"

"Any day of the week and twice on Sundays, Mrs. Jackson."

In the double shower, the hot water rushed over both of them. Stan raised her arms above her head, and then let his hands trace down, caressing her to the ends of her fingertips. He was reminded of his commitment when he touched the engagement diamond and wedding band. Showered and clean, they stepped out.

"Is that all, Flash Jackson?"

"I'm just getting started, Mrs. Jackson."

Stan lay on the bed after Paige disappeared into the bathroom to finish dressing, their favorite groove playing in the background. It was hard for him to move. Paige was as much woman as any man needed. *Why do I continue to wreck my marriage,* he thought. *What if she finds out?*

"You OK in there?" she called out.

"Yeah. Barely. I feel like I've been through a hurricane."

Paige walked back into the bedroom and lay next to Stan. "Judi gave me a referral for a fertility doctor we can see."

"We don't need a baby, Paige. We need to spend more time together. That's my fault."

"Can we spend time together today? No boards. No deals. Just me and you?"

"You know we can. Just me and you." *And the persistent guilt of Vegas.*

Paige made another cup of coffee and scanned the *Orthus County Post* on her laptop downstairs while she waited on Stan to come down for their day together. "Municipal Bankers Cash in on Blind Pools, Inner City Kids Pay the Price." The lead article outlined the blind-pool financing issued for the MOTrail but only partially spent. The excess was accruing interest on Dunham Schauble's books. The unspent funds were slated for evicted residents' transfer payments promised during the tax-foreclosure proceedings and new housing, but Dunham Schauble refused to spend the money. Paige was surprised Onward Orlando would allow Enzo to include clauses in the bond memorandum authorizing his discretion for any costs exceeding the price of the MOTrail. Jim had labeled Dunham Schauble's closing commissions as "icing on the cake" in the article, as it described how they doubled their municipal underwriting revenue by collecting legal fees for prepared contract documents always written to favor the investment bank. Jim quoted a Dunham Schauble spokesperson, Kirsty McPhee, explaining the complexities of tax-abatement deals, and that the steep legal fees should be considered a value, in retrospect. The article's comments icon was constantly swirling as taxpayer advocates lit up the page with responses chastising the dealmakers. It was getting harder for her to feel sorry for Stan's public miscues.

Stan's phone pinged over on the kitchen counter. She got up from her papers and went over to read it. We need to meet. Are you coming back to Vegas? Should I come to Orlando? Paige read the number but didn't recognize it.

Stan hit the bottom stair with the old electricity. "OK, Your Fineness. Where can I take you today?"

She cut her eyes over to the bottom of the stairs. "Who in Las Vegas needs to meet you?"

He squinted his eyes and asked, "What are you talking about?"

"Your phone has a text from Las Vegas."

Stan took the phone from her and read the text while he pulled a water bottle from the refrigerator. "Oh, the City of Las Vegas Board of Education Chair. He wants to see our new facilities at Orlando Downtown District. I think he's trying to get the Las Vegas Development Authority to give him the same deal Onward Orlando gave us."

"Then why does he want you to go back there?"

"He wants me to meet his development authority. Their board chair was gone the last time Sterling flew us out." He leaned over to kiss her from the refrigerator door, but she ducked and went back to the table and sat down again.

"Don't try that, Stan. If some whore from Las Vegas has her eyes on you, it's over. Damn it, Stanley. Are you seeing someone else?"

"No, baby. I'm telling you the truth. Don't believe that bullshit you hear from Judi and your friends at your office." She measured his actions while he opened the bottle of water, and leaned against the kitchen counter with confidence she'd only seen from truth-tellers. "They want me to explain how we did it. Not just anyone can finance a rails-to-trails project in a tax-allocation district and then parlay the deal into new office space. That's why people want to meet me. Not because I make it happen, but because I MADE it happen. That's it. Try to have some faith in me."

Her instincts were telling her to cross-examine him, but she knew a marriage required trust that wasn't useful in the courtroom. "It's just," she paused, "I see the young girls looking at you. I know you're no angel, but I married you against the wishes of Judi and dad. You better not make me look like a fool. You'll be very sorry if you do, Stan."

She didn't look up as he moved over to the table and sat down with his water bottle. As he flipped through the top pages of the newspaper, he glanced at her laptop. "What the hell is this?"

"You mean Jim Pinson explaining to the public how blind pools are executed? And how the evicted residents got stiffed because Enzo Ruiz decided not to build the housing they were promised? Or pay them for moving?"

"Of course, that's what I mean. He forgets we're building a trail to revitalize a rundown railroad track. Do you know how much political capital this is costing me with my friends? This is where Darrell and I grew up."

"You better watch DC, Stan. He'll set you up for the fall. Getting rid of his old neighborhood is only the beginning of what he'd use against you. His first priority is DC. His second priority is the teacher's union. He doesn't have a third priority." She slid the laptop in front of him, grabbed her coffee cup, got up, and poured out the last drops into the sink.

Stan kept reading, shaking his head. "Jim Pinson, nor anyone else for that matter, has any idea how hard it is to put something like this together. There is no money for visionary projects. The voters would never vote for it, but it brings jobs and growth."

"You're saying Jim's wrong to tell all of Orthus County you issued a two-hundred-million-dollar bond to build a one-hundred-and-fifty-million-dollar MOTrail. Then you got new offices in the Orlando Downtown District. Dunham Schauble got a fifty-million-dollar operating loan, and you didn't spend the money on new schools. Yeah, I feel ya', Boo." Paige had meant for her sarcasm to hit the mark. She'd grown numb to Stan's daily political conflicts of interests, and the text message had her on edge.

"Just drop it. It's perfectly legal, and it's standard operating procedure. Enzo wouldn't steer us the wrong way. He and Bob need me just like Mayor Tisdale does. I should be getting paid what Sterling Johnston makes. He's no smarter than me."

Paige rolled her eyes. "Just because it's legal doesn't make it right. Now I'll drop it."

"Good."

They gathered their things and headed to lunch at the MOTrail Meat Market. Paige reluctantly believed his story about the text. She'd half-convinced herself after all these years that good sex meant a good marriage. But she also was beginning to be convinced he was having good sex with plenty of other women. As they drove along, she blurted out, "Do you know Ezzy King?"

"The Charter School Baroness? Yea, I know her. She's making my school system look like a joke." His left arm was draped over the steering wheel and his right hand was on Paige's thigh.

"She sent word to my office she wants us to tour King Christian Academy. They're celebrating their anniversary with a big reception." Ezzy King could make or break political careers, and Paige didn't dare turn down the invitation. "She invited both of us."

"Paige, she does this every year. It's a fundraiser, pure and simple. I'll go because I know what this means to you. It's obvious you want higher office. It's also obvious you deserve to be elected to anything you set your mind to, but that takes money. Ezzy is powerful and rich. I'll only ask one thing. I don't want to stay long."

"It's in August. The week before school starts."

"Perfect timing. I only have one hundred and thirty schools to open. Should be a breeze." He chuckled. She laughed softly in return and began silently counting cracks in the sidewalk as they cruised by.

Paige's phone chimed with a text from Judi. Hey Sis, how was your day with Mr. Worldwide?

OK, I guess, Paige replied. Flash and I have been together all day.

I wish I could sing to you like when we were kids to make you happy.

Paige sighed as she texted back. Me, too. Happy Fourth of July, Judi. We're fine.

CHAPTER 17

King Christian Academy had been established years ago with a full elementary school and a hundred students. Ezzy liked to call them the Pioneer Class. As acting headmaster, she used every opportunity to reward them. They had so little to enjoy, and she had so much to give. She used the alumni reunion to bring together headmaster, teachers, and students before the school year began. The first fifth graders were now rising juniors. KCA built a new school for the oldest students as they reached the next level. Middle school construction began before the elementary school was finished. The high school was completed as the oldest pioneers reached seventh grade. Parents of scholarship students worked at the school five hours a week, and Ezzy gave them their choice of cafeteria, front office, campus maintenance, or after-school day care. She granted all legacy King Citrus employees first enrollment priority. Ezzy had built the school for them.

Only baseball, basketball, track, tennis, and golf teams were offered, because football required too many players. Every room was fitted with laptops, computer tablets, and Wi-Fi. The Engineering Building provided classrooms, chemistry labs, and materials testing centers. KCA sponsored two solar-car teams. The school's pride and joy was the Agricultural and Animal Sciences program. Students were able to research and invent different cultivars of the rarest plants and vegetables. The adventurous studied animal life sciences and genetics at King Farms' stables. Competition and academic rigor were fostered. Ezzy had instituted a "three strikes and you're out" policy, but no one had ever been expelled. The parents told her it's because the kids were too loyal, and grateful, to throw away this opportunity on childish games. Ezzy utilized biblical principles to guide the culture without requiring ardent faith. The proverb corresponding to the day of the month was posted on a video screen in the cafeteria.

Before Ezzy built KCA, many of the local kids were either homeschooled or truant. If they did go to Lochloosa, they caught a bus at 6:00 AM, or earlier. Depending on the bus, it either spewed smoke or ground gears all the way to school. Ezzy's father, Jepson, required her to ride the bus as a child. "You're no better than anyone else," he would say. The Orthus County School Board didn't have the resources, or will, to serve such rural areas. Lochloosa was the picture of rural poverty then and now.

High rises and urban noise pollution faded into lush countryside. Stan's long arms stretched over the steering wheel, the air conditioner working overtime. They saw the beginning of the boundary fence surrounding King Farms. "Good Lord. How much fence surrounds the property?" Stan asked.

"Well, I know it's thirty miles of highway frontage, twenty on this stretch alone." Paige researched everything about King Farms and King Christian Academy.

"That's absurd. What does she think? People are going to steal her oranges?"

"No. But I'm sure a roving thief with a trailer would like to cart off a horse or two, Stan. Don't be so rude." Over the rolling hills, they raced past the endless brown, three-railed fence. "It's so pristine. I can see so far back onto the property." Paige marveled at the live oak hammocks that reached out of the swamps into emerald green horse pastures.

"See the golf course?" Stan asked.

She'd studied every inch of the school map she'd read online. "An eighteen-hole golf course, four indoor basketball courts, a baseball complex with four fields and batting cages, teacher and student living facilities, stables, and an agricultural research center? It's a totally balanced science and technology-driven campus. And it's huge. King Farms is over a hundred thousand acres. KCA is just a small part of it all."

Stan interrupted her. "And doesn't pay property taxes on any of it. She used her inheritance for a school poor kids can only dream about. Her teacher- and staff-compensation arrangement is a disservice to all of them."

"Stan, you don't pay property taxes either. And, by the way, KCA teachers have higher average salaries than Orthus County teachers."

"She leaves her teachers to find their way through the stock market. We guarantee our teachers a respectable and dignified retirement. Why are you always fighting me?"

"You sound like a variable annuity salesman defending those pensions. Ezzy hired a nationally recognized 403(b) provider. They do financial planning for every member of the staff. Their custodians know more about diversified portfolios than your principals."

Stan shook his head as they drove past the small airport. "Who is supposed to use the airfield, huh? Her local grove employees? It's technically part of the school, you know. She gets a tax abatement for an airport."

"So did OSK when they bought the land from Ezzy."

"Oh, my God. Are those tennis courts?"

"Twenty of them with lights plus a sports science facility."

They approached the main campus, where three buildings anchored the entrance, separated by long, open concourses with views of the sports facilities in the back. In front of the main building, blue and white buses looped back and forth to the airport.

Three four-story curved buildings sat side by side with the middle building set as the apex. Glass wrapped every floor separated by horizontal red-brick facades connected with white mortar. English gardens and fountains in a round piazza invited guests into the main entrance hall of the center building. The large front parking lots were filled with passenger vans, local cars, along with TV news vans and expensive cars with out-of-town plates. Construction traffic was carefully traveling around the backs of the building to a large construction site. Paige noticed large building foundations behind the main campus. Off in the distance, large cranes poured concrete into a massive structure.

Stan found a parking spot and parked. "Well, we're here," he said as he opened Paige's door. "Let's get this over with."

Paige emerged from the car into the noon sun. "Stan, please try to behave." She straightened out the front of her summer dress. "This is a fabulous academic center. Please, just for the day, appreciate it for what it provides this very poor part of Florida." She smiled at him and drew near as they walked toward the entrance piazza.

They stepped up onto the concrete sidewalk, and Paige noticed Stan scanning the curved glass around the never-ending building corners. She sensed his jealousy before he spoke. "Paige, my job is providing education to the children of Orthus County. This place makes a mockery of our efforts, but I will behave, for you."

Ezzy was greeting guests in the center of the large three-story room as Paige and Stan entered the building, Paige smiling at all the students on hand in their bright KCA uniforms. Governor Gordon Sikes was present along with other dignitaries in suits, while a couple of his staff huddled near him holding notepads and buzzing cell phones. She and Stan politely waved as he waved back, barely looking up from the staffer talking to him. The Orlando and Jacksonville news channels were set up, presumably recording for the six o'clock spot.

Paige caught Jim's eye briefly as he passed by, and nodded in his direction. Stan followed as Paige joined the processional of cordial hellos only a few feet away from Ezzy. "Paige, Stanley, thank you so much for coming," Ezzy said as they approached.

"Thank you for inviting us." Paige took her proffered hand. "You've done an outstanding job. Your students are so blessed."

"We're the ones receiving the blessing, Paige. Please make yourselves at home while you're here. Stanley, we're glad you could join us. I know this is an extremely busy time for you."

Paige watched his face twitch before he answered. "I will. No one can deny this is an amazing thing you've created, even if you had institutional help."

"Everyone needs help to build a dream. We've had a lot of help from the local community. Our parents have gladly accepted roles here to offset tuition costs. Progress Orthus provided us with tax abatements because we provided them park land they needed for buffers between neighborhoods and MOTrax stations. I'm sure you've had help along the way as well?"

"That's right, Ezzy. We all need a little help." Stan moved ahead toward the fountain as Paige nodded and shook Ezzy's hand one more time.

Paige glared at Stan as she slowly caught up with him.

"What's that for?" he asked.

"I asked you to behave. You're being a jerk," she whispered.

"Come on, Paige. You heard what she said."

"What?! You promised, Stan." Paige saw Ezzy glance over, and stopped herself from saying anything else.

Ezzy made her way over to a large service table covered in white cloth, where people had been snacking on pastries and other homemade appetizers that, according to the signs on the table, originated on King Farms. She picked up a glass, filled it from the crystal lemonade dispenser, and tapped its side with a spoon, calling the room to order. "Everyone, thank you all so much for coming. The entire facility is open to your wandering this afternoon. Please don't be shy around the lemonade dispensers. We have plenty more where that came from." Her face glowed into the gathering as she looked around the room. "The buses will leave in thirty-minute intervals. You can keep your recorders on while we venture around the campus, but please use my quotes only." Paige chuckled with the rest of the room, as she tried to capture Ezzy's smile. "Our very capable staff is on hand to show you our process and facilities, but please allow me to review any quotes you are considering from them. They delight in expounding on our students' high achievements, both past and present. It's our favorite part of the Annual King Christian Academy Reunion. I will take any prepared questions from the press now." She nodded toward a raised hand. "Yes, Action News Jacksonville?" Cameras flashed.

"How much state funding do you receive?"

"Like all other Florida charter schools, our state funding has been cut in half in the last ten years to approximately four hundred dollars per student."

"Can you give us a total?"

"I want to be as open as possible, but we're growing so fast, it's hard to pin it down, but around three hundred and fifty thousand dollars."

Paige noticed Stan slowly turn his head toward the back. She politely turned around to see one of the corporate visitors, arms silently folded, looking back at him. She took no notice of the exhaling press corps. "That's it?" the reporter responded.

Ezzy gestured behind her to the immense structures in her background. "Yes. That's it. KCA is fortunate to have many visionary, and, I might add, generous benefactors. Next question. Jim, *Orthus County Post*?"

Jim held up the audio recorder. "What will your effect be on the Lochloosa Cluster thirty miles to our West?"

Ezzy's smile had the natural effect of disarming the crowd. "Jim, I can always count on you for thoroughness." A few in the audience chuckled. "We started KCA for the children and parents of King Citrus employees when King Citrus moved south for a more stable operating environment. King Citrus, and by association, King Farms built this academy so our people wouldn't be left without." She folded her hands in front of her. "We're so far from Lochloosa that many children either weren't going to school or were so distracted by the commute that their studies suffered. Through no fault of the Orthus County School Board, and Dr. Stanley Jackson is here with us today, we wanted to make something unique. Our enrollment populations do overlap, no doubt, but we have subsidized our enrollment from other surrounding, rural counties."

Paige looked up to see Stan's face twitch again.

"Any other questions?" Ezzy asked.

A guest raised her hand. "It will take a week to see this place. When can we start?"

Everyone laughed. "We can begin…" Ezzy noticed Stan's raised hand, "after one more question. Dr. Jackson?"

"Yes, Stanley Jackson, Orthus County Superintendent. How are you able to retain teachers given their lack of a guaranteed retirement, tenure, and work-place bargaining privileges? What guarantees can you afford the parents of students taught by teachers with no teaching certificates?" The media's instantaneous note recording was not lost on Paige, as they would use any sound-bite opportunity, but when she saw the benefactors lower their eyes in obvious disapproval, she was embarrassed for him.

"Thank you again for coming, Dr. Jackson."

"Thanks aren't necessary. I'm here."

"Right." She walked with her hands clasped behind her in front of the crowd to be closer to Stanley. A power move Paige didn't miss and knew Stan wouldn't either. "We have filled all of our teaching vacancies every year by the end of the prior school year, yielding a teacher waiting list almost as long as our student waiting list. King Christian Academy receives applications from all over the country from very qualified teaching professionals and other industry leaders with graduate degrees. They are empowered and employed here at will. Many of our vacancies are filled by retiring college professors from Florida, FSU, and UCF. Most charter schools take advantage of absent union dues with lower teacher payouts. King Christian Academy has decided to pay our teachers on balance a higher salary than they might receive elsewhere. We are fully staffed and have an ample employee pipeline to resource future growth."

"That higher salary even includes their lost pension and two months of vacation days?"

Ezzy seemed to be pausing for effect, Paige admired, and then she continued. "Stanley, I appreciate your candor. Our mission is giving children the most powerful start they can receive anywhere in the nation. Why should we take risks for our employees using yesterday's retirement model? That would detract from our mission. We have, however, accommodated ERISA law and provided our wonderful staff with a state-of-the-art retirement plan. We also offer the full twelve weeks of vacation and sick days, but rarely does anyone take more than five because we pay double for summer. We are one of a fortunate few companies able to attract and retain the highest caliber of personnel with not only benefits, but world-class facilities as well."

"And with that, can we get started on the tours? I'm dying to see the place, Ezzy." The governor stepped in, ending the dialogue. The crowd scattered like broken ice. As guests strolled toward the buses, he stepped over to Stan, nodding first at Paige. "Hello," he smiled as he shook her hand. "It's great to see you."

"You, too, Governor Sikes."

"Stan, you've had enough fun," the governor cautioned. "The press is here. Dial it back. I know you're under a lot of pressure from the unions. So am I. But that's no reason to bark at Ezzy. This is a good thing she's doing."

"Yes, sir, Governor," Stan admitted. "You're right. It's a lot of pressure."

"I know I'm right. Paige, can you and Stan ride on the bus with me? I'd like to run a couple of things past you. Try and pick a bus with no reporters, will ya'?"

"You bet, Governor."

"You two call me Gordon. It's going to be a long day."

Bathroom lines formed and guests gathered up the remaining appetizers as the guests prepared for a long afternoon of tours. Paige waded through the throng of donors vying for Ezzy's attention. Their eyes met and they moved away to the side.

"I am so sorry, Ezzy," Paige offered.

"That's quite alright, Paige. I'm no stranger to straight talk, especially from the public-school sector. We're a threat to their power structure. I'm glad you accepted my invitation for both you and Stan. He doesn't know it yet, but I need him."

"Oh?" Paige wasn't surprised, but she was charmed. "By allowing you to expound on the advantages of charter schools over public schools? In front of all these reporters?"

"You're as insightful as I've heard. Would it be OK if I borrowed Stan during the tour when we get to the sports complex?"

"You can have him as long as you want." Her mouth curled at the corner and she raised one eyebrow.

"My friends tell me marriage is very difficult. Unfortunately, I wouldn't know."

"It's even harder than that sometimes."

"Well, buck up. Today is your interview with the governor. Your performance as District Attorney has opened eyes around the state. You're a star on the rise."

"Thank you for that vote of confidence. I'll count on it in the future."

"Do."

Paige smiled at her, feeling a connection to Ezzy's spirit as they walked toward the buses.

CHAPTER 18

Ezzy stood at the front of the bus following the governor's, her hands lightly gripping the support poles on each side of the aisle, as she answered reporters' questions. Jim pointed to the two large concrete slabs behind the main campus as they drove by. "What are your plans over there?"

The other passengers followed her gaze out the bus window. "As I mentioned," she began, "our growth seems boundless at the moment. Our facilities and resources have drawn the attention of parents across the country. Those slabs are the foundations for new dormitories. Boys on the right. Girls on the left. Over to the far left, you'll notice the staff facilities for full-time teachers from out of state, or those who choose to live here instead of in town. All of our inhabited buildings are equipped with the latest LEED technology and Wi-Fi. The building off to the back is a separate but smaller dining hall that doubles as a recreational space. We thought our students staying overnight should have a special area not related to their daytime activities. The faculty, of course, have similar facilities on the other side of campus."

They drove past the baseball fields and the track-and-field complex, and pulled up to the giant cranes pouring concrete. As the tour exited the buses, Ezzy found Stan. "Stan, I was serious. You're welcome to ask or comment on anything here. We're an open book." She looked into his eyes to make sure he knew she meant it.

Stan nodded, offering a cautious smile in return. "Thanks, Ezzy. I'm sure you are."

Ezzy had known he wouldn't be easy to win over, so she pushed down her frustration with his stubbornness, and corralled the visitors into a group before splitting them into halves. She needed to fill a new high school football stadium with football teams Stan scheduled, and the governor had requested some time alone with Paige. Two vanloads of reporters, political handlers, and reporters were drawn to the construction like bees to honey, while she noticed Jim lingering behind Paige and the governor's small group of capital staff.

As Paige and Governor Sikes's entourage moved toward the baseball fields, the reporters began snapping photos of the facilities and getting live video collateral of earthmovers and cranes rumbling around in choreographed chaos near the rising stadium in the background.

Ezzy triangulated toward Stan as he drew near the site. "Damn, Ezzy," he said without looking away from ongoing construction. "I wish I could've gone to school here."

"This facility would've suited your unique skill set very well. I'm building it for men like you."

She stood silently, letting him take in the roar and rumbling of progress, the smell of red clay and concrete, and the heat of the noonday sun.

The reporters meandered back toward Ezzy and Stan and formed a small group around them. Ezzy waited for questions.

"Ok, I'll say it," Stan said, coming out of his trance. "It's the biggest football stadium around. When will you put a team on it?"

"Thank you, Stan. As soon as we can find someone to play us."

Stan scratched his cheek with his forefinger as he looked over the site. "I know a couple of teams that might invite you to their stadiums," he said with a smirk, "but you must have football operations together by next spring when scheduling takes place."

"We stand before you, hat in hand, Superintendent Jackson. We'd like to have at least some of the games here, but we understand the challenges you face. You've been very gracious with our other sports schedules. We're a small school and need all the help we can get." What she didn't say was the coaching staff she was forming only played larger schools for non-conference games, instead of taking the guaranteed victory of a lesser opponent.

"Just keep me in the loop on your progress throughout the year, Ezzy. I'll see what I can do."

She could tell he respected the view before him, but filling a football schedule with the largest schools in the state required his help. "Fair enough," Ezzy said. "We'll keep our end of the bargain. Any of the Orthus County teams can join us for our Spring Jamboree here at T Sam King Field. Our dance card is filling up, though."

Ezzy had to hold her joy for her seniors in check when Stan stretched out his open hand. She reached out hers in return and smiled. "You gotta' deal, Ms. King," he said as the cameras rolled.

If her luck held, the six o'clock news would report King Christian Academy would enter the Orthus County football rotation for the following year. Papa T Sam had always told her, "If you can get it in the news, it happened."

Paige followed the governor and his staff, assuming that was the scenario Ezzy had wanted: uninterrupted time with Stan. Trailing at a safe distance behind them was a group of people in business suits who kept checking their watches and never seemed to say anything, except to smile when the governor smiled. The man who'd given Stan a dirty look was trailing near the front of the group. They listened to every word, and then she noticed Jim following them as well, though he seemed intentionally out of earshot. She'd uncovered criminal activity immediately upon joining the DA's office years ago. When the State Attorney wouldn't move fast enough after several requests for indictments, she reached out to the governor as a last resort. Knowledge of complex financial matters was her source of confidence, and everyone with a political heartbeat knew Governor Sikes had reached his two-term limit and had amassed enough power to retire comfortably with his pension up in the Florida Panhandle. Paige wanted to be his handpicked replacement.

"With only two men old enough to be her father following them, Governor Sikes stopped, looked at her, put his phone in his pocket, and got right to the point. "You've been doing a bang-up job down here, Paige. What're your aspirations?"

"I have many, but protecting your policies and following in your footsteps would probably serve me well." She opened up to him about her ideas and vision for reform. His reactions confirmed they were ideologically in sync. She surmised her brand of reform wouldn't normally interest the governor, but his lame-duck status provided him an unleashed, bully pulpit. Her confidence only grew when his staff nodded appreciatively through her breathless project list.

"Paige, Bob Drolland is in over his head," the governor said when she'd finished outlining the changes she had in mind. "Progress Orthus has issued debt way out of proportion to its economic development mission. You probably know more about it than I do, but this recession is going to stretch already thin budgets."

"Governor, I know Orthus Regional Hospital has gone to bare-bones operations because they can't make their bond payments.

The young docs with any talent are leaving. The private practices supporting the hospital are referring cases to out-of-network hospitals." She crossed her arms and kept talking without interruption. "Orthus County's bond rating will plummet if they don't support the hospital. If the hospital defaults, the blind pool that supports the hospital and OSK will implode. You know, they both collateralize the debt."

She saw the blank stare of surprise in his eyes when he responded, "No. I didn't. Please, continue." The governor and his two advisors, including the man from the atrium leaned in.

Paige continued in her best professor's voice. "Dunham Schauble will often hold a lot of their client's debt on their books. It's part of the fill-or-kill obligation they have with the municipality. They keep the highest-yielding debt for themselves. The high-yield municipal-debt market gobbles up most municipal junk bonds. Investors can't get enough of a tax-free, five-percent yield. It's feeding the monster." She took a breath and exhaled. "A municipal bankruptcy will touch many lives inside, and out of, Orthus County."

As a few of the staffers began to close ranks around the governor, he asked, "Are you saying if Dunham Schauble holds too much of this stuff, they go down the tubes along with Orthus County?" He looked around at his financial advisors, who continued looking at her.

"That's correct, gentlemen."

"What about the bonds of other counties they hold?" one staffer asked.

She tried to lay out the structure as plainly as possible to keep Bob, Enzo, and Patrick's intended distractions from muddying the water. "They do a lot of business in Chicago, Philadelphia, Atlanta, and Baltimore. Any bonds they were obligated to pay in those cities would be toast, too."

"Why?"

"Even if those cities are making their payments, it won't matter. The bonds Dunham Schauble is responsible for, like the ten million per year for the blind pool, won't get paid, because they will go down the tubes with Orthus County."

"Holy Christ, Paige. How close is Bob to bankruptcy?" the governor asked above a roaring row of lawn mowers moving in a staggered arc across the outfields of the baseball diamonds.

She caught Jim out of the corner of her eye adjusting his watch and twisting it on his wrist. "Bob has given away so many tax abatements, it'll be hard to plug the holes," she said. "The tax abatements are even worse on Stan's department. For every Progress Orthus tax abatement, the school board loses twice as much. The police and firefighters are threatening a strike because they haven't had raises since the last recession. This recession is going to be a double whammy because you're demanding more infrastructure spending, and both Bob and Stan have to fund the pensions to bring them back in line with guaranteed market returns. It's a mess with no way out, except for, well, you know."

Gordon swatted away flying insects floating around his face. Then he walked over to one of the baseball bleachers and hiked his shoe up on one of the seats as the group formed around him. He leaned over to retie his shoelaces and asked, "Are you trying to say a double bankruptcy by both Orthus County and the Orthus County School District?"

"That'd be a worst-case scenario. Stan's office has only begun its foray into the development authority trap. He won't discuss it with me, but I know his budget is three times bigger than Bob's. They have liabilities right now of around nine billion. Only two hundred million are revenue bonds. Remember the MOTrail project?"

"Yeah." Gordon laughed. "I heard that's what paid for Stan's new offices?"

"Case in point. Only part of the revenue bond was spent on the MOTrail. Dunham Schauble is using the rest on office space and their racing team. But the MOTrail is a drop in the bucket compared to Bob's scenario. He's been issuing bonds to support pensions, retirees, downtown districts, hospitals, airports, golf courses. You name it; Bob will finance it. A recession will be the worst on him. Pensions have to be paid."

"Well, I was right." He brought his shoe down and slapped his hands clean. "You do know more than me. The donor types are very impressed with you. I've never heard a politician talk like that. Putting that string of dominos together must have taken years of experience. I may need to make a call to my broker."

Paige continued. "Governor, this stuff is complicated. Development authorities have been on a debt binge for years. When the last recession hit, the Feds created so much regulation banks couldn't lend. Guess who filled the void? Development authorities. They have zero underwriting requirements. They'll loan to whatever government developer gives them the best deal. Free market financing for multi-family apartment complexes has been twisted into distortion from a lack of oversight. Progress Orthus masks its unaudited financial statements with rosy scenarios with no downside."

The man Paige noticed spoke up. "She's right, Governor. Our commercial banking division usually won't do the deals Progress Orthus will. The headline risks are higher than lending to a church. If the church defaults, do you foreclose? If one of Bob's friends gets a bribe from a contractor, are we perceived in the papers as guilty by association? We're leaving the Chamber of Commerce because Patrick McDaniel uses the downtown space like his own Progress Orthus headquarters and car dealership."

The governor shook his head. "I lived in an apartment in my twenties. I never heard of this type of transaction."

"Governor, when you came out of college, this scheme wasn't being used," Paige said. "Development authorities expanded from the blight business decades ago, and now the pensions are unsustainable, too. It's worse than you think."

"You're depressing the hell out of me, young lady."

"Sorry about that. I can't shake it. I see it all around us."

"Would you take over if I have to put an emergency manager in place?"

Paige crossed her arms and bowed her head, frustrated with the reality that no one just gives you the governorship. She'd have to earn it. "I love finance. I love the law, but Orthus County's problems might be too big for me. I don't want to get blamed for the meltdown that's about to occur. Very tough decisions will have to be made. Union leadership will come from all over the country like they did in Detroit. I'll be made to look like an Uncle Tom."

She was used to his widening eyes, as people were often startled by her direct style of engagement.

"Desperate times call for desperate measures, Paige," the governor said. "Leadership positions like mine come with a heavy price."

"But I'm not desperate. Orthus County is. If I were to do this, I'd need to know I had your full support. Teachers unions will crucify me for being inhumane. Wall Street will send armies of attorneys down here claiming they're first in line for payment. Pensioners, already retired, are going to have their pension paychecks and healthcare eliminated."

"Paige, I can't do this forever." The governor pulled his glasses off and wiped them on his tie. "My third term is up next November. I need someone to lead Florida through this recession. I want my legacy to carry on. I've done a good job based on my popularity in the polls. If you are seeking higher office, this could be your coming-out party."

"I'm seeking higher office, but this will be no party. If I get your full support, your endorsement, and the backing of your financial infrastructure, I'll do it."

"What does my 'full support' look like?"

"In addition to a signed executive order naming me emergency manager at a press conference in Orthus County, I'll also need a couple of executive orders from you putting the unions on notice we aren't messing around."

"I could probably swing that. I have a few ideas in mind already, but what about infrastructure?" he asked, putting his glasses back on. "Some places on your highways are damned near impassable, and what about that Bob Drolland interchange? Any chance Orthus County can help the state with it?"

"Nearly impossible. I'll have my hands full making sure the credit-rating agencies don't drop us all together. If I take some unprecedented steps maybe, but hard to imagine they would allow us to borrow even more."

"Not even a couple hundred million? What if you sold some county assets? Like maybe the hospital?"

"We might have to do that anyway."

Gordon nodded.

Jim kept his distance, working on a story while he typed away on his tablet.

Sheriff Bolek was in full uniform waiting at the school when they came back around. The tour made its final descent from the buses as the visitors scattered out into the parking lot. Bill met Ezzy as she stepped off the bus, and walked over to Gordon's bus with her before he stepped down. When Gordon came into the exit door, Bill greeted him. "Well, hello, Governor! It's been too long. Ezzy told me you'd be here."

"Bill Bolek? What're you doing out here? I haven't seen you in a coon's age."

As they shook hands, Bill patted Gordon on the shoulder. "Protecting and serving, Governor. You good? You've been doing this a long time now." He'd known Gordon since their days playing high school football against one another in Thompson County and going on the same college football recruiting trips. Bill watched Gordon's career surpass his after he opted for the Police Academy, but he enjoyed the old memories and the access they provided to the governor. In the event of budget shortfalls, Bill could solicit Gordon for emergency budget funding, knowing he was doing nothing more than reaching out to an old high school friend. "How high are the weeds on your farm, Gordon?"

"Too high and need mowing. Give me a call sometime and I'll let you come do it. Me and my people have a plane to catch at Ezzy's runway. Thanks for having us out, Ezzy."

"Anytime," she said.

"Have a safe flight," Bill added, and then noticed Jim passing by with the other reporters heading to their cars.

"Hey, Sheriff," Jim called out. "Would love to stay and chat. Got a deadline."

"Don't let me keep you. I hear the watchdog of democracy never rests."

"You got that right." Jim's chuckle carried across the parking lot.

"Hey, Stan," Bill said as he and Ezzy joined Paige and him next to the entrance fountain.

"Hello, Sheriff. Everything OK?" Stan asked.

"Why wouldn't it be? Though last time I saw you MOTrax was flying off the tracks."

"Sorry I didn't stop to visit. I guess I was in shock."

"Yeah, sure. Can I borrow Paige for a minute? I won't take much of her time." Bill turned to Paige. "That okay?"

Bill caught Stan's double take in his side vision, but kept his eyes on Paige.

"Sure," Stan said. "I'll be at the car." He looked over at Ezzy as he walked away. "Let me know when that stadium gets built. I'll see if I can get you on the calendar." Bill stared holes through Stan when he glanced at Paige and tapped his watch.

After Stan was out of hearing distance, Bill turned back to Paige. "I've been doing some digging. There're some things you should know about Bob. I'm also pretty close to some information about First and Last. I wanted to be sure before I included you, because of Stan's relationship with the suspect."

"Stan and I don't discuss any of his relationships. I don't trust him with confidential information. I've been doing some digging, too. We need to talk, but it's been a long day. Can I catch up with you in a couple of weeks? I'm in trial through Labor Day."

"Sounds good. Good luck in court." As Paige walked away and got in the car with Stan, Bill felt sorry for his boss for being stuck in it with him for another hour.

Bill smiled at Ezzy. "Ms. King, can I interest you in a tour of your property? I'll drive."

"Well, Sheriff Bolek, I thought you'd never ask." She smiled up at him as she took him by the arm.

CHAPTER 19

The dust rolled behind Sheriff Bolek's Suburban on the twisting, sandy ranch road. Ezzy thought of her childhood and inspection cruises with her father that inspired the new direction of King Farms, as she and Bill coasted through groves of experimental fruit. Hints of citronella floated on the late-afternoon breeze. "Can you smell the sweet grove?" she asked.

"Smells like candy in the pharmacy I hung around when I was a kid." Orange-colored lemons hung from manicured fruit trees, and trimmed vines were loaded with yellow scuppernongs. The road led them around pastureland, and it divided fenced livestock on the right from the swamp bottom on the left. The crackling dash-mounted police radio echoed the voices of Bill's employees attending a two-car accident resulting from a broken traffic light. She was further reminded of the reality of Bill's job by the shotguns clipped to the roof above her head. A fallen tree lay across their path as they came around the corner. Bill slowed the truck to a stop and turned down the police radio. "Be right back."

"Can you move that tree all by yourself, Bill?" Ezzy asked only to flirt.

She glanced at Bill's massive frame ambling around the front of the truck. He turned back to her in the passenger's seat. "Want to come watch? Maybe we walk a while? You can stretch those long legs."

"I'm with you. Let's do it."

Bill leaned over to grab the limb and didn't notice the rattlesnake. Ezzy's eyes widened as it struck, but before it had time to recoil, Bill pulled his Glock and fired two shots, sending the snake back several feet with both rounds. Ezzy stared at the sheriff in shocked silence. He grinned at her and said, "You OK, girl?"

"Yes." She exhaled.

"Sorry about that. Just a reflex. That was a big one."

She walked over to make sure it was dead, picked up a long limb from the fallen tree, scooped it up, and threw it off the road. "There's plenty more where that came from. I can smell it from here. Are you OK?"

"I'm not leaking—that I can see anyway," he said looking down at his boots. "I think I'll make it."

"I thought you'd been bitten. Orthus Regional is twenty miles from here." She pointed at his hip, reminding him to holster his gun, and walked over to where he stood while he bent over and checked for a bite. She took his hands in hers, turning his arms in her grip and said, "I don't see anything. Yep, you'll make it." They embraced and she whispered in his ear. "Just a little ole' rattlesnake." They separated, still holding hands. "I don't know if you've heard, but I'm bad luck around boyfriends."

"What are you talking about? Face of an angel. Generous as Mother Teresa. Smarter than me, and that's hard to be." He chuckled. "If you're bad luck, I need more of it."

She laughed through her poker face. "But I'm really busy, and have so much to do. I haven't made much time for, you know, romance."

"I know and I don't know. Being sheriff isn't a cakewalk either, but you're under a different sort of pressure. You have the school, the land, the politics. Your dad and King Citrus have put all their trust in you. That about cover it?"

The school and the King legacy were all she ever thought about. She'd never been lonely, but she thought of Bill almost all the time now. She squeezed his hands. "That about covers it." They turned and walked down the dirt road, releasing their hands as they approached the fence. A thin line of flowering weeds accented the fence-row edge protecting the livestock grazing in the distance. The post tops formed a dotted line that disappeared around the next rolling hill and supported a home for dragonflies dancing among the flowers at the bottom of the fence, occasionally bumping into butterflies feeding on the nectar. Ezzy ran her fingers through her hair, lifted by the wind blowing across the green pasture. The other side of the road, from where the snake had emerged, dipped down toward a creek hidden by a lush swamp thick with magnolia, live oak, and bay trees.

Bill's eyes twinkled when he looked at Ezzy. "I have no idea how you do it. My job's pretty straightforward: find the bad guys and put them in jail. You have to convince people to do the right thing and then hope they do it. Jobs and families are relying on you to stay in business. You're fighting for profits."

She appreciated his respect and understanding more than she could say. So instead, she reached out and rested her hand on his. Thunder rumbled in the distance, and clouds had gathered in the western sky.

"Afternoon rain shower," Bill said, but neither of them made a move to leave. "Right on time. Maybe it'll go around us."

"The politics part is the worst," she finally said, taking her hand back. "I would never be involved with it except they pay the asking price for King Farms' property." She leaned against the rail to look out over the cattle. "I gave Bob and Orthus County all that park land because the last thing King Farms needs is a residential real estate operation next to a MOTrax station."

She felt the top rail of the fence adjust as Bill leaned over as well and turned to look her in the eyes "Hey, whatever you say. I'm behind you one hundred percent."

"It seems like all the property they buy from us is just wasted. Have you ever driven by that industrial development outside of Sanford?"

"You mean the big blank space inside that long fence just on the outskirts of town?"

"That's it. They put an industrial park far enough from any highway or airport that no one uses it except small contractors needing storage space. They had to cut the rent in half just to get a towing company interested."

Bill laughed. "My friend Ronnie owns the towing company. He does a lot of work for the sheriff's office. He waited for the City of Sanford to beg him to move in there."

She had struggled to understand the financial mechanics of economic development authorities when she was first appointed to Progress Orthus three years ago, but now her understanding was solidified as to how they acted as both a private enterprise and a municipal entity. "The only development authority project I can think of that seems to function at a profit is the OSK Airport. I wouldn't send my dog to Orthus Regional Hospital unless he had a gunshot wound."

"Maybe we should send that snake." They both laughed. "Let's drive a little while. Your legs look fine." She smiled and grabbed his hand as they turned to walk back to the truck. When they arrived at the tree, he moved it by himself.

When they were back in the Suburban, Ezzy confided in him. "I think I might resign from Progress Orthus."

"Can't say I blame you." Bill put the truck in gear and rolled forward down the fence line.

Ezzy continued. "Bob is a fool and Patrick has financial problems. They're weak. Stan is going to lose the best thing he ever had."

"I know that's right."

"Know what's right? That Stan is going to lose Paige if he's not careful? Why do you care?"

"Who's Paige? What's she look like?"

She tamed her jealousy when he grinned wide. "Don't mess with me, Bill Bolek."

His smile didn't diminish as he readjusted his sheriff's baseball cap, cinching it down over his thick brown hair. "I wouldn't mess with you. I'm not crazy."

She brushed his free hand resting on the console as he turned the wheel around the next corner and leaned into her. When his lips reached her cheek, she faced him to steal a kiss. Her fingers were still tingling when Bill said, "Bob Drolland is a fool. He's making a lot of mistakes. Jim has him on video taking money from a developer?"

Ezzy thought through her Rolodex of names. "Which developer?"

"Jim said he was some guy that built transit stations or something like that." The big truck rolled through a large mud puddle formed by a small stream flowing across the road.

"Must be Gene Dodd. He rides the coattails of Sterling Johnston around the country building TODs and sports stadiums. Those guys grease the skids as well as they pour concrete." She shook her head. "Probably didn't take them long to figure out what makes Bob tick: campaign contributions. Enzo Ruiz has been paying to play for a long time in Orthus County."

"Who?" Bill asked.

"Did you see that guy in the pinstripe suit at the county commissioners meeting?"

"As a matter of fact, I did. I watched you watch him walk into the room."

"Bill, you won't ever have to worry about Enzo and me. He gives me the creeps and likes much younger women anyway."

She guided him onto a slightly elevated road through the swamp, surrounded by palmetto bushes and scrub oaks. The large tires maneuvered over a wooden creek crossing shrouded by live oak limbs and Spanish moss that marked the center of the darkest part of the cool swamp. When they came out the other side, the truck rolled around Citrus Lake. An alligator rushed into the water and disappeared as the Suburban cruised by. Three ospreys were using the late afternoon hot air drafts to hunt together. They took passing shots at a bald eagle hunting next to them, but the eagle defended its position.

"So where does Enzo fit in?" he asked.

"He's the Dunham Schauble financial advisor. He sells the bonds Bob and Progress Orthus issue for all these new economic development projects."

"And?"

"He named his yacht Touch Down after the Touchdown, LLC, he drafted for Bob, Patrick, and himself to operate OSK FBO. Does that tell you anything? He's more arrogant than Sterling Johnston."

Bill turned and looked into her eyes. "The FBO?"

"Fixed-base operator." As they drove next to the lake, frogs jumped into the water from the bank like sprinkled pebbles. "Bob and Patrick have exclusive rights to sell jet fuel, service jet engines, and rent cars at OSK. No one else is allowed to bid on the business. They charge four times what the three FBOs at Orlando International Airport charge." She got mad every time she thought about it.

"I wouldn't know anything about servicing private planes, but it sounds like their business model might infringe on a whole list of legal codes?"

Ezzy suppressed a laugh. "You'll see how an FBO operates and, yes, I think theirs is illegal. I was hoping we could fly up to Mackinaw Island before the snow starts to fall. Do you have any vacation days left?"

"You mean that super swank hotel in Michigan?" They drove around the large sweeping corner of the dam keeping the lake full of water. The birds of prey swooped and dove with the air drafts. Black clouds thickened as plumes of white boiled ever higher from the top, forming classic thunderheads.

"That's the Grand Hotel, but yes, it's on Mackinaw Island. You game, Sheriff? I'll make it worth your while. I have some friends up there."

"Well, all the sheriff's department witnesses are lined up for Paige's prosecution calendar. I could probably skip out for a couple of days. How long?"

"We should go for a week. You like catching fish, right?

"Only the kind that swim."

"Does salmon on fly rod do anything for you? I haven't had a vacation in a year. Maybe we can go after school starts, when everything settles down. Late September maybe?"

"Salmon? They get a lot bigger than shellcrackers. Hell, I haven't had a decent vacation in years."

"You hunt with your North Florida buddies all the time." She regretted her words as soon as she said them, only to be reassured by his answer.

"You think deer-camp lullabies beat ten seconds with you? I'm in. Do I need to do anything?"

"I'll have my executive assistant book everything. You clear your calendar."

"Ms. King, I might decide to make an honest woman out of you."

"Bill, if you do, you'll be the luckiest man alive."

"You got that right." He smiled at her. They rumbled past a warehouse-size building with an open-sided pole barn attached on the back. The raised-metal-seam roof covered an open dance hall and a deck that extended out over the lake shoreline.

"What's that building?" Bill asked.

She picked up her phone to flip through her calendar and to distract her from the memories made there. "We call it the Fish Camp. It's been there since I was a little girl. We've renovated it a couple of times but kept the back deck the same."

"Can I see it?"

She tamped down her disappointment, wishing for a moment he were a little less curious about her life. The building held such bittersweet ghosts for her that she wasn't sure sharing it with him would be easy. "Sure."

Bill pulled into the white gravel parking lot next to the pole barn. They got out, walked over, and stepped up on the wooden flooring. A black blanket of clouds moved to block out the sunny sky as they walked over to the center. A violent summer thunderstorm began to pound on the metal roof. The sound of rain above and the shortened lake view in the distance had always given her a sense of peaceful isolation. The tumbling rain streamed off the side of the roof into the lake like a hotel waterfall. The world around them vanished. She moved a little closer to the edge, giving him his privacy when he began scrolling through his phone. Unexpectedly, he moved closer to her, his hand outstretched, with his phone playing "The Time of My Life." Ezzy rolled her eyes, laughed, and looked into his chiseled smile and brown eyes. "Sheriff Bill Bolek, you are one hundred percent real from your baseball cap to your work boots."

"Why, thank you, Ms. King. May I have this dance?"

She took his hand and placed her other on his shoulder. "I thought you'd never ask."

CHAPTER 20

Stan pulled into the Grady High School parking lot one week before school started. He was there to speak to a group of administrators and teachers union representatives about salary freezes, proposed sick-day reductions, and pension reform. His phone rang as he stepped out of the car and he shook his head before he answered. "What, Candi?! I told you to stop calling me."

"Flash, you think you can get off that easy? You come to Vegas for a little fun and make a baby. That's on you."

"Flash?" He asked, instantly feigning ignorance to a nationally recognized nickname. He looked at his watch and headed across the parking lot, knowing the crowd inside would be getting restless. He imagined DC would be in there ginning them up.

Candi lowered her voice. "Don't bullshit me, Baller. I know who you are. My roommate told me who you were as soon as you left. You're married to the Orlando DA? You're some kind of school teacher or something now?"

"Look. Fun is fun. You got paid. It's over. Don't you have other ways to make money?" He heard slot machine bells ringing in the background. "Christ, you work in Vegas. You sound like you're in a bar right now."

"Got paid? I'm not a hooker, but I am at work if that's what you mean. I dance here."

Flash heard someone in the background say, "We're on in fifteen minutes. Wrap up those phone calls."

Candi continued. "Flash, baby, come see me again. I have your baby. He's going to need a daddy. I'm not going to be a baby-mama. You're a pro football player and he's going to need you."

Stan stopped in his tracks. "He's a boy? How do you know? You keep talking like it's mine. You don't know." Stan was motionless, hoping she would cave under his questioning and drop the obvious paternity act.

Candi sniffled into the phone. "Damn it, Flash. I'm not a prostitute. It's your baby. I didn't know at first if it was yours or not, but I know people out here in Vegas. I would never be telling you this if I didn't have proof."

"Proof? What proof?" Flash heard a commotion of girl's voices in the background again.

"One of the bartenders at the club is a programmer, or a hacker, or whatever they do. He hacked into the Osprey's healthcare records. I got your DNA. It matches the baby's."

Suddenly, he felt the weight of his actions combined with a feeling of panic knowing she was making medical decisions without him. "You took a DNA sample of my unborn son? You didn't even ask me? Those tests are dangerous."

"No, baby, they don't do it with the long needles anymore. He's fine."

"Damn. You sure it's a boy?" He stopped and turned to pace in the parking lot. The entrance door to the high school was only a few feet away.

"Yeah, baby. It's a boy. He's going to be big and strong just like his daddy."

In a moment of vulnerability, he couldn't hide, he said, "Me and Paige can't have kids."

"Do you want to be in his life, Flash? I want him to know his daddy."

"Whoa, whoa. I don't know about all that. If Paige finds out, I'm done." *Probably done anyway*, he thought.

"Flash, I ain't getting rid of this baby. This is my baby and you're famous. We can do this my way or the public way, but I'm keeping this baby."

He slowed his breathing and his racing heart. "What's your way?"

"A million dollars to keep this private. Two if you want to know him."

His jaw muscles flinched. "Are you out of your mind? I was a seventh rounder. I don't have that kind of money and we damn sure ain't getting married." He rubbed his free hand over his forehead, desperately hoping she would understand his circumstances.

"Well then, I'll send a couple of emails to Jim Pinson. You know who Jim is, right? He writes all those articles about Orthus County."

Stan began regretting not calling her back over the summer. "Look, we can work this thing out. Can you come to Orlando? I can't come back out there. Paige is already sniffing around my cell phone. And don't send any more texts. I almost didn't get out of that last one, Fourth of July weekend."

"To hell with Paige. You're my man now."

"Candi, we can work this thing out, but I'm not your man, ever."

"Then you best come up with the money and you can be whoever you want. I got an attorney, too, because I thought you'd try to play that shit. You can't leave me with this baby, Flash." Her voice started to quiver. "That's not right and you know it."

Flash winced and tried to slow her down. "Give me a couple of weeks. I need to put some things together."

"Flash, you know anything about babies? They don't wait. I'm in my second trimester. My due date is January and my hospital bills are piling up. I need help now."

"Give me two weeks. I'll call you back."

"Can't you call before then? Don't you want to know me?" she sobbed.

He stopped pacing between the cars and leaned against the brown brick gymnasium. "Take it easy, Candi. I'll call you."

"OK."

"OK, bye."

Stan pulled the entrance door open and walked in. Teachers stood against the white-washed, cinder-block halls. Dented, scratched lockers were stacked behind them. The old asbestos floors peeled away at the edges from years of neglect and provided a distraction from the glares he could feel. As he approached the auditorium doors, a couple of police officers held them open. Jim Pinson stood in his path. Stan groaned. "What are you doing here?"

"Reporting the news, Dr. Jackson."

Stan passed around him and two other men nearby wearing Lochloosa Bulldog hats. Retirees from the look of them. Union hard liners from inner-city Orlando schools lined the sides of the packed basketball court. Banners and posters reading "Protect Teachers from Bullies" and "Flash Jackson Gets High Rise Offices: Teachers Get 50-Year-Old Schools" were raised over their heads. The newsletters he'd intercepted from the national teachers union organizers rallying school employees to show up warned him this was the sort of crowd he'd be meeting. He'd become familiar with the intimidation and pressure they supplied through the media, but the new threat of a Supreme Court ruling allowing their class-action status when suing for delayed retirement-plan payments was real.

Stan approached the stage from the center aisle, barely muffled boos and loud whispers greeting him from both sides. DC's Grady High School golf shirt was a beacon of safety at the bottom step of the stairs up to the stage. Stan offered his hand and DC shook it like an old friend. "How you doing, DC?" Stan asked, still hoping DC had delivered his ideas impartially to his union constituents.

"I'm good. I hope you are." They started up the steps together. "You OK, man?" Darrell asked. "The union leadership is here and they want answers. And not the kind you've been giving me. I hope you're ready."

Stan shook his head, DC's position now clear. "Yeah, I'm ready, Judas."

"You got big balls, Flash, calling me Judas. You're the one here to bust up the unions. They're about to take you to the woodshed. Follow me." Stan followed his lead to center stage, where DC put his hands on the podium and waited for the audience to quiet down. "Thank you everyone for coming today. We know you're busy prepping your classes for the new school year. So, without further ado, I'd like to introduce the Orthus County Superintendent, and Grady High School's own, Dr. Stanley Jackson." A few people in the audience clapped—hardly a standing ovation, given his failure to restart the retirement contributions his predecessor had discontinued.

Talk past the questions, he reminded himself as he stepped behind the podium. "Like Darrell said, we know you're working on learning plans and getting classrooms ready, and the last thing you need is a presentation from me. As you've probably heard, the school board has proposed a few changes to buffer our budgets from tax-revenue shortages, pay you more, build new schools, and provide our students with the best possible learning resources. We're pushing the reset button on our children's futures. This year, we'll begin Orthus Children 10. The Orthus Children 10-Year Plan has several components. We'll continue to support you as you support our children. You have been, and will remain, our greatest resource, and our children's living role models.

We've outlined a worst-to-first plan that includes renovating four more high schools, seven middle schools, and six elementary schools to minimize overcrowding." His microphone cut in and out, and the crowd grew restless as he grew annoyed. "We'll build at least one brand-new high school, two middle schools, and three elementary schools. All classrooms will be provided state-of-the-art learning resources. New chemistry labs will be the envy of the nation. Auditoriums such as this one will get new production equipment to encourage our students to explore their creativity. Cafeterias will undergo equipment build outs to increase efficiencies with a focus on healthy menus and diets." On the last sentence, the microphone died altogether. Stan looked over to see DC unplugging the cord. Stan walked around the podium and raised his voice.

"However," he continued, "compensation changes will accompany Orthus Children 10. The changes are an improvement. We'll continue to honor our commitments to your retirement and retiree healthcare, but the provisions of our pensions must be reformed in order for them to be available for all of our teachers. If changes are not made, our newest teachers will be denied a dignified retirement. Our new system will give all teachers under the age of forty a ten-percent pay increase. You'll receive a twenty-five-percent match of your contribution in order to keep our teachers' compensation competitive with the private sector. We can no longer afford to double your contribution. Everyone over forty can take the same deal, or opt out and stay in the existing system."

A shout came from way in the back. "Flash, you're lying to us. You just told us you were giving us a pay raise. You haven't paid our retirement match since I started. That's supposed to be my social security."

"Everyone, retirement-plan provisions are deeply complex, but I promise you this is a better deal. In return for the increase in pay and the contribution decrease, your pension balance will be rolled into your 403(b). Everyone under forty will receive seventy-five percent of their current pension balance plus one percent for every year over forty. There will be some cut backs, though. Going forward, you will have eight sick days and four personal days during the school year."

Boos from the crowd erupted. "We're better than that, Flash!"

"Settle down, everybody. That's a small decrease from the ten and six deal you have now. We have to eliminate some of our part-time teachers' expenses." More boos echoed off water-stained ceiling tile.

"We're making other improvements to the plan as well. We're increasing the DROP program from five years to six years."

From somewhere in the middle of the throng of teachers a voice yelled out, "So we have to work longer to get the money?"

"Hey, now! The DROP program is a bonus for you all. We have to reward our senior teachers who work longer."

"You can't do that, Stan! Who do you think you are?" The chorus of opposition was growing.

"Hey! Hey! Calm down. Calm down, everybody." Stan was waving his arms with his palms down as he tried to control the crowd's building momentum.

"Orthus County is going through a recession. Tax revenues are dropping. We have to borrow money just to keep up with the eight-percent guarantee on your retirements. The longer we wait—"

"We pay for your new offices, Stan! You think you're better than us?" The crowd shouted questions, not even waiting for him to answer anymore. "Yeah, the longer we wait, the more money you spend on trails where minorities used to live! Your very own neighborhood. How could you do that?"

Stan noticed DC at the bottom of the steps, smiling and nodding to someone in crowd. The irony of DC's betrayal was a small but vaguely expected surprise to Stan, but the last heckle was too personal to have come from anyone else. He continued, "Folks, please. Let me finish. If we don't make these changes now, our students will continue to suffer in cramped classrooms and dilapidated buildings. The pension will not be there for young teachers when they retire." No one was listening, and he knew that. "Please,

please. You'll have access to the best financial advisors in the private sector."

"You're throwing us to the wolves of Wall Street?! How much are you getting paid to screw us, Flash?"

"Are you kidding me? Your retirements will be worth twice as much ten years after you retire. Did you realize you're getting almost no return on your investment after you begin drawing your pension? What happens if you have a medical emergency? Or inflation goes up higher than your monthly benefit?"

The teachers union organizer walked down the aisle to the front of the room, a small black button attached to her suit jacket—a wireless microphone. Stan sighed and folded his arms across his chest, waiting for his death knell. He hadn't stood a shot from the second he'd walked in.

The woman's soft voice filled the room. "Settle down. Settle down, everyone. Dr. Jackson has a point. Orthus County is under a lot of financial pressure. Bob Drolland has issued more debt than any other county of its size in the country. He owns an airport. He owns a hospital. Soon he'll own MOTrax developments." The depth of DC's betrayal was confirmed when she reached the front of the stage below Stan's podium, looked up at him for a split second, and then turned on her heel to face the audience. "The recession is starting to bite Orthus County and bite hard," she said, raising her voice. "But it's not biting the Orthus County School Board. Is it, Dr. Jackson? Yes, the recession will hit hard. The financials are stretched thin, folks, but not for Dr. Stan Jackson. He works in a high rise most people only dream about. Your Orthus County leadership talks about lowering taxes, then gives commercial developers tax giveaways. Then they put it back in their pockets." She turned back to Stan. "Dr. Jackson, we have a contract. A contract we negotiated with you and your past boss many, many years ago. It is illegal for you to even suggest these changes without talking to us first. You haven't even paid us for the work we've done over the last seven years."

He stared at her in disbelief, and wondered if she'd ever stepped foot in Orlando before, much less guided pension negotiations with the Orthus County school system.

"Yea, Flash. Illegal." The chorus grew, and any shred of actual discussion left the building.

The organizer continued. "If you try to make those changes, Dr. Jackson, we'll sue. And if you don't reinstate your contributions to our pension, we'll sue. And we'll win, Dr. Jackson, we'll win, and while we wait, Dr. Jackson, we'll STRIKE." She paused between each word and slowly chanted, "Strike, Strike, Strike..."

Darrell rallied the rest of the audience, "STRIKE, STRIKE, STRIKE, STRIKE..." The organizer began clapping her hands to the word as it rang through the building. The posters and banners bounced up and down in the rhythm of the chaos. Jim's cameras rolled.

Stan sighed. His elevated pedestal in front of the crowd had become his schoolroom chair in the corner of shame. He walked off stage and left the building from an exit he remembered from high school. His eye caught the fractured glare across the parking lot from his windshield as two men scampered away. Stan considered chasing them, but he froze when the whole car came into view. "Shit! Shit! SHIT!" He turned around in the hot August sun, plowed both hands over his scalp, and began to calculate his way home because he couldn't drive a car with broken windows and slashed tires.

"You probably ought to get out of here." He turned to see Jim pulled up next to him. "You need a lift?"

Stan nodded. "I guess so. You can drop me off at the shopping center up the road, but I need to get away from that crowd."

"Things that bad, Dr. Jackson?"

"You heard it in there," Stan said as he climbed in. "You tell me." Stan paused and looked straight ahead. He was well aware who he was talking to, but the world was closing in, and Jim's friendly voice had the hint of an off-the-record conversation.

"I saw you on the phone when I arrived. You looked pretty stressed. Got a lot on your shoulders, Dr. Jackson?"

"I got it coming from all sides."

They rode in silence a couple of blocks until they reached the shopping center parking lot. "Here we are, Dr. Jackson. I can drive you to your office if you want." Jim pulled up to the curb at the main entrance.

"Thanks, Jim, but I need to take care of the police report so my insurance pays, and they'll need to see the car. Look, man, I don't know you and you don't know me, but I got a job to do just like you. I know you're going to write this story, with pictures and video. Try to remember I don't control financial math. I know your parents are good people and your mom is a great teacher, but these pensions are too rich. They can't go on forever. The deal I offered them is a better deal. You know it, but they don't."

Stan stepped out of the truck as Jim asked one more question. "How will you pay for the pension rollovers?"

Stan rested his hands on the doorframe. "If the teachers union gets on board, we'll double team a general obligation bond campaign. Let the voters approve a rollover bond and be done with it. The government's got no place in the retirement-plan business. The Orthus County School Board has too much liability. The pension plan's broke."

Without waiting for a response, Stan turned and walked away toward the shade and air conditioning of the grocery store.

He was relieved when he read the headlines the next day. The *Orthus County Post* had a picture of his busted-up Salvatore and the video of the meeting: "School Board Finances Thin - Teacher's Union Rejects Pay-Raise Offer."

CHAPTER 21

The TV blared over the main bar at First Chance Last Chance, mocking Bob's 11:00 AM hangover. Next to him, Patrick picked through the bowl of stale nuts until Bob grabbed it from him, stopping himself from hurling it across the room.

"Morning, fellas'."

Bob winced at the sound of Craig's voice as the barkeep and owner stepped out of a back room, a keg hefted over his shoulder.

"What are you doing here?" Bob asked, though he realized too late he didn't care. "I thought you just worked nights."

Craig lowered the keg. "I work when I need to. Regular called in sick." He nodded toward the television set. "What're the Gators going to do today? Bob, the usual?"

"Start the march to the SEC Championship. That's what. Scotch on the rocks. Bring me a plate of those fried egg rolls, too."

"Patrick?" he asked while he finished changing out the keg.

"Whatever Bob's having sans the fried food?"

"Two scotches and fried egg rolls coming up. Hangover, huh?" Craig filled the glasses with ice and liquor before shouting the food order back toward the kitchen. Bob winced again.

Craig grinned at him, like he knew what an asshole he was being. "Gators are the three-thirty game right after FSU takes care of Wake Forest. Finally, we're past the warm-up games and into the conference opener. You guys sticking around for the whole thing?"

Bob downed almost half of his drink on the first tip. "Don't know. We're meeting some people in here in a bit."

A man in a dirty, oil-stained Orlando Ospreys jacket ambled up to the bar. Bob could smell him before he was within feet of him, likely a vagrant from the makeshift camp. "Hey, Craig. Man, you got any leftover bread or sandwiches from last night? We thirsty out here, too. It was a long night."

"Get the fuck out of here before I call the police." Craig put the plate with Bob's egg rolls on the bar.

"The PO-lice?" The man scoffed. "Fuck you. You ain't callin' the PO-lice. They'd take us both in. C'mon, man. Just something to tide us over until the traffic picks up this afternoon. Hey, fat man, let me have one of those egg rolls."

Bob didn't even bother looking up from his food. "You smell like a sewer hole. When's the last time you had a shower?"

"Fuck you, too, fat ass."

Bob laughed, took a drink, and set his glass down. "Boy, I am the cops. Now beat it," he added as he shoved an eggroll in his mouth.

The vagrant sniffed before ambling off. "Fuck both of ya'. I'll be back later for my pickup, Craig."

"Hey, Bob, you need any stardust?" Craig asked, dumping the nuts from last night into the trash and pulling out the refill container.

Bob caught the look of shock on Patrick's face. "Good God, no." Craig's liquor license would have to wait another few weeks thanks to the little show he was putting on. "Patrick, if you want any of the white stuff, Craig here is your man." Bob shoved another fried egg roll in his mouth.

"No. That's OK." Patrick chuckled. "Uh, I haven't touched the stuff since college."

Craig laughed. "That's really sweet, man. Good for you. Bob, you getting anywhere on my alcohol license? That sheriff of yours had a couple of guys in here poking around. They said I had another month or they would shut the place down."

"What?" Patrick turned away from the TV and looked at Craig. "They can't close this place down. First and Last is the only reason people come here. The kids are doubling up in their apartments because of the recession. Vacancy rates are at all-time highs. Mayor Tisdale is going to have to pull from the General Fund to pay the Orlando Downtown District bond payment."

"Yeah, I know. I'm working on it, Craig," Bob said, knowing full well he wasn't. He finished off his scotch and chased it with another egg roll. He felt the sauce running down his chin and caught it with a napkin before it could drip onto his shirt.

Craig slid another scotch toward him and continued to wipe down the bar. "Damn, Bob. Business is slow. I'm moving more blow than drinks. People come in here with their own liquor bottles and order sodas. I can't ask them to leave, because no one else is coming in."

"Craig, please." Patrick's tone was so earnest Bob had to stop himself short of patting him on the head, or just punching him for effect. "I'm uncomfortable with the insinuation this place is a drug den. Ridership on MOTrax keeps dropping. That means fewer people are coming here, which means less money goes to mass transit. When are they going to complete the construction fixes from the train wreck?"

Craig shook his head and put a toothpick in his mouth. "I don't know. MOTrax works in fits and starts. At least the one train is single tracking through here."

Patrick nudged Bob. "Sterling and Gene just walked in. MOTrax is with them."

Bob shoved the last half of the last egg roll in his mouth and raised his glass. "Craig, move our tab to our table. And keep the drinks coming."

"You bet, Bob," Craig answered, an edge to his voice. "Your liquor tastes aren't cheap. You need to get me some help with the license."

Like Bob "needed" to do anything. He'd do as he damned well pleased. He shot Craig a glare as he headed to a table. "I'll get it," he lied.

Kate Brown from MOTrax stood next to Gene with some young buck off to the side, his hands in the pockets of his shorts. Sterling was already seated, legs crossed and his hands folded together like he owned the place. *Stupid prick,* Bob hated them all, just in varying degrees.

"Hello, Bob." Gene shook hands with Bob and Patrick. "I think you know Kate, and this is her chief of staff, Lawrence Donatello. They work three floors up from Stan's school board offices."

"I know Kate." Bob shook her hand lightly, not bothering to wipe off the eggroll oil first. "I gave her variances this summer. She owes me."

Bob could see how Patrick was clearly taken with her. She'd been recruited from Philadelphia because of her experience with TODs, and having a pretty, young face in front of the camera didn't hurt either.

"I've heard so much about you and your support for walkable livable communities, Bob," she said as she took a seat, the others following her lead. "What you're doing for MOTrax will put us on the world map as the first in carless cities."

Bob had no idea what any of that meant, and was pretty sure she was just kissing up anyway, so he didn't care either. He looked at Patrick and Sterling, then back to Kate. "Yeah, sure. Our traffic is awful. Anything we can do to get cars off the road, we want to support."

"Kate, we enthusiastically support your mission," Patrick said with more of that technocratic gamesmanship he oozed with. "Lawrence, thanks for joining us."

"Thank you, Patrick." Lawrence adjusted his bowtie. "Sterling's dynamic designs have set the new standard. High-density living spaces will drive people out of their cars and onto mass transit. Carbon dioxide emissions will be a thing of the past. Riding MOTrax will be the only viable solution for transportation in the future. I'm glad you invited me."

Bob considered taking a bathroom break while the chief of staff finished his spiel. He glanced around at the bar filling up with the game-day crowd, and wondered what was taking Craig so long to show up with more drinks. He'd need several to get through this meeting.

"Bob, we've generated five separate designs for the MOTrax stations with Kate's involvement," Sterling said. "There will be approximately eight hundred apartment units per station. We've included a holding place should you need administrative offices in one of them, or your space will be a hotel, whatever you prefer. We'll call it community space for now. The uniquely designed station parcels will accommodate the options and amenities young people expect. They'll be able to choose from Mission Style, Colonial Williamsburg, Metro Glass and Steel, Desert Southwest, and Stone Block."

The waitress finally showed up to take their drink orders. Bob figured Sterling could do with a few frozen drinks himself to ease the pain of removing the stick up his ass.

Bob tried to get comfortable in the tight booth he knew Sterling had picked specifically to *make* him uncomfortable. "Did you say eight hundred apartments per station? Won't the sewer and new roads be expensive to build? Who's paying for that?"

"Sewer? Who said anything about sewer?" Kate asked. She seemed rattled, and Bob hoped he'd contributed.

"Which station are my new offices in?" he asked.

"We'll put them one station north of here, closer to your house. It'll cut your commute to five minutes." Sterling said.

Gene broke into the conversation, appearing eager to show off his construction expertise. "Bob, we included parking decks, but studies have shown high-density apartment complexes actually decrease traffic. We'll gladly pay for the sewer improvements and the parking decks, but it's going to cost about twenty million per station. It comes right out of the bottom line, but the rezoning you approved will help. Shared parking in your parks surrounding the sites will defray some of those costs as well."

"I'm not drunk yet, Gene. Did you just say traffic decreases with high density? Kate, you might not understand how government works, but new development requires new infrastructure. I don't care what little Larry has been telling you. The building we are sitting in generates overcapacity that still hasn't been addressed. Just ask the neighbors."

"Bob, when these apartment complexes are filled, peak drive times will not allow local traffic flow." Lawrence's interjections tempted Bob to pound the table, as he twisted his glass on its coaster and looked at the others. To Bob's annoyance, Lawrence continued. "The residents won't even be able to enter the streets. If they were to attempt to drive, the queue of cars would assemble inside the parking decks. People will be forced to take MOTrax. Ridership will increase and so will revenue." He was clearly regurgitating what he'd heard from his professors. Not a lot of critical thinking going on at the table, but Bob just shook his head as part of his role in the negotiation.

Gene continued. "Like I said Bob, we've included infrastructure for the developments, but we need the money for each site. Patrick, can Progress Orthus make it work? The capital-market lenders get scarce when affordable housing is involved."

"For all five?" Patrick asked, on cue from Bob's preparations with him earlier. "We're almost at our debt capacity now. I guess we can price a phantom bond higher than the infrastructure costs to make the negative cash-flow number work. Then no new debt gets issued." Bob ran his finger around the top of the glass and glanced toward Kate to see if she noticed Patrick was his puppet.

"Yes, Patrick, all five," Gene went on. "As long as we get the one hundred million in tax abatements, you and Enzo can price the phantom bond as high as you want. We'd retain ownership of the land. Progress Orthus would technically own the development on top of it. We'd pay Progress Orthus the admin fee and you abate all Orthus County and city taxes for each site."

"Can't you get government grants for putting up the poor people?" Bob asked, hoping to see a reaction from Kate. Then he started tapping his empty glass on the table and tried to get the waitress's attention. "I thought that was part of the grand scheme of your train? Getting poor people to work."

She grabbed her own glass with both hands. Bob got what he was waiting for when she sat up higher in the booth. "Bob, affordable housing initiatives and federal grants to support those initiatives are part of everything we do. We would do it without government assistance. They need places to work. Employers need affordable employees. If there weren't any housing for our work force, restaurants and dry cleaners would have to charge more."

"There's affordable housing right outside the door. Ask the guy you walked by on the way in. He loves it out there." Bob laughed at his own joke. He could see Kate looking at Patrick for help, and getting none, which made him laugh even harder.

Patrick cleared his throat. "Kate, can you speak with your MOTrax security guards to see if we can have them removed?"

"They have as much right to stand wherever they want as any of our other riders," Kate said, her face reddening.

"Typical," Bob said. "Why don't you sell the property to a developer that builds apartment complexes? Then you'd have all that upfront money to make the trains run on time. You wouldn't have to worry about sewer, traffic, or bond payments. You wouldn't have to deal with me."

The condescension in her voice fed his contempt. "Bob, we'll never sell the property." Her tone tightened, and Bob could see she was working herself up to a lecture. "We're as competent as any private sector developer when it comes to multi-family real estate construction. This is not rocket science. It's MOTrax's mission to provide mass transit to all races, religions, and socioeconomic backgrounds. If we sell that land, we're defeating our own purpose."

"Good grief. You really believe all this stuff? You're living in a bubble created by your own ideology. You ever heard the term cognitive dissonance?"

"Of course, I have, Bob." Kate sipped the wine the waitress placed in front of her. Bob grabbed his drink off the tray and swallowed.

"Oh, right. You really do believe your own hype. Let me get to the point. You don't pay any property taxes on the land now and you own it. You get a one-cent sales tax from all of Orthus County. Now you don't want to pay any taxes, period, for twenty more years? There's got to be something in it for me."

"If Progress Orthus won't provide the tax abatements, we'll get them from the small cities along the line where the TODs are located." Her aggressive answer stoked his intrigue because of the lips it was coming from and the lack of ever hearing it from the endless string of MOTrax directors. "They seem all too willing to do end-runs around you since the new cityhood wave started. In return, we'll pay our administrative fee to their development authority instead of yours. Who knows? Maybe they'll gang up against Progress Orthus with their newly minted North Orthus Development Council."

Bob ordered another drink as the waitress was walking away. He knew Kate was right. Progress Orthus needed the fees paid by all the tax-abatement deals to keep Patrick's offices opened and the coffers full. "You people. You create government-subsidized trails and bike paths. That makes the land more expensive, but you don't want to pay the property taxes. The 'affordable workforce,' as you call them, has to move out because they can't afford the property taxes in the new development. Then you move them onto mass transit lines and rip off the school system to do it. Whatever you say. Sounds like social engineering to me, but as long as you pay for sewer and traffic." He took a long draw from his glass and looked at Gene.

"We can get the state to pay the current residents in the blighted areas to leave," Gene said.

"Hope you figured that into your budget," Bob retorted, knowing Gene would continue to mention tax breaks and ask for favors until he stopped him. "We're not paying it."

Patrick looked at Bob. "We can provide the tax abatements using a synthetic tax-allocation district. The MOTrax administration fee will go to Progress Orthus. Eliminated Orthus County schools and city taxes will go straight to the bottom line." Patrick pulled out his phone with a financial calculator. He pushed a couple of keys. "The total bond will be about three hundred and fifty million dollars. Does that sound good?"

"Sounds pretty standard to me," Bob responded. "We screw the cities and the school district out of their taxes. We get paid, traffic and sewer gets fixed. Storm water and police are on the cities' dime for the developments. No public vote on the new debt." He finished his drink.

Patrick shrugged. "We'd have to take a vote on the tax abatements at the next Progress Orthus meeting, but it shouldn't be a problem. If that's OK with you, Bob?"

"We can probably figure something out." Bob waved to the waitress to hurry with his drink. "If anyone at Progress Orthus decides to balk at the tax abatements, let me know. I'll make the necessary changes."

"Perhaps there are solutions around these challenges," Sterling said. "We can all drink to that. A toast?" Bob raised his glass in a half-assed attempt at feigned solidarity, hoping Gene had relayed to Kate this was her sign to leave. "Here's to the effortless travels of our society around the marvelous environments we will build."

Kate sipped her wine and excused herself. "Gentlemen, thanks for meeting me, but I have errands to run. Lawrence, I'll see you at the office Monday. Have a nice weekend, everyone."

"I'll follow you out," Lawrence said. "Some friends and I are ride-sharing this afternoon. I'm the first pickup."

"Neither of you took MOTrax?" Bob asked, already knowing the answer. *Hypocrites.*

Lawrence seemed too taken aback to answer. Kate smiled politely. "Not today, Bob. I'm sharing a van to the mall. Probably the same one Lawrence is taking."

"Why not ride one of your buses to the mall?" Bob called out, as she hurried toward the door, Lawrence hustling to keep up.

"We'll put out a press release," Gene said, drawing Bob's attention back to the table. "We'll explain the advantages of new TODs."

May as well plan early for the coming neighborhood resistance, Bob thought, and offered a nod. He rose slowly, his buzz having hit just the right level. "If that ragtag bunch of activists want to sue for sewer and traffic, we'll appeal all the way to the Florida Supreme Court. They'll pay for the settlement costs, new sewer bonds, and attorneys' fees." He remembered the double-taxation-without-representation quote someone had used in a letter to the editor in the Orthus County Post. *If the shoe fits...*

CHAPTER 22

The sun was baking the concrete parking deck in the downtown Orlando summer. Lawrence turned to Kate in the shaded ride-share kiosk as they waited on the van. “Bob’s not nice.”

“He’s a first-class asshole, Lawrence, but he harbors financial value for MOTrax. He’s the key to tax abatements that make our projects possible.”

“What just happened in there?”

“Which part?”

The ride-share van arrived right on time. Kate followed Lawrence up the van steps, sat down across from him, pulled out her laptop out, and logged onto the Wi-Fi. She opened a project file showing the costs of one TOD and turned it around so he could see it. “Progress Orthus is going to issue a three-hundred-and-fifty-million-dollar bond, probably through Dunham Schauble, except it’s only a bogie number. We won’t actually borrow any money. They issue a paper bond, and give us one hundred million dollars in tax abatements.” She pointed to the expected profit margin. She hit one button that eliminated the taxes from the project costs, and the final cell on the spreadsheet went from negative to positive.

“Why issue a bond then? Why not just eliminate property taxes on the new improvements?”

"Great question. Florida is a transaction state. Development authority law was created to allow authorities like ours, Onward Orlando and Progress Orthus, to finance projects without a public vote. When all of the legislation was being crafted in the seventies, transparency advocates required any tax abatement be part of a transaction."

"So citizens could follow a paper trail?"

"Something like that. Most of the cities on the MOTrax North Line didn't give their local leaders redevelopment powers except Smithson, when years ago they created the tax-allocation district for the automobile manufacturer."

Kate saw the blank look in poor Lawrence's eyes and tried again. "When a city votes to allow redevelopment powers, the leadership has the voter's permission to create improvement districts or tax-free zones. They're called tax-allocation districts. The citizens on the North Line denied that authority to their new city mayors, so we needed a work-around. In steps Dunham Schauble's phantom-bond strategy. Progress Orthus needs to keep doing tax-abatement deals to keep the revenue flowing into their bank accounts. It's perfect. Progress Orthus will have ownership of the development, but not the land. We'll get the same advantage as a tax-allocation district, as in, no new taxes on the improved property." They pulled to the next stop. Passengers got on, while Kate shifted her knees to the side so others could get off.

"So why three hundred and fifty million if we only need a hundred?"

She turned the laptop back around and closed it. "That's the hardest part of the equation. To review, we need a transaction, right?"

"Right."

"And we need a hundred million over twenty years, or five million per year; one million per TOD, right?"

"Sure."

"Dunham Schauble will issue a zero-coupon bond for twenty years that has a phantom payment of five million per year, which is about what our taxes would be with the new development, but we'll have to use an eleven-percent interest rate on the bond to get to five million per year. That results in a three-hundred-and-fifty-million-dollar zero-coupon bond. Remember when Patrick called it a synthetic tax-allocation district with negative cash flow?"

"Yeah. Is that what this is?"

"Exactly. It's a government hybrid to get around the voters' rejection of redevelopment powers, but in this case, we'll use it to get around not only Bob's tapped-out bonding capacity, but also the voter rejection of unauthorized debt. Wait til' Gene gets Bob drunk and negates our administration fee to Progress Orthus, too."

"What's a zero-coupon bond?" The van rounded the corner into the mall parking lot.

"What?" She knew he was just out of college, but someone had to tell him. "Lawrence, I don't want to sound like your mother, but you need to start investing sooner rather than later."

"I've got a pension, don't I?"

"Yes, but you're going to need more than that. A zero-coupon bond is a bond you buy for a discounted price. In return, you get a larger payoff at maturity based on current interest rates. You don't receive any income along the way. It's called phantom income. That's why you get a reduced purchase price. Just like this deal. A bond gets issued for three hundred and fifty million because the phantom payments are . . . ?"

"Five million per year? But to us, not to Progress Orthus?"

"Exactly. They're negating our tax bill that happens to mathematically equal the phantom payment we won't pay. In essence, we used the tax abatement to come up with the bond price."

"Why does it get twisted in a pretzel like that?"

"Enzo is genius. He created phantom bonds so development authorities can keep the wheels rolling in the cities without redevelopment powers. The deal meets the standard of a lease-buy-back transaction, so we retain ownership of the land but not the developments. Now he uses phantom bonds for metro-area development authorities that have exceeded their bonding capacity. He should get more than five-percent commissions, but that gets added on top of the bond, unless he gives them an hourly rate that equals the same five percent." Kate began to rise, but then sat back down as the van waited in a traffic jam at the main entrance of the mall. They weren't going anywhere for a couple of minutes.

"Would Enzo get double the commission if the bond got doubled?"

"Yep. Enzo will get seventeen million for this one alone. The bond will just sit on Dunham Schauble's books until the maturity. Orthus County will show only the abated taxes as lost revenue, not a bond. Then we'll make one transfer and close out the mortgage at the end. When the bond matures, there's no more lien on our TODs."

"Dunham Schauble won't sell the bond on the open market like all the other projects we finance?"

"No. It's called a failed-to-deliver mechanism. They'll sell it to themselves, and Progress Orthus pays Enzo his commissions. It's just a holder so we can get our tax abatements. I'm sure Bob is back there right now haggling his cut for doing the deal."

"OK. You're stretching my comprehension, but what happens if Dunham Schauble has financial trouble, y'know, defaults on their loans? Does anyone owe any money to anyone?"

"We wouldn't because no money will change hands on the JLMS, LLC, building out the North Line."

"What about the loans from Onward Orlando on the South Line?"

"Those are non-recourse loans."

"What does non-recourse mean?"

The van started to move again, although, she thought, the air-conditioning was a good reason to prolong the conversation.

"Just what it says. In the event one of the MOTrax South Line LLCs defaulted, our lenders have no recourse."

Lawrence shook his head. "Who would lend money that way?"

"You worry too much. Loans facilitated by Onward Orlando would be re-characterized as equity financing in bankruptcy court. In other words, if we didn't pay, in your end-of-the-world scenario, a bankruptcy judge would treat Onward Orlando and Dunham Schauble as stock holders in the South line MOTrax LLCs and would be paid as such, getting nothing. Number two, our little LLCs don't have any assets that could be sold to placate lenders, well, other than empty apartment complexes next to MOTrax stations, but that's not going to happen, because people are swarming to TODs, and you're watching too much financial news."

"You're right. That *is* complicated. Almost too complicated."

"It is, but it has to be this way to get around the voter. Guess what else? Phantom bonds for the North Line will provide us with off-balance-sheet financing for capital expenditures that appear as our expense, but not our liability, which gives us more access to the bond markets for future loans on the South Line. They're a legal masterpiece."

"How do you know all this stuff?"

"It's the way all TODs are financed. We did the same thing in Philadelphia and Baltimore."

After several minutes working its way through the parking lot, the van was finally at the mall entrance. Kate stood to get off.

He moved over to her seat. "I think I'm really going to like my stint here at MOTrax," he said. "Thanks for the lesson. I'll forget all of it as soon as we get to the theme park."

"Enjoy the roller coasters. The bottoms are worse than the tops. See you Monday."

As she stepped to the pavement, she thought about all the tax breaks she'd ever negotiated. She'd encourage her developers to commit funds for infrastructure costs, only to reassure them their commitments would be quietly omitted from the contract agreements. The tax freebies flipped her construction bottom lines from negative to positive, and gave her the flexibility to pad MOTrax pensions with the profits. Regardless of Bob's insinuation she lived in a bubble, her future was tied to the success of the new urban designs to not only get people out of their cars, but to bolster the fragile MOTrax balance sheet. Naturally, her adversaries should expect she'd use every strategy available.

The scotches were beginning to take their toll on Bob's speech as he sat around the table with Gene, Sterling, and Patrick, glad Kate had left with her obnoxious college rookie so they could negotiate in private. He winked at Patrick, while Gene and Sterling looked on. "You think you want a taste of that MOTrax director, Patrick?"

"Whatever, Bob."

Long afternoons drinking and watching college football were Bob's last remaining pleasures in life, and the sooner he made his deal, the sooner he'd be able to relax. "Have the Coyotes given us any word on moving?" he blurted out.

"They have," Gene said. "Smithson Galleria is having trouble retaining equity partners. The insurance companies are backing out, and it's given us a ray of hope."

"They've engaged me to design their baseball stadium," Sterling said. "You and Patrick walked right past the one in my office last Easter, but you didn't recognize it."

Bob shrugged—like he gave a rat's ass. "Guess not."

"They want a rendering integrating the stadium into Smithson Downtown District, and it'll take up almost half of the project site. No longer is the project hijacked by insurance company executives with unreasonable demands for ghastly building designs." His glass hovered above the table as he swirled his wine.

"Great," Bob said. "I can't think of a better reason to build an interchange with my name on it. What is Johnston Limited going to pony up for the MOTrax tax abatement? Three hundred and fifty million is a lotta' juice."

"How about exclusive rights to concessions at the new Coyotes stadium?" Gene asked.

"That sounds pretty good. Right, Bob? What do you think? Fifty-fifty split on all concession dollars?"

Patrick's eagerness disgusted him, but Bob choked back a rebuke and smirked. Then he turned to Gene. "Who's going to run it?"

"You can use the same service contractor the Coyotes use now. They manage operations, and you get a ten-percent facilitation fee," Gene answered.

"Then it does sound pretty good. It sounds better at a seventy-five twenty-five split."

"Damn, Bob. How did you come up with that math?" Patrick asked.

"I came up with it the day I found out you and Sterling left me out of your apartment-complex deal. How're the loan payments by the way? Hurt much?" He finished his drink and leaned over for the glass of wine Kate had left on the table.

Bob expected Sterling to smile at Patrick, because he knew his penchant for enjoying the silent torture of others, and he didn't disappoint. Patrick looked away from Sterling's gaze. "It hurts a ton, Bob. My dealerships are short inventory because I have to pay Sterling's attorney every three months."

Sterling punctuated the point by lifting his glass again and said, "Business is business, Patrick. Your dealings with my attorney are not my concern. He only demands contractual obligations you afforded yourself."

Bob could see the amusement Patrick provided Sterling, and couldn't help himself. He had to revel in it, too. "Patrick, you've known since college not to leave me out. My extra cut will be a reminder for the next time. The only reason you're the Progress Orthus Chair, or a partner at Touchdown, LLC, is because I allow it."

"My OSK airport split is barely enough to keep the mortgages paid. The recession is killing me, Bob."

Bob could see how Patrick's financial stress could be great leverage when his discovery was interrupted by Sterling. "Now, now, boys. Let's don't get our panties in a bunch. Everyone will gain from Smithson Galleria."

"Listen, guys," Gene said. "The Coyotes Stadium isn't a done deal. Bob, you're close to your bond cap. Hell, twenty-five percent of your property-tax revenues go to interest payments. You're going to get pinched by this recession, too, because your hospital is a problem. The Coyotes need four hundred and fifty million. The Smithson City Council needs two hundred million for their new downtown district. A bank isn't going to give it to either of them. The voters of Smithson would never vote for a bond to build a courthouse and a City Hall when the existing facilities are still fairly new, much less two more multi-family apartment complexes to match the four at Smithson MOTrax Station. There's only one pot of money that big."

Sterling leaned toward the table and looked Bob in the eye, before turning to Patrick and then Gene. "We must determine when and where to include Dr. Jackson," he said almost in a whisper. "Has he spoken to any of you?"

"You don't worry about my finances, Gene. You do your job and I'll do mine." Bob inhaled deeply as Gene sipped his beer.

Gene slowly put his beer down and checked his watch. "Whatever, Bob. No, Sterling. I haven't heard anything from Stan. I've left some messages, but nothing. Warren Sanderson has invited us to meet him in his personal suite at a Coyotes game to discuss the details. I'll set up the arrangements and be in touch. I'll make sure Stan gets the invite. I need to get going. Got a long flight back to Dallas."

In the parking deck, the men headed toward their cars, but none of them noticed Jim Pinson. Since he'd videotaped Bob taking money, he read the OSK departures and arrivals app to see Sterling's plane movements every day. He noticed Sterling's plane was coming in from Dallas. In the hopes that lightning might strike twice, Jim had arrived at the Orlando Downtown District's parking deck about an hour earlier and noticed the red sedan, as well as Bob and Patrick's SUVs, and decided to stick around. He texted Paige. We should meet. I have something you should see.

Let's get something on the calendar, she replied.

Back inside First and Last, the undercover officer at the bar texted Sheriff Bolek. A cook just walked out the back of First and Last with a suitcase. Came back in with a gym bag.

On vacation, Bill responded. Make sure you put that tracker on Bob's car.

D-U-N. I did it on the way in. Enjoy the weather. There's a tropical storm scheduled for this weekend here.

CHAPTER 23

Bill put his phone away. "I feel like I'm looking in a mirror." Ezzy and the carriage driver laughed.

"Buck and Bonnie have drawn carriages here for years," Ezzy said. "But you're right, you and Buck have a lot in common." She put both arms around Bill's neck and kissed him. "I hope you have fun this week."

"Flying onto this island with your plane was a pretty good start. I'm assuming Buck is compassionate and generous?"

"Not quite. More sneaky and egotistical." The good feeling running through her heart almost vanished again when she thought about Bob and Patrick's politically maneuvered gas monopoly. "If OSK had affordable gas, we could have been here sooner."

"We're past all that, babe. Let's have some fun." Ezzy stifled the annoyance of an additional hour added to the flight plan in order to honor her own boycott of Touchdown, LLC.

"Welcome back to Mackinac Island, Ms. King," the carriage driver said. His top hat towered above the roof of the carriage from his driver's seat perch.

"Always good to be here, Shorty. How are you?"

"Shorty?" Bill laughed.

"I played basketball in college," Shorty said. "Been working here since I retired. I have to say, this is the best job I've ever had. Where else can I wear coattails and riding boots every day?"

Ezzy hadn't ever been with a man so secure in himself, especially one with such an unassuming sense of humor. "You got any openings?" Bill asked.

"Not much need of your services here, Sheriff." The carriage gently rolled down the path with the clip-clop of horse hooves.

"I was thinking of a promotion to carriage driver. Where do I sign?"

"I'll have them slip an application under your door, but this isn't for everyone. You start at the end of the production line with a shovel, if you know what I mean?" Shorty turned back and smiled at them.

"That's what I do now," Bill retorted.

Their laughter breezed up to the tops of the blue spruce forest, and Ezzy let the carriage take her back in time as it traveled through the wooded interior of Mackinac Island. They passed a few other carriages on the dirt road covered in spruce needles, sun gleaming off the hand-polished wood exteriors. Horse hooves ticked like a fairy-book clock in her head. Kettle corn and fudge shops lined the quaint avenue through the middle of town, just as they always had. Butterflies floated on the mid-day breeze across unending rows of wildflowers bordering the streets. Families rode bicycles between houses and restaurants. Late summer tourists absorbed the waning wonder of Northern Michigan before the long winter began. Yellow birches and red maples painted the landscapes of mansions on the water. Before them, Ezzy saw the hundred-foot-long, double-mast wooden schooner berthed in the Yacht Club, and waited for Bill to say something.

"Whoa, is that it? Now that's a boat," Bill said when he put his arm around her.

"Isn't she beautiful?"

Shorty pulled up on the reins in front of the small harbor where ferries moored allowing their passengers to disembark. "Whoa, Buck, whoa." He tied off the team to the cleat mounted on his bench, got out, and opened the carriage door.

"Oh, Bill. You're going to love it." Her assistant had set this trip up so many times, the travel agenda had become second nature to Ezzy. She could sail, cycle, rest, and see Mackinaw Island all in one week.

"I don't know. If I get seasick, it won't go well."

"You'll be OK. People don't get seasick on sailboats, honey. We ride between the waves instead of banging through them."

The boat captain came out of a bulkhead on deck. He hopped out of the boat and placed the step-style gangplank on the edge. Shorty followed behind them carrying two bags. "Aye Yai, Ezzy. Hello, Bill. I've heard a lot about you."

"None of it is true," he replied.

"I didn't think so. I'm holding judgment until I see your sailing skills." Ezzy's concerns were put to rest as soon as Scott cut a grin that put the sailing trip in motion.

"Then you're in for a big surprise, skipper," Bill said with the sarcastic wit she'd come to appreciate.

"I'm Scott, the owner and captain of Inherited Wind. This is Edwin and Mo. They're my first mates, chefs, and best friends. We're all here to make this a dream vacation for you."

"Hey, Scott. The boat looks shipshape," Ezzy said as they embraced. "Brass is shining in the bright sky."

"It's a great day for a sail, Ezzy. Let's get underway as soon as you two are ready." He grabbed both bags from Shorty and said, "Thank you, sir. I got it from here." Scott handed both bags to Edwin who stowed them below deck.

Bill handed Shorty a tip with the ease Ezzy appreciated in generous men while the money disappeared into the lapel of his coat-tailed-jacket. "We'll see you in a couple of days if we don't die first."

"Your room will be ready at The Grand upon your safe return. Fair winds and following seas," Shorty declared. "The clear sky looks ominous, but I think Scott can handle it." He laughed and turned to walk back to the carriage. Scott held Ezzy's hand as they all boarded the teak deck.

"See you in a few days, Shorty!" Scott yelled down the dock. Then he pulled up the gangplank, tossed the line back in the boat, and hopped to the helm. "Bill, the state room is below through this hatch. Watch your head and always walk the stairs backwards. There are two heads topside. One for us and one for Ezzy."

"Thanks for the tip, Captain," Bill said and walked toward the bulkhead opening. Ezzy chuckled to herself watching him crawl down the open hatch to the spacious cabins below to look around.

"Edwin, pull the mooring lines while I move us away from the dock. Mo, store the rope coming over the gunnel."

"Aye Yai, Captain," they called out in unison.

She knew he was going to enjoy himself by the smile on his face when Bill climbed back through the hatch minutes later. "This is exciting, Ezzy. Have you seen our room?"

"Yes. It's amazing, isn't it? Scott had to renovate the interior, but both masts and the hull are in great shape. And now it all seems brand new. The teak is original."

"Sheriff, want to help?" Scott said.

"Sure."

"Edwin, you and Bill haul up the aft sail." The resemblance to his father was undeniable when Ezzy caught his glance before he yelled up to the front of the boat, "Mo, haul up the foresail. We'll all get the topsails together." She leaned on the deck rail of the ship encircling the perimeter of the boat, turning her head with Bill's motion as he made his way behind the wheel to the stern of the ship.

"Aye Yai, Captain," Edwin said. "Follow me, Shair-eff'. Nothin' but a ting'." The sound of Jamaican patois carried her further away from the swirling storms in Orthus County. She inhaled the clean lake air whipping the canvas in the wind as it expanded into the sky.

"Cleat hitches secure, Captain," Edwin and Mo yelled in succession.

"Let's all get the topsails," Scott commanded. Then the crew joined her near the center mast and boom where she'd been standing and watching. Leaning into her role, the hand-over-hand hauled rope became heavier with every unfolded yard, then the sails popped into full form inhaling the breeze. She could feel the boat begin to glide faster toward the Mackinac Bridge up ahead.

"We should arrive tonight around six, Ezzy. You can hang out below deck or ride topside. Bill, we have hand-crafted beer in the keg freezers and plenty of bottles. Mo is making sandwiches for lunch. Enjoy yourselves."

"Thanks, Scott. It's so good to be here again," Ezzy said. He had his father's looks and brains. Ezzy and Bill walked up to the bow, stepped up to the elevated lounge platform, and relaxed back in the Adirondack deck chairs underneath the foresail.

Bill clicked the buttons on the armrest, looked at his hands as he reclined, and released the buttons. "How do you know Scott?" he asked.

She turned away, closed her eyes, and dropped her head back. "Oh, I've been sailing with him for years?"

"He's much younger than you, right?"

"Scott is Garland's son, my first fiancé."

"Oh." She could almost hear the smirk in his voice, and opened her eyes. "Didn't think to tell me before we got here?" he asked.

She smiled back. "Not really. I've known him since he was a boy. Not just anyone can sail around the world for a living. They've built quite a little business for themselves."

"What was he like as a kid?"

"Totally devoted to his father. His mom passed away long before I met them."

"Poor kid. I wouldn't wish that on anybody."

"When his father died in the plane crash coming to meet my parents, Scott stayed behind in Manhattan. He was just a boy when I lived in New York, but we were like kindred spirits. I felt responsible for so long."

"Babe, a plane crash is a horrible thing, but you couldn't prevent that."

She turned her head without raising it and said, "I know. Guess who told me that first?"

"Who?"

"Scott. This sweet sixteen-year-old boy came up to me at the funeral and said, 'Ezzy, I know this wasn't your fault. My dad loved you and so do I. Please stay in my life. I don't have anyone now.' I cried on the spot." Her voice quivered at the end and she wiped her eyes.

Bill grabbed her hand and squeezed it. "So, have you, you know, stayed close?"

Bow waves trailed off the sides of the boat in the pattern of geese flying south for winter, cresting gently as they followed passed the stern. The sincerity in his touch awoke something inside her, and she wrapped her hands around his and leaned up from the chair. "Sure we have. I helped Scott through the estate-settlement process. It's hard for a teenager to understand Wall Street estate-planning attorneys, but he was far brighter than they imagined. Takes after his father like that. I made sure his father's friends kept in touch with him. He had a job all lined up after Harvard, but took the gains from his investments and bought this boat after graduation. I knew he was sailing at Harvard, but the sailboat was a little bit of a surprise to all of us."

"It sure looks like he knows what he's doing."

"They sail to the Caribbean every year in the off season." Scott had looked so shocked when she suggested it on her second trip, until she convinced him idle boats and minds waste away without challenge. "Most of their business is pleasure cruises out of Chicago or Traverse City. No telling what that's like, what with the Detroit bankruptcy wrecking people's vacation dollars."

"Hey, look. We're sailing under the Mackinac Bridge. It's huge." Bill looked up and back over his shoulder as they passed under it.

"You should see it in the winter. Long icicles hang off the suspension wires shaped like the wind. Michigan is no pleasure cruise after November, but if you embrace it, there's nothing to make you feel more alive." She reached over and caressed his hand, slid one shoe off with the other onto the honey-colored teak. Bill followed her lead and kicked his off, too.

"Anyone hungry?" Ezzy turned to see Scott carrying their lunch on a tray.

"Hey, Scott." Ezzy yawned and stretched her arms.

"I brought turkey wraps up from the galley. Bill, I brought you a Hop Cat IPA from Grand Rapids." A cold spray of foam burst out when Scott cracked the cap of the beer bottle. He handed it to Bill and put the serving plate on the table between their chairs. "For you Ezzy, your favorite, Black Star Merlot. Mind if I join you?"

"Please do. Thanks for the beer."

Scott bent to one knee on the broad deck where they were sitting, under the waving banner bearing the ship's name high atop the main mast. Wind blew through his shaggy blond hair as he poured the glass of wine.

"How have you been this year?" she asked, picking up her lunch.

He smiled. "The sailing has been remarkable. Best sailing weather yet for Lake Michigan and Huron. Not as many trips, though."

"Really? Why not?" She took a bite and waited for his answer. He flopped his hair back into a small ponytail, his arms and hands sweeping through the air—so much like his father.

"This whole area serves Chicago and Detroit tourists. Detroit keeps getting smaller, and Chicago's not far behind what with all the people moving away because of the recession. Plus, we're not cheap, so boating is the first tradition to get axed when a recession hits, but this boat is large enough we can sail down to St. Barts for the winter and get a full year. Then we have our Spain trip during the spring, thanks to your inspiration and what not."

"Do your dad's friends on Wall Street still call?" she asked.

Scott nodded. "They're my steadiest customers. They usually apologize for not coming more often, and remind me to tell you they stay in touch."

"Good. Let me know if they don't. Your father made a lot of people very rich."

"Sure did. You're looking at one of them." He said it in a way that reminded her of the corporate donors and dealmakers she had dealt with—confidence without arrogance.

Bill finished a bit of his sandwich and tipped the bottle. "I get the feeling a lot of your dad's market skills have rubbed off. This boat is impressive."

"Maybe. If he were here, he could teach me to trade, but I wouldn't trade this job for anything on Wall Street. Although I do have a Bloomberg Terminal in my cabin."

Ezzy smiled, put down her sandwich, and leaned back. "Say it ain't so?"

"Yep." His eyes squinted, hiding his father's green eyes when he smiled. "I have the biometric encryption unit and everything. It accesses the mainframe via satellite from my hard drive. Four monitors show me everything I need to see. All my research and history are uploaded to the cloud automatically. I can trade anywhere in the world anytime, day or night. Usually when my sailing guests are asleep and Edwin has the helm, or when he and Mo are partying in the harbors."

Her fading memory of Garland reminded her of the hours upon hours of reading and analysis he absorbed before making any decision. "How often are you doing research?"

He shrugged his shoulders and popped open a grin. “I’d do it all the time if I didn’t have the ship.”

“You like it that much?”

“Not really *like* as much as, well, I don’t know, am born to it, I guess. I see patterns emerge. Fundamental trends in the market will veer away from standard deviations occasionally. After reading enough financial statements, I can understand company strategy.” He stood up from his kneeling position and crumpled his lunch wrapper into a ball. “It’s not easy, but a common denominator of successful arbitrage is picking out inefficiencies. When inefficiency appears, the market exploits it.” He leaned over and held out his hand for Bill’s trash.

“Do you do a lot of trading?” she asked.

“Some, but my investments are more outsized bets made in single transactions. Dad’s trustees run the trust funds like Fort Knox, so I don’t do anything with them. They buy domestic and international sovereign fixed income and blue chips—basic plain-Jane stuff. My investments are more like a hedge fund, but with enough clout to buy custom-structured securities at the big wire houses.”

“Speak English, kid,” Bill said as he put the beer bottle on the deck.

“Sorry, Bill. That’s why I prefer the boat job. My dad was very wealthy. He put most of his money in a trust for me with required stipulations on when, and if, I can access the money. You know. Normal stuff. I have to have a job. Can’t be strung out on drugs, etcetera.”

“Sounds normal to me. Like I would know. Ezzy, will you hand me another one of those Hop Cats out of the cooler?”

“I’ll be right back after I throw the trash out.” Ezzy handed him hers before he jogged off.

Then she pulled out a cold beer and handed it to Bill, who had already uncorked the bottle Scott left and filled Ezzy’s glass. Scott came around the ship's side leaning to the inside with his hand running along the roped edge. He hopped back on the platform, standing upright with one hand resting on the boom, listing to one side in the summer wind.

Bill took a sip. "What do you mean by wire houses?"

"When you have enough money, you can get Wall Street banks, or big investment houses, to create specific bets, or plays, for you. Then they take the other side of the bet on the trading floor, or hedge themselves in the next room over with an insurance product, usually before you've left the closing table. They're supporting liquid markets. It's what they do."

"Have you found anything particularly interesting? Ezzy asked, piqued by his depth of knowledge. Her emails and phone calls to cajole bankers to stay in touch with him had obviously paid off.

"Some things, but it's only a hunch right now. I've been watching the municipal bond market for a couple of years."

"You have my undivided attention." She sat back up in her chair. "What's your hunch?"

"I used the bankruptcy metrics of Detroit, Stockton, Harrisburg and the Puerto Rico default to gauge major metropolitan finances."

"And?"

"Inefficiency exists…everywhere."

She smirked when Bill laughed and said, "Well sure, kid. That joke's as old as Roman literature."

The ladder of O-rings attaching the sail to the mast clinked like a xylophone from top to bottom as a gust of wind released and then filled the sail full force. Ezzy watched Scott's eyes dart back and forth on the deck as he spoke. "I mean the financial stability of our entire municipal system. The deviations have a wide range across municipalities of differing sizes and demographics, but most major metropolitan areas are awaking to Detroit and Puerto Rico-like problems."

"What do you mean, 'Detroit and Puerto Rico-like problems'?" Bill asked.

His eyes stopped moving when they met Ezzy's, and he said, "In many ways, exactly like theirs. Archaic pension systems and economic development debt were hidden until a system shock was delivered by the housing crisis. Fannie Mae and Freddie Mac's easy money inspired lackadaisical quality-control systems and market inefficiencies; inefficiencies that are now creeping through development authorities that fund real estate ventures where traditional banks won't lend."

She'd heard the Fannie Mae causation narrative before and considered it political at best. "But aren't banks always claiming they won't lend to multi-family apartments because regulations are so stringent?" She'd always assumed the regional banks didn't want local municipal business, and the financial crisis was so bad it washed out the possibility of more Black Swan events. She also hoped his Detroit and Puerto Rico comparisons were isolated problems, and any of his conclusions came from odd-ball brainstorming sessions on long trips at sea.

Scott propped himself against the mast and took a swig of beer. "What they mean is, they won't lend to any projects with hair-brained affordable-housing initiatives or minimized parking spaces in areas where people prefer cars. They can't lend money to build marine ports or mass transit, because they can't match the negotiating leverage of a government system. State development banks have the category killer of tax-exempt income providing an unending supply of lenders that fund large government projects with socialized risks and lower borrowing rates. Social engineering doesn't have the profitable track record banks need to lend. They get to stay out of risky markets, and label municipalities as competitors with unfair lending advantages. Then they use the label as a truncheon when negotiating with their regulator, the Fed, for laxer capital requirements. Talented industrialists and developers will always need money, even during a banking crisis, which spawned the current lending environment of tighter commercial bank-lending regulations and development authority easy money. The current municipal-debt underwriting system is driven by aggressive politicians with no banking experience approving projects on the advice of commissioned bond salespeople."

Ezzy's three years on Progress Orthus's board were clicking in her mind like a slideshow. She'd struggled with Progress Orthus's and MOTrax's borrowing inconsistencies since she sold them King Citrus groves and distribution hubs. When she'd asked her personal banking connections why they weren't banking Orthus County's business, they'd told her because Bob Drolland and Patrick McDaniel were the bank, and intentionally cut them out.

"And just as global demand was drawn to Fannie Mae's triple-A-rated implied guarantee paying higher interests rates than treasuries," Scott continued, "bond buyers are gobbling up tax-exempt municipal debt that's appearing as fast as Orwellian downtown mini-malls labeled mixed-use developments. Passive investors have fueled the municipal-debt market for the last three decades without asking any questions of the governments issuing the debt. Since the financial crisis, development authorities have shifted the inefficiency into hyper-drive."

Ezzy had to remind herself to breathe. A future with Progress Orthus would mean going against her core principles. Part of her had known that from the start, but part of her also wanted to be wrong about those suspicions. She wanted to believe people were as good and decent as she wanted them to be. Patrick's willing submittals to Bob and Enzo's suggestions, her park gift soon to be flooded with apartment-complex overflow parking, the improprieties she knew existed at OSK, and now Orthus Regional Hospital missing payments . . . it all amounted to her feeling a little duped—and a lot pissed as hell.

She struggled for control of that anger. This should be a dream vacation, not the boiling point for her problems with work—or the world, for that matter. She focused on the sound of the O-rings on the main mast, the occasional pop of the canvas, and the bow slipping south through Lake Michigan. She took a deep breath, hoping her voice wouldn't betray her emotions. "How many other municipalities will end up like those you've mentioned?"

Scott tipped his beer and shrugged in a kind of resignation. "Where my hunch has its most value is the domino effect that Detroit, Puerto Rico, and other major defaults have started, but they're different. Detroit is a city; Puerto Rico operates like a state. Puerto Rico can't file for bankruptcy, but it can't make its bond payment either. Detroit set the precedent for large, orderly municipal bankruptcies, while Puerto Rico will be the standard bearer for states." He took a swig of beer and shook his head. "The carnage will bleed into municipal bond funds. The market isn't pricing risks correctly."

"Are you moving against the trend?" Bill asked, darting a glance at Ezzy. He had to know she was more than just curious.

"That's the part of the journey I'm in now—how to exploit the inefficiency. I'm working on some things with interested counter parties. I've already shorted a few investment houses. Ever heard of Dunham Schauble? They issue most of the bonds down in Florida."

She groaned inwardly. "Of course. They issue all of Orthus County's and Progress Orthus's debt."

"They're nationwide. Their biggest clients are Chicago and Philly, but counties like Orthus, with powerful development authorities, are getting in on the action to feed the hungry muni-investor."

"Our hospital bond is coming due," she said, almost embarrassed. "We had to cover their payment this summer from a tax-anticipation note."

"I didn't know you were involved with them. That is NOT good, Ezzy."

"I know. I joined the board of Progress Orthus a few years back to guard a donation I made to Orthus County. My position is one of the reasons we took this vacation, away from the constant but desperate political maneuvering." She leaned back, took another sip of wine, and wished she'd asked for something a little stronger.

Bill said what she was thinking. "The corruption and the politics are like one big dark cloud. Everyone knows things are bad, but they can't quite put their finger on it."

"When the trends don't conform to logic, I dive in," Scott said. "As you can see, Sheriff, I have a lot of time to think."

"Well, let me know when you need some investors, Scott. Right now, I'm long old police cars and forty-five caliber bullets." He set his empty bottle on the deck next to his chair, and she caught his eye as he looked back up. In addition to the worry she was feeling over her own work, she didn't need to worry about his. He laid his hand on hers and gave it a gentle squeeze.

"You think your police cars are old?" Scott asked. "Try clean water shortages in San Juan, or graffiti-stained buildings in Downtown Detroit." The men laughed like old buddies, but she couldn't join them in the gallows humor, and could barely hold it together as they continued to jab. "But your old bullets? Now that's been the right call for months. Ammunition manufacturers can't make the stuff fast enough." He took the last swig of his beer, bent over to pick up Bill's, and said, "When the cruel mistress of leverage turns on the politicians, and the money gets tight, public safety concerns rise, which is job security for you."

Bill slid his shoes back. "I guess that's good news. They're not paying the teachers what they owe them, but us cops always have jobs. Robberies and murders don't occur in heaven, and money doesn't spend up there either, son, so make sure you get started on the entry tickets early. Got any more of those Hop Cats?" he asked. "That's damn good beer."

When Scott left to work his way back down the side of the ship, she couldn't suppress it any longer. "You know, Bill. I had a dream about you."

He raised an eyebrow at her. "Was I naked?"

She frowned again. "Not this time."

"Oh, c'mon. Now you're just messing with me."

His spark reminded her this was his vacation, too. She wrapped her hands around her wine glass and leaned over to kiss him on the cheek. "I'll tell you about it later." She sipped from the glass. "It's so much better when you're here."

"It certainly is." He smiled at her as Scott came back around the bulkhead from the galley and handed the beer to Bill before pouring another glass of wine for Ezzy. Then he set down a plate of cheese and almonds on the deck table between them.

"Smooth sailing, huh, skipper?" Bill asked, and relaxed back in his chair.

"The knife hasn't rolled off."

"Huh?"

"On the cheeseboard. It hasn't rolled off." Ezzy looked down to see the knife rock back and forth between two blocks of cheese.

Bill chuckled. "What do y'know? Smooth sailing, indeed."

"You see the Grand Traverse Lighthouse over on the left?" Scott pointed into the southern horizon off the bow. "See Big Bear and Little Bear Islands on the right?"

"Yeah, man, this is something else." Bill winced from the first sip of the new beer. "Are those sand dunes?" The sun reflected off his outstretched forearm, creating the illusion of a wood-handled sledgehammer as he pointed off in the distance.

"Precisely. Giant sand dunes. We're almost there. We'll anchor off the coast of Glen Arbor. You'll be watching the sunset for dinner."

"Sounds divine, Scott. You boys wake me when we get there."

"I'll go hang out with Scott, babe. Maybe he lets me drive the boat."

Scott reached out his hand to help Bill out of the chair. "I was counting on the help. I need a nap, too." Bill's mouth opened with surprise. "Just kidding. I need you to trim the jib and haul sail, Bill."

Ezzy laughed, her fear rumbling just below the surface. She laid her head against the headrest and watched them walk back toward the helm, thinking of two alternate futures: with Bill and without him.

CHAPTER 24

Dark orange, violet, and yellow butterfly wings daisy-chained the length of the porch, feeding on sweet geranium nectar. Sunrise reflected off the lanterns hanging high overhead. The bridge stood like a shining steel altar in the distance, while Bill sat alone in a rocking chair overlooking the Straits of Mackinac. He took a sip of his coffee as Ezzy came through the screen door to join him.

"Good morning, beautiful," he said. "It's good to wake up on dry land. Scott's boat is nice, but Grand Hotel living suits me better."

"It certainly does. Why didn't you wake me when you left the room?"

"Because you tossed and turned all night. I thought you needed the rest."

She brushed the hair from her eyes. "That was very sweet of you. What're you reading?"

He held his phone screen up for her to see. "The *Post.* Want some coffee?" He nodded toward the waiter arriving behind her with a cup.

"Desperately." She took the cup from the waiter, and then dropped a light kiss on Bill's lips before she sat down in the rocking chair next to his. She nodded toward his phone. "So what's going on back home?"

"Oh, just more stuff I have to deal with when we get back."

"Like high school stadium construction and school expansions?"

"Less difficult." He smiled. "More like mortgage evictions in slum neighborhoods created by mortgage evictions. Car wrecks because traffic lights don't work. Break-ins all over town. All that on top of the tropical storm dumping torrential rain. It's becoming a mess."

"That's a shame." She nodded hello to a couple who walked in front of them on the porch.

"Yeah, but the stuff you never expect is the worst."

"Like what?"

He looked around at the hotel guests beginning to mill around on the porch, and lowered his voice. "Well, the sewers aren't working now."

She made a face. "I knew the pipes were old, but have they really gotten that bad?"

"Jim's story this morning says the tropical storm cut the power. The pumps shut off, and now there're sewer fountains around the lake down by Orthus Park and the Orlando Downtown District. Take a look." As he turned the screen toward her, he turned his expression to mock horror. "Jim wrote we're suffering from municipal diverticulitis."

Ezzy leaned over, looked at the picture of water gushing from three manholes in a line along the lake side, and twisted her lips in disgust. "That's horrible."

"Want to know the worst part?"

"Do I?"

"The pumps were so old the power failure shorted out the electronics. We don't have any more in supply and all of central Florida is trying to get new ones. The waste-water treatment plant south of town is funneling raw sewage around the plant, directly into the river."

"Things are getting bad, aren't they?"

"That's pretty bad. Bad enough to have environmental enforcement on site, monitoring the situation. I don't know how much longer I can do it." He shook his head, turned his phone off, and took another sip of coffee.

"You mean you're thinking about retiring?"

He shrugged and turned to her. "Policing is all I know."

"I think about it all the time." She didn't lift her eyes from her coffee cup.

"*You* want to retire?"

"No," she breathed a heavy sigh before looking up again. "I've a school to run."

It hit him. "Oh, you mean *my* retirement? Why? Afraid I'm going to drop out early so I can live the life of a kept man?" He regretted the joke the moment he said it. "Ezzy, that's not what I—"

"You dope," she said, her eyes misting over. "I'm talking about the danger. I see the news, too, Bill. Shootings are on the rise. It seems like everyone's gone crazy."

"Whoa! Wait a minute, Ezzy. We don't talk about that. Not on the force, and not here."

"Well, we *need* to talk about it." She raised her voice. "*I* need to talk about it."

"Ezzy, I'm in a dangerous profession." He kept his tone gentle. The ache in her voice reminded him she'd already lost one man she loved. And though he found himself loving this woman more than reason should allow, she had to hear him out. "I'm not on the front lines, but my people are. If ever there was a moment where I had to take a bullet for someone, I'd do it. We have the best training and equipment money can buy. Not a lot of it, but we got it if we need it. We try to minimize risks with professionalism and diplomacy, but sometimes . . ." He let his voice trail off.

"I need to hear more assurance than that, Bill. I'm falling in love with you. And if something were to happen to you . . ." The emotion got caught in her throat, and it was like she was squeezing his heart with a vice.

He reached over to brush away a tear on her cheek. "Oh, come on now. I love you, too, Ezzy. I don't take unnecessary risks. I never have. And like I said, I'm not on the front lines anymore."

"I know. I know. I'd never be the one to keep you from what you love. I just think about it, that's all."

Clip-clopping on the carriage road drew his attention away as Buck and Bonnie appeared on the road that ran along the porch's edge. Ezzy wiped her tears one last time and smiled at Shorty as the carriage came to a stop in front of them.

"Good morning, you two," the driver shouted. "Everything OK?"

"Morning, Shorty. Everything's good. It's so beautiful here it's hard not to feel a little blue about having to leave," Bill said.

"Did you do OK in the salmon stream?"

"Unbelievable. I had no idea there were so many, and that they'd be so big. I tore 'em up."

"He missed four before lunch, Shorty, but he picked it up pretty quick." Ezzy was the only woman he'd ever seen fly-fish, much less the first woman to ever catch more than him. "How are you?" she asked.

"Couldn't be better. Big football day and I'm off at lunch."

"Say, I was wondering," Bill mused. "Where does a football fan watch games on Mackinaw Island?"

"I'll be at Goodfellows down on the main strip."

"Mind if I join you? I don't think I can bike another mile or get another massage."

"Come on down. Mostly Big Ten, but some other games, too."

"See you after lunch." He looked toward Ezzy. "That OK with you?"

"Of course, but be dressed for dinner because tonight's our last night, and I have something special planned. I'll ride around the island again today and then take my last nap until Christmas."

"Then it's a date, Shorty. I'll be down after lunch."

TV sportscasters' voices filled every corner above the bar. Bill climbed on the barstool next to Shorty. "Who's winning?"

"The Buckeyes are getting their hats handed to them and Michigan is running through the eastern division. It doesn't get any better." Shorty raised his glass and toasted the guy sitting next to him. "What're you drinking, Sheriff?"

"Cold beer, but you were right. I don't recognize any of these teams. Are they intramural squads?" Bill glanced around the room full of fans, wearing their team logos on vacation.

"Right, Sheriff." Shorty looked up at the TV in mock disgust. "Michigan's got the biggest line in the nation and the national championships to go with it."

Bill waved down the bartender and ordered a Hop Cat as Shorty took another sip from his over-sized frosty mug before him. "Aren't half your players from Florida?" Bill smiled at him.

"Recruiting the entire country comes easy to our head coach. He's got way more to offer than oppressive heat." Shorty turned to him and winked.

"Fair enough." Bill chuckled. "Is this where you spend every Saturday?"

"Every Saturday I have to work the buggies." The bartender set the beer in front of Bill. "The wife's back in Kalkaska."

"Where's that?"

"About two hours south. Outside of Traverse City. You don't think we live on this island, do you?"

"I don't know. I suppose I just assumed." Given all he'd heard about Mackinaw Island—and all he'd seen since arriving—Bill realized what a naïve assumption that was.

"Houses on the island are in the millions. We moved to Kalkaska after I retired." Shorty looked into his beer. "Or after Detroit retired me."

Bill took a sip of the beer. "You got caught up in the bankruptcy?"

"That was a while ago, but yes. I was a casualty of municipal bankruptcy."

The room erupted with cheers when Michigan scored on an interception returned for a touchdown. "What did you do?" Bill shouted over the bar crowd's rendition of the school's fight song.

"I was in the Public Works department. My degree was in Public Administration. As soon as I got out of college, I went to work for the city of Detroit. Worked there for twenty-nine years. Then lost it all."

"Lost it all?"

Shorty shifted in his seat and turned to Bill. "The emergency manager fired almost the entire department except my boss and four assistants. We lost our healthcare and twenty-five percent our pensions, and we don't have any Social Security. None of us contributed, so we don't get it. The last six months at work was the worst time of my life."

Bill shook his head. "No way. The stress must've been terrible." The bartenders jogged back and forth to take more orders as the football game went into halftime.

"I can't imagine what you see in your job, Bill, but looming bankruptcy is a gnawing kind of stress. Everyone knows it's coming, but no one can do anything about it. The unions tell us our retirement plans are safe and our healthcare is covered, then one day they're not. I have a small retirement I saved myself and the reduced pension, but if I get sick, I'm on my own."

"Kids never think about that stuff." He tried to remember the last time he'd thought about an escape route if Orthus County got any worse. The State Patrol had already offered him a new position in Tallahassee.

"I'm only fifty-five." Shorty rested his elbows on the bar, both hands extended above the beer mug with his fingers resting on the rim of the glass. "I was supposed to be five years into retirement, living the good life. Now I have to come up with almost half of our monthly budget for healthcare. Wife's in the same boat. She worked in the accounting department. Thank the Lord our house was paid for. We sold it and moved to Kalkaska when she got a job with a local CPA. The cost of living is a lot less up here, and it's a lot more peaceful."

"So why don't you get a job in Kalkaska?" Bill asked.

"In a recession? No one is hiring. The Grand Hotel was the only thing I could find. I drive up here to the ferry on Monday mornings and go back on Friday afternoons unless I get a Saturday morning shift like today. Granted, my office is hard to beat, but we're only open six months a year. My entire summer income goes to healthcare. Want to know the funniest part?"

Bill raised his eyebrows. "There's a funny part?"

"Hey, getting out of the Detroit rat race and moving up here gave us a new lease on life. And now I've put this job on my resume."

Bill laughed. "Why's that funny? You work here, don't you?"

Shorty lowered his voice and leaned closer. "A fifty-five-year-old guy putting 'carriage driver' on his resume? After working in public works for almost thirty years? It's all about perception—the perception of the people I'm trying to land interviews with. So I leave off the Detroit job, put in 'carriage driver,' say I'm willing to be an intern—that's a trick the college kids taught me—and suddenly I'm just another out-of-work college kid."

Bill cocked his head and lowered his voice, too. "And all that gets you more interviews?"

"You bet it does. Keeps me from looking like an over-the-hill, down-on-his-luck retiree hoping for one last show. No one checks my age when they set up the interview. And when I show up, they can't ask." Shorty poised his glass high in front of them. "I've certainly been getting plenty of interviews anyway."

Bill met his glass in mid-air. "Here's to second careers." He caught the bartender's attention, pointed to their now-empty glasses, and held two fingers up. "Do you ever hear from your friends back in Detroit? Are things getting any better?"

"Sure, they call me, and wish they were me. As for Detroit, if you believe the politicians, things are great. They filed for bankruptcy, making them debt free except for my tiny pension we managed to negotiate, and then the Detroit Downtown Development Authority went back into debt for a new hockey stadium. Can you believe that?"

"I get the feeling I'm about to." Bill picked up one of the beer mugs the bartender set in front of them. "I work in a large metropolitan area. Bankruptcy, pensions, and low morale are all the talk at the national sheriffs' convention. I figure my time is coming."

"Good luck. Now C'mon, Sheriff," Shorty said as the teams came back onto the field. "Blue needs a touchdown so we can sing."

"Go Blue!" Bill shouted. Michigan scored on their next set of downs, bringing the crowd out of their chairs, hands raised in the air while singing "The Victors" once again. Bill and Shorty touched glasses like old friends.

"My, my! Don't you look handsome, Sheriff Bolek?" Ezzy said as they stood in front of the room mirror.

"I look like a hundred-year-old alligator standing next to you, but thanks for giving me an hour to sleep." He looked her up and down. "Good Lord, Ezzy. God ain't made a girl prettier than you. Not that I've seen anyway."

"Thank you, Sheriff. Can I take you to dinner?"

"Been looking forward to it all day. Where're we going?"

"The Woods."

"Been in 'em all my life. This should be good." He took her hand as they headed down the wide staircase to the porch. The wide carriage pulled up to The Grand's front-porch valet stand. As they climbed in, he could see the reflection of passengers in the mirror hung from the carriage ceiling behind the driver, in their vacation best and filling the back three benches, singing college fight songs, drinking wine, and laughing.

"You're going to love this place," Ezzy said, and then nudged him and pointed out the sun setting over the Straits of Mackinac as Buck and Bonnie climbed the scenic view.

A stone and wood barn appeared on the hill past all the houses. The sand carriage trail went past the front door and around the front yard like the North Florida driveways of his youth. Couples sipped whiskey outside the front door, in the quiet dusk. Smiling at Ezzy with his arm around her, he waited patiently for everyone to exit before stepping down onto the soft sand. They entered the small wooden doors to the front room, and most of the traveling troupe headed straight for the bar. Bill looked around at the mounted deer, elk, pheasant, and geese lining the walls, but before he could comment on them, the concierge at the podium called out their table. "King? Party of two?"

Bill glanced over in time to see the concierge lift her head from the reservation book in front of her. "Ezzy King?"

"Hey, Suzanne." Ezzy embraced the woman, who had walked around the front of the podium to greet her like an old friend, which, Bill realized, she probably was.

"I didn't know you were in tonight. Hello, handsome." She stretched her hand out to Bill. "I'm Suzanne. I've known Ezzy for years. Welcome to The Woods."

Bill shook her hand, giving her the same wide smile he'd had on his face all week. "I'm Bill Bolek. Nice to meet you."

"Please let me know if there is anything you need." She dropped his hand, grabbed Ezzy's shoulders and said, "How have you been?"

"Missing this place. That's for sure."

Suzanne turned and opened two swinging doors. "Follow me." She led them through to the main restaurant, Bill gazing around the dark, century-old dining room humming with romance under the Elkhorn candle chandelier, while the flames of the hearth flickered on the faces of the diners. Suzanne took them up a half level to a private table. “Is this still your favorite spot, Ezzy? If not, we’ll put you anywhere you like. Eric will be your waiter as usual.”

“Perfect, Suzanne. Thanks.”

“Enjoy.”

Bill held Ezzy’s chair while she sat down and Suzanne disappeared back behind the swinging doors. “How do you ever return to real life after spending time here?” he asked as he took his own seat.

“It’s not easy,” she said with a smile, and then lowered her voice when the waiter approached. “But I get to take the best part of it back home with me this time.”

“Good evening, Ms. King and Mr. Bolek, I presume. Welcome back. Can I start you off with some drinks?”

“Yes. Thanks, Eric. Nice to be back. I’ll have a Chardonnay.”

The waiter looked at Bill. “Mr. Bolek?”

“The same. I’m starving. What’s good?” Bill took one of Eric’s menus and opened it up.

“I’m glad you asked. Our steak is great, and so is everything else. How about a ten-ounce peppercorn encrusted filet with red sherry and morel sauce. We also have wild-caught salmon, but if you’ve been here more than a week, that’s probably a non-starter. If I eat another one, I might start swimming upstream looking for a good time.” They all laughed. “The salmon is grilled on a cedar plank with butter and garlic glaze.”

“That sounds great, Eric,” Ezzy said. “I’ll have the salmon.”

“Steak for me, please,” Bill said. “I’ve eaten more salmon than a black bear.”

“Very good. I’ll be right back with your drinks.”

After Eric walked away, Bill reached across the table for her hand. “Do you think you’ll ever consider marriage again?” The candlelight from the table and the wall sconces highlighted Ezzy's cheekbones. Her face glowed like one of the female attendants in the seventeenth-century hunting scenes adorning the walls.

Her voice lifted. "I wondered when you'd open up about it. I mean maybe, but we're both so busy. I hadn't thought about it much until we got on the boat last Saturday, but this week has been incredible. I could travel anywhere with you, Bill."

"I feel the same way." He brought his other hand on top of hers and said, "Where do you want to go next?"

"King Christian Academy," she said with a start. "There is so much to do. I need to dive into work when we get back. Our larger enrollment next year and all the new construction are going to take most of my time until the Christmas break."

Bill nodded. "I know the feeling. Based on what Shorty told me at lunch, my next two years are going to be crisis management."

"What did he say?"

"I gather the common theme of bankruptcy is a really bad last couple of years for county and city employees who make it to the last round of cuts, only to get the rug pulled out from under them in the end."

"How so?"

"Remember how I described that feeling of anxiety among my staff? Everyone feels this angst because things break and aren't replaced. No-brainer fund appropriations don't get funded. I feel like we're slogging through mud all the time. Bob and his constant promises make it worse. I want to believe him, but I don't want to wake up at the end of my career and find out I'm fired with no retirement or healthcare. If things don't change someone's going to get…" Bill caught himself and looked up at Ezzy.

Ezzy gently put her elbow on the table and placed her face in her hand. She looked up at Bill with her head to one side. Her blue eyes beamed like moonlight. "You remember that dream I had?"

"Which one?" He searched his memory. "Oh, yeah."

"Well, you died in it."

"Oh?" He tried to react lightly. "That's not good. How do I die?"

"It's not funny, Bill. You were wearing your uniform."

"Babe, I'm not going to die. You know what the cops' wives say?"

"I have no idea. You're the only cop I know, other than your people who keep holding the door for me. What do cops' wives say?"

"If I'm brave enough to suit up," he paused, "you have to be brave enough to let me." The motto didn't sound nearly as honorable as when he'd practiced it.

"This is all so new. I never thought I'd fall in love with a cop." She sat up straight again.

"Here's some good news. We're in Northern Michigan and we love each other." Bill took her hand and leaned in to her as their lips pressed.

After dinner, they came back to The Grand ballroom for their last night. Ezzy's mention of her dream had cast a shadow over the rest of the evening, and he felt an emotional wall building between them as they sat alone together in the ballroom as the band began warming up. "Can I have this last dance?"

"I don't know," she said. "I don't feel much like dancing."

"C'mon, babe. This might be our last time. Let's live in the moment."

"Damn it, Bill. Your choice of words is ruining my mood."

"I'm sorry, Ezzy. I'm one-hundred-percent male. I can say stupid things when I'm talking to women. Look, I've been doing law enforcement my whole life. I admit it's dangerous, but do you know how many times I've actually pulled my gun?"

"I don't know. How many times?"

"Four times. Four times in thirty years, none in the last ten. I'm the sheriff, but my job is mostly managerial now. But know this: I love you and I want to make a go at this. Are you with me?"

She sighed, but he could tell he was getting through to her. "Yeah, Sheriff," she said. "I'm with you. But for my sake, please be careful."

"I'll be fine. Don't you worry about a thing." The band started playing and Bill reached for her hand. "That's our song. Will you please dance with me?"

"Of course, I'll dance with you, Bill. I'll dance anywhere with you. How much did you have to pay them for this?"

He pulled her in close. "They said it was on the house for you."

CHAPTER 25

Enzo wheeled out of the Downtown Tampa Dunham Schauble parking deck, the Saturday morning sun shining bright on his silver Audi. One hand rested on the wheel and the other on the stick while he waited for the light to change. He smiled at the young blonde associate in the passenger seat, and Kirsty smiled back with the ease of new romance. Her mini-skirt cover-up had shifted back far enough that he could see her black bikini underneath. The small, interlocking gold loops hung around her neck partially covered by her sun-kissed hair. Enzo turned his eyes back to the light when it turned green, and he raced ahead, the tires chirping when he shifted into second. He slowed when he passed a black Crown Victoria, thinking it might be an unmarked car, but when it didn't follow him, he sped up.

Launching the car into fifth gear, he reached 90 mph across the Howard Franklin Bridge. "The things your team is doing with the computer systems are outstanding."

"What about the other things I can do in your office? I could double your bond issuance in San Francisco, if you'd let me go out there with you."

He'd heard the hint before. He understood her ambition. Hell, he respected it. But that didn't mean he wouldn't use it to his advantage. "Technology is why I hired you. One day I'll teach you the trading desk, mi amor. I promise." Enzo pulled his hand off the stick, opened the sunroof, and ran his fingers through his hair. Then he reached over between her legs and pulled a cigar out of the glove box, and rolled it in his hand while the lighter torched the end. The seven-day workweeks had blended together over the summer. "You have a very complex mind, but your beauty is the *ceriza en la punta…*"

"Or cherry on bottom. Whatever you like, mate."

Enzo weaved in and out of traffic as they drove through St. Petersburg. The sooner he could hand off operations to the next generation, the sooner he could move the Dunham Schauble racing team up from road courses and into the big leagues. The St. Pete Firestone would be the perfect entry point for his Formula One racing dreams.

"We're going by Bob Drolland's condo first, before we drop the boat at Pass-A-Grille." He gave her the easy decisions, assuming she could be placated with empty power. "Then you can decide where we drop anchor." He'd been around young international Harvard students long enough to know, and if she was no different from her classmates, he could string her along with designer dresses and yacht rides indefinitely, but her ambition gene was stronger than he'd seen from the recruiting trips in years.

"Is he the Orthus County client?" she asked.

"Yes. He's a whale, both figuratively and literally, and he's issued over four billion dollars of bonds in the last nine years. We sold all his investment-grade general obligation debt on the open market, and the other half is unrated high-yield revenue bonds that get split up between the members of our syndicate to do with as we please. The others sell most of theirs. We keep a little for the income and some skin in the game. We keep some of the proceeds of the blind-pool bonds on the books, too, but most of that is held at Wall Street banks. That's what they built the airport and the hospital with.

"Doesn't owning blind-pool debt give us a lot of counter-party risk if their hospital debt goes bad?" She learned so quickly, the challenge of keeping her in an IT closet was going to be problematic. "Regional hospitals are ticking time bombs in the muni-market."

He didn't need her to tell him that. "Technically, yes, but I manage those risks by being inside the meetings. Should Progress Orthus ever decide to default on any debt, I simply convince them not to, but they don't know we hold it on our books. Those rubes do what I tell them, because the Orthus County commissioners and Progress Orthus don't know the difference between bank debt and bond issues." He shifted the car into a lower gear as they came to a stop, hoping the roar of the engine would idle her questions.

"Is Bob the chairman of Progress Orthus?"

He paused while the cross traffic drove in front of them. A police car entered the intersection, with the driving officer wagging his finger at him. "No. Bob is the Orthus County Commission Chairman."

"Oh, so he has ultimate authority for a go, no-go vote to issue the Progress Orthus bonds?"

"Correct." He pulled the barely street-legal Audi through the light, out of the police car's view, and dropped it back into second before stopping at the next red light.

"What kind of revenue has he generated for Dunham Schauble?"

He pushed down his irritation at her incessant questioning. She was young. She was learning. She didn't mean to sound challenging. "One hundred million dollars in commissions, another forty million in interest income from the bonds we hold, and attorneys' fees for financial advice on how to issue them."

"Why do we hold their debt on our books?"

He sped up in the bend of the curve and scoffed. "Because we have to. Our offer to the client is fill-or-kill. Whatever we don't sell, we buy."

"What's the difference between the bonds we own and the blind-pool bond proceeds on our books?"

"You ask a lot of questions, *ceriza*." He leaned over the console to kiss her on the cheek and she met him in the middle, smiled, and kissed him back.

"Don't punish me for wanting to learn." Her Australian accent was melting his remaining impatience.

He blew smoke through the sunroof and licked his lips. "The bonds we can't sell we have to buy. We hold them on our books and keep the tax-free interest income. On the other hand, the blind pool is debt issued, but not spent, sitting in our custodian bank so we can use it for operations when we need to. It's like a low-interest loan to Dunham Schauble. We pay ten million per year in interest, but that's hands down the best loan on the street."

"Different sides of the same coin?" she asked, amazing him again with her veteran bond broker's understanding of the nuances.

"Sure" was the only thing he could think of to keep her in the dark. "You keep working on my computers, and I'll run the operations."

"Okay, boss."

He turned to look back to his left for cars coming, and slammed the stick into third, generating enough stir in the passenger seat to blow her mini-skirt back up. "Bob's condo was a gift from Dunham Schauble for the hospital bond issue," he confided before he thought better of it. "My boat was a gift to myself for the airport."

"Well worth it, I'd say."

"The cost of doing business," he said as they glided past the Don Cesar Hotel. "It's right down here." Exquisite beachside condos zipped by on both sides of the road.

They pulled through a gated condo community and up to the security stand. The officer leaned out of the guard shack. "Hello, Mr. Ruiz. Bob's expecting you."

Enzo drove into the garage, parked, and threw his cigar on the ground outside the lobby entrance door. They took the elevator up to the 15th floor.

Bob answered the door in a bathrobe. "Top of the morning, Enzo. Hello, young lady."

"Good morning, Mr. Drolland. I'm Kirsty McPhee. This place in bonzer. Can I look around?"

"Sure. Help yourself. Drinks are at the bar," he said, and held the door open as they walked in. "As you can see, I've already started. The bathroom's occupied, but it's right down that hall." He held his drink up in the bathroom's direction and chuckled for emphasis.

Kirsty helped herself around the condo and began making a drink at the bar. Enzo followed Bob out to the balcony overlooking the beach. "Bob, I understand your freewheeling lifestyle, but please, I don't want Kirsty to quit the firm. Can you please put on some pants," he asked, and laughed at Bob's nonchalant attitude?

"What's the matter, Enzo? Does my appearance make me less valuable to you?"

"If you must know, you look practically worthless." He rolled his eyes and turned away as Bob's man kimono opened. "Dear God, Bob. Please. Sooner rather than later."

"I didn't know you were such a puritan, Enzo. I'll be right back." He worried what Bob might say to Kirsty, but he could see she had her back turned to him, standing at the marble counter mixing a drink. Bob was watching her, though, and when Kirsty shifted subtly, Enzo sensed she could feel Bob watching her, too. After Bob turned away to walk down the hall, she came out with a couple of mimosas.

"Here you go," she said as Enzo closed the door behind her and took a glass from her. "This view is fantastic. No surf, but the volleyball keeps me moving. I play on those courts over there." As she pointed out over the beach, the wind blew her top open, exposing the black bikini. "Hey, up here." She lowered her eyelids, smiled, and handed Enzo his drink.

Hiding his momentary sense of weakness, Enzo leaned against the railing and nudged her when Bob and a young woman emerged from the bedroom. Her makeup and hair were askew, and the white bathrobe Bob gave her fit like an overcoat. She kissed Bob on the cheek in the open doorway as he shoved a fistful of bills into her hand.

Kirsty looked at Enzo and laughed. "That guy is a slob."

Bob pulled the sliding glass door back and stepped through, wearing pants and a linen shirt. "What's all the laughing about out here? You got a problem with my entertainment habits?"

"Not at all," Enzo said. "A man of your position has many tastes. Itches need scratching, right? Let's walk down to the poolside and get some brunch. You game?"

"Follow me," Bob said and waddled toward the door.

The detective downstairs counted the floors up to the balcony, "...13,14, 15...15th floor," and then he texted Bill the information. Bill knew the condo address from the tracking device on Bob's car, but had asked the detective for the floor level to shrink his ownership search.

Enzo maneuvered to put Kirsty closest to Bob when the waiter seated them near the beach. "Good morning, Mr. Drolland. Can I get you and your guests more drinks?"

"Damn right, you can," Bob answered. His bravado when spending other people's money amused Enzo since the day he met him. "I'll have another scotch. Kirsty, can I get you anything?"

"Thanks, Bob. Sure. I'll have another mimosa." She sipped the last of her drink through the straw, and set it on the table, while trying not so dutifully to keep her cover-up closed in the wind. She leaned back in the chair, stretched her legs out in front of her, and pulled the wrap off. "You don't mind if I get some sun. Do you?"

The waiter appeared flustered. "Ma'am, we require cover-ups while on the patio."

Bob shut him down. "Hey, I'm an owner. As you can see, the rules require an exception today. If anyone has a problem with what you see before you, tell them to send me their bar bill. Enzo, you want anything?"

"I'll have the same," Enzo said. Kirsty was using male avarice to her advantage. Again, he had to admire her methods. The waiter walked away in a huff.

"Bob," Enzo continued. "This place is as nice as the day I found it. Do you still like it?" Enzo knew Bob needed to be reminded of the constant stream of luxury he could provide, as long as Bob was willing to play.

"I'll like it a lot better when I get the unit above me and make it two stories. My finder's fee for the MOTrax TODs should be enough for purchase and renovation. You can buy my new upstairs. How's that sound?"

"I'll begin the process Monday. How much have the Coyotes inferred they'll need for their new stadium?"

"Should be at least four hundred and fifty million for the stadium and two hundred million for the Smithson Downtown District. What will you do with your fee, 'mate'?" Bob licked the sweat off his upper lip before he took a sip of his drink. The accompanying look he gave Kirsty made Enzo's stomach turn. It wasn't jealousy he was feeling; it was genuine nausea.

Enzo looked at Kirsty, trying to transform the moment back to casual from lewd. "What do you think, mi amor?"

"I can teach you to surf the pipeline, boss."

Enzo leaned back and smiled at the woman young enough to be his daughter. The waiter brought their orders and left, casting a glance at her bikini-clad body when she ran her fingers through her hair to mock his rebuke. Enzo waited for Bob and Kirsty to reach for their drinks, while he looked at the unobstructed view of the beach.

"Gene is setting up a meeting for all of us in Warren's stadium suites," Bob said. "You won't need to be there, so I'll relay all the details for your document production."

Enzo reached for his drink. "Whatever I can do to finance your future, Bob. It will be a slightly different deal, but Orthus School Board will provide the bonding capacity and you'll be the conduit. You'll own Smithson Downtown District and Coyotes Stadium now that Smithson Galleria evaporated with the departure of the insurance companies. The Coyotes will rent from you. All you need is an LLC name."

"I follow, but just make sure the deal I spell out is outlined in the documents. That's why you're the bond counsel; I don't want this messed up with an outsider. I've got to figure out a way to get Flash interested between now and then, but I think I know what he likes." He gave Kirsty the same look again, adding a raised eyebrow this time.

Enzo cleared his throat to save Kirsty from having to respond. "Dunham Schauble will serve at your pleasure, Bob. The bond memorandum will be iron clad."

"The taxpayer will not be obligated for one dime of this debt, right?" Bob asked.

Bob asked the same question before any signed deal. "Of course, Bob. Revenue bonds are never taxpayer-obligated debt."

"Good. The press release will say the bonds are completely supported by the revenues generated by the Orlando Coyotes and Smithson Downtown District. Who doesn't love baseball? The

Coyotes fans will be closer to their favorite team. The stadium will finally be located next to a MOTrax station."

"Perfect. The 'everyone loves sports' idea is a nice touch," Enzo said. Bob's greed was profitable for Enzo, but he wouldn't mind if the man showed a little more gratitude, considering how the corporate bond market would never lend to such an imbecile.

"How will you retain the taxes Orthus County or the school board won't get?" Kirsty asked.

Bob paused and folded his arms, his short fingers barely touching his elbows. "The Coyotes will build Flash Jackson a high school, along with his precious football stadium, on the north side of the property where a couple of our colleagues own an apartment complex. He's insisting the football stadium be the largest in the county. Progress Orthus will buy the land from our colleagues as part of the larger deal structure." Bob sipped his scotch again while Enzo thought of the debt load Patrick was under, knowing Sterling wouldn't think twice about putting him into bankruptcy and taking his share. Bob put down his glass. "I'll have the Coyotes pay an administration fee to Progress Orthus replacing the lost taxes, tell the voters we got a good deal, and then do with it what we please. School board tax losses aren't my concern."

Enzo raised his glass above the poolside table. "To government transparency and a growing property tax digest." Their glasses touched. "Thanks for the drinks, Bob. We're headed to the yacht. Want to join us?"

"Not on your life. A sixty-five-foot Sea Ray with a stiff south wind is not my idea of fun, but I'm sure you two will enjoy it. The motion should provide some inspiration." Enzo tried to avoid eye contact with Bob, and was even more embarrassed for Kirsty when Bob winked at her, but she delivered like a pro, smiled, and winked back.

Enzo drove by the detective parked across the street, on the phone with Bill. "Yeah, there he goes, Sheriff. The security around here is for shit. I put the tracking device on Enzo's car when the gate guard was smoking a joint in the parking deck. Did you come up with a condo owner?"

"Uh huh. Listen to this," Bill said through the phone. "The owner of the condo is Get Well Soon, LLC, which is a partnership solely owned by Bob Drolland. Guess who holds the mortgage?"

"Dunham Schauble Financial Services?"

"Yep. What a dipshit. I bet you a box of donuts it was a payoff for something, but we'll let Paige figure all that out."

"You're on, boss. No one said criminals were smart, and I love donuts. These guys catch themselves."

CHAPTER 26

Patrick sat center stage behind the commissioner's wood podium, in Bob's chair at the front of the county commission auditorium. He wrapped his fists around the armrests, pickets loosening at the base from a decade of Bob's wear and tear, and tested the limits of its integrity by pushing the pegs back into their base. "Can't we get a new chair?" he asked. This seat was a jolting reminder of the suffering he'd endured, rooted in Bob's pompous authority, of Bob's authority over him, only confirmed by the repeated answer from staff: *"Bob likes the chair."* Ezzy's seat directly to his right was becoming increasingly awkward with her new-found principles. The other board members typed on their phones, waiting for him to call the meeting to order. He looked over the audience, which was bare except for those paying homage to Sterling, as he acknowledged the ever-present hangman's noose of Sterling's capital calls for new money to keep their apartment complex out of foreclosure before it could be sold to Progress Orthus.

The only thing more disconcerting than daily calls from Sterling's lawyers was Jim Pinson's rolling camera on the back row. His videos of Progress Orthus meetings had been posted on line for the last three years at Ezzy's request, but public apathy left him to harness the raw financial power of Progress Orthus. Patrick used the standard hyperbole about economic development, instructing his website designers to highlight fictitious new jobs pulled from thin air, resulting from enterprise zones, increased tax revenues buttressed by tax giveaways, and low-income and subsidized housing concessions wrenched from developers in return for rezoning requests approvals. Patrick hadn't expected the new accounting rule requiring tax abatements to be listed on the Orthus County financial statements, not to mention dropping revenues from the ongoing recession, but no one read Jim's paper—not anyone he knew anyway. Enzo Ruiz, Gene Dodd, and a few MOTrax officials sat on either side of Sterling, appearing as his servants.

Patrick looked up and down the panel as he pressed his lips against the microphone. "Looks like everyone is here, so I'd like to call the meeting to order." He shuffled some papers while the board replied "Present" as their names were called. "Thank you, everyone, for being here. I'd like to call the September meeting of the Orthus County Development Authority to order. Progress Orthus is dedicated to making Orthus County the most business-friendly and transparent county in Florida. Thanks especially to Johnston Limited Partners for joining us. We all look forward to seeing your ideas for the MOTrax stations, Smithson Downtown District, and the Smithson Galleria. Please bear with us. We need a few more minutes to go into executive session to discuss real estate matters. I'd like to—"

Ezzy interrupted him. "Patrick, I've been listening to this body repeat its commitment to transparency for three years now. Can we please have this entire meeting in public? Quite frankly, I'd like to get this over with and move on." Stunned, Patrick looked down at Sterling, Enzo, and Gene glancing back and forth at one another, and then to Jim, who was smiling and newly attentive to his camera.

Quickly, and a little too close to the microphone, Patrick said, "Ezzy, I completely appreciate your valuable time, but some matters aren't suitable for the public purview. Executive Session is for real estate and human resources discussions."

"You can't be serious. Half the Progress Orthus staff is working for your Salvatore dealerships."

He grabbed the gavel, his exit to privacy hinging on quick and obedient compliance from the commissioners, having been protected until now by the veil of process. "All in favor of executive session by a voice vote?" Five members spoke, including him. "Aye."

Patrick knew it was coming before he asked. "All opposed?"

Ezzy calmly said, "Nay."

"Motion passes." He hoped no one would ever inquire about Ezzy's claim and he was out of the public eye for at least one more meeting. "We're adjourned for Executive Session." He put his hand over the microphone. "What the hell is wrong with you, Ezzy?"

"Nothing. I'm back from vacation, I've got a school to run, and I'm growing weary of your presence, but why would anything be wrong?"

Patrick stood up from the chair and almost fell when one side of the armrest tipped unevenly in his hand. He looked under the chair for damage, instead of his first reaction, which was to pull both armrests out by the pegs. Enzo was waiting for him toward the side of the stage, his face twisted up in smug superiority.

Patrick facilitated the selection, and appointments, of all five of Bob's hand-selected board members, including Ezzy, after he'd sifted through his political IOUs to find them. They consisted of a concrete supply company CEO, a land-use planning attorney, one of Bob's college buddies serving with him on the county commission, and Ezzy, a recent—but becoming an unwelcome—participant. Patrick had already directed TREP to sign unrelated purchase orders to the concrete company, in return for the CEO's "yes" vote tonight. The land-use planning attorney was Bob's golf partner, and Thomas Stutts, the county commissioner from the Orlando district, who also served on Onward Orlando's board. Patrick came through the door after they'd taken their places around the table, and waited for Enzo to follow him in and shut the door. Then he gathered himself and looked to Enzo. "Can you please make this short and to the point? Apparently Ezzy's in a God-awful hurry."

"Sure, Patrick. Hello, Ezzy."

Patrick rolled his eyes when Enzo pulled on his shirtsleeves, revealing the DS cuffs.

"Mr. Ruiz, please retain some sense of composure. I will always be Ms. King to you."

"Of course. I'll get right to it." Enzo opened his files.

"Do," Ezzy added. "You are paid to advise, not waste our time."

Enzo's hands were motionless in front of him except for the grip of the pen, which he rolled between his fingers. "As you were all made aware via private conversations, Orthus Regional Hospital is very likely to default on the bi-annual twenty-million-dollar bond payment in November. Bob has given us all indication the payment will be funded via the Orthus County tax-anticipation note, just like the scenario this past summer. Given the seriousness of the event, it seems even more urgent we move forward with the MOTrax Station abatements on the docket for tonight. JLMS, LLC, the development partnership created by Johnston Limited, TREP, Inc., and MOTrax, is asking for one hundred million dollars in tax abatements for five MOTrax station transit-oriented developments. Based on current market rates, we'll need a three-hundred-and fifty-million-dollar phantom bond. Progress Orthus will utilize a synthetic sale-leaseback transaction with a twenty-year bond maturity. No funds will be issued, borrowed, or transferred. JLMS has renderings as part of their proposal you'll see once we're back in the main auditorium. Does anyone have any questions?"

Patrick was about to say no, when Ezzy interjected. "Why doesn't Bob allow the hospital to default so it can be put in a conservatorship, and unlock the value inherent in bankruptcies? This body is made up of corporate professionals with banking relationships.

Our bankers adhere to regulatory oversight. They would be required to find us in default given the same scenario the hospital now finds itself in. Bankruptcy allows for constructive elimination of poorly managed assets. There are plenty of hospital systems that want that property."

He avoided having to explain the ownership structure, and the collective liability they all held with the hospital and asked, "Is that why King Citrus owned all the regional banks in Central Florida? Because you needed a monopoly?"

"No, Patrick, King Citrus used forward-thinking technology allowing us to dominate the frozen juice market for over four decades. There wasn't enough money to grow our business, so we improvised, and built the banking system for ten counties." He hated defending Bob's actions, and tried to think of the spin as Ezzy's words came flowing out. "Why doesn't Bob add a one penny sales tax as a November ballot referendum for highway infrastructure? They're going to need it for the streets around those stations. Isn't that what the Orthus Regional Commission demanded in order to build the interchange into Smithson Galleria? It's an off-year election, so most people wouldn't even show up to vote." He held her stare before she looked at the others in the room. "That's standard operating procedure anyway, right?" One of the board members shrugged his shoulders and another swiveled in his chair with his palms open. The concrete company owner excused himself to go to the bathroom.

"The MOTrax developments are solid gold investments," Patrick said, trying to steer the conversation back to current business. "Lending standards are so stringent that young people aren't buying houses, and multi-family apartments are full all over town. MOTrax will benefit from increased ridership driven by livable communities within walking distance of a train station."

Patrick felt cornered by Ezzy's laser focus when she asked him again, "Where will the money come from to stave off the hospital default? Parks or police or roads? The ORC told us not three months ago that we have the worst roads in the state. Why are we financing multi-family apartment complexes for MOTrax when we should be trying to save a hospital?"

Patrick stood up and paced, talking as he walked. "This is a completely different scenario, Ezzy. We don't have the money to save the hospital, and the MOTrax stations aren't costing us anything."

"Patrick." She bowed her head. "If it doesn't cost us anything, then why does Bob have to put it on the financial statement? MOTrax patrons are clearly not enamored with their service, as seen by the annual surveys and the half-empty parking lots. Why not have MOTrax sell them to competent developers who have traditional banking relationships? Then we could focus on the problems we already have, like a hospital that needs our attention. Don't you think, Enzo?"

Enzo smiled and shrugged his shoulders. "Yes, Progress Orthus should be focusing on making all of its payments, including the ones you owe for the hospital. I believe Bob is preparing measures for his responsibilities, but that is protected information between me and my client, the county commission."

Patrick sat back down. "Forget about the hospital. MOTrax will have to build out infrastructure to support the apartments. Sewer and new intersections must be built to handle the additional density. All of that costs money, Ezzy. We're not making Bob put a tax increase on the ballot when he doesn't have to. Now, can we please focus on the business in front of us?"

"Patrick, correct me if I'm wrong, but every other developer has to pay for all those costs from bank financing." She had both elbows and her palms on the table, and looked around at each of them separately. She reminded Patrick of a hawk visualizing its surroundings, and he felt himself instinctively shift in his seat. "Your proposal eliminates their bank financing costs, their sewer construction costs, and their new road costs. They won't even have to build parking spaces, because Bob has allowed shared parking on the park land, I gave him." She paused. "On publicly owned parks. Do you hear yourself?"

Patrick shook his head. "The taxes being abated will come back to us in the form of fees MOTrax will pay. In return, the bond matures and goes away in twenty years."

"Oh, Patrick. This deal will abate Orthus County, and school board, taxes for twenty years. We get our abated taxes in the form of admin fees, but those fees come to Progress Orthus, not the general fund, and I've been to Progress Orthus's offices in Orlando. MOTrax's admin fee will be wasted on overhead, like the secretarial pool that actually does more work for you than Progress Orthus."

"That's not true, Ezzy, and you know it."

"Of course, it is, Patrick. I had timesheets faxed to me yesterday because I'd heard rumors."

The concrete company owner returned from the restroom, closed the door behind him, wiped his hands with a towel, and tossed it in the trashcan. When Patrick finally caught his attention, he said, "What? Can we go back in yet?"

"The sooner the better," Patrick said. "I simply wanted to inform the board of the upcoming Orthus default." He corrected himself. "I mean missed payments. All in favor of ending the executive session signify by saying, 'Aye,'" Unanimous. "All opposed?" Silence.

They paraded back on stage, Jim's wide-eyed stare in the back of the room enticing him to look back only to see Ezzy's sullen face. He turned away from her to lean down to sit in the chair, pushing the loose armrests' pegs into their holes, half of them cracked at the end. It leaned awkwardly to the right and lower than Ezzy's. As if on cue, Ezzy scooted her chair a few inches away.

He made sure everyone had taken their places and settled in, and then paused to honor the procedural drama. "We're back.

Thanks for the interlude, Sterling." Patrick noticed Ezzy out of the corner of his eye opening her notepad and unscrewing a pen top. The room was silent except for Jim's typing in the back. "We're very excited to see what you've planned for the MOTrax stations. After your presentation, we'll vote on the requested abatements."

As Sterling stood, his gold Rolex was visible just below his tailored sleeves and sport jacket. He walked over to the easels, nodding briefly to Ezzy, who was smiling at the impressionistic renderings glowing with pastel hues and dark-inked lines. Then he positioned himself between the stage and the prearranged artwork.

Patrick had seen Sterling's graphic artists turn out renderings hours before a Progress Orthus meeting, when no other printing services were open, only to be amazed to see new renderings the next morning in response to an idea he'd had while presenting. The baseball stadium prototype at the OSK office was their pride and joy, and their prolific passion put voters at ease and kept questions at bay. Patrick pulled his eyes away from the five uniquely themed apartment-complex images embossed on the white boards, and focused on Sterling's prophecy. "Members of Progress Orthus, you stand on the precipice of history. Nowhere in the country has transit-oriented development been so well received and designed. These drawings will give you a glimpse of the future, of carless travel that will only come when old methods are challenged and the future is embraced. The urban lifestyle housing you see can become home to thousands of new families who want to play where they live, and live where they work. The MOTrax's North Line will connect new generations of pedestrians to their lives at Smithson Station, and as a bonus, I've taken the liberty of introducing you to Smithson Galleria, which will be built in conjunction with the Smithson Station TOD."

Patrick got lost in the patchwork of dreamlike painted light and open spaces of the fifth rendering of the MOTrax-Smithson Station.

Two ten-story boutique apartment complexes wrapped around the MOTrax station, while a five-story plantation-style Smithson City Hall matching the facades of the residential apartments was neatly tucked into the far corner of the empty MOTrax parking lot, and connected the apartment complexes to a public park for overflow traffic. Standing in the shadow of four twenty-story corporate towers on the opposite side of the development was a shopping district with its own movie theatre, restaurants, and a farmer's market, seamlessly connecting Smithson Station in the foreground to Smithson Galleria in the background. Miniature animated figures scurried around on bicycles and walked in the shopping district, but even with the money Patrick owed Sterling, he found it hard to stay awake. The chore of listening to him pontificate about young, hip residents who wanted to go to the Orlando International Airport, Coyotes Stadium, or Osprey Field by hopping on a MOTrax bullet train from the large renovated station was part of the hard work of patience. Patrick didn't know if Sterling was right about MOTrax-centric transportation, but he sure sounded confident about it. It reality, it made no difference to him what the plans for the property parcels were. He just needed a cover story to sell the slum they owned together on the edge. He tried to picture a baseball stadium where the corporate towers were, and was relieved when Sterling finished with a flare, waved his arm at the drawing, and faced the panel. "Are there any questions?"

Ezzy's voice in his left ear slapped him awake. "Yes. First of all, why would you include a project we aren't financing and have no interest in?"

Patrick pulled his shoulders up tight. She hadn't requested to be recognized, which was a flagrant show of disrespect for his procedural authority. Obviously not caring, she kept talking. "Smithson Galleria is no concern of ours. The limits of our financing ends at the parking lot of the MOTrax station, not a speculative real estate project on the site of an old automobile plant."

Sterling unfolded his fingers from in front of his belt and swung his hand around to the drawing. "Ms. King, four of the stations will stand on their own. The fifth station, and most northerly, will connect Smithson Station, the shopping district, and the Galleria together into one coherent walkable, livable community. It would be a travesty not to design them as a whole."

"Mr. Johnston, that's fine, but for the remainder of my questions, I'll focus on our liability. Are there any financial forecasts showing ridership increases that would reverse the existing downturn at MOTrax?"

"Ms. King, we aren't that far along, but I'd have to defer to TREP."

"Okay." Her rapid-fire questions were two steps ahead of him, but Patrick tried to keep up. "Mr. Dodd, has Transportation Real Estate Partners generated spreadsheet financial forecasts showing profitability for the new construction, and how quickly will you need the financial assistance?"

Gene stood up and buttoned his wrinkled suit jacket as he crossed over to the podium. "I can have that profit forecast forwarded to you this week. We'd like to start construction in January."

"You don't have any forecast with you?" She offered Gene a condescending smile that made even Patrick squirm. This wasn't at all going as he'd planned—not as *any* of them had planned. Except Ezzy, of course. "This line of questioning isn't any different from what banks normally ask you, is it? If you're far enough along to have a start date, maybe you can make a guess as to how profitable this will be."

"I wouldn't want to speculate on a profit and loss statement, but I'll have them sent overnight."

"We're not getting anywhere, gentlemen," Ezzy continued. "Let's try a few more. See if you can answer at least one before we call it a night. Will infrastructure improvements be made before, or after, the apartments are built? When will the MOTrax stations be renovated? They look brand new in the renderings. Are you renovating the MOTrax stations, Sterling? Gene?"

"My design creations speak for themselves," Sterling said before Gene could speak, his hands now refolded in front of him. "Orthus County would be wise to move forward with these projects. There are no other firms that can deliver this kind of product."

Ezzy leaned up to the microphone and lowered her voice. "Surely you expected questions, Mr. Johnston? When I request loans from banks, those are just the first of many questions. Progress Orthus is acting as your banker, and we're tied to this project in a way you are not. You're simply providing the design and construction. Progress Orthus is taking all the risks of a private equity banker, with only *possible* rewards we *may* see in twenty years. We won't be able to use a competitive bid process because you, and TREP, were hand-selected by MOTrax before financing was ever acquired. I know of at least five qualified developers very interested in building this project without the profit-eviscerating amenities of mixed-use retail and affordable housing. They certainly weren't interested in ruining our parks with parking overflow from the apartments. Two of those developers made official offers to MOTrax to buy the land, but were rejected on the grounds MOTrax would own these properties for mass transit in perpetuity. Orthus County will have to pay for the additional police coverage." She turned to Patrick. "And we're voting tonight to pay for your infrastructure, or whatever else you want to spend abated taxes on. We're stuck with each other, so try to be at least minimally prepared next time." Before Patrick could respond, she added, "But there will be no next time, will there, Patrick?"

He inhaled, trying to settle the anger that had welled up inside him as she'd spoken. Then he exhaled slowly, and offered her the same smile she'd given Sterling just moments before. "Ezzy, Orthus

County will benefit from Johnston Limited's engagement with these new projects, and I appreciate and want to honor your questions, but you seemed in a big hurry when we started." He slowed his pace of speech as they approached the formality of a public proclamation of opinion with the weight of law. "We'd all like to get home to our families, so I move we hold an immediate up or down vote on the agenda item."

Immediate seconds came from the concrete company owner and the land-use attorney. "Counselor, could you please read from the notes?" Patrick continued.

"Sure, Mr. Chairman. All in favor of enacting the Memorandum of Understanding to issue a three-hundred-and fifty-million-dollar lease-buyback, phantom-bond transaction for the benefit of JLMS, LLC, herein after referred to as the applicant, please signify by saying 'Aye'. 'Aye' came from four of the members. 'All opposed?' One silent, but forceful 'nay' from Ezzy.

Patrick had gloated enough, and adjourned the meeting as the balloon of tension began to subside. Ezzy had left before they had to personally face each other, though he knew they eventually would. He walked down to the front row to shake hands with Sterling, Enzo, and Gene, as everyone from the group stood to congratulate him.

The *Orthus County Post* headline greeted him the next morning as he turned on his computer at work: "MOTrax Giveaways Questioned by Progress Orthus Member - Approved Without Answers." The worst part was the comments section lighting up. Patrick had a vague recollection of Ezzy acknowledging Jim on her way out of the meeting the night before: an alliance he hadn't counted on or prepared for, but one he'd have to be aware of from now on.

CHAPTER 27

Bob's top-floor office had his University of Florida diploma on the wall, and not much else. The fourth floor had a view over a parking lot draped in live oaks. Other pictures of Bob's nine years leading Orthus County hung around the office in no particular order. He breathed into his hand as he walked in, not recognizing the man sitting in front of his desk. "May I help you," he said, disgusted at the smell of his own morning-after scent.

Before the man answered, Bob remembered he was thirty minutes late for a 9:00 AM appointment. The man closed a file folder sitting on his lap, put his pen in his shirt pocket, and stood. "Frank, from the state auditor's commission."

Bob threw a couple of boxes of donuts on the desk between them, came around to his chair, flopped back, and flung the donut-box lids open. "Morning, Frank. Grab a donut." Debbie walked in with his first cup of coffee. His hands shook as he picked it up. Last night's residual buzz kept him going. A bracer of what he liked to call "papa's helper" on the way to work made the commute bearable, but the dryness in the back of his throat put him on notice that he'd soon be in worse condition. "Sorry I'm a little late. Had my oldest son's play last night. The whole family went out after with a bunch of our friends from the PTA. Debbie, hold up. Frank, can I get you anything? Coffee? Debbie, can you get Frank some coffee?"

"No thanks, Bob. She already offered. I'm good." Debbie shut the door behind her. "Look, we have a bunch of questions. We've sent you emails, but you only answer every couple of days."

"Don't you want to know the name of the play?" He finished the first donut out of the box, grabbed a second, and reclined with his feet on the desk.

"Sure, Bob." Frank twisted in his chair, and checked his watch. "What's the name of the play?"

"All the Kings Men."

"What part did your son play?"

"Willie Stark. Who else?" Bob wiped his mouth with his sleeve and grabbed another donut.

"Bob, we went through the cash-flow projections with Finance. Hopefully, you're aware your cash deposits go below two million on some days. There's no room for error. Is the hospital going to make the November payment?"

"Sure, they are, Frank." Bob flipped through the call messages on a side-table computer Gloria had emailed earlier.

"You can't access the line of credit from the tax-anticipation note anymore, either, y' know? It's tapped out, too."

"Do you have any kids?"

Frank re-opened the file with a huff, obviously irritated, and joined the long list of Bob's enemies who lost focus from his needling—a list Bob was pretty proud of. "Yea, I've a son and a daughter, both in college." He turned one of the pages in his file. "Have you spoken to the airport administrator about filling the gaps in the event of an Orthus Hospital default?"

"Why would I do that, Frank? The hospital's going to pay. Where're your kids going to school?" The dull ache in his forehead was metastasizing into another thunderclap headache, like the ones he'd been getting the last few months.

"Bob, stop avoiding my questions. We've been here three months, and we're no closer to helping you sort out your finances. The governor wanted our audit completed months ago, because while we've been here, your credit rating has dropped below investment grade, and he wants answers. I don't work for you. I work for the governor, but I'll tell you as a municipal financial expert: any more hiccups, and you go to the bottom of the barrel. No one's going to lend you money anymore, and your existing debt will be owned by powerful adversaries demanding grave concessions."

Frank continued to probe, but Bob's headache had momentarily deafened him. Then as soon as it had appeared, it disappeared, and he was left with a dull, manageable thud. He regained his composure with the leverage afforded by two months to the next hospital payment date. "Frank, I'm sorry you're having to go through all this. We want to be as much help to your investigation as we can, but until you have the power to make decisions around here, I need to get to work making them." Bob's telephone rang. "That's probably my ten o'clock. Sorry to cut this short, Frank." He picked up the phone. "Tell him I'll be right out," he said before Debbie could speak. As he hung up, Frank asked another question about the blind pool, where the accounts were held with the excess proceeds, and why Orthus County hadn't listed them as tax abatements on their annual report. He blurted out the only answer he had: "Because we only had to start listing tax abatements this year." Bob had already gotten up from his chair and headed toward the door to slow Frank's momentum until he could open it.

The Orthus County administrative parking lot was full, with cars continuing to pull in. Bill checked his watch as he parked. 9:45. It was too late in the morning for these to be employees just showing up. He made his way toward the door and passed a crowd of employees smoking cigarettes. "Morning, Sheriff," one of them called out.

"Morning, everyone. Tough day already?"

The officers working the metal detectors were sheriff's deputies and stood to attention when he came through the door. "Morning, gentlemen. Ready for the beat again?"

"Morning, Sheriff. We're ready when you're ready."

Bill stood aside from the security lane to allow passage, while people pulled phones and car keys out of their pockets, and returned them when they passed through the metal arch to the other side. "I'll think about it," he said. "A couple more months of this, and maybe you won't unintentionally discharge at the gun range, Crowley. Or fail another PT exam, Bozeman. Have you dropped a few pounds?"

"Started running the day I failed PT, Sheriff. The sooner I'm on the beat, the better."

Bill loved his people like a father, which meant doling out administrative disciplinary action. Bozeman and Crowley were veteran cops in it for the long haul, so Bill gave them 'Drolland Time' at the Orthus County metal detectors.

Their sentence had reached three weeks, and Bill was feeling sorry for them. As he stood cajoling them, he began thinking about all the people coming in from the 9:30 break. He leaned over to the officers and half-whispered, "Unemployment doesn't seem to be hurting recession-proof Orthus County administration, does it?"

Bozeman whispered back, "Everyone's got their own offices, including the receptionist. Half these people have to park across the street in a public lot. Auditors are crawling all over the place, Sheriff."

"Well, gentlemen, I need to go to work. I'll check around to see if we have any openings for reformed rule-breakers."

"We'd be very grateful, Sheriff," Crowley said.

Bill dodged around the crowd of people waiting for the elevators, and bounded up the wide granite staircase to the fourth floor and into Bob's waiting area. He leaned into the special office for the receptionists. "Morning, Debbie. Morning, Anisha. I'm here to see Bob." They were both texting on their phones when he leaned in.

Debbie looked up, almost coming out of her seat. "Oh! Hey, Sheriff. Can I get you some coffee?"

"No. Thanks, though. Gives me an itchy trigger finger if you know what I mean?" He winked at both of them and smiled.

Debbie flushed. "Whatever you say, Sheriff. Those auditors drink most of it anyway. They're into everything." She picked up the phone and opened her mouth to speak, but was apparently cut off. "Yes, sir," she said before putting the receiver back in its cradle. "He'll be out in a minute. He's finishing up with the audit manager. I'd say pretty eager to finish up, too."

A moment later, Bob's door clicked, and opened to Bob slapping a man on the back. "Thanks for keeping me informed, Frank. Let's reschedule another meeting so I can get some more answers for you. We'll get through this thing together." He turned back into the room. "Bill, come on in."

Bill watched the auditor exit the room through the doorway. "Thanks, Debbie," Bill said. "Let's see how quickly he rushes me out next."

He came through the door just as Bob was squeezing himself between a bookshelf and his desk. Bill could see the early morning fog lifting off the parking lot through the window, and from the smell of things, off of Bob's hangover, too. "Morning, Bill. Give me a second." He picked up the phone. "Debbie, can you bring me another very large cup of coffee with three aspirins? Sheriff, want a donut or coffee?"

"No. I'm OK."

"That's it, Debbie."

Bill laughed openly. "Late night, Bob?"

"Yea. Molly and Trip had a play, so I stayed home and overserved myself. Watched the Coyotes lose another one in the ninth. Last in the division with no bullpen, and no chance at the playoffs. What the hell? It was a good reason to toss a few back."

Debbie brought in the coffee and aspirin—obviously a routine she was used to. Bob popped the pills in his mouth and took a gulp of the coffee before setting it down on the table, his hand still shaking. Being around crime had presented Bill with a full profile of the functioning alcoholic. Seeing one before him, he wondered where his daytime bottle was hidden. As Debbie closed the door behind her, Bob shook his head in appreciation. "Damn, it's good to have help like that. Don't you think, Sheriff? Makes a man almost happy to show up at work when I get to look at that anytime I want."

"I'm a cop, Bob. Distractions like that get people killed."

"Yeah, sure, Bill. I'm glad you came in to discuss the salaries because I need a favor, too. Sorry I couldn't give your people raises. You saw the auditors out there. I can't take a shit without them asking me how much toilet paper I used. You know Governor Sikes put them in here, right? That asshole told me I should be grateful it wasn't an emergency manager."

"I didn't notice, Bob. I don't come here that much, and can't tell the difference between city staff and auditors. What is it you need?" Bill folded his hands in his lap.

"You know Craig Walker? Owner of the First and Last at Orlando Downtown District? I set him up in the restaurant business because we were friends in college."

"Uh, huh. I've heard of him."

"Well, look. Those liquor licenses are expensive as hell. This recession has hit him pretty hard, and he just needs a little time. You can understand the situation he's in, right? If First and Last is shut down, the Orlando Downtown District will become a wasteland with a big vacant space. Vacant spaces drive apartment rents down. Onward Orlando needs that revenue because the Orlando Downtown District wasn't cheap."

Bill paused, looked down, and then looked Bob in the eye. "Y'know, Bob, my men made a commitment to protect and serve. They realize their job puts them in harm's way every morning they walk out their door, or every evening they leave their dinner tables. They put on their badge with two priorities: apprehending lawbreakers and keeping the peace. They trust me to handle the paperwork, the police cars, the media, and the salaries. They protect the citizens of Orthus County from Downtown Orlando all the way north to the swamps of Lochloosa. That's as far as their ability can, and should, take them. They're conflicted about striking, and now they're distracted at work. That's when accidents happen, Bob."

Bob leaned over the desk, rubbed his forehead, most likely trying to make his head stop pounding, and took another sip of coffee. "And we're very proud of them, Bill. They do the good work I hired them to do, but Craig needs a little time."

Bill bristled at Bob's self-promotion, but continued without acknowledging his suggestion of leniency for Craig. "I can't barge into a man's house without a search warrant, nor can I arrest a man walking down the street with a gun and a concealed carry permit, and unfortunately, I can't reach over and drag Craig Walker's sorry ass out from behind his bar and shake the cocaine out of his head."

"Pardon me?" Beads of sweat welled up on Bob's forehead, and Bill figured it was probably a combination of the shakes and the realization that Bill wasn't the idiot he hoped he was. "Do you have some proof of that accusation?"

Bill tried to suppress a laugh, but gave up. "So, Bob, my men and women put themselves in harm's way every single day, while you spend endlessly on projects no one elected you to construct. My men and women have families to support just like you. They haven't had a raise in over three years because of your misallocation of resources, and now you use the recession to deny them the raises they're being offered at neighboring counties. You aren't giving me the resources for the equipment I need to keep them safe, and you aren't providing the Orthus County Sheriff's department with the things we need to do our job."

"Now wait just a minute, Bill. You're getting a little ahead of yourself."

"Bob, do you know where you sit in this power structure?"

"What the hell is that supposed to mean?" he asked.

"Bob, sheriffs and governors have a special relationship. If you don't approve my budgets, I'll take it up with Gordon."

"Who?"

"Governor Gordon Sikes, and Thompson County Press Gazette Offensive Player of the Year my senior year in high school. Now are you beginning to see the bigger picture, Bob?"

The bags under Bob's eyes were moistened with sweat now, too. "You can ask Governor Sikes for more equipment," Bob said. "But I control the salaries around here. You're crossing a line, Sheriff Bolek. Keep it up, and I'll make you pay for it. Understand?"

Bill got up from his chair and walked around to Bob's side of the desk, now seeing the daytime bottle behind the computer tower next to his screen. He leaned over, put both hands on the table, and saw an accounting statement on the company letterhead of Touchdown, LLC, that Bob must have forgotten to hide in one of his stupors. Bill hovered in the plume of Bob's day-old alcohol and said, "Bob, I asked you a question. Do you know where you sit in this power structure?"

Bob rolled his office chair back away from Bill and looked up. "I don't know what you're talking about. What do you mean 'power structure'?"

"It is illegal for elected officials to take bribes. It is illegal for elected officials to engage in business activities that might be a conflict of interest."

"Fuck you. I don't know what you're talking about."

Bill picked up the profit and loss statement from Touch Down, LLC. "Like owning a jet-fuel monopoly at OSK under the name of Touch Down, LLC? Looks like you guys cleared a pretty good August. What's this paperwork say? Two hundred and forty thousand dollars? Who do you have to split that with? Is that legal, Bob?"

"We're running a business serving the executive air traffic of Orlando. Someone has to do it."

"So, you *are* splitting it with someone. Ever taken an envelope full of cash from a developer, Bob?"

"Hell no. Plenty of developers contribute to my campaign, but I'm not that stupid." He tried to reach around Bill for the document, but Bill moved in front of him, grabbed it, folded it up and stuffed it in his shirt pocket. "You can't take that. That's private property. That's my private business document."

He turned toward Bob as he fell back toward the chair, and moved closer to where their knees were almost touching. Bill reached down and grabbed both arms of Bob's chair. "Let me speak slowly so you can hear me through that pounding headache of yours, Bob. Everything in this office is the people's business. I need my men to know I'm looking out for them. You've got till the end of the year to reconsider the Orthus County Sheriff's Department pay raises, and if I don't get them, I'll remind you of where you sit in the power structure, Bob."

Bill turned and walked out the door. "Have a nice day, ladies. If you don't, it's your own fault." They both laughed, and he pitied Governor Sikes' auditors who were scurrying around looking for the information he had in his pocket.

As soon as Bill walked out, Bob yanked the bottle of scotch from behind the computer, and filled up the remainder of his half-empty coffee cup. Sweat was dripping off his forehead onto the desk as he swallowed hard, trying to shake off the vibration in his head, until he realized it was the phone ringing. "Yes, Debbie?"

"It's Donald from OSK on line one."

"Thanks." He clicked over. "Yeah, Don?"

"Morning, Bob. I had the strangest conversation with an investment banker buddy of mine out here at The Hangar."

"What now?"

"Someone told me both the OSK Airport and the hospital are connected somehow. You know anything about that?"

"No." The alcohol infusion kicked in, providing him some pain relief and the liquid courage he wished he'd had when Bill was in the room. "What do you mean?"

He put the caller on the speakerphone, reclined, and took another drink. "Well, Bob. Let me explain exactly what this person told me so there's no confusion. He said you guys used an arcane, but legal, development authority bond called a blind pool to finance the hospital and the airport. He said both the hospital and the airport collateralize the same debt. Said it works like a line of credit or something. Here's the part that concerns us over here at the airport. He said if the hospital misses a bond payment, the airport is obliged to make the payment for them. Is that what you understand, Bob?"

He and Enzo had skipped over that part when explaining the terms to the public. Enzo had told him when they issued it that the only way he could get a hospital bond was to attach a small airport with helicopter landing ability, and an aviation services hub. "The hospital isn't going to miss a payment, Don. If they do, we'll just vote to pull it from the county's general fund."

"Good, because I can tell you, it's bad enough we have the highest jet-fuel prices in the state hurting our profits, but there's no way we can handle the hospital's mortgage on top of our own. Are we clear? It wouldn't do your political career any good for everyone to know you get twenty percent of the FBO proceeds."

"And it wouldn't do you any good if your airport experienced a gas shortage. Or the INS showed up with deportation warrants for your maintenance crews. Watch your step, Donald."

"I didn't stutter, Bob," Don said before hanging up.

Bob put the phone back in the receiver, took a long tip, and turned to the window with the scotch shaking in his hands, watching Bill walk through the parking lot.

Bill walked past Bob's SUV on the way to his truck. Location trackers were the oldest trick in the book, which was probably why they worked so well.

CHAPTER 28

Jim Pinson walked through the metal detector at the Orthus County Courthouse. The two deputies waved him through as he picked up his laptop and recording equipment on the inbound side of the metal arch. "Good day, Officer Bozeman." Then he looked back to the deputy behind the screener. "You, too, Officer Crowley." They both nodded as he threw his bag strap over his shoulder and walked toward the wide staircase. He weaved in and out of cross-walking assistant district attorneys, local defense council, county commissioners, and sheriff's deputies, which he usually counted on to provide something newsworthy, but today he'd brought the story with him. As he stepped onto the granite tile of the second-floor courtrooms, families of victims and defendants filled the hallway with court cases recessing for lunch. He looked down the hall and saw Paige exiting one of the courtrooms with her team in tow.

"Hey look. It's Jim Pinson from the *Post.* What's got two thumbs and got a murderer to confess on the stand?" one of the male attorneys asked as Jim approached the group. He poked his thumbs on his chest, and the other two associates laughed.

Jim had never met him, so he looked at Paige, who turned to the attorney and teased, "Easy does it, Jonathan. The gun was in the car. Orthus deputies found him two hours after he shot the victim, and we found his fingerprints at her house."

"Hey, at least you let one of us say anything at all," Jonathan said as the group broke into laughter again. Jim hoped the young gun grew into a sound-bite machine. Every courtroom needed an ego as big as this one.

Paige smiled. "Congratulations, Jonathan. Your future convicting high school dropouts looks bright."

As they spoke, a middle-aged man and woman walked up to the group. "Mrs. Jackson," the man said, "me and my sister want to thank you and your staff for what you've done. We tried to move mom away from that place, but she wouldn't, said it was home. You know how they are." He wrapped his arm around his sister, whose face was wet with tears she must have been crying since before she'd left the courtroom. "We don't have enough police protection down there. The streets around Mom's neighborhood near the Coyotes stadium is filled with crime, and it's getting worse."

Paige took a packet of tissues out of her purse and handed them to the lady. "It's true," Paige said. "Police protection should be a higher priority for our county leadership. Unfortunately, our elected officials are missing the mark since the recession and current budget cuts. We can only hope tragedies like yours will serve as a wakeup call. We're very sorry for your loss."

They gave Paige a warm embrace and turned to walk away, but not before Jim got their names and permission to use the video, possibly for a campaign ad, but he'd keep that idea to himself for now. Paige looked at the young attorneys and said, "That's why we do this, people, and don't forget it."

Paige led Jim through the crowd, up some side stairs, and into a conference room. "Sheriff Bolek told me you had something," she said as she set her bags down next to a chair and Jim began setting up his equipment on the table. "Try not to make me wait so long in the future. I gave you some leeway because I know Ezzy, and you two seem to know one another."

He felt like he was sitting in the principal's office. "I have to follow my hunches, Paige. I have a voice, too, y'know." He clicked play on the laptop screen, and the crystal-clear video from last May framed Gene Dodd and Bob Drolland in a dimly lit, crowded parking lot, MOTrax signs in the background on the wall. Jim pointed to Gene's extended hand from the car window giving Bob an envelope. As Bob walked away in the center of the screen, he opened it as the camera zoomed in. "Watch this," Jim said and pointed at his hands, where hundred-dollar bills were plainly visible. He fast forwarded the video, clicked play again, and pointed at Bob bent over and dropping bills on the ground, then bumping his head on the elevator, and thumbing through the stack.

Jim clicked stop and turned, expecting more than the blank look she was giving him. Much more.

"What am I supposed to do with that?" she asked.

"What? You have a county commissioner accepting a bribe."

"Jim, I have grainy footage of Bob Drolland counting cash given to him by a man in a car that's hard to recognize."

"Well, wait a second." He clicked through to the next video image and pointed at Gene Dodd getting out of his car, removing his sports jacket, and hanging it on a hook in the back seat. Jim zoomed in on his face.

"Okay, so your video is good footage, but the importance of it will rest on who gave him the money."

"That's Gene Dodd. He owns Transportation Real Estate Partners? TREP. Ever heard of 'em? He and Sterling are the named partners on almost every government-financed transit-oriented development, and sports-stadium complex from here to Los Angeles. They got the contracts for the MOTrax station redevelopments." He plugged in a flash drive to make her a copy.

"Got it. I'll dig into Mr. Dodd, but Bill and I have been working on an investigation since you told him about this video. This will provide some circumstantial evidence, but we need hard proof."

He slid the flash drive across the table, put his laptop back in his bag, and tried to dig up his best school-boy Romeo act. "What has your investigation turned up so far?"

"Sorry, Jim. We appreciate all you do for the force, but I can't discuss any of that with you."

"Okay. I get that. How about this? What loose ends do you need to tie up? Maybe my local knowledge can help."

She paused, her mouth screwed up in thought. "We need more info on the relationship between Dunham Schauble and Bob. Can you get copies of the blind-pool contract Progress Orthus signed with the hospital and OSK? We're trying to keep the investigation undercover until we have everything, but Progress Orthus wouldn't have to give them to us without a subpoena."

"What about the Freedom of Information Act?"

"Development authorities are immune from FOIA requests. Do you think Ezzy would give them to you?"

"I don't know. I'll see what I can do. I don't know how to say this, but Sterling, Gene, Bob, Patrick, and Mr. Jackson were getting mighty chummy the night I took this video."

"Oh, yeah? How chummy?"

Jim looked away, shrugged his shoulders, and winced. As a reporter, he was used to sharing news people didn't necessarily want to hear. But telling Paige her husband was in cahoots with this crew still wasn't easy. "Well, Flash came down from his office and joined Sterling and Bob at the table after Bob had come back in from the parking deck. Then Gene came back in, sat down, and started talking. Then it looked like Stan got angry with Bob, and Sterling raised his glass for a toast. I couldn't put any of it together, but it looked unofficially official."

"Did my husband accept any money or do anything illegal?" An edge had entered her voice. Whether she was worried or just plain pissed off, Jim couldn't tell.

"Not that I saw," he reassured her. "But it doesn't look like he and Bob are hanging around the golf club together."

The sigh of relief that rushed out of her took him by surprise—and seemed to surprise her as well. "Thank goodness. Please don't keep anything from me anymore."

"I won't," Jim promised. "Enzo will do anything to be the bond salesman on all Orthus County bonds. There's got to be evidence on his office computer of any misdeeds."

"We're working on that but aren't sure how to get on the inside. You're right about Enzo, though. We've already uncovered a smoking gun on St. Pete Beach but need more. Do you know anything about Patrick McDaniel, Progress Orthus Chairman? Both Patrick and Bob are silent partners on the fixed-base operator company at Orthus County Airport. They have a monopoly on airplane service, gas, the works, and not so coincidentally, they've had it since the airport was constructed. It's a conflict of interest, which should be enough to haul them to jail, but citizens are desensitized to it because deals like that are so common voters chalk it up to the way business is done."

Jim rubbed his chin and looked up at the ceiling. "I figured out the airport connection when Bill asked me this summer what a fixed-base operator was. What about the new Australian smoke show that works for Enzo? Kristy, or Kirsty, or something? Last name is McPhee. She probably knows something. She's with Enzo at some of the commission meetings."

"What could she know?"

"I did some research on her when I saw her name on the sign-in sheet. She went to Harvard Business School, but her undergrad was at University of Queensland. She majored in Computer Engineering and worked at some worldwide cloud-based computing company before going to Harvard. I never heard of them, but then again, I'm not a computer programmer."

"That's it." Her eyes widened for the first time.

"What's it?"

"She'll need citizenship eventually. Girl like that doesn't want to go back home. She's here for the money, the fame. She's only got a work visa, but she'll need something more permanent to stay in the states."

Jim almost finished her thought. "If she believes Dunham Schauble is about to go down, maybe she does a solid for the attorney general's office in return for some help at the INS."

Paige nodded, and he could almost see the to-do list she must've been writing in her head. "I'll handle all of that. Anything else?"

"Maybe, but this is a long shot." He folded his hands behind his head trying to reconcile his hunch, needing to try it on someone he could trust. "I think the Coyotes are about to move, but I don't know where, and Mayor Tisdale is worried about it, too. That's what we were talking about that day you saw us drinking beer on the MOTrail. Smithson Galleria would be the perfect spot, but all the renderings at the last Progress Orthus meeting showed multi-family apartment complexes, high-rise office towers for insurance companies, and a downtown district. I mean, that's crazy, right? The Coyotes wouldn't move, would they?" Then he leaned forward, putting his hands back on the armrests.

"That would crush Orlando," she said.

Jim continued. "The Coyotes' bond matures in two years and the Ospreys in four. If Mayor Tisdale is going to hand out more tax abatements, it'll be to the championship Ospreys, not the bottom-of-the-division Coyotes." He looked at her for any confirmation he was wrong, or at least barking up the wrong tree—something to poke a hole in his theory.

"But wouldn't Onward Orlando be left with loads of debt for neighborhood improvements around the stadium, not to mention the remaining debt on the existing stadium? The new schools Mayor Tisdale promised those neighborhoods last year aren't even started. The scene of the murder we just convicted is in one of those neighborhoods, and they happen every week."

If she was following his logic, he couldn't tell, because her facial expressions hadn't changed since he suggested her office could help with an INS work-around. He leaned back. "Like I said, it's just a hunch. What do you mean new schools? I thought that was Stan's job?"

"It is, but he's not doing it. He's too concerned with Flash. He comes home late from First and Last all the time, and he doesn't know I have an active investigation into his party pals. When we do talk, it's all about how he deserves more money and how Bob and Patrick shouldn't get all the breaks. It's disgusting."

Jim thought about his wife hurrying in from the garage to him if he got home from work before she did. He thought about how they snickered at each other's dark jokes during formal events, how they supported and encouraged each other, and loved one another through every crisis. "I'm sorry, Paige. That's terrible. I don't know what I'd do without Rebecca."

"Tell her you love her every day, because it never gets old."

"I will. Thanks for meeting me."

"By the way, my daddy likes shellcracker fishing as much as anybody and wants to go."

He leaned back hard against the chair, letting it tilt back against the wall like a front-porch rocker. "Taking a sheriff to Lake Lochloosa almost got me ex-communicated, Mrs. Jackson. I'm sure Judge Olmstead is of a very high caliber, and a justice of the peace is exactly more of what Lochloosa needs, but bringing the long arm of the law to some of my friends' doorsteps might get me disowned.

But I'll surely see what I can do. The early warning will be a big concession I can take to my people." He savored her laughter and smiled. "Let me know how else I can help."

Paige pulled her bags off the ground and set them on the table. "Thank you for the video, Jim, and please tell Ezzy hello from me."

"Will do, Paige."

Before leaving the county offices, Jim called his wife to let her know he'd be home early.

CHAPTER 29

The crowd noise from above the concrete was deafening in the basement corridors of the stadium as Stan arrived at the executive elevator. The glass doors opened, and the elevator operator wearing a Coyotes stadium security guard jacket greeted him. "Hey, Flash Jackson! They're expecting you in the owner's suite. The new kid just rounded the bases. Maybe we can pull one out."

"Let's get to it. Go Coyotes!" He stepped onto the elevator and tucked his phone into his jacket pocket.

"You don't remember me, do you?" The operator pushed the elevator button, folded his hands in front of him, and smiled as the doors closed.

Flash placed his face from his reflection off the glass door as the elevator rose through the concrete, but not his name. "No, sir. Refresh my memory."

"We grew up together over near the tracks. I'm Lucius Teale."

"Luscious Lucius! I knew you looked familiar. What are you up to, man?"

"Working this elevator and scalping when I can, but we can't give these tickets away. It ain't the breezy life you got, but it pays the bills." He shifted from one foot to the other and ran his hand over his head.

"You still live in our old 'hood? I see DC all the time at Grady High School."

"Naw, man, I live right around the corner. I moved away when you all built the MOTrail, about the same time DC moved. I couldn't afford the taxes no more, so I moved thinkin' the new stadium bonds were goin' to clean the place up. Turns out I should've stayed 'cause MOTrail don't reach all the way to my old house like they said." Stan didn't want to tell him he lived in MOTrail's anchor residential development that'd seen the most growth. "The Coyotes finally started sprucing things up around here, though, but they got a ways to go, know what I mean? What's DC up to?"

"He's still bustin' my balls like always."

"Ain't that right. How 'bout you? You gettin' along OK? You lookin' good." He slapped Stan's triceps a couple of times.

Stan ducked in a pseudo boxer's pose. "Yeah, Lucius. I'm good. Wife's getting older, and the girlfriend wants more money, but ain't that the way?" The elevator bell dinged.

"Yeah, you got that right, too. This is your stop, Flash. Can I get an autograph before you go?"

"Sure." He signed the parking-ticket receipt and slid out as the doors were closing. "Have a good one."

The owner's box restaurant-size room was adorned with pennant banners, All-Star posters, and original Coyotes memorabilia. It was a staggering distance from watching football on the Ospreys sidelines as a professional participant, but it wasn't the first owner's box he'd been in, and the last thing anyone would see from him was fan-like worship of spectator opulence. He walked across the wood floors showcasing a Coyotes logo made from a Heart of Pine, wooden inlay below him, while he took special notice of the glass wall encasing a media distribution center complete with a broadcast studio on one side of the room. Raised tables made of inter-connected home plates, surrounded by stools with leather-glove-shaped seats, popped up in the middle and added the usual themed-based décor he'd seen around all the leagues. One entire side of the room was a bar with baseball-topped draught handles, bar chairs made of bases, and awnings supported by bats stacked from top to bottom. Noticeably missing was any National Championship trophies, which is why he played football in this town, not baseball. He made the last couple of steps toward the wide windows and lounging area where Coyotes owner, Warren Sanderson, and Sterling, Gene, Bob, and Patrick were looking out over the ballpark.

As he walked over, Warren stood and bellowed like everyone else who wants something, "Flash Jackson! Completely my honor. Can I get you a drink? Welcome to the best seats in Coyotes Stadium."

"Hey, Warren. Man, this place feels like home, if your home was on a space ship. Sure, I'll take a beer." He shook Warren's hand and started toward the bar area.

Warren walked next to him and smiled. "It'd be a whole lot better with an October miracle, but we've got some good prospects coming up from the minors to replace our weakness on the mound."

"You gutting the team didn't help much either." He arrived at the tall stainless-steel refrigerator behind the bar before Warren, and opened the door.

Warren reached around him and pulled out two bottles. "Yes, Stanley, we made some strategic moves in the off season." Warren popped the two beer bottles open on a baseball-cap shaped bottle opener mounted on the side of the bar awning, and poured the beers into two tall, frosty glasses. "Here you go. Help yourself to anything here. Our new kid just hit a grand slam. Maybe we pull one out for the fans here at the end."

Stan's phone pinged with a text as Warren walked back over to the viewing area with the others. Hey Flash. I miss you. Stan dialed, and headed to a private part of the bar to call her back.

"I told you I'd call you," he said when Candi answered. "What do you want? I bought you the plane tickets. You'll be here in three weeks. Stop texting me."

He'd almost gotten used to her crying every time he reminded her this was a short-term relationship. "Damn it, Flash," she said, sounding angry instead of hurt. I just wanted to tell you I felt our baby kick. He's getting big and strong like his daddy."

Stan lowered his voice and turned away from the large picture-window viewing area. "Hey look. Sorry. I've got a lot on my mind. School started, people are riding my coattails, and you want money. Lots of money I don't have."

"Don't bullshit me, Flash. I know you're rolling in it. Besides, babies ain't free. You made it, so you're going to pay for it."

"Listen, I'm working on some things. Just be here in three weeks and we can figure something out. I want to make sure you're really pregnant."

"Oh, I'll be there, and I'm really pregnant, asshole. Can I meet Paige?"

Her asking price of a million dollars warned him in the beginning she was out for serious dough, but bullying him about his personal life was a new low. "No, you can't meet Paige! You'll get paid and then I'm putting your ass back on a plane. Now I've got to go." He disconnected the call and walked over to the expansive couch where they were all seated.

Patrick broke the awkward silence by getting up and moving over. "Flash! Thanks for coming. Let me make some room."

Stan forced a smile. "Damn, Warren. This thing seats like a whole offensive line." He set the beer on a napkin on the glass table, the frost quickly melting away.

"Nothing but the best," Warren bragged.

"Hey, Flash," Gene said. "Good to see you. Bottom of the second. Four-O, Coyotes."

"Trouble on the home front, Flash?" Bob asked. "Wives can be like that, especially if they have a law degree. I should know."

Stan kept his eyes on the field. The mood he was in, he was likely to punch Bob in the face if he had to look at him. "It's all good, fat boy. You wouldn't know anything about my business. Maybe you need to get a better handle on your wife."

Out of the corner of his eye, Stan could see Sterling twitch. "Stanley, I hope all is well this afternoon. How's your new school year going?"

"Same as always. Unions are threatening to strike if I don't give them a raise. Kids are running the place. Thank God football season is in full swing."

"Word on the street is Grady's got what it takes to go all the way," Patrick said.

Stan looked at him as he would any other amateur making amateur predictions in the middle of the season. Instead of telling him to shut up—which was his first instinct—he figured he'd go for polite. "They're stacked, but you know what they say? It's hard to get to the top, but it's even harder to stay there. If they don't get overconfident, they can be a good team, from what DC tells me anyway."

"Good for Grady. Shame they still share a stadium with two other high schools," Patrick said.

Stan scoffed. "If Bob wouldn't give every single developer that comes along a tax abatement, they wouldn't have to share stadiums."

Bob slammed his glass down hard enough for the ice to hop around the rim. "Flash, if I didn't build a hospital and an airport, your high school buddies wouldn't have a place to go with gunshot wounds, and my buddies wouldn't have a place to land their private planes."

Stan felt himself jumping up before he had a chance to think about what he was doing. He glared down at Bob, towering over him with every inch and ounce of his six-foot-two frame. "Say it again, mother fucker."

Bob looked away. "It was a joke," he muttered.

"Come on, guys," Warren said. "We're here to make a deal, not start World War Three. I could've been in the Caribbean watching the game with my kids."

Sterling set his tea on the table. "Gentlemen, please. Let's discuss our collective opportunities. Stanley, I think we have some ideas you might like."

Stan sat back down, his fists still clenched. Bob grinned behind his raised glass, and was within arm's reach for a black eye.

He heard Gene's voice calling his name. "Flash, look. You know how much we want this Smithson Galleria project, right?"

The mention of today's business brought Stan back to his senses. "Yeah, the *Orthus County Post* makes it seem like you'll do anything. One of your state senators already called me with an offer for a high school."

"That's right," Patrick said. "There's an apartment complex on the north side of the site the owners are willing to sell, and it's big enough for a high school. It could have the biggest football stadium in the county, bigger than the one Ezzy is building at King Christian Academy."

"You have my attention," Stan said. "You need me to issue a bond for a downtown district for the Smithson mayor's City Hall, a giant apartment complex, office towers, and retail to go with it? There's a movie theatre and everything, right?"

"There've been some changes, Stanley," Sterling said. "We decided the insurance company wasn't a good fit for our vision."

"I heard they backed out. As soon as they met Bob, it was over. Charming guy, Bob." Stan smiled, leaned over, and grabbed his glass of beer off the table.

"That's unfounded speculation," Bob said. 'I've done plenty of deals around here. If insurance companies don't like our bargains, they can go screw someone else out of free money."

"Well, now. I don't know much about real estate, but it sounds like you need some renters." Stan took a long sip of beer and set his glass back down.

Gene smiled. "Flash, you don't think we got rid of the insurance company without a better plan, do you?"

"Flash," Warren chimed in. "You probably already figured this out, but the Coyotes want the spot."

"What?" Stan looked around at everyone else. They'd obviously already reached a pre-arranged consensus.

"We're moving to Orthus County so we can build inside the Smithson Galleria footprint," Warren continued, "where the insurance company towers were supposed to go."

Stan shook his head. "No shit? The Coyotes are moving to Orthus County?"

"With your help, we are." Warren got up and walked between Stan and the ongoing game, holding his beer glass to his side. "I've hired Sterling to design the stadium. We've tried and tried, but Mayor Tisdale won't work with us on our maintenance costs, or any other challenges we face, and it's costing us too much to stay. Our home office staff has been negotiating since last year for repairs, but we haven't had any luck. Plus, MOTrax doesn't come to the stadium and never did. It's just better this way. The Coyotes have provided so much to the City of Orlando, but the parking problem around the stadium isn't going away. The roads are awful and we need a smaller stadium that's useful all year long."

Stan was still catching up to the realization a mid-market sports team was about to move out of a major metropolitan downtown. "What about litigation costs? You know Mayor Tisdale is going to be livid. Don't you still owe them money? Serves them right, though. They did the same thing to me for two years."

"Flash, look around you. I'm a billionaire because I prepare for every outcome. Sterling, you're better at this than me. Can you explain? We just want to play baseball."

"Stanley, the upgraded MOTrax Smithson Station will deliver residents, government participants, and patrons to our Smithson Downtown District. As riders exit the renovated train station, they'll look out over a piazza framed by a new City of Smithson

Court House and City Hall. Throngs of young people from all economic walks of life will reside in the mixed-use enclave. The collective development will be the envy of every metropolitan region in the country. No cars—only pedestrian-friendly sidewalks and bike paths. Patrons and residents will enjoy first-floor retail topped by twenty stories of multifamily, high-end apartments. The sight lines from the street view of the downtown district will look east, out onto a grand promenade complete with fountains, baseball-themed statues, portable venues, and interactive, experiential games."

"Promenade my ass," Bob said. "It's going to be a parking lot, with a single exit dropping cars right on top of it from the Bob Drolland Interchange."

"Ignore Bob for a moment, Stanley." Sterling shot Bob a look that had the surprising effect of shutting him up. "Coyotes fans in the outfield will view the branded home-plate background, seats, press boxes, and suites rising into the western sky supporting the apartment-complex towers visible above the stadium opening. It will be a monument unto itself. No more entrapments of downtown Orlando, no more late arrivals because of cars jamming the streets, only walking and biking to a day at the ballpark. The Coyotes sunset will be the envy of professional baseball."

Gene spoke up again, assumingly to hot box him into making early concessions, but he was nothing more than a fixer lurking around for Sterling. "What do you think, Stan?" he asked, and paused when Warren's phone rang and he walked over to the bar to answer it.

"Where will people park, unless Bob was right and his interchange would drop people into a parking lot?"

"We're working out those details," Gene said while twiddling his thumbs, "but the intention is to build a walkable community centered around professional baseball."

He chuckled at the absurdity of the idea, but played along. He needed the payday to get Candi off his back. "I'm a baseball fan, sure, but what's it going to cost? Last time I asked, it was four hundred and fifty million dollars."

"Six hundred and fifty million for the best sports stadium in the world and the biggest high school in the state," Gene said.

"What else you offering besides a high school?"

"What do you mean, what else are we offering?" Patrick asked. "You're getting a high school out of this."

"That was two hundred million dollars ago, last I checked with Gene," Stan said. Getting rid of Candi would require more than a new high school.

"Well, what about another car?" Patrick asked.

"My insurance took care of the union damage. What else you got?" he said.

"How's two hundred and fifty thousand a year sound?" Bob asked. "You can have part of the stadium concessions contract."

"You bullshitting me?" Stan turned to Bob, understanding Bob'd been holding the cards all along.

"Nope, you're getting half of Patrick's take."

"What?" Patrick asked. "How're you going to do that, Bob?"

"Shut up, Patrick," Bob said. "You want to sell that apartment complex or don't you?"

Patrick's shoulders slumped and he leaned back into the couch.

"The Orthus School Board needs something more than a high school, Patrick," Stan said. "Add two million per year into a community-improvement district around the Grady High School cluster, plus my people need maintenance contracts."

Bob held out both fists, his short fingers unfolding while he counted out loud. Then he turned back over the back of the couch and yelled, "Warren, can you swing two million into a community-improvement district around Grady High School?"

Warren put his hand over the bottom of the phone. "If it gets this deal done and I can get out of here."

Bob turned back. "Deal, Stan?"

"That all you got, fat boy?"

"Take it or leave it," Bob said.

"I want our concessions LLC to have a line of credit from Progress Orthus immediately, and I want a checkbook."

Patrick leaned back in disbelief. "Damn it, Bob. One of the Progress Orthus board members was getting a maintenance contract. What do you want a checkbook for, Flash?"

"Shut up, Patrick, and don't ask me again."

"The maintenance contracts are spoken for, Patrick," Bob said. "Stan has mouths to feed, too."

"What's next?" Stan asked. "Is this just like the MOTrail deal?"

Patrick lowered his voice and spoke through his hands covering his face. "Yep. Operation Grand Slam is what we're calling it for privacy. The only difference is Progress Orthus is your conduit, not Onward Orlando. I'll bring it up at the next meeting."

"Don't be so mad, Patrick." Stan patted him on the back like he would a rookie that made it to the last tryout, only to get cut. "This is three times bigger than the MOTrail deal. My board will do it, but they need favors, too."

"Wait a minute, gentlemen," Warren said as he walked back over in front of the couch. "You can't just announce this thing at a Progress Orthus meeting. I have to tell Mayor Tisdale personally, and only after that can it be announced, and only in a way that will make the fans want the move. This has to be done right."

Looking back over his shoulder into the stadium, Stan saw fans leaving in the seventh. After a quick check of the scorecard, he knew why: three errors had cost the Coyotes their early lead, and now they were down by two. To add insult to injury, there were base runners on first and third, and Stan saw action in the Coyotes bullpen.

"Warren, it would be wise to tell Mayor Tisdale nothing." Sterling said, not having moved from his relaxed position on the couch. "I've successfully completed stadiums all over the world—many times for cities with several professional sports teams like Orlando. If this were to leak out, the deal would be scuttled in a matter of hours. For this deal to have any chance of completion, it should be announced closer to financing approval."

Warren looked at Sterling hard. "You're right. This is going to be a shit storm for a year or two. Bob, have you spoken to Enzo?"

Bob poured another scotch from the bottle sitting in front of him on the table. Stan wondered why he didn't just get rid of the glass and drink straight from the bottle at this point. "He's sitting on go. He'll be the bond counsel and the underwriter. He'll sell most of the issue on the open market and keep a little for himself, but I don't care what he does with it. We just need the municipal bond buyer's money."

"Alright, the timeline looks like this," Warren said. "The morning before Progress Orthus approves the bond issue, we'll hold a presser in the studio next door for the morning-drive radio shows. Nothing negative. We'll focus on the year-round use of event space with multiple attractions. Concerts, world-class retail, experiential game play, and baseball. I'll get with my marketing people to arrange everything. Sterling, you're all set with graphic art, right?"

"Of course. I have a prolific artist already creating what I just described."

"Good. Thank you all for being here. I have a plane to catch. Security will let you out. I'll be in touch on the press conference." Warren shook Stan's hand before he walked out. "Thanks, Flash."

"Us, too. We need to get going." Sterling and Gene followed Warren out.

Stan had no interest in watching baseball with Bob and Patrick, and headed toward the open door. "I'm following you guys." On the way out, he emailed himself, GET CONCESSIONS CONTRACT IN PLACE. GET CHECKBOOK.

"You really know how to screw a guy, Bob," Patrick said once the others had left.

"You're going to split five hundred thousand dollars of bottom-line income with Stan, while I provide the urban utopia you and Sterling have been dreaming of. Please, tell me: How did you get screwed?"

"I deserve that power as much as you."

Bob laughed, poured one more scotch, and unloaded on him. "Deserve? Operation Grand Slam? What kind of bullshit is that? You think you're in the goddamn CIA? Who invited you to this meeting? Who made the deal with Warren and Gene? You deserve what I give you. You want this power, run for county commission, but I mean it, Patrick: keep it up and you'll lose your chair on Progress Orthus."

Patrick shook his head and left.

Bob drank by himself until a security guard came around with the cleaning crew. He'd slept through the Coyotes loss in the ninth.

CHAPTER 30

Paige fought the traffic on the way to work, the long red lights and merge lanes giving her plenty of time to think about the strange texts on Stan's phone from Las Vegas. She hadn't been able to find a match between the phone number and the Las Vegas School Board's cell phone numbers she'd obtained from a federal database. His credit card statement showed round-trip tickets for someone to fly to Orlando in October, but she knew his assistant bought all the plane tickets. She flipped the channel to sports-talk radio to avoid another story about missed corporate earnings and the continuing recession. The local news anchor broke into the syndicated football pre-season predictions: "Breaking news. We're here at the Orlando Coyotes home office, at Coyotes Stadium, for a press conference called by Warren Sanderson, Orlando Coyotes owner. We'll come back to you after their comments."

Jim's tri-pod-mounted camera stood in the corner of the room near the entrance where Warren walked in. The entire media could see through the glass wall to the owner's suite, and Jim thought of Lochloosa High School's press box where he used to announce games as a favor to his dad after he graduated. Warren's arrival in the room, surrounded by handlers and PR staff, ignited clicking cameras and shuffling chairs as the media squeezed closer. A screen behind and above Warren materialized from the shadows, triggering Jim to refocus his video. The screen captured the moving angles of a drone flight path that gave a three-dimensional tour of a baseball stadium, which didn't surprise Jim. He'd just been waiting on the announcement, day by day growing more confident in his research. Baseball-themed museum easels held mural-sized canvas artwork underneath the giant screen TV.

"Good morning, ladies and gentlemen," Warren began. "I have terrific news for Orthus County. The Orlando Coyotes Stadium and all Orlando Coyotes operations are moving into our new home connected to the Smithson Downtown District in Orthus County. We plan to be an integral part of a new urban design that will transform our fans' dreams of all-inclusive experiences into a reality, while coming closer to where they live. A newly renovated MOTrax Smithson Station will transport fans from all over Metro Orthus County to our new home. Coyotes' fans drive all of our decisions, but our fan base lives far away from here in downtown Orlando. The stadium will shine with world-class innovations including a fan-based outdoor promenade, private suites encircling the entire stadium rim, and a smaller, more intimate baseball experience. We will miss our partnership with the City of Orlando, but we must proceed into the next chapter of the Coyotes organization. We've been family for over eleven years, but have decided this move will be the foundation of our success for generations to come. Stadium construction will take about two years, so we have two more years at Coyotes Stadium. Now I'll take limited questions from the press."

Jim was first. "Will Orthus County or its school board provide any financing for the new stadium contract?

"Currently, there's no contract signed, but we're sure the move will happen. We can't discuss any of our financing options as they're still in flux, but we're moving. Next question."

The *Orlando Journal*'s Coyotes beat writer, whom Jim had met a few times, didn't wait for Warren to pick someone else, and directly confronted him. "Is Mayor Tisdale aware of this decision?" The *Journal* funded a large hometown portion of the Coyotes advertising revenue.

"In an effort to remain true to our fans, all negotiations were kept private until this press briefing. We have been negotiating this deal with Orthus County leadership for over six months. Next."

Reporters were raising their hands in unison, another spoke out. "What will the City of Orlando do with the existing stadium?"

"Onward Orlando is a competent group with many talented individuals driving their decisions. Our nation thrives on sporting events. Onward Orlando is the owner of the stadium. They can easily find another group willing to lease or buy the stadium, but that's their decision, and we have no control, or interest, in it. Next."

The Orlando local charged ahead, having followed the team for years and knowing only what a local would know. "You mentioned the MOTrax Smithson Station will get a renovation? When will construction begin? Are any other stations scheduled for renovations?"

"We'll leave the scheduling to MOTrax officials, but the transit-oriented developments will be a great start."

"But you said the station. The TODs have their own financing source, apart from the MOTrax stations. What is the future of Smithson Galleria and the insurance companies expecting to inhabit that space?"

"Again, all of those operating decisions are for MOTrax leadership. Your question regarding Smithson Galleria, or the insurance companies, is above my pay grade and should be directed to MOTrax or Progress Orthus."

Jim hurled a curveball. “What will keep the Coyotes from moving to another stadium when your tax abatement ends at the new stadium?”

“We haven’t received any tax abatements to date, although we’re working with Progress Orthus on a few opportunities. We hope to have a long and fruitful relationship with Orthus County. The Coyotes organization seeks long-lasting relationships in order to build traditions that serve generations of fans. Baseball is a game of traditions, and we want to capitalize on those traditions that Americans hold so dear. Jacksonville News 5. Go ahead, Sam.”

Jim asked another question before he lost the floor. “Why not increase ticket prices instead of taking tax breaks?”

“Our stadium will provide the surrounding areas of our ballpark with thousands of new jobs, and years of economic development to the community. Tax breaks are a no-brainer, and the taxpayer is not obligated to any of the debt. Jacksonville 5, go ahead, if Mr. Pinson doesn’t mind.” Jim kicked back in his chair. He’d get the story lines from his recorded video.

“Are the Coyotes responsible for the remaining bond debt still left for the stadium?” the Jacksonville reporter asked. “I think it’s around fifty million dollars.”

“No. And seeing no other questions, we’ll continue to release information as we move forward. Thank you for being here on such short notice. Go Coyotes.” Cameras starting clicking again, and then faded back to quiet.

“One last question,” Jim shouted, still reclining in his metal folding chair. “What happens to Orthus County if professional sports fans stop watching for some unforeseen reason?”

Warren stopped at the bottom of the platform staircase on the side of the stage, the drone video above the stage on a continuous loop, and looked at Jim as if he’d ask him what’d happen if the sun didn’t rise. “Professional sports are part of the American social fabric, and there's nothing that'll keep our fans from coming to stadiums—large and small. Since before gladiators fought in Rome, humanity has adored sports and physical drama."

The local beat writer passed by Jim as the crowd thinned. "Maybe the Orthus County Coyotes will get you to write a ten-million-dollar check for the logo space on the centerfield wall, a members-only luxury outfield café, and a foam-ink pen race in the seventh inning," he said. "I think the *Orlando Journal* checkbook is closed."

Paige looked around at the other cars maneuvering through rush hour, and judging by the looks on the drivers' faces, they must've been listening to the same news she was.

"There you have it, folks," the announcer said. "The Orlando Coyotes are moving to a new stadium in Orthus County. In one of the most recent examples of undercover negotiations, Coyotes owner, Warren Sanderson, is moving the team from their home of over ten years since league expansion. We'll have more information as this story continues to unfold over the coming hours, days, and weeks. Now back to our regularly scheduled show."

Paige texted the mayor. You alone?

While she was still looking at her phone, Jim texted her, You hear?

Brian returned her text. My phone is blowing up, but I'll answer if you call.

Paige texted Jim. Major blow. More to follow. Great questions in the press conference.

She pushed the call button from her steering wheel, and Brian answered without asking who it was. "Hey, Paige. Those sons of bitches. I'll be damned if I'll stand by and watch them walk out on the forty-seven million dollars they still owe the City of Orlando. Where do I get that kind of money? What the hell am I going to do with a baseball stadium?"

"That's why I called. What can I do to help?"

"Right now, I don't know, unless the DA's office has some legal advice. I don't even know where they got the money. I thought Bob was tapped out. Progress Orthus is about to be on the skids for the hospital."

"Brian, I think they got it from Stan." She pulled around another corner and into the parking deck of the Florida Attorney General's offices.

"What? Oh, my God! The nerve. What business does the school board have with a baseball stadium?"

"None. I've been doing some research on a few things that are connected. I couldn't believe Stan would do it either."

"Oh, Paige. It just dawned on me. I'm so sorry. Did you and Stan talk about it? Does he know you know?"

"No, and please don't tell him. It's been difficult, but I'm up to it. This is bigger than Stan and me. I'm going to lose you going into the parking deck."

"That's ok, I need to call that pompous ass, Warren Sanderson."

"Let me know…" the signal was lost as she drove up the levels of the parking deck.

The receptionist answered the phone, "Coyotes Home Office. Go Coyotes. May I…"

"This is Mayor Brian Tisdale. Please put Warren on the phone."

"Good morning, Mayor Tisdale. Mr. Sanderson isn't in the office right now. Is there something I can do for you?"

"Yeah. Have Warren send me a check for forty-seven million dollars." He slammed the phone down and dialed Warren's cell. The call went to voicemail after the first ring. Brian hung up again and called the city attorney.

"Hey, Brian. What a load?!"

"First things first, Roger. We need to file an injunction immediately, and then file a lawsuit against the Coyotes. I need those filed by this afternoon and e-file a copy to the courthouse and Warren's office."

"You bet. I like your style, Mayor."

"It's just business. If they're going to leave us high and dry, they get what's coming."

He planned his next moves while continuing to avoid calls from the press until he could speak to Warren. When Warren finally called the next day, Brian was hosting his city attorneys in his office, filing paperwork, and advising on the language in the lawsuit being shaped.

He put his index finger to his lips, quieting the group, yanked up the phone and said, "I thought those injunction letters would get you on the phone, Warren."

"Look, Brian. Save yourself the time and energy. Go talk to your attorney, and call off the dogs. You can't win, and you'll only waste money trying to fight it. I saved enough money on my salary cap to pay the exit fees. Read the contract, I pay twenty-five percent of any remaining lease payments should I decide to leave the stadium. We don't own it. You do."

Brian put him on speaker so the legal team could listen. "Warren, in no way is that acceptable. You signed those lease agreements with Onward Orlando before I ever got here. What the hell am I going to do with a stadium specifically built for baseball?"

"I'm sure the deal I would've made with you would've been more favorable to the City of Orlando. You're shrewder than the administration you replaced, which is probably why you were elected. It's why I supported your election. I'll support you again, but you're right; I didn't make those deals with you, but they're valid contracts."

The managing litigator rolled his chair back up to the head of the table, picked up a blank sheet of paper, and waved it over his head like a flag.

Brian ignored the symbolic surrender, looked him directly in the eye, and said to Warren, "I don't need your support, asshole. The heat will continue because you might have unlimited access to baseball players, but I have unlimited access to legal staff."

"The rhetoric isn't necessary, Brian. I wrote the contract. I can help you if you'll let me."

"You've helped enough already."

"I know people at the University of Central Florida. They might need your stadium. You have options."

"Not many. Damn it, Warren! This is really going to hurt the citizens of Orlando. We have to make those missed payments from the police and infrastructure budget. Forty-seven million dollars is a lot of pension payments, plus those neighborhoods around your stadium are expecting upgrades for putting up with your bullshit for eleven years."

"Your stadium, Brian. You had pension and infrastructure problems before today's announcement. It's two of the reasons we're leaving."

"And you don't give a damn. Be looking forward to more attorney phone calls. I have to play the hand you dealt, but I play as good as anyone."

"Do what you have to do, Mayor. See you at home plate."

CHAPTER 31

Shining in the western sky, the sun set behind the Orthus County Administration Building, the parking lot full since lunch, cars still circling the area looking for open spaces as employees headed home from Downtown Orlando. Patrick had arrived early to hide from the crowds, but hustled up to the side of the building from the back door to gauge participation one last time. Packed crowds overflowed out onto the sidewalk, dotted with people holding signs that read "Build Schools, Not Sports Stadiums," "Apartment Complexes Don't Teach Kids Anything," and "Hands Off Our Pensions." The extra security detail Patrick had demanded for tonight's meeting had been granted, confirmed by the six Orthus County Sheriff cars parked up front. Patrick watched Ezzy land two-footed on the pavement from her truck and walk past a couple of officers who tipped their hats like they worked for her. On one of his last walk-arounds, he'd asked the deputies not to arrest anyone but to be there as a show of force. Looking back on the interaction, he hadn't been given half the respect Ezzy was getting for just walking by. Patrick had already seen some of the other commissioners arriving, and decided to jog back around to the side entrance. He didn't want to have to greet Ezzy away from the stage, his safe zone of procedural predictability. He managed to dodge her, only to come face to face with a mob scene growing inside, and a line of speakers already at the podium. People with orange shirts filled one side of the room, the words "Coyotes Fans Won't Move" emblazoned on the front and "Coyotes Stadium Is Our Home" on the back. He recognized teachers union sympathizers from fundraisers he'd attended, wearing brown and standing on the other side of the room. The other commissioners had joined him on stage as Ezzy climbed the side stairs to the platform. He looked up and down the row to his right and left to signify he was about to begin calling the role. "Good evening, Ms. King," he said into the microphone. "I assume you are present. Better late than never."

"Oh, I don't know," she said, leaning into her microphone. "Please don't let my tardiness interfere with your plans."

Patrick drew his shoulders up when the room filled with laughter. "What's with you lately, Ezzy?"

His effort to keep her in line melted into public embarrassment when she answered, "I'm busy running a successful organization. You wouldn't understand, so let's stop wasting everyone's time and get on with it."

Patrick rapped the gavel, trying to regain composure. "Thank you, everyone, for joining us for the October meeting of Progress Orthus." He rapped the gavel several more times. "People, people, please. Tonight, we'll be voting on a memorandum of understanding to request public debt issued by the Orthus County School Board in the amount of six hundred and fifty million dollars for the applicant, Smithson Coyotes Stadium, LLC." Boos erupted. "The debt will finance the construction of the Coyotes Stadium that will replace the blank space left in our city from an irresponsible car manufacturer, and will connect to MOTrax-Smithson Station and the new transit-oriented development previously planned and funded. Because of the large audience, and your demonstrated raucous nature of opposition, I'd like to make a motion for transparency's sake that we extend the speaker time to thirty minutes instead of our normal ten. Do I hear a second?"

Just as he'd hoped, Ezzy said, "Second."

"All in favor of extending the public comments to thirty minutes, please signify by saying 'aye'." It was unanimous. "Okay. I'd like to take this opportunity to remind our audience of procedure. If you'd like to speak tonight, please fill out a comment card located on the back table." He watched the people in line at the podium begin to exchange puzzled looks. Others in the back stared at a small table with a stack of comment cards his staff had placed there after he'd walked on stage.

The man at the podium said, "Mr. McDaniel. I've been standing here for almost an hour, and there's no way I'm going to fill out a comment card and lose my spot."

"Sir, I appreciate your passion and willingness to be involved in our process, but the procedures are in place for fairness to all." About half the podium line walked to the back row and formed a new line to fill out comment cards. The new line almost reached to Jim's camera set up next to the door.

The front half of the podium line stood their ground and stared holes through him, their arms crossed. "Mr. McDaniel, you'll have to put your procedure aside for tonight. I've been a season ticket holder for twenty years," the man said. "All the people behind me are either season ticket holders or Orthus County taxpayers, and we *will* be heard."

"Sir, I'll remind you I have the force of an executive officer trying to hold a public meeting, enforceable by law." People in plain clothes began to form the second half of the line at the podium.

"What's that supposed to mean, Patrick?" asked the angry woman standing second in line.

"It means our sergeant-at-arms role is provided by the Orthus County Sheriff's Department, and if you don't have a comment card filled out, you have two options. Go fill one out and wait your turn, or sit down. If you continue to stand at the podium without a comment card, you'll be removed forcibly." Patrick's anxiety faded when one of the officer's moved closer to the podium with his hands on his utility belt for emphasis, but the two that had deferred to Ezzy in the parking lot stood their ground on the side.

"You think we're going to leave here without telling you your deal is a load of crap?" the man asked, glancing back and forth from Patrick to the approaching officer. "That we won't stand for it? You got another thing coming, Patrick."

The officer approached the man and whispered something Patrick couldn't hear, but then raised his voice and asked, "Do you have a comment card, sir?"

"A comment card? No, I don't have a comment card," the man yelled. "What is this? Kindergarten, officer?"

"Ok. That's it then. Off you go." He grabbed the man under the arm.

"What the hell are you doing, officer?" The remaining original speakers began to move back.

"Sir, you're resisting a very direct and polite request to follow the rules and remove yourself from the podium." The officer pulled him over to the wall and pushed him up the side aisle with his arm held against the small of his back.

"Can everyone see what is happening?" the man shouted, looking back over the police officer's shoulder. He caught Patrick's gaze. "I am being removed from a public comments section to tell Progress Orthus, and Patrick McDaniel, we won't stand for it." Patrick saw Jim's camera in his hand as he followed him up the side aisle and out the door, ensuring the unwanted attention would continue to pressure his deal.

The remaining officers moved toward the podium as both the orange- and brown-shirted protestors moved to the back, leaving only the speakers in plain clothes, whom he'd met with earlier that day.

One of the orange shirts in the back yelled out, "When did they sign comment cards?"

A brown shirt yelled back across the room, "They just walked in."

"Destiny, will you please read off the speakers," Patrick interrupted their dialogue as quickly as he could. "As you hear your name, please approach the podium, state your name, your home address, and your comment. Each person has three minutes, but please be brief and respectful of everyone's time that would like to speak."

He'd met each of them personally this morning, when they introduced themselves as friends of Warren's, and showed them how to fill out comment cards. They'd used fake names and addresses for all their comments, as the first man rambled through two minutes: "Thank you for this opportunity you've given Orthus County. The economic benefit from a new baseball stadium will provide us the economic boost we'll need during this recession. Thousands of jobs will be created, local economies will flourish, Orthus County schools will benefit from higher tax revenues and a new high school. I couldn't be more excited." The timer dinged and he capped off his soliloquy. "I respectfully request Progress Orthus issue the new debt in the name of the free markets and progress for all socioeconomic backgrounds. Go Coyotes!"

"Thank you for your comments." Patrick checked the muffled boos. "Audience! Please respect the decorum of this meeting. As you've seen, the rules will be observed and executed, but it would be much easier if everyone would respect the rights of others."

The next nine speakers gave renditions on the same theme he'd approved, before one of the orange shirts from the back of the new line at the comments card table shouted out. "This is bullshit. You aren't respecting the process, Patrick. No one in opposition will have any time."

He caught Ezzy shaking her head, fueling their disruptive nature, when the last speaker ended with, "Please move forward with this nationally recognized opportunity for higher school funding and economic development only made possible by new sports stadiums." The crowd booed all the way through the last three sentences. Patrick delighted as raw nerves sentenced two more community activists to a personal escort out of the room. Now three officers guarded removed citizens outside and three officers tried to maintain calm inside. One watched from the back, and the two officers he'd recognized from outside moved in front of the stage and stood in front of Ezzy.

"Thank you, Orthus County, for your feedback," Patrick concluded. "And thanks to both the opposition, and the supporters for being part of the process. We value your opinions. With that, I'd like to take a vote among the panel, as I'm sure you've had time to think this thing through and get your questions answered. All in favor of acting as conduit for Orthus County School Board for the issuance of six hundred and fifty million dollars of revenue bonds for SCS, LLC, please signify by saying 'Aye'."

Orange shirts were standing up and booing, the crowd bursting at its emotional seams. Most of the board members looked blankly into the distance as they responded. "Aye."

Patrick turned in his chair and stared at Ezzy. "All opposed?"

Ezzy stood up. "Nay."

"The ayes have it. We're moving forward. If there's nothing else, I make a motion we adjourn."

"I've got a few things I'd like to wrap up before we finish." Ezzy grabbed the microphone in front of her seat, pulled several sheets of hand-written notes out of her purse, and backed away from the table.

Patrick rolled his eyes. "By all means, Ezzy, please go ahead."

She looked down at him with her unfolded papers resting at her side. "The votes we've taken to issue debt for the new Coyotes Stadium hold reckless disregard for the voters of Orthus County, Patrick. You've indebted the taxpayer with over a billion dollars in new debt over the last three months. You had the gall to stack tonight's podium with your friends, who most likely stand to gain, while opposing voices were silenced." Patrick looked around the stunned audience, orange and brown shirts aghast. People still filling out comment cards looked up from their chore, and Jim laughed as he typed on his laptop. "You've acted with impunity with their hard-earned tax dollars, while our children suffer from your incompetence, our teacher's work with last century's tools, and our police and firefighters put themselves in harm's way without a raise in three years. Rome is burning, and you couldn't care less."

He exhaled when she looked away to peer into the other commissioners' eyes. Gene smirked at him, and Sterling, sitting next to Gene, had nothing more to offer than a shrug of his shoulders.

Ezzy set her notes on the table in front of her, glancing down as she continued. "We're appointed by our elected officials with almost no required accountability to the taxpayer. I would argue our fiduciary duty to the taxpayer takes on an even higher standard because of the trust we've been given. Yet, you act out of vanity for your own desires, ignorance, and selfishness."

"We've been told by our own regional transportation consultants, and Governor Sikes, that we have the worst roads in the state. Our school system is demoralized from years of scandal, dilapidated buildings, and the loss of our children's self-esteem resulting from their dropping test scores. We've given away hundreds of millions of dollars in tax revenue, without any consideration of the schools that money would build, the teachers it would hire, the roads it would fix, or the police force it would sustain."

She looked up from the paper, out to the crowd, and delivered what Patrick would later call raw meat. "What the hell is the City of Orlando going to do with an empty sports stadium? Since when is a baseball stadium, a multi-family apartment complex, and a downtown district considered a county service? When will any of you provide actual proof of the jobs created that you so often quote? When will you provide proof of actual taxpayer benefits from this mythical economic development you parade around? You can't provide it, because it doesn't exist.

I've said enough. You've made up your minds without me, and I can no longer waste my time in support of such a corrupt authority blinded by greed, power, and self-interest. As of this meeting's adjournment, I resign." Applause tore through the room the moment the words "waste my time" left her lips, and erupted into a standing ovation as she finished. Patrick's banging gavel did nothing to quiet them down as she dropped the last page of notes on the pile.

Ezzy exited stage left, walked down the steps, and up the middle aisle of the room as the applause grew even louder. With Patrick watching her every step, she reached the first row of seats, reached into her bag, and pulled out a large brown envelope. At the top of the auditorium steps, she walked over to where Jim was sitting, people continuing to clap as she dropped it at his feet.

Patrick felt the blood rush to his face. He was pretty sure he knew what was in that envelope, and equally sure he'd lost control of more than just the meeting.

Bill was waiting at the door for Ezzy and followed her out to his truck behind the building, where he'd parked for a quick getaway. He stopped when he heard Ezzy consoling the removed citizens who were still fuming. "Thank you all for being here. It takes a lot of courage to stand up against ingrained corruption. This might be the bravest thing you've ever done. Hopefully, it's worth it."

She hurried around the corner and almost into the tailgate of his truck. "How did it sound?" she asked as he pulled her in tight.

"Ezzy King," he said as he released her and got down on one knee, "you're the most honest woman I've ever met. I wasn't going to do this right now, but I can't wait another minute after what you just went through. Your heart is as pure as God's love. You're as beautiful as a summer sunset. Please marry me. I want to spend the rest of my life with you." He held out the diamond ring. "This was my mom's."

Ezzy teared up. "It's so beautiful, Bill. Yes. I'd do it tonight if I could, but you deserve more. I won't let you get away. Now get in the truck. There's a mob in there, and I'm done talking."

The next morning's *Orthus County Post* read, "Progress Orthus Loses Its Leader - Pathway Forward Foggy" and "Coyotes Bonds Approved by Progress Orthus - Concerned Citizens Silenced."

CHAPTER 32

"I can't believe he's stiffing the school board like this." Darrell paced around the Grady Middle School teacher's lounge, glancing back and forth at the president of the teacher's union "What's Flash thinking?" Stan's late arrival, requiring him to spend more time alone with her between classes, was working his last nerve. He'd probably forgotten Darrell had a lunch hour to patrol coming up in forty-five minutes. Though that likely wouldn't have made a difference to Stan anyway.

"You have every right to be upset, Darrell. He's doing this to spite you."

"To spite me? What's that supposed to mean, Angela?" He looked at her seated on the other side of four cafeteria tables shoved together, lit by rows of exposed fluorescent light.

She shook her head, like he was a fool for not knowing the answers himself. "You should've known he was out to get you when he started talking about pension reform."

"Yeah, but he's explained that to me before. He almost makes a good point."

"Now I'm losing confidence in you, too." Her small wiry frame twisted up in the seat. "If you think pension reform is good for Mother Union, you're on your way out."

"I didn't say I agreed with it. Hell, I can barely understand it. But lending the Coyotes all that money . . ." he said, trying to regain traction. "For Chrissakes, we could've bought fifty new high schools."

"You don't have to understand it, Darrell. He's making you look like a fool. He knows it, I know it, and your teachers know it. If you don't come around in the next ten minutes, I'll have you replaced."

Darrell chuckled. "You can't do that. I'm elected by my fellow teachers." Her support was critical to advance in the organization, but at the moment, he was counting on his inner-city Orlando popularity for leverage. "Plus, I'm about to shut him down." He pointed at Stan through the window as he entered the main building.

"Oh yea?" she asked, looking out to where he was pointing. "How are you going to do that?"

"Flash is elected, too. He needs me. If I'm not with him, he doesn't get elected."

She smiled. "Now you're getting it."

"If he thinks he can go make a deal with the Coyotes and Progress Orthus without consulting me, he's got another thing coming." He was building up his own momentum, knowing Stan was probably turning the corner at the principal's office.

"That's the DC I supported," she said. "Who would replace him if he didn't get elected?"

"I would," he answered before he had a chance to think about it.

"Would you?"

"Hell, yes, I would." Her question seemed more like a call to arms than doubt. "I can beat him. Do *you* think I can beat him?"

"Maybe. Are you fully committed to the teachers of Orthus County?"

"Sure, I am." And now he was.

"How committed? Are you willing to organize a strike or plan marches?"

"I guess so." Then he reminded himself he was in an impromptu interview. "Yes. Hell, yes!"

"Then maybe you could be superintendent, and maybe I'd be willing to help. Let's see how your dress rehearsal goes."

"Deal."

Stan climbed the front stairs of Grady High School. He passed an electrician working on the faulty circuit breakers. "Hey, brother. Found this in the parking lot. Maybe you need it."

"Sure, Flash. I need all the extra screwdrivers I can get."

"Don't electrocute yourself," he said after he handed it to him and then stood there for a moment, feigning an interest in the man's work. He was in no rush to answer DC's demand to see him.

The electrician stood up from his crouching position and reached out to shake Stan's hand. "What're you doing here?"

"Trying to keep Darrell in line," he said, returning the grip. "Thanks for keeping the lights on."

The electrician laughed and turned back to his work. "Good luck in there."

DC was pacing around the room when Stan walked in, and the teacher's union president, Angela Kirby, was tapping the end of her pen on the table.

"What the hell do you think you're doing?" DC blurted out.

Stan grinned. "Coming here for this meeting you requested."

"Don't act like you don't know what I'm talking about. You give the Coyotes six-hundred-and-fifty-million dollars. You trying to get rid of our pensions? Man, keep this shit up, and we'll see how next November goes."

Stan turned and smiled at Angela. She'd never been his favorite person, but most of politics was about spending time with people you didn't like too much.

"What are you smiling at?" she asked.

"Who do you think gave DC his nickname?" he asked.

"Dr. Jackson, you're treading on thin ice. You should take Darrell very seriously."

"You got my boy, DC, all riled up, Ms. Kirby. How long do you think DC and I have known each other?"

"How should I know? And why do you think I'd care?" Normally his stature and celebrity status were intimidating enough to remain unchallenged—at least until he got home at night—but Angela kept attacking. "You've been trying for years to screw the teachers out of their livelihood, so you obviously don't care what he thinks or who he represents. You might've known each other for years, but that doesn't make you friends."

DC was still pacing when Stan pulled out a chair right next to Angela, sat down, and looked her in the eye. "I've known DC long enough to know he won't ever go against me in an election." Her mouth opened. "What? You don't think I know how you operate? How long before I walked in here did you tell him he could be superintendent?"

DC stopped pacing, as Stan had expected, and sat down across the table from them. "Wait just a minute, Flash. She doesn't run me. I run me."

Stan turned to glare at Darrell. "Shut up, DC. I'll deal with you in a minute." Then he turned his attention back to Angela. "Now listen up, lady. You come down here from New York, you and all your Ivy League types, and tell my people . . ." He pointed at DC and raised his voice. "*My* people that I'm trying to rip them off, that I'm lying to them, and there's plenty of money to go around."

She pushed her chair back and stood up. “We only tell them what they can’t figure out for themselves.”

“You tell them what you need to tell them to keep yourself in power. Look around.” He leaned back in the office chair and waved his hands around, pointing at holes in the wall and water-stained ceiling tile. “There’s rats running through the gym and roaches in the cafeteria because we can’t afford exterminators. There’s an electrician out there right now that basically lives at the Grady cluster because these are the three oldest schools in the county.”

“You’re the one making the unprecedented power grab,” she said with her arms crossed, glancing back and forth at DC. “Pension reform is nothing more than a veiled attempt at staff reductions via tenure elimination.”

“You need to go back home. Ms. Kirby. You’re the problem. Now get the fuck out.” He leaned forward in his chair and put his elbows on the table while looking at Darrell. “I need to talk to DC. Alone.”

“This will all be over for you by Friday. You can’t kick me out of a public school, Stanley Jackson.”

“Sure, I can, but I won’t.” He paused for effect. “This is DC’s school. He’s going to do it.”

“You’re over-stepping your bounds, Dr. Jackson.” She looked at DC, obviously expecting him to come to her aid.

Stan tilted his head forward. “DC, deep down, do you believe her or me? Get her out of here, so we can talk.”

DC sat down. “Ma’am, I appreciate all the help you give us down here, but Flash and I need to talk.”

Stan never took his eyes off DC.

“Darrell, you do this, and you’ll never be superintendent,” Angela said.

“Flash is my superintendent. Now please excuse us so we can finish. I need to get back to work, because the lunch bell is going to ring in ten minutes.”

"I'll take you both down." She grabbed her purse and satchel from the chair. "I'm coming after you first, Stan Jackson."

"Good luck," Stan said. "Did you bring your paint and body guys with you this time?"

"I thought you'd like that. Expect more," she said before slamming the door behind her on her way out.

The room shook with the impact, and a package of crackers dropped in the vending machine.

"DC, what the fuck was that all about?"

"Sorry, man. She was talkin' all that shit."

"Look, I have to fix this. The bank accounts are empty and Orthus County is a sinking ship. You read the papers, right?"

"You going to try and tell me again you're out of money and we're going to go bankrupt like Orthus County?"

"I know you've heard this song and dance before, and I don't know what I've got to say to get you on board, but I'm changing the retirement plan."

"Fuck you, Flash. You just loaned a baseball team enough money to build a whole new school system. You must've gotten something for it. I'm not stupid."

"They're going to pay for the bond."

"Don't try that shit with me, Flash. You explained it pretty good' last Spring. We lose all the tax revenue."

"Like I said, what's it going to take to get you on board?"

"Now you're talkin'. What've you got to offer?"

"I'm getting two million dollars a year coming straight here to the Grady cluster. We can fix a lot of problems with money like that."

"That's nice. What about me?"

"You willing to work on a cleaning crew once the stadium is built?"

"What? You mean like push a broom and shit? I don't clean toilets, Flash. I damn sure ain't cleanin' the new stadium's."

"What about running crews that do?"

"I've already got a job."

"You don't have anything to do from June to September. The baseball season only runs from April to October."

"You know better than that, Flash. We start two-a-days in August and drill all summer. The last thing I need is a second job."

"What if it paid an extra fifty grand a year for six months of work? You can hire whoever you want."

"Who would I work for?"

"No one. You'll run all your operations through me. I've got the main contract. You'll subcontract to me."

"I guess that works. All under the table, right? I don't want to pay taxes on it."

"You running my campaign next year?"

"Damn right, I am."

"Then we'll pay you in cash, but you can't spend it on new clothes and cars, man. You can't tell anyone. I'll set your maintenance contract up on annual renewals just to make sure you don't step out of line again. Calling me out like that in front of that Yankee nut cookie. You ought to know better by now."

"Yeah. Sorry about that Flash." DC thumbed his nose.

"Cool. I've got to go. I'll see you Friday night at Grady versus Lochloosa. It's for all the marbles."

"Damn straight. We're going to kick their country ass."

After he left DC, Flash walked past Angela leaning against her car in the parking lot. "Hot out here, ain't it?" he said.

"Yeah, you fucking asshole." She flipped him the bird. "You pulled my door lock out, and gouged a scratch down the side of my car. I already called the cops."

"That's not my style, lady, but check the other side. I think I saw a flat tire, too. Maybe the cops will change it for you."

CHAPTER 33

Patrick strolled through the main showroom of McDaniel Salvatore and passed the elevated reception platform surrounded by the newest Salvatore Motors sedans. “Morning, Gloria.”

“Morning, Patrick.” Her smile had greeted him almost every day since he’d opened the dealership.

The General Manager’s office door was open. Patrick leaned in. “Morning.”

“Morning, Pat,” Stuart said. “You traveling the dealerships this week, or stuck here with us?”

“Stuck here with the best Salvatore dealership in the country. That OK with you guys?”

“Sure is. Hey, you got a minute?”

“Yeah. What’s up?” Patrick asked.

“The Salvatore CFO called twice about our late payments. We’re behind on months of accounts payable to them.”

“What? I set up a deferred payment plan last Christmas.”

“I know. She says we were ten days late last month.”

“Damn it. The summer’s been slow,” he said, yanking his hand off the doorframe. “Is Salvatore with us or not?”

“I don’t know,” Stuart said. “Would you call her, please?”

“Yeah, I’ll call.”

Patrick heard the laughter before he stepped into the kitchen. "Gentlemen, anybody hitting their marks yet for October, or is this just free coffee?"

"Patrick, it's a Salvatore. We hit our marks every month," the smug sales manager said.

"Good. That's what I wanted to hear, Carl."

Patrick headed to his office, with his coffee mug in his hand, when he heard Carl speak up again—quietly enough that he was sure he hadn't meant for Patrick to hear him. "We could sell a lot more if you got some Lux editions on the lot. Last year's sedans sell like used cars."

Patrick stepped into his office and closed the door to the roar of laughter. He shook his head and sat down behind the desk, where a note read, 'Call Sterling's lawyer'.

First things first, Patrick dialed Salvatore.

"Hey, Tanya. Is Sarah in?

"Sure. I'll get her."

The Salvatore CFO answered. "Good morning, Patrick."

"Hey, Sarah. Stuart asked me to call you."

"Good. I don't know how to say this, Patrick, but we set up your deferred payments last winter. You made a new contractual obligation to make a lower payment spread over more years because Bretto likes you, but I'm not paid to like people. I'm paid to keep Salvatore North America solvent. You're now eleven days late on your monthly payment."

"Sarah, we'll get you paid. Don't worry."

"Patrick, that's another thing I'm not paid to do: worry. You've got till the end of the week to make that payment. Are you capable of meeting your obligation?"

"Of course, I am. Should I be worried Salvatore Motors is going to take over my dealerships?"

"Although we have that power in our distribution contracts, yours might not be worth it."

"What do you mean?"

"Your debt to us is equal to the costs of the cars on your lot. How about we take possession of your inventory, and your debt free to Salvatore?"

"Our dealership is worth more than that."

"Patrick, we're done here. Make double the payment next month, or we'll let bankruptcy court decide how much your dealerships are worth. We'll get your cars first, take the loss on our books, and move on." The phone clicked in his ear.

He dialed Sterling's attorney.

"Good morning, this is Jenson Conner's office. May I help you?"

"Good morning, Megan. This is Patrick. Is Jenson in?"

"Sure. I'll put you right through."

"Hey, Patrick. Everything good? We need the fourth-quarter balance paid on Johnston Limited Lofts, LLC. Sterling isn't going to take your shares in exchange for mortgage payments any longer. You'll need to come clean or file."

"Things are great, Jenson," he said, leaning back in his chair and looking out the window. He imagined how good it would feel to pay off these parasites when the apartment slum was sold. "I don't know if Sterling told you, but we're close to selling the property. Progress Orthus is preparing a bond to buy it as part of the Coyotes Stadium deal."

"Yeah, he told me. But until closing, you have an existing capital call of a one hundred and fifty large.

"Aren't rents high enough to pay some of the debt?" Patrick had never looked at the financial statements of the apartment complex, because Sterling was so sure it could be sold.

"Renters? The residents who didn't move out because of the sandstorms blasting across the demolished car plant, we evicted.

That place should be condemned. Anyway, send your share in before Christmas, please. My escrow team would like some time off during the holidays."

"Like I said, Jenson. We'll close before then. Is there anything else you need?"

"Nope. That's it. Sterling says hello. Have a great week."

"Yeah, sure."

Patrick sent a few emails and walked around the showroom to shake off the constant reminder of the proverb about the borrower being a slave to the lender. When he got back he had a message from Salvatore Motors North America president on his voicemail, "Patrice, good morning. This-a Bretto. Can you call me? Salvatore North America has proposal for you." Bretto's friendly voice was the shot in the arm he needed. Getting a personal call from Bretto, next in line to replace his father as CEO, probably meant good things for Patrick.

A crisp Italian accent answered on Patrick's second ring, "Weila, this-a Bretto."

"Good morning, Bretto. This is Patrick down in Orlando."

"Weila, Patrice! How you doing in the South Florida sunshine?"

Patrick didn't mind the mispronunciation of his name because it was surely meant in kindness, or a translation error, but either way, Bretto had been calling him that for a couple of years. He answered, "Selling cars so we can ski the Alps at the annual meeting."

"Thats-a what I like to hear. Say, we have idea for you to see. We making some moves to make-a more money. What if you took over North Central Florida, but consolidated Ocala, Sanford, Gainesville and Orlando into one showroom?"

"Never thought about it," Patrick said, and was ashamed to admit it. "I didn't know we needed more stores north of here, but I guess it'd make sense if I had more territory."

"Sure, sure, Patrice. How could you know? That's-a why we want to first run by you. You have any land down there?"

Patrick paused, not believing his luck, and said, "Interesting you should ask, Bretto. I think I might have a couple of ideas. Can you come down?"

"I plan to be there in two days. Is that enough time, Patrice? Sorry for late notice, but I've many, how you say, pans in the fire."

"Whoa, two days? That is short notice. Are you flying into OSK?"

"Yes. Is that-a what you prefer? I can come later if this not good time."

"This is a great time." Patrick said, perhaps a little too eagerly. "I'll pick you up at OSK."

"That sounds-a good, Patrice. See you in two days. Ciao!"

Patrick and Bretto walked up the stairs of the indoor airplane hangar connected to the main terminal, and headed through to The Hangar, OSK's homecoming bar and restaurant, with the best hamburgers in town and martinis to match. Patrick tried to get a hostess's attention as bartenders delivered drinks and brought back empties for the Thursday night happy hour. Bretto gazed at the model airplanes hanging from the ceiling, and Patrick turned to the noise of a jet throttling up to full power, watching it through the large glass window overlooking the runway. After the plane left the ground, he turned back to see Bretto smiling at a waitress who was walking away. "The young girl is getting us a table."

The waitress came back quickly with menus and table settings, placed them near a window, and stuffed a hundred-dollar bill Bretto must have given her into her pocket. "Patrice, how come you sell so many cars but not so many as-a last year?"

"Like my sales people say, Bretto, 'It's a Salvatore'; they sell themselves. We're down a little, but only with the SUVs."

"Thats-a funny, but true. My father put the engine of a jet in the body of a Venus. We make fastest European production cars in history, and we're best-a selling European sedan in US of A. What kind-a pasta they got here, Patrice?"

"I don't know if Hangar Italian is what you want, but everything else is good," he said, hoping the talk of declining sales wasn't the reason he'd asked him here. The waiter came over to take their orders. Patrick handed him his closed menu. "I'll have the Jet Burger and a cold beer."

"And you, sir?" the waiter asked Bretto.

"I'll have-a what-a Patrice have. He's a lucky man."

The waiter thanked them and walked away. Bretto looked back up at the airplane models, but Patrick wanted to know what brought him down to Orlando with such a rush proposal. "So what's the new strategy, Bretto? You want to consolidate a couple of my lots? Anything else?"

The waiter brought over their beer and Bretto said, "We want to change our strategy a little bit." He held his forefinger and thumb close together. "We want to go back-a to small production lines, faster luxury sedans, and no more SUVs. SUVs too expensive to build. Good ol' US of A is-a going through big recession. Mommas not buying big-a trucks for bambinos anymore. We won't need as much real estate. That's OK with-a you, right?"

Some of the beer Patrick gulped almost came back up. "Um, sales might be down, but they're not out. SUVs are still a large component of revenue, Bretto. Salvatore isn't making any more, period? Like none?"

"How many SUVs you sell this year, Patrice?"

"Right at two hundred and fifty."

"You sold-a two hundred twenty-two. You-a, how you say, close enough for communist work. Guess how many you sold-a last year?"

"Around four hundred?"

"That's-a right. How many five-fifty sedans you sell?"

"You probably know that, too, but I'd say around six hundred.

"That's-a right, Patrice'. How many you sell last year?"

"Five hundred and fifty?"

"Right again. You sell less SUVs and more sedans. It's not your fault, Patrice. It's-a happening all over US of A. Salvatore is-a small and nimble. We Italian. We go where money go. We want you to move four dealerships into one. Since we won't make-a anymore SUV's, maybe you get a higher price for your inventory."

The lower-profit sedans wouldn't support his debt load, and he'd never considered not having SUV sales to prop up margins. "I'm assuming Salvatore would like to help support this move financially?"

"Of course-a we going to help you, Patrice. We don't leave you out in the cold. We help-a you, you help-a us."

Sterling approached the table. Patrick had alerted him to the possible architectural engagement, and assumed Sterling would reward him for the introduction. "Good afternoon, gentlemen."

"Hey, Sterling. This is Bretto Rossi, CEO of Salvatore Motors North America."

"Buongiorno, Bretto, and welcome. What brings you south? Aren't your headquarters in New Jersey?"

"Buongiorno, Sterling. It's-a very nice to meet you. Yes, I needed a break from Patrice's sales numbers flying across my desks. I needed to-a come see for myself."

"This would be a great place to expand your operations." Patrick envied Sterling's ability to connect to his audience.

"Very good, Sterling. I like-a your machismo. Florida has been good to Salvatore Motors. What-a you do?"

"I design buildings all over the world for magically successful people like you."

"Ah. Maybe this chance encounter Patrice set up good for both of us. Patrice and I looking for a building designer. Maybe he think you-a good fit for our image."

"I'll form your image in glass and steel, Bretto," Sterling continued, looking down at both of them.

Bretto laughed. "You, how you say, speak-a my language."

"Ok, then," Patrick said, trying to regain control of the conversation. "This might be too good to be true, but tomorrow we should ride up to Smithson. I'll pick you up in the morning and we can take a look at the property I had in mind. Sterling, can you join us?"

"Sure. I'll meet you there," Sterling said. "Around ten thirty?"

"Want to-a join us for a drink, Sterling?"

"I'd love to, but I still need to tie up some loose ends in the office downstairs."

"You have-a office at the airport?"

"It gives me the mobility I need for my projects nationally and internationally."

"You going to be an interesting architect to know. Nice to meet you, Sterling. Ciao!"

"Ciao, Bretto." Sterling shook his hand and left.

"Perfetto, Patrice! Let's drink-a more American beer and watch-a American football."

Patrick pulled the Salvatore SUV through the desolate parking lots of the abandoned apartment complex, boarded-up windows masking every building. Late fall weeds grew through the cracked concrete under the long Florida summer sun. Johnston Limited Lofts, LLC, was a wasteland of its owner's making. If Patrick had to split stadium concessions with Stan, this parcel would become a McDaniel Salvatore dealership. High school be damned.

"Patrice, this look-a like a war zone. What-a we doing here?"

"This is an apartment complex Sterling and I own together. The plan is to assemble it with the blank canvas in front of you."

"Your-a blank canvas looks like an airport with no buildings, Patrice." As he said it, a jet turned high in the sky after its ascension from OSK.

"That, Bretto, is the future home of the Orlando Coyotes. It will be the epitome of modern multi-use facilities."

"Perdono? What-a multi-use mean?"

"Bretto, you see before you the reason I brought you here. This war zone will connect to that future community that is now a white gravel desert. This is the perfect place for the new Salvatore Motors Sunshine Complex. Our new dealership on this lot will provide high-end luxury cars to the masses living, working, playing, and driving in that village. Think of the visibility being right next to a brand-new baseball stadium."

Patrick was relieved he had him alone in order to drive the conversation without Sterling's interference.

"Sunshine Complex? Patrice, now-a I know why you sell so many cars. You a visionary. Everything so new in US of A. Paint me a picture of your dream, fratello."

A cloud of dust rose from the far side of the vast emptiness. Sterling's Salvatore i575Lux approached from the rim road and then around to the Johnston Limited Lofts site where they stood. "Good morning, gentlemen," Sterling said as he climbed out of the car.

"Ah, Sterling. Buongiorno. That's-a my padre's favorite idea. I hope-a you like it, too. Why you come from way over there?"

"Bretto, this car is whisper-quiet power wrapped in velvet. Pure genius. Please pass those thoughts along to your padre'. I thought we were meeting on the site of the new stadium. Patrick, what are your thoughts?"

Patrick wasn't prepared for the glare coming from Sterling, and tried to remember if he'd set the meeting for the old Smithson Galleria site or the Johnston Limited Lofts site. "Good morning, Sterling. I was showing Bretto this view of the new Coyotes Stadium site."

Sterling's intensity softened into a smile. "Sure. What do you think of the site, Bretto?"

"I think either site is large enough for-a Salvatore Motors. How high can-a we build?"

"Elegant simplicity, Bretto." Sterling said. "I'm beginning to see where your magical success comes from; simple questions demanding simple answers. How high would you like?"

"Oh, none of our dealerships are higher than three or four stories," Patrick answered in an effort to remain relevant to the conversation. "Any fourth story is usually a facade."

"How about-a ten stories?"

"Brilliante, Bretto." Sterling said. "But it would need to be on the site where I was parked. This parcel isn't zoned for buildings that high."

The earth seemed to shift beneath Patrick's feet. "What dealerships are ten stories?"

"Oh?" Patrick noticed Bretto's eyes squint, and his temper seemed to heat up. He said softly, "You don't own any of-a the Coyotes land. Si?"

"Uh, si. Uh, no I don't."

"That's-a OK, Patrice." His tempo picked back up as quickly as it had slowed. "We still need a dealership on this-a lot, too. What about your-a, how you say, Salvatore Motors Sunshine Complex connect to our new corporate headquarters at the boundary?"

Patrick looked at Sterling, who was smiling at them both and seemed to have the answers Patrick was grasping for. "Corporate

Headquarters? Salvatore Motors is moving from New Jersey? This is the first I've heard about it."

"Bretto," Sterling jumped in. "We're on the same page. I'll design exactly what you want. Do you need to see anything else?"

"No. I have seen Patrice's vision and heard-a your ideas. I need no more. We get-a right to work on designs, no?"

"That's great, Bretto. This will be a wonderful new beginning for Salvatore." Patrick said.

Still looking for clarification of his financial life raft, Patrick asked, "Both facilities, right?"

"Si. You OK, Patrice? You look-a pale."

"He's fine," Sterling said. "Society should build schools with Patrick's passion. Maybe somebody will, but it won't be on this lot."

"I like-a schools. Maybe Salvatore becomes a, how you say, a charity?"

"A not-for-profit?" Patrick asked, glad they were already talking past the deal they'd just made.

"Not-for-profit," Bretto said. "What's a not for profit?"

"It's another name for a charity," Patrick replied, even happier he might be of some tax assistance to Bretto.

"No. It's-a bankrupt." Bretto laughed out loud. "That's-a funny, no? Sterling, you know-a what I mean, si?"

"Of course, Bretto. That's very funny. Let's go get some lunch."

"Ah, Sterling. You-a, how you say, put-a you money where-a you mouth is. For my padre, can I ride-a with you?"

Patrick watched as Bretto followed Sterling to his car. "My pleasure," Sterling said. "Would you like to drive?"

After Bretto closed the driver's-side door, but before Sterling had opened his, Patrick caught his intense glare. "Follow us, Patrice," Sterling said with a grin, and then opened the passenger door after Bretto cranked the car and revved the motor.

CHAPTER 34

Jim's coverage of the undefeated Grady High School Panthers had been much the same as last year. They marched through another record-breaking season under the tutelage of an army of Panther parents and supporters, led by Florida Gator All-SEC linebacker, Darrell Cross, with only one district rival left to dismantle before entering the state-championship bracket for a repeat performance of last year's mauling. His hometown Bulldogs of Lochloosa struggled early in the season with a quarterback change, but stood with a record of eight wins and one loss. The new sophomore quarterback, Jamal Kendrick, was faster than any player since his brother, John, to play in a Bulldog uniform, but only time would tell if he was tougher. While Grady exuded the confidence of a defending state championship during their warm-ups, Lochloosa was witnessing the rebirth of its program. The Bulldogs stunning string of five upsets leading up to tonight's game dictated that tonight's winner would represent Orthus County in the playoffs.

Matt and Beth had made the hour-long trip south to Grady Field on the request of Jim and his wife, Rebecca, to come to the inner city to watch football. Jim didn't have to twist Matt's arm too much because of the high-stakes reward both teams sought, even if he'd had to promise Beth there'd be enough police officers to patrol the perimeter parking lots of the event. He was certain they both needed a break from the teachers' strike rumors, and Beth's looming retirement neither of them ever mentioned.

Once they got past the ticket counter, Jim said, "I'll meet you guys in the visitors' section after I get us some drinks and peanuts." Then he and Rebecca peeled away to the concession stand as he shouted back, "I think someone you might know saved you a seat."

Matt's face relaxed as he stepped onto the edge of the turf, the stiff green grass in the end zone begging him to get back in the game, the second guessing getting worse every fall as his bones ached a little more than the year before. The song of cicadas high above the stadium lights, and the crackling sound-checks coming from the press box, provided the backdrop of the only career he'd regretted leaving. Beth came to his side and put her arm around his waist and her head on his shoulder. "I thought we were thinking about our retirement years," she said.

He put his arm around her shoulder and kissed her on the check. "Yeah, yeah, our guaranteed retirement is going to be guaranteed boring unless we find something to do when the fish aren't biting." He thanked God she still laughed at him after thirty-five years of marriage. They walked around the running track, making brief hellos to the Lochloosa faithful.

One of the old-guard parents came up beside him. "Should be a good one, Coach Pinson," he said "What do you think of our chances?"

"Grady's always been fast," Matt said. "But we have speed we haven't seen yet, and Coach Manning's got us peaking at the right time; the fewest mistakes wins."

Grill smoke wafted over the warm autumn night, the full moon high overhead. "This atmosphere is electric," Beth said before abruptly breaking away from him on about the fifty-yard line. "Oh my goodness. It's Ezzy."

Ezzy was waving from the bleachers on the far ten-yard line. She had placed herself out of the main noise, because she wanted Matt and Beth's undivided attention when discussing King Christian Academy's upcoming growth. They took their seats next to her with broad smiles.

"It's been so long, Ezzy," Beth said. "How are you? Tell me everything."

"I couldn't be better, and seeing you two reminds me of all the good in my life. Go Bulldogs!"

"You got that right," Matt said. "Go Bulldogs! By the way, Ezzy. I talked to your dad last week about some welding problems they were having on the new irrigation systems in the groves outside Fort Myers. He's real proud of you. All he could talk about was King Christian Academy."

"The students are responding to our strategy, Matt, but we didn't know how fast it would grow, or the challenges it would bring." She allowed her voice to rise with excitement. "Or how to meet those challenges, but we're learning fast."

Beth leaned in. "The way you're inspiring those children is a blessing for us all."

Ezzy looked up and threw a fake punch at Jim when he and Rebecca arrived at end of the row with cardboard trays full of concessions. Ezzy smiled at Rebecca laughing at Jim, who almost spilled his tray. "Dang it, Ezzy. I'm a grown man." Ezzy, still chuckling, took one of his trays and passed it over to Matt and Beth, and made room for Jim to sit next to her so they could share information without blocking Rebecca's view. "Thank goodness I didn't spill these drinks, but did I bring enough cokes for all of us?" He asked with a wink. "Am I missing one?"

She counted five in the both trays, still wondering why he'd winked. She looked up at Matt, who was watching the players take the field, and then saw Beth looking at her hand. Beth crossed her hands over her heart before grabbing Ezzy's hands. "Oh my goodness, Ezzy, your engagement ring. It's so beautiful. Oh, how wonderful. When and how?"

Ezzy was still trying to get used to the questions, but was more than happy to answer. "He's over there in the end zone with some of the off-duty guys." She tossed a look that way. "They do seem to have a lot of fun." She caught Bill's eyes and he tipped his hat before a smile spread across her face.

"Congrats to both of you," Matt said. "But Lochloosa lost the toss, so we get to watch Jamal right away, if that makes any difference to you ladies."

Rebecca leaned over. "Give the lady her moment, Coach, but thanks for the update. Ezzy, can I see your ring?"

Ezzy wiggled her fingers over Jim's nacho tray. "What do you think?" she asked Rebecca.

Rebecca shook her head. "I love it. You two are like Lochloosa royalty." The thud of toe meeting leather that sent the football flying out of the end-zone turned their attention to the deep receiver as the sophomore QB loped out to the twenty-yard line to form the huddle and start Lochloosa's drive.

"When is the wedding? How far along are the preparations?" Beth asked.

"Beth, you're so kind, but we're planning a small affair. Bill and I are past the wedding parties and the rehearsal dinners. We might take a cruise or something." She thought of Scott's text last week joking he was going to buy a second boat with his gain, and then chided her to peek at Dunham Schauble's dropping stock, widely attributed to the recession.

"We're so happy for you both. Such wonderful news," Beth said.

"That is really fantastic, Ezzy," Matt said, turning away from the action for a moment. "Bill seems just your type, strong as a bull with the head to match."

"Oh, stop, Matt." Beth nudged him.

"Jep said you all were doing so well that next year you'd take overnight students."

Beth gave Ezzy the classic Mrs. Pinson raised eyebrow. "Is that true, Ezzy? Is your idea an evolving success?"

"Yes, Beth, thanks for noticing. I've tried to fashion our culture around models of success I've seen in my life. Clear guidelines coupled with accountability and reward, incredible teachers, and warm, productive learning environments. I'm having the time of my life, but it's growing so fast."

"We watch the news. You're adding football?" Matt asked. "Have you been able to fill a team? Your track and field squad seems like a pretty good group. I see their names on Jim's website all the time. Your golfers probably aren't begging for it, though, huh?"

"You'd be surprised. My golfers are my biggest football advocates. They play golf because they can't play football. We made it to state last year and came in third. But we competed against the best and gave ourselves a chance to win in the end. That's all we ask of them: compete, get in the game. Just like you taught us kids in the grove, Coach."

Jim interrupted, his thumb to his mouth like a microphone. "The Bulldogs are on the ten. Jamal Hendricks takes the hike, reverses in motion to a passing running back. He fakes the hand off, bolts to the sideline and . . ." Ezzy rose to her feet. ". . . cuts up to score."

She high-fived all of them while the crowd erupted into a long breath of "Jaaaaaa-MAL."

"Touchdown Bulldogs!" Matt yelled. "That's what I'm talking about. That kid's got some wheels!" The extra point sailed through the uprights.

"There're four Lochloosa players on the field right now that live within minutes of KCA," she said to Matt. "Jamal's sister has been at KCA since the start. She's our star tennis player."

"Have you scheduled any games?" Matt asked.

"King Christian Academy has embarked on the next phase of our five-year plan," she said, feeling the kind of satisfaction you can only feel bragging to family. "It was never our goal to become a boarding school. We simply wanted to meet the needs of the locals King Citrus left behind, but we're the ones who receive the blessing. Sixty-five percent of our kids are going to college. Forty percent of our college-bound students were given scholarships. Our campus drapes over one of the most historic and beautiful places in Florida, and enrollment applications are coming in from all over the country. King Christian Academy should accommodate outside demand the only way we know how: with the welcome embrace of the future."

She exhaled, hearing the crowd grumble about a Grady field goal that occurred. The scoreboard read 7-3, but Matt, Beth, Jim, and Rebecca were focused on her. "Now to the point. We'll admit boarding school enrollees next year, adding hundreds of kids per class from K through twelve. Their accommodations are already under construction and they'll be completed by spring, in time for the alumni reunion next August."

"Ezzy, this is so exciting. How're you going to handle the new workload?" Beth asked. "Where will you find teachers?"

"As usual, you've pinpointed our largest challenge. Out-of-state boarding school enrollees bring with them a demand for Language Arts, French, and Spanish. We're expanding KCA to include new classrooms, an auditorium for speeches and debate, production studios, and a theatre. I'm searching now for my new Language Arts Executive Vice President."

"Every great school needs those programs. Communication is the vector for creative thinking," Beth said with the demeanor of a seasoned professional educator. "I can't wait to see it."

"I'd like to take you on a personal tour next weekend if you have time. I'd love to get your ideas about improvements we could make to the facility."

"That would be magnificent. I hope I don't fall in love with it, or I won't be able to leave."

"That's my goal, Beth. I'd like you to manage the first group of programs. Make it yours. Put your stamp on it."

Beth's gaze widened like a deer in the headlights on the long Central Florida highway. "Oh! Oh, my goodness, Ezzy. I . . . I can't. I'm retiring next year."

Matt laughed out loud. "Retiring? To do what? Come home and watch me sell bait?"

"You know what I mean, Matt. You've always wanted to travel. Now we can."

"Honey, all I need is to see your face every morning. It doesn't matter where I am. Lochloosa's as good a place as any."

"Matt, are you sure about that?" Beth asked. "Ezzy, we'll have to think about it together, but I definitely want a tour. Oh, my, I just can't get over it. That's such a gracious offer."

Ezzy watched the game for a few series to allow them to digest her offer, because she had more to say, and the delivery needed to be perfect. Watching Lochloosa defend the Grady offense reminded her of fire ants devouring beetles. She stood and cheered when they intercepted another Grady pass across the middle. For the next few Bulldogs offensive plays, she couldn't follow the backfield action, and neither could the Grady defense. She measured Lochloosa's Coach Manning, whom she'd considered for coaching duties, when he jogged to the 30-yard hash mark following a blatant but missed personal foul committed by a struggling Grady defensive lineman unable to contain Jamal.

The concrete slabs of the visitors' section vibrated with the foot-stomping chant of the crowd, "Hur-ley, Hur-ley, Hur-ley." She'd heard the talk—that the LHS QB Club was sick of the dry spell, that the losses to not only Grady, but also to lesser teams with no tradition, had the town in a sports funk. His choreographed frustration erupting, he ripped through the young referee, no doubt reminding him of how high the stakes were and how missed infractions cost games. He turned back to the sideline, barking as he walked away, and Ezzy cheered when Lochloosa ran for a first down from fourth and inches.

Matt pumped his fist in the air and turned to her. "That man has a will to succeed I've never seen in anyone else. Players run through brick walls for him. I don't guess you know, but Hurley was the offensive mastermind behind my championships. I can hear him now: 'Every defense from Miami to Milton knows what we'll do. We'll work harder than them. We'll beat them in the spring. We'll beat them in the summer, and we'll beat them in the fall.' KCA could use a guy like Hurley."

"Indeed," Ezzy said, smiling. "I promised the juniors I'd let them play senior football if they stuck with us. Well, they did, and it's payback time. Trouble is, I have absolutely no idea how to start a football team from scratch. The golf, track, and baseball coaches are all willing to help, but they have their hands full with their sports and class load." She paused and glanced at Jim.

Jim leaned back and raised his hands. "I know where you're going with this, Ezzy. No need to look at me for support. If mom and dad are happy, so am I."

Ezzy turned back to Matt. "They all said I should ask you."

Beth looked at Matt, and Ezzy saw her eyes soften and water. With a steely grin both of his sons inherited, he replied, "What did you tell them?"

"That they deserved an A for their humility and a raise for their advice. Monday morning, they'll all be waiting to find out what you say."

Matt glanced at Beth's smiling face. "Is that stadium we saw on the news ready?" he asked.

"The coaches said you'd ask. We're putting the finishing touches on the scoreboards and locker rooms now. The coaches said if you're in, they'll do it, but they asked if they could have the spring off to turkey hunt."

"They'll give up spring gobblers for spring training. They always do."

She wanted them both to want it. "I'll make it worth their while. Yours too."

"Your athletics department is rolling pretty good now. Why me?"

"Because you'll start the culture I'm looking for. It's the culture you and Beth taught all of us. I want it imprinted on my program."

"Your football staff is the best assistant staff in the state. They've got more experience than FSU and Florida combined."

"That's on purpose, Matt, but we need you to put it all together."

"Would I be able to play Lochloosa? Or Grady?" he asked, pointing his thumb at both sidelines. "If we're not playing the best, we're not challenging the team, and that's no good for the players." Lochloosa was platooning a stable of running backs to compliment the young quarterback, allowing the hallmark Lochloosa run-offense to demoralize the Grady defense.

She'd hoped Stan had taken her seriously when she'd asked during his tour months ago, but took him at his word and replied, "I'm working on it, but I think it can happen."

"That's a lot, Ezzy, and I'm honored. But I don't know. Like Beth said, we'll have to talk about it."

She waited for him to look at Beth and then look back at her before she continued. "Jamal's sister said he's very interested in KCA. If he comes, the other three will come with him. The coaches tell me those four, and the out-of-state kids, would form unstoppable chemistry with you at the helm. While you think about it, can I count on both of you for a tour?"

"We wouldn't miss it for the world, Ezzy." Beth spoke for both of them, and hugged Matt. "We'll be there. Thank you for thinking so highly of us."

"Oh, we'll be there alright," Matt agreed.

Jim finished a bag of peanuts with Rebecca. "Mom's got some leverage, but dad, you should take the job before Coach Manning wins this game."

The Bulldogs drove for another score, and led fourteen to three at half time. Both teams ran into the locker room past where Bill was standing, and he broke away from the other officers in the end zone and headed in her direction.

"How's everyone tonight?" he asked, leaning his long arms through the bottom rung of the bleacher railing.

"We're good, but we're Bulldog fans, so it comes with the territory. Who you rooting for Sheriff?" Matt asked.

Bill reached into his jacket. "Does this Bulldogs hat tell you anything? But only if we win."

"Don't let him fool you," Ezzy said. "He's got a Grady hat on the other side of his jacket." The night sky filled with bands playing fight songs, and giant moths hovering above the field, their transparent wings glowing from the stadium light.

"Congratulations, Sheriff," Beth said. "You both deserve all the happiness in the world."

"Beth, there's no doubt I outkicked my coverage. I'm lucky to get a girl like Ezzy, and I'm going to try and make her very happy."

"We'll see about that," Matt said. "Pretty tall order."

"Easy does it, gentlemen," Rebecca said. "She's sitting right here."

"Thank you, Rebecca." Ezzy smiled.

"Who came up with Bulldogs, anyway?" Bill asked. "Why not Gators or Ospreys or something?"

Ezzy responded with Bulldog pride, "That might be the best story in Orthus County."

"Oh?" Bill said. "Any story you're telling, I want to hear, Ms. King."

"Lochloosa is unincorporated Orthus County. We used to be North Orthus County High School." She spoke past the tongue twister from decades of repetition. "We had to vote on a mascot back when we were in high school, because we were the first class to have sports."

Ezzy saw Jim and Rebecca smiling at one another, but stayed in rhythm, "Our local LHS Teacher of the Year, Beth Pinson, offered a solution." She looked at Beth. "This is your story to tell."

"Oh, Ezzy!" she laughed warmly. "Must you always put me on the spot?"

"It's my favorite story, too, Mom," Jim said.

Beth took a deep breath. "Bill, Orthus County was named after Florida pioneer, Tobias Orthus, from the 1860s. Conscription was the best way for the Confederates to get North Florida males into the Civil War. Being a pragmatic man, Tobias decided the Seminole adults were more reasonable than conscription patrols. They both had the tenuous relationship of a common enemy and travelled south in parallel journeys necessitated by survival. Seminole children could attack Tobias's chicken coops and cows, but they couldn't throw him in the stockade."

Bill turned his arms hanging through the railing over with his palms facing upward. “Finally, someone who can tell the real Seminole story. For crying out loud, we're reasonable people.” Ezzy loved his easy way around her local family.

“Well, Bill. Tobias Orthus's last name happens to coincide with Greek mythology. Orthus, or more correctly, Orthrus, translates to two-headed beast, or dog, so I offered our students a traditional mascot, with a unique connection to our past. The kids loved the Greek mythology theme, and we all agreed. ‘Bulldogs’ would carry Orthus County's past into Lochloosa's future.” Ezzy waited for Beth's concession she always saved for last. “Unfortunately, the story of Orthrus often ends in suicide. Both heads kill the body while competing for food, but that didn't matter to the kids.”

“If Tobias wasn't Greek, what was he?” Bill asked.

“Maybe English,” Beth replied, “having started his journey from cattle farms in North Florida.”

“Probably French,” Matt said as the teams took to the field again. “He was running from a war, you know.”

Jim turned to the group and recited his mom's favorite slogan, “Good teachers broaden our horizons,” and Ezzy smiled in the fall night air.

The Lochloosa band took its place back in the bleachers, and Bill took his place over at the end zone. As he walked away, he motioned to Ezzy like a schoolboy with his thumb against his ear, and his pinky near his face. “I'll call you after the game?”

Her heart leapt as though she were sixteen again. God, but it was good to be in love with that man.

Grady received the opening kickoff and ran it out to the thirty. For any chance in the second half, the Lochloosa defense had to play their best game.

Jim nudged her. “I talked to Paige.”

"And what did she find? Did she get the memorandums of understanding and the bond documents I gave you?"

"Yeah, I gave them to her. Patrick's face was priceless when you dropped them on the floor in front of me, but Ezzy, it's more than we thought."

"Oh, no. What has Bob done?"

Matt stood up from the bleachers. "Catch it, Catch it. Interception! Run, run," he shouted as the Lochloosa defensive back tucked the ball away, and swerved past Grady offensive lineman and the quarterback, streaking down the side-line. "Fifty-yard Pick Six! We're rolling." She cupped her ear to hear, but the visitors' section was pandemonium after the successful extra-point try, and the Bulldogs led, twenty-one to three.

Below the roar, Jim said, "It's not just Bob. He and Patrick have the exclusive rights to sell jet fuel at OSK for the blind pool they created for the hospital and the airport."

"I knew that the first day my pilot bought gas for my plane. I asked Donald, the airport operator, why so high, and he said 'cost of doing business,' which told me everything I needed to know."

Jim leaned into her ear. "He also got a condo in St. Pete. Did you know Sterling and Patrick own land adjacent to Smithson Galleria? Patrick, Sterling, and the president of Salvatore Motors, Bretto Rossi, met out there last week. We went to high school with the motor-grader operator that keeps the site level."

"That explains a lot. I wonder if Patrick drove away the insurance companies for the new Coyotes Stadium, or if they backed out on their own."

"Who knows?" Jim said, "Maybe a little of both."

The game continued back and forth, until Grady scored the next touchdown on a long drive. 21-10.

Jim leaned toward her again. "I think Sterling is hanging Patrick out to dry. They've owned the property together for a couple of years now. Most of the tenants left as soon as our man graded the site. The wind and dust off the site blows right onto their low-income apartment complex. Even poor people have options way out in Smithson. That is, until Progress Orthus drives them all out."

"I'm so glad to be done with them," Ezzy said, embarrassed she hadn't figured out their schemes sooner, and hoping she'd left early enough to avoid the public blowback.

"What I can't figure out is why Sterling and Patrick seem like friends. He's probably calling Patrick about mortgage payments that aren't being made from lost rental income, don't you think?"

"Jim, I guarantee you Sterling is not making those calls. His lawyers are. When Sterling meets with Patrick, he probably doesn't even mention it. A tiny apartment complex like that is nothing but a pawn in a larger maneuver. He's probably forgotten Patrick is his partner, and wouldn't care if he hasn't. Sterling Johnston is ruthless."

"They pressured Stan Jackson to get the school board's loan. I get the feeling they're offering him more perks than a new office building."

"Are you close to finding out what it is?"

"I'm always close, Ezzy. These politicians have been doing these shady deals so long they get sloppy. What do you think about the Dunham Schauble letter-of-intent-to-review from the SEC?"

"What?"

"This morning's market news reports. You didn't see it?"

"No. I'm running a school, but that would explain the falling stock price. What happened?"

"After your outburst at the Progress Orthus meeting—"

"Outburst?" she interrupted. "Jim, I'll not sit by and do nothing while Patrick continues to profit, handsomely I might add, by votes he's making with no accountability to us. I assume you pay taxes?!"

"Yes, Ezzy. I pay taxes. I didn't mean to—"

"I gave them park land with solid commitments it would be left that way in perpetuity, and now MOTrax is going to use it as apartment-complex parking. I've discovered to oppose is to dishonor his altar of progress led by the battle cry of "highest and best use'."

"I know. I know," Jim said.

Ezzy lowered her voice when Rebecca glanced over. She hadn't meant to cause a scene. "Jim, do you think financing a baseball stadium, and a new city downtown district, in the middle of a recession is a good idea? This is dangerous stuff. Wall Street firms will send their best lawyers down here to camp out for months, attacking the County Commission at every chance, all in the name of protecting their shareholder's rights. We, the voters, will temporarily lose control of our surroundings."

"Not in Lochloosa," he said, looking out at the football game. "No one controls that place."

Ezzy didn't smile, but asked, "So Dunham Schauble got a SEC letter-of-intent. Did the news say why?

"Some kind of shady stuff in Chicago."

"Half those letters of intent-to-review are bullying tactics by the SEC, but they have the force of law. It might be nothing, but I'll talk to Paige about it. I'm meeting with her next week to discuss my years at Progress Orthus."

"You should've seen Patrick's face while he was banging that gavel," Jim said, laughing.

"I did, dope. You put the video on the *Post*, and thanks for not zooming in on my face again. Nobody likes a stalker, Jim."

"Sure, whatever. I talked to Paige this morning after the Dunham Schauble news broke."

"What did she say? I know someone who's been tracking Dunham Schauble for a while. He's taken a heavy short position on their stock."

"She said the math for Orthus bonds doesn't add up. There's a couple hundred million not accounted for. Paige spoke to one of her law school classmates in Chicago who did a little digging. The same thing is happening up there. I'm out of my depth with finance, but she said blind pools allow for overfunding, but there's no requirement for escrow at the custodian bank, or in this case, Dunham Schauble,"

Ezzy turned to him. "And half of Progress Orthus bonds aren't rated. Sometimes municipalities don't rate their bonds, because the insurance is too expensive to tell Wall Street what they already know."

"What's that?"

"That they're junk. It's like excluding your grade point average on your resume if it's too low."

"I told you I was out of my depth."

"Maybe Paige thinks Dunham Schauble is using the over-funded bond as its own personal bank loan."

"Is that possible?"

"I guess. How well do you know Enzo Ruiz?"

"That snake charmer is way out of my league, too," Jim said, shrugging his shoulders. "Other than giving him fashion advice at the meetings, we don't talk."

"All you Lochloosa guys are the same. Walking around, acting like you're going to kick everyone's ass."

"C'mon, Ezzy. He wears pinstriped suits."

"What's wrong with that?"

"Every day?"

"I see your point," she laughed and pointed her finger at him. "You just need to behave around adults, Jim. You've got some credibility now. Don't screw this thing up you've created."

"What? The *Post*? Or my skills in international brand campaigns."

Rebecca chimed in. "Both," she said. "We've got our future to think about."

"Good advice," he said, laughing. "I've already started on King Sodas. It's in Mandarin and Spanish."

"How did you know about that?" Ezzy asked, slightly concerned a media outlet had information about her family's publicly traded company, but relieved when Jim winked at her.

"No one covers Orthus County like the *Post,*" he said. "But your secret's safe with me. When do you want to see the slogans?"

The crowd shouted, "Five, four, three, two, one!" The visitors' side erupted into cheers with toilet paper rocketing out of the bleachers and students storming the field. Over in the end zone, she saw Bill put on a KCA Saints hat.

Orthus County Post headlines the next day read, "Lochloosa Back on Track - Runs over Grady."

CHAPTER 35

The Private Investigator read his text message from Bill. Sugar Daddy is on a plane to Chicago. Proceed to Tampa to apprehend target. Meet at the Don.

Kirsty stepped out onto the sidewalk in front of the Dunham Schauble high rise in the mid-morning Tampa sunshine on a bustling Thursday morning. Crisper autumn days allowed her to get away with more style than the promotional volleyball-court bikinis sports agents begged her to wear. She strutted across the street for coffee in her best thigh-length man-stopper she wore when Enzo travelled, her thigh-high suede boots providing the only warmth from the tropical fall breeze. When the sole of her foot landed on the curb in front of the retail windows, she looked down, swept her hair out of her eyes, and soaked in the morning stares. She thought of the never-ending surfing circuit and her odds of still being on top if she'd stayed in a few more years. The ultra-competitive tournament schedule and lurking wave wolves made the Dunham Schauble experiment much easier to swallow. Because Enzo hadn't given Kirsty any trading authority, or training, she spent more time out of the office when he travelled. There was no money to build out the new computer system either, but the dresses and jewelry he bought her kept her in the hunt for a more permanent situation.

She walked into the coffee shop, put her laptop down, and parted the crowd in front of the glass pastry case. “The usual, Ms. McPhee?” the barista asked.

“That’s right, mate. Coffee du jour, black, with enough room for a cowboy on top.”

After she creamed her coffee in the extra room provided in the cup, she sat back down and saw a note taped to the laptop: “Answer your next phone call unless you want to get deported to Melbourne.”

She looked around and caught two businessmen still in line checking her out, but no one with any seemingly bad intentions. Her phone rang and she answered without saying anything.

“Good morning, Kirsty,” the voice on the other end said.

She lowered her voice, and smiled into the phone. “Who is this, puffer? I’ll live wherever I please. What do you want? Leaving anonymous notes on my laptop is not a good way to start a conversation.”

“I’m doing you a favor.”

“I’m about to hang up.”

“Dunham Schauble is in trouble, big trouble. I can show you a way out,” he said before she had a chance to do it.

“Who is this?”

“I represent the Orthus County Sheriff’s Department and District Attorney Paige Jackson. You can meet me in the parking lot, or in Mrs. Jackson’s office under a subpoena. For the next few seconds, it’s your call. After that, it’s ours.”

“Where?”

“I’m in the black Crown Victoria. Orthus County Sheriff’s plates on the back. Get in. We’ll take a ride.”

“Pull away from the coffee shop and pull into the gas station next door.”

"Why? You don't want to risk being seen with a cop?"

She ignored his question. "Have your badge ready, or I'll scream bloody murder."

"Fine. See you across the street."

Once she'd crossed the street, she located the car. The driver—a middle-aged man with thinning blond hair—held out a badge where she could see it, and she climbed in, carefully putting her laptop in the seat pocket. She tugged her dress back down as she closed the door and shifted in the seat. "What do you want with me?" she asked as she turned to face him. "I'm a busy lady."

"Yes, you are."

He pulled the car out of the gas station, and she held out her hand for the badge he'd already returned to the visor. "Let me see that thing," she said.

He handed it to her. "Take a long look. We're in the car about thirty minutes. That OK with you?" She jerked a little when he gunned the car out into traffic without waiting for her to agree.

"What about Dunham Schauble, Officer Staton?" she asked. "I'm working the trading desk today."

"I think you can take a day off since Enzo's in Chicago, don't you?"

"Depends on who's asking and why." She said as she brought one of her boots back enough for suede to dip below her knee. A flash of her leg was usually all it took. But this guy wasn't taking the bait. She opened her clutch and pulled out a cigarette. "Where're we going?"

She lit it and cracked the window, blowing the smoke toward the window's gusty edge. He reached across her and took the cigarette out of her hand before crushing it in the ashtray. "Anyone ever tell you it's rude to light up in someone else's car? And we're going to the Don Cesar. Private room," he said. "District Attorney Jackson has come to you, but you should be respectful. She's friendly, but don't cross her. I wanted to transport you back to Orlando in a squad car, but they want to help you. I guess that means you have some redeeming value."

"Cops make everyone nervous. The cigarette was just to take the edge off a bit." She adjusted her knee again. Still, he didn't give her a second look. She sighed. "What kind of trouble?"

"Pardon?"

"On the phone. You said Dunham Schauble was in trouble."

"You know Bob Drolland?"

"I've met him."

"You ever been to his condo on St. Pete Beach?"

"Maybe."

"Do you have any access to Dunham Schauble financial records?"

"You ask a lot of questions." They crested the mid-point of the Howard Franklin Bridge. "Drive faster. You're a cop, right? I need to get back."

"I guess you're used to Dunham Schauble cars on the track and Enzo's driving. The speed limit's sixty-five, but don't worry, you'll be back soon enough to get all your work done—the work you do anyway."

"Don't kid yourself. Our computer system is a five-year-old dinosaur. I'm the only one that can pinpoint the bottlenecks, because I have to do it every day, so at least pass all these blue hairs. If one of those bond traders downloads a virus from a porn site, I'm getting a call."

"I thought you said you worked on the trading desk," he said.

Her spine tensed. His lack of interest was throwing her off her game. "In my spare time. I went to Harvard, remember. Did you read my file?"

"I created your file. You also surfed every pipeline from Perth to J Bay. Are you aware of the legal limits on bribery and what impacts they can have on perpetrators?"

Instinctively, she reached for another cigarette.

"I'll throw that one away, too," he said, nodding toward the pack she'd taken out. "It's illegal for elected officials in America to accept gifts, or assets, exceeding one hundred dollars in value. It's the same in Australia, just in case you were wondering. District Attorney Jackson is about to close the net on all this bullshit."

"So?" She asked. "I just build software. What's any of that got to do with me?"

"You're a non-resident working with a temporary visa at a company that is going to experience a very rocky year. Maybe they're not around next summer. You need a landing strip."

She turned to him and grinned a half-smile, revealing the dimples that would throw most men off balance. "Maybe I do, maybe I don't."

He laughed, and she felt the heat of her thwarted efforts rise up in her face. "Girls that go to Harvard, the ones I know anyway, usually end up lurking around the information systems at their new jobs," he said. "Maybe you're not as inquisitive?"

She ran her fingers through her hair to straighten it, and tugged her skirt down again. "I know my way around the cloud."

"Thought so. What's Enzo doing in the Chicago offices?"

"Underwriting bonds. That's what we do, but it must not be in the file?"

"The squad car would have been much better suited for you. Whose bonds this week, *mate*?"

"Chicago needs a lot. Philadelphia is streaky, but consistent. Metro Atlanta is a hotbed of different municipal debt, and we're competing in San Francisco. But Enzo put an office near his alma mater and Sterling's headquarters so we could start a sailboat racing team.

"Any of those clients get beach condos? Or better?"

"My answers are the same. It depends on whose asking."

"Have you been in any meetings regarding the Securities and Exchange Commission inquiry?"

"No, but I know what the SEC wants to know."

"The market is crushing your stock price from that intent-to-review letter. What do you think that means?"

"The market doesn't know half of what I know. When is someone going to make me an offer?"

"We're almost there, Ms. McPhee. You'll get your offer."

Kirsty saw the head valet before he saw her. When the Crown Vic pulled up, the valet hurried to the car door, opened it, and waved his hand around him toward the entrance like a butler. "How is the overhand serve, Kirsty?"

"Get out with me on Saturdays and find out, Joey," she said as she climbed out. "You boys doing ok?"

"Never better," he called out over the car as he waited on Officer Staton to vacate the seat behind the wheel.

"I got it, kid. We're parking my car right here." He flipped the badge as Joey backed away from the car and Officer Staton pulled forward up onto the curb.

She followed the PI through the lobby to a set of double doors he at least had the decency to hold open for her. They entered a room filled with empty chairs around small tables. Three chairs were arranged together next to a large resort window she'd seen from the beach, but never from the inside. A tall woman in a business suit who'd been looking out the window turned and smiled, her hand extended. "It's very nice to meet such an aspiring and gifted talent, Ms. McPhee. I'm District Attorney Paige Jackson."

Kirsty tossed her hair to one side and smiled a nervous smile, but didn't extend her hand, in honor of the forced transportation. "I'm extremely nervous about this entire meeting. Your man here practically tried to get my clothes off all the way here. What is it you want from me?"

"You should've let me haul her to Orlando in the squad car, Paige. A long hot ride works wonders on attitude. I warned you,

Kirsty. This is a one-time opportunity," the PI said as he took a seat near the window.

Paige gently rested her hand on Kirsty's forearm. "All of our cars have video cameras, so rest assured that if Officer Staton was inappropriate at any point, we'll deal with him. Now please sit down."

The flush of humiliation hit Kirsty's cheeks again, and she watched Paige's long fingers fold her business skirt under her knees as they sat down together. "Let me get right to the point, Ms. McPhee. Dunham Schauble has broken many laws, including bribery and financial fraud. The FBI Financial Crimes Unit is aware of your activities at Dunham Schauble and believes you are the head of information systems. Is their intel correct?"

"Not really. I'm securing vendor proposals for a new platform build-out, and constantly teaching Enzo how to turn the computer back on. I don't have much of a role there."

"I understood you were the, let's see here . . ." Paige pulled a business card out of her file. "Chief Information Officer, unless CIO means Chief Intelligence Officer. Which is it?"

"Information," she said. "So what? I'm twenty-four. No one will believe a junior champion surfer from Australia had the capability to mastermind an embezzlement scheme like this one."

"That's correct, Kirsty: embezzlement. I knew you were a smart young lady. How good do you think your job prospects will be after doing a perp walk in those high-heel boots on national news?"

"Based on American social media? Pretty good. What's your point?"

"In return for your assistance, we'll grant you US citizenship. If you do not, you will be deported after a very public airing of your activities, real or perceived. Do you understand?"

"I know a little about a lot, but that's it. I'm just a sheila trying to make ends meet. I'm trying to get all the redundancies in the system eliminated for faster speeds and lower hardware costs, so I'm not sure I can help you."

"Your ends seem to be meeting fine, Kirsty. Look, I've been in your shoes. Well, I've never worn those shoes, but I was fresh out of college once. Hey, I married a professional football player, and worked courtrooms for a living. You have great potential, but you've come to a crossroads that leads back to Melbourne or Wall Street. Ever seen anything related to Touch Down, LLC? Funny name for a boat, don't you think? Or Get Well Soon, LLC? Anything like that in any other cities?"

Kirsty swallowed. She wasn't so much out of options as aware she hadn't had any to begin with. Enzo was taken by her. For now. But would he stand by her if the DA followed through on her threat to deport her? "Now that you mention it," Kirsty said. "Maybe. I always like to self-insure when I can. Condos on Lake Michigan, Sea Island weekends, Vegas gambling trips. If it works in Orlando, it works anywhere. Do you have contacts at the INS? How quickly can I become a citizen?" She needed to fine tune the deal before she gave them the mother lode of flash drives containing all the contracts, off-balance-sheet slush funds, and transfers to and from the blind-pool account.

"Your application papers have already been drafted." Paige pulled them from the file next to her chair and extended them. As Kirsty tried to take them, Paige tightened her grip. "Take a look at the paperwork, but I do have to get back to Orlando. If you'll indulge me, do you have anything on digital file we can compare to the audited earnings reports?" She pulled back the papers as Paige released her grip.

"No, but I can," Kirsty lied while reading the application. Her laptop was a treasure trove sitting next to her on the table. "When do I get citizenship? This is just an application."

"We can process almost immediately using asylum procedure. Not many people seeking asylum from Australia, but it's a workable solution for urgent matters like these."

"Whoever filled out my application missed the World Junior Regionals in Kiama my senior year of high school."

"Apologies for the oversight." Paige reached toward her with a pen in her hand. "It shouldn't matter, but if it does, we'll add it in an amendment. Please sign so I can forward to the INS." Kirsty took the pen, but still couldn't bring herself to sign.

"Is Dunham Schauble an active trader in blind pools and phantom bonds?" Paige asked.

"They're legal," Kirsty said. "We underwrite all types of municipal-debt strategies. Those are just two types. Why do you care?"

"What do you do with the excess funds generated from bonds issued, but not spent on construction projects?"

"The cash we pull from the over-funded blind pool account gets used for operations. The rest sits waiting for maturity. What's the big deal?"

"What if the municipal bonds of your clients you were holding on the books defaulted? What counter-party risks would that trigger?"

"Never thought about it. I know we'd immediately get capital calls to boost our capital base on our bank loans. Maybe our stock takes a hit for a few months, but nothing long term." She didn't care. Enzo never gave her any stock.

"How about the racing team?"

"Those cars are expensive. The cost of one race is my salary, but the drivers are cute." Paige's questions were coming faster than any Harvard finance professors had asked them.

"How leveraged is Dunham Schauble? Your annual statement says forty percent of the balance sheet. Does that include the over-funded blind pools you're using as personal loans to upgrade your software, or appease politicians, or enter auto races?"

"The over-funded blind pool transfers included, our debt is probably around seventy percent of our balance sheet."

"Ms. McPhee, Dunham Schauble is in a very precarious position. If Orthus County Hospital bonds default, the Orthus King Airport will have to pay. If they don't have the money—and they don't—the Orthus County taxpayers will have to bail them out, which can't happen fast enough to avoid default because the General Fund is empty. Therefore . . ."

Paige's voice trailed off as the last piece snapped into place for Kirsty. "Therefore, not only will the hospital default, but so will the airport bonds, because they both support the blind pool." Kirsty looked out the window. "We hold more of the Orthus blind pool than any other, and we don't have the cash to meet our capital requirements should we have to repay the escrow account. So we'll have to sell more stock and then watch the stock price plummet. How soon is Orthus Hospital's next payment?"

"November first."

"It's still only a short-term event. As Enzo always says, 'If Orthus or Chicago doesn't pay the bond payments on the bonds we hold on our own balance sheet, we'll get our money in court."

"It didn't work that way in Detroit, and it won't work here. I'll make your attorneys look like vultures feeding on the carcass of municipalities. Who do you think Bob Drolland will pay? The pensioners or Wall Street bond holders?"

"You know Wall Street bond holders are really just small people owning mutual funds, right?"

"Look, Kirsty, you can get through this, but you need our help. When you get the digital copies, give them to this very pleasant man who gave you a ride over."

"Can I give you a ride back, Ms. McPhee?" Officer Staton offered.

"Thanks, but no thanks. I can get my own ride." She'd had enough of being taken down for the day. She signed the application before handing the paperwork back to Paige. "I'll be in touch."

Kirsty walked out to the empty pool deck next to the beach. A young waiter approached her. "Can I get you anything, miss?"

"Sure, I'll have a chardonnay. I'll find my own seat." Normally she'd have offered him a wink, but her energy had been drained.

She sat down in the open sunshine looking toward the beach, the motionless sky surrounding her like a sapphire shell, the ocean breeze caressing her every thought as she leaned her head back. She ran her fingers through her hair, when her phone rang her back into the moment and the crisis.

"Mi amor. Why aren't you answering your phone?"

"Just came up from a morning run on the beach to the deck of the Don, lover, but then I'm headed into the office. How was your flight to Chicago?"

"So far, so good. Tim just needs me for the CEO appearance so we can close the Chicago Board of Education. How was the run?"

"Didn't set any records, but close. The sand is packed perfect when the tide is out." The waiter appeared with her Chardonnay. "Thank you. Can I see a menu?" The unblocked breeze washed out the sound in the phone.

"Where are you?" Enzo asked.

"I decided to have brunch here."

"Good for you. How you coming on the technology transfer?"

"Working night and day when you're gone. I'll get a long way this week so we can be ready for rollout in a month."

"You're a princess. Call you tonight. Stay on the boat if you like."

"I need to be near the office. It's crunch time. No time on the beach till this is finished."

"I'll take you with me to San Francisco for the Football National Championship in January. The Ospreys are still undefeated. How does that sound?"

"I thought we were surfing in Australia?" Her travel plans had already changed, but she knew she needed to play along for the time being.

"Let's do both."

"There's no plan too big is there, mi amor?" She felt something tighten in her chest, but she pushed it away. No time for ties. She'd known that from the beginning.

"Not for you. Call you later."

"I'll be in the office working. Later, Tater."

A checklist was forming in her mind of the documents she would give to the PI Sunday morning, and she was already devising a plan to keep Enzo occupied while she delivered them. *Silicon Valley is calling, mate. Enzo can hire another secretary.*

CHAPTER 36

Paige and Bill showed up at the Progress Orthus offices on the second floor of the Orthus County Chamber of Commerce building in Orlando. As they walked through the double-glass doors, with all the Chamber of Commerce corporate members etched down the door on the left like stationary, the receptionist hung up the phone after seeing Bill's uniform.

"We're here to see Mr. McDaniel," Paige said.

Startled, the receptionist looked toward her dual computer screens, the mouse in her hand moving frantically. "I don't have you on the calendar."

"We're not on the calendar," Bill said. "We're here on professional business; our professions."

Ezzy's resignation from Progress Orthus last week couldn't have been a better catalyst for a change-agent like Paige. She'd decided her case against Patrick was harder to prove than her case against Bob, and would give him the benefit of the doubt in return for turning state's evidence. Development authority law circumvented Freedom of Information Laws, so she'd gotten all their contracts from Ezzy, in addition to long conversations with her about the nuances of each deal. Compiled with the video tapes of Bob and Gene, Bill's delivery of TouchDown, LLC's quarterly statement, the mortgage financing on Bob's condo, and the SEC's letter-of-intent-to-review flooding the Wall Street headlines, she believed she had probable cause to begin making arrests. Her final suspicions were confirmed yesterday morning when Kirsty insinuated Dunham Schauble used blind-pool proceeds as a slush fund for political kickbacks and a racing team. Orthus Regional Hospital's looming default, which would trigger Orthus County's default notwithstanding state bail-outs, philanthropic life-lines, or a pension annulment, needed the immediate attention of an emergency manager, and the best way to do that was to clean house early. She and Bill had devoted the entire summer to the investigation, Kirsty's offer yesterday, and Patrick's interrogation today.

"Thank you," Bill said when the reception led them down the aisle. "This shouldn't take long."

They followed her through a maze of real estate analysts, county maps, and filing cabinets until Paige spotted Patrick through his glass office walls. Everyone in the cubicles had their eyes on Bill's badge.

When they got to his office, Patrick was already waiting by the open door. "Good afternoon, District Attorney, Sheriff. What brings you this way? Can I give you a tour?"

"That'd be great, Patrick," Bill said, taking the early lead, as Paige had asked him to in order to keep Patrick confused until she felt he was on the ropes.

Paige nodded. "We'd love to see the wonderful things you're doing for Orthus County."

"Follow me. I'll show you some of the projects we're currently financing." Patrick turned back to her as they walked down the hall. "No one ever comes here." He led them past renderings of several apartment complexes, all five of the MOTrax development sites, some downtown districts, and the recently financed Coyotes Stadium.

"Wow, this is a lot of projects, Patrick," Paige said, having analyzed the contracts on every single one except the baseball stadium. "How're you able to keep up?"

"Well, we get administrative fees that cover the county's abated tax revenue, so we can hire staff and pay for office space. We've been around so long, we're a pretty smooth operation."

"I heard something about those admin fees," Bill said.

Paige listened as Patrick rambled through the litany of his own perspectives that created the problem she was going to spend the next few years fixing. He spoke as if he were divulging a legal but institutional secret when he said, "Government developers don't mind who they pay, or what it's called. They just want their tax bill cut in half, so they pay us half of what their tax bill would have been. We finance their projects with very competitive rates. Just ask the bankers here at the Chamber."

"Now that you mention it," Bill said, "this place does look like a bank. You got a lot of people working here."

"Precisely," Patrick said as they got to the last easel, which held one of Sterling's drawings. "Sorry this place is a bit cramped, but we won't be here much longer. We're moving our offices to the MOTrax-Smithson station next to the new Smithson City Hall that MOTrax is building." He laughed. "We're financing it, so it's in their best interest to give us the space, and besides, the Chamber has become argumentative over some of our real estate endeavors. Some of their members feel threatened by our success."

"The bankers or the developers?" Bill asked.

"Both, I guess." Patrick raised his eyebrows and crossed his arms. "So how can I help you today?"

"Let's go back to your office, Patrick," Paige said, tiring of his incredulous presentation of legally permissible government real estate speculation. "We've got a few questions."

"Oh? I'll be happy to help you however I can," he said, waving his arms back down the hall. "I'm right behind you."

"No, you lead," Bill said.

Patrick's look of dismay at Bill's command reminded her of the first speaker he'd had escorted out of the Progress Orthus meeting the night they approved the Smithson Coyotes Stadium deal. Jim's video was the best reality TV she'd seen. After she walked through the door behind Patrick, Bill closed it with a bang. "Seems like we have an audience, Patrick," Paige said when all the heads in the office turned toward them.

Before he could respond, one of the analysts opened the door, and Patrick said, "Sandy, can't you see we're busy in here."

"Yeah, Patrick, sorry about that. You asked me to bring the McDaniel Salvatore third-quarter reports as soon as I printed them out. Can I leave them on your desk?"

"No. Please come back later," Patrick said. "And don't let anyone else in here." After she closed the door, he asked, "So what is it you need to know?"

"Are you aware of the Orthus County finances?" Paige asked.

"Somewhat. I'm not privy to everything, but I have some local knowledge." He smiled with his hands folded in front of him on his desk, looking from her to Bill's badge.

"Then I guess you know Orthus Hospital is going to miss their payment next week, and I'm sure Bob is telling you it'll come from the General Fund."

"That's right, and there would be no reason to doubt him. We certainly won't let that bond default, because it's imperative we stay true to all of our bondholders. If we ever defaulted, that's it; no more park bonds, bridge bonds, nothing."

His explanations veered into political policy that was anything but legally transparent, so she ended the philosophical debate. She had business to do and time was wasting. "That's not going to happen, Patrick. The General Fund is empty, and the bank holding the tax-anticipation notes has made too many allowances for Bob's overdrafts already. It's tapped out. Are you understanding the gravity of this situation?"

"Then OSK will pay for it, or we'll cut the pensions," he said, sounding as if those changes could be made by a wave of his wand.

"Patrick, bondholders are only secured creditors on paper, not in reality. I'll negotiate with Wall Street attorneys, and they'll learn the hard way Orthus County has a constitutional obligation to protect the public safety, health, and welfare. I'll make sure our hospital, sheriff's department, fire department, and charter schools are funded with whatever spare change I can find, but from now on, Wall Street, and Dunham Schauble, are at the bottom of the list."

"You? Who put you in charge? Orthus County hasn't filed for bankruptcy, and you wouldn't have any authority if it did."

"When the governor announces my appointment as emergency manager of Orthus County, I'm going to cancel all of the airport contracts, all of the hospital contracts, and all of the MOTrax projects. I have Governor Sikes's full support."

"But the credit-rating agencies will act immediately to downgrade our debt, and the bond markets even faster, raising the interest rates for the MOTrax developments and the new stadium."

"Patrick, ratings agencies started using the global rating scale during the last financial crisis. Your bonds are two notches too high already. The market will simply bring them back in line, but no one will know, because we're not doing either of those deals."

"In other words, you're going to illegally transfer the blind pool's investor payment seniority to an unsecured creditor, like employee salaries and pension funds, discard the legal votes already taken by Progress Orthus, and that's after you become the self-appointed emergency manager."

"'Illegally' is rich coming from you, Patrick. Bankruptcy proceedings are driven at the negotiating table. Enzo and his clients are going to walk away with nothing, and so are you."

"What do you mean me? I don't hold any of those bonds."

She shook her head and looked at Bill, who sat expressionless staring at Patrick. Even she would've been intimidated by the sheriff's sustained eye contact. She turned back to Patrick and was pleased to notice Bill seemed to be having that very effect on him. "Are you familiar with your oath of office to avoid even the appearance of impropriety?" Paige asked. "What were you thinking?"

His throat moved as he swallowed hard. "I think I might need an attorney."

"What do you know about Gene Dodd?" she asked.

"He's one hell of a developer and a solid businessman."

"You sure about that?" Bill asked, and then smiled at him. But it wasn't a friendly smile.

"You do know he's building most of the projects on our financing list, correct? He's a good man."

"Pretty strong endorsement, Patrick," Paige said. "Does he drive a small red sedan around town when he flies Sterling's plane back here from Dallas?"

"I have no idea. He probably ride-shares, or gets one of the driver services at OSK. How should I know?"

"How about Sterling's plane? Who fills it up with gas?" she asked.

Patrick inhaled deep. "The airport FBO? But again, how should I know?"

"Because you're a silent partner in Touch Down, LLC, and you receive income from jet-fuel sales and maintenance contracts." Bill said. "Does that jog your memory?"

Patrick's forehead glistened with sweat in the coolness of the air-conditioned office. "Look, I'm just a small silent partner. Flight traffic is down, and planes are staying in the hangars longer. We're losing lots of money from the recession."

"That's not what this profit-and-loss statement that I got off Bob's desk says." Bill pulled the folded paper from the front pocket of his uniform and tossed it on Patrick's desk.

"Patrick, we know Bob has been ripping you off for a long time," Paige said. "I've got all the contracts Progress Orthus signed. You finance Bob's deals and you get a cut, but what you don't know is Bob is getting an extra cut."

"I've always known it, but I can't do anything about it. Plus, it's all legal. He can kick me, or anyone else, off the Progress Orthus board anytime." He leaned back in his chair and stared toward the ceiling. It was the look of defeat she'd seen many times in the defendants she went up against. She imagined he was looking into a rear-view mirror of Bob's misdeeds, and she almost felt sorry for him as his eyes began to glaze over with tears. "You can't arrest me on some legal notion of impropriety."

"No, but I can have Sheriff Bolek arrest you on a number of charges ranging from theft to embezzlement. I have the signed warrant for your arrest in this file, and I'll throw in a conflict-of-interest violation to make it stick at least through appeals court. We can make it very uncomfortable for you while we prosecute Bob for bribery. But it doesn't have to be this way."

"What the hell does that mean?"

"Patrick, have you ever known Bob to take a bribe? Or Gene to offer one?"

"No, Paige. Really, I've never seen him take any money from anyone."

Bill scoffed. "You mean other than jet-fuel sales, engine repairs, and a condo in St. Pete. I guess you're planning a Salvatore showroom here at Progress Orthus so the staff can start selling cars for you, right after Sandy finishes analyzing your third-quarter results?"

Patrick exhaled as his elbows landed on his desk, his hands pushing his hair back.

Paige pushed play on her phone and laid it on the table. "Take a look at this video." She watched his eyes when the video shots darted back and forth between Bob and Gene. "Patrick, is that Gene Dodd in the video?"

"That's him, alright." Patrick nodded, his face reddening in what Paige could guess now was anger. "That's a hell of a lot of cash, isn't it?"

"I'm going to arrest you publicly, possibly here today, in front of all your employees, if you don't help us."

Bill dangled a pair of handcuffs in the air high enough to get the attention of everyone watching from their cubes.

"Sheriff, please. Put those things down," he said and looked at Paige. "What do you want from me?" He rubbed his head in his hand, his shoulders jerking with emotion.

"I want you to tell us everything you know about Bob's condo in St. Pete," she said. "Your business connections at the airport and any other deals Bob has set up with Gene Dodd or Sterling Johnston."

Patrick nodded, chewing his lip, and then took a deep breath. "Enzo bought Bob that condo when we did the hospital. He's buying him the floor above it for the MOTrax deal, but that's it."

"What about the airport maintenance contracts?"

"We set it up with the airport developer as soon as the second funding tranche from the blind pool was distributed. We have a guy that runs everything, but Bob and I take ten percent a piece."

Bill reached back over and picked up the Touchdown, LLC, quarterly statement. "This statement says Bob's cut is twenty percent. He's a slippery one, isn't he Patrick?"

"Whatever. I don't need the money. My Salvatore dealerships are doing just fine."

"Is that why Bob and Stan both drive Salvatores?" Paige asked.

"That's exactly why, Mrs. Jackson. I don't see you hauling Flash in for anything."

"What's Flash done? Losing money on the MOTrail isn't illegal. Did he, or you, get anything from the Coyotes Stadium deal?"

"I gave him his car the unions trashed this summer, and he got a new high school with a football stadium for financing the Coyotes deal."

"You gave him the car long before Smithson Galleria, or the new stadium, were in the public purview. What was it for?"

"The MOTrail deal."

"But Progress Orthus wasn't the conduit for the MOTrail bond. Onward Orlando was."

"I gave it to him as a favor to Mayor Tisdale. That high rise he works in wasn't free either."

"You gave Stan a car on the suggestion of mayor, and you received no compensation for the gift. Stan negotiated better office space, and another high school, in return for issuing a bond to build the MOTrail and the Coyotes Stadium, so be very careful you answer my next question honestly, Patrick. Is that all?"

"Yes," he hesitated, "that's it. Guess that doesn't sound illegal."

"Why, no. It doesn't," Bill chimed in. "Did you know Grady High School shares its stadium with two other teams? That's a shame, isn't it, Patrick? I bet one of the abatements from just one apartment complex will pay for a new football stadium. What do you think?"

"How would I know?"

"You keep saying that. You're either the dumbest guy in the building, or you live on Mars," Bill said. "Seems to me, you are exactly the person to ask how much a sports stadium would cost, asshole."

"One last question, Patrick," Paige said, still not convinced Patrick was being completely forthcoming. "Sterling owns a slum adjacent to the Smithson Galleria project. You know anything about that?"

"What about it?"

"It's called Johnston Limited Lofts, LLC. Are you, or Progress Orthus, any part of that?"

"There's nothing illegal about my real estate partnerships."

"The purchase was made three years ago, about the same time Stan got his new car, but way before any Smithson Galleria or Coyotes Stadium designs. Wouldn't that strike you as opportunistic, Patrick?"

"Call it a lucky break. That's all I've got to say."

"That's all we need today, Patrick. I need all the documents you have on the St. Pete Condo and Touchdown, LLC, on my desk by Sunday. If you want to hire an attorney, Sheriff Bolek will be back over here to escort you to jail. You can call one from there."

Bill dangled the handcuffs again and smiled. "Unless you're not here because you've moved offices. Then I'll come find you there," he paused. "Or wherever."

CHAPTER 37

Stan could see her in the passenger-side rearview mirror, coming down the Orlando International arrivals sidewalk, her white feather maternity dress accentuating her knees and calves that had been honed for the dancer's stage. He sent Candi a text: I'm in the Silver Salvatore convertible just up ahead of you. Then he turned his eyes back to the mirror as he connected her movement to the sound of clicking heels off the terminal wall coming toward him, the sun glinting off her over-round sunglasses holding her hair out of her face. Fading out of the mirror, and into view through the open window, she bent over, smiled, and said, "Hey, baby. Can a girl get a lift?" Only having met her once, he'd forgotten how striking her cheekbones were, but barely got his fill before she opened the door, dropped down in the seat, and pulled her legs in. She looked at him and asked, "Did you miss me?"

"Not for one second," he said.

"Aw, that's too bad. I missed you," she said pouting her lips while she pulled the lipstick out of her overnight bag that was still sitting on her lap in front of her baby bump.

"Well, at least you weren't lying to me about the baby. You're big, but damn, for a pregnant girl you're holding it together."

"This body should be insured." She threw the lipstick back in the bag, snapped it shut, and tossed it in his backseat.

"You got that right," he said as he pulled his sports car away from the curb and pointed it north toward the Orlando Downtown District, but not quite that far. "How's the baby?"

"Ready to get out and get around."

He nodded to the back seat. "Is that your only bag?"

"You bought the tickets. One night's not much with my baby's daddy, but I'll take it."

He looked around as they exited the terminal back out onto the interstate, and only saw a bunch of cars, people he didn't recognize, and the black Crown Vic that had dropped off its ride-share fare.

"You checking to see if any of your football pals notice?"

"Why are you so paranoid? I don't hang out with my football pals anymore," he said, telling himself to calm down, as an emotional battle raged within him; responsibility for a new human pitted against his commitment to Paige. "Just to be clear, this is not convenient."

"But you did play professional football, and you did make this baby, so you better make it convenient." Her forceful nature fanned the flames of resentment building up inside him, which were briefly postponed by her maternal blush.

"I've been working on some things. I'll show you when we get to the restaurant."

"Where you taking me? I'm starving. I haven't been on a Saturday night date in forever."

"The restaurant in the hotel where you're staying."

"Is it nice?" she asked, smiling and looking around the inside of the car. "Like the ones in Vegas?"

"Not quite, but like the ones in Central Florida, it works."

"I didn't wear my best pregnancy dress to stay in a dump. You better start taking this serious, because you got a baby on the way, a real baby, and I'm the baby's momma, and everyone knows who you are. You're married, and you make the news." She twirled her finger in the air and said, "You're about to make the news again if you don't act right. Now take me to a nice restaurant."

He gripped his hands tighter around the steering wheel. She was beautiful, and that was his baby in her, but he didn't know much beyond that—not how he felt, what his future was going to look like, or how long he could hide any of this from Paige. "Calm down," he said. "The Summit Building is great. I do a lot of business dinners there."

One exit south of the Orlando Downtown District, he pulled off the interstate and into the Orlando financial district where he wouldn't be easily noticed. She craned her neck around to look up the side of the office tower and said, "This is beautiful, Flash. I knew you loved me."

He rolled his eyes as his foot hit the pavement certain she was just pushing him into an emotional corner to fleece him, and he jogged around to hand the keys to the valet and help her out of the car.

"Name?" the valet asked.

"Latrelle."

"Thanks, Latrelle. We'll have your car right here when you return."

"Thanks," Stan said, and opened her car door.

Candi unfolded her legs out of the car seat. "Why you ballers always buy these low-ass cars?"

He and the valet chuckled as Stan lifted her from the waist, helping her to stand up.

"Let's go." He followed her passed the valet stand, and into the pink marble and glass lobby, Chihuly blown glass adorning the sky-lit ceiling, illuminating her white dress like a Chinese lantern floating across the large polished floor.

"Is this where you work, baby?" she asked, her eyes wide at the extravagance of the place.

"Not really. I just come here because the rooftop bar is private. I work north of here."

"Are you ashamed of me?"

"Not with those legs, but you said it yourself, I got a reputation to uphold."

"From what I see on the internet, you got a big reputation, and it includes a lot of girls like me."

"You read it on the internet so it must be true, huh?"

"Hey, where there's smoke there's fire. You can't bullshit me, Flash."

He pushed the elevator button to the Garden Deck.

"Where're we going?" she asked.

"You'll see. This place is special."

As soon as the elevator doors shut, she grabbed his hand and kissed him. "I have to pee."

He smiled down at her, feeling the spark of lust in his temple ignite a welder's torch of regret. "They have restrooms here."

When the elevator opened, he was relieved when she looked out past the roof-top tables and the Orlando skyline. "Damn, Flash, I can see so far. The sunset is so many colors." She closed both of her hands around the hand she was holding and whispered into his ear, "I should come here more often."

"I thought you'd like it. We get a couple of extra minutes of sun up here."

"Good evening, Mr. Thibodeaux." The concierge said. "Table for two?"

"Mr. Thibodeaux?" Candi looked at Stan with a half-smile. "Who's that?"

Her barely disguised insolence was already wearing thin, but he ignored her. "Yes, table for two. Thanks." He leaned over her, and whispered in her ear. "I brought you here because it's beautiful and private. Please cut me some slack. The bathrooms are around the corner and down the hallway next to the edge."

She smirked again. "Better hope I don't jump."

"I haven't been that lucky in a while."

"Miss, there are glass barriers for just that purpose," the concierge interjected. "But please enjoy the view."

"I'll get us a table. See you when you get back."

As she walked away, the concierge said, "Follow me, Mr. Thibodeaux."

When he sat down at the white-tablecloth-covered table in the corner, the concierge handed Stan two menus. "Is this table okay?"

"This is great. Thanks." He handed the concierge a hundred-dollar bill, counting on the secrecy he'd been afforded there for so long. "For the table and the discretion."

"Of course, Mr. Thibodeaux," he said, slipping the bill into his coat pocket before it saw the light of day, and then walked away.

Candi's clicking heels sounded like the count-down clock on a bomb, and he turned to see her walking around the glass edge, undeniably pregnant, but also undeniably a Vegas showgirl, as her dress caught the sunset, revealing the perfect image of new life.

"You know how to enter a room," he said, noticing all the other men in the restaurant looking at her, too, wondering if it was jealousy or pride he was feeling, and why. "Who wouldn't want to be seen with you?"

"Nobody. That's who," she said, and put her purse down. "Can I have one of those menus?"

"Sure. Get anything you want," he said, trying to turn off his man appeal just this once.

The lighthouse-shaped propane heater behind him curbed the chill of the cool autumn breeze, as the waiter arrived in white shirt-sleeves and black pants, put a bread bowl on the table, and poured olive oil and balsamic vinegar into a dish. "Can I start you off with drinks?"

She handed him the menu. "I'll have a Chardonnay and the pumpkin soup to start. I didn't have lunch."

"You sure about that?" Stan asked. "What about the baby?"

"One glass won't hurt anybody. Sounds like you need one, too."

He handed his menu to the waiter. "Just a beer, thanks."

"Of course, I'll be right back with your drinks and to take your dinner orders."

He caught her eyes and decided to begin the scene he'd run through his mind all summer. "You're sure this baby's mine?"

She pulled a lab form from her purse and handed it to him.

Stan read over an original copy of his DNA records from the Ospreys Football Organization. "How did you get this?" he asked, having been in this situation before, but never accompanied by a DNA test.

She plucked a slice of bread out of the bowl, ripped it in half, and dipped it in the bowl. "I live in Vegas with the best hackers in the world. That's how. Flash, this shit is real. I want a million dollars, or I'm telling everyone." She finished her last word by taking a bite of the soaked bread between her fingers.

"I told you I don't have it," he said. "I only played four years in the league. Didn't your Vegas friends tell you anything about my short career?"

"I'm pregnant, Flash. How do you think I feel? I make money off this body, and now I can't." He listened unfazed while she rambled on, hoping she was getting closer to the end. "Now my mascara's running," she said, wiping her eyes with the napkin. "You sure know how to make a girl feel special."

"Now the shoe's on the other foot. You don't give a damn about me or your piggy bank baby," he said, shaking his head and determined not to fall for her eyelashes and guilt trips. “Look, I worked something out and I got a new contract with some people that’ll pay me extra, but I’m a school superintendent because I need the extra money. My bank account emptied about the time I stopped playing football.”

“What’re you offering?”

“I can pay you fifty thousand now and fifty thousand a year for five years.”

She let her hands fly up above the table. “That’s nowhere close to what I need. I make one hundred thousand a year dancing, and you’re asking me to take a pay cut to take care of your baby. I know you don’t have any kids with Paige, but this baby’s going to be beautiful and rich.”

He’d contacted Gene because he knew he’d minimized the fallout from some of Sterling’s unpleasant encounters. Gene had advised him to demand proof, and then to start slow and hold out as long as possible. “I can pay fifty thousand for ten years. You’re fine now, but in five years you’ll look like my wife, and nobody’s hiring showgirls that old.”

“I can work this body for at least another fifteen. Keeping my mouth shut is extra. You have to do way better than that.” Her cool business approach to the conversation, about the lifetime costs of having a baby was not something Gene had prepared him for. She put another piece of bread in her mouth, while he could barely think about food.

The waiter brought the drink orders back. “Are you ready to order dinner?” He placed the soup in front of Candi as she swallowed the last piece of bread.

“Yes. I’ll have the misto salad and the veal parmesan. Can you fill this bread bowl back up, too, please? Thanks.”

“Of course. I’ll bring some right over.” He turned to Stan and said, “Sir?”

“Steak is fine,” Stan answered, saying the first thing that came to his mind, because he couldn’t concentrate long enough on the menu to make a decision. “Medium rare.”

“Very good, sir. I’ll get you some more bread, ma’am.”

“You sure are hungry,” Stan said.

“Flash, I could do your workouts—I mean, if I wasn’t pregnant.”

“I got a glimpse as you walked over here to the table. Your body is solid even with that baby.”

“Solid enough to have sex later?” she asked.

“That dress is testing my will power, but I need to get home to Paige.”

“Have you lost your mind?” She pulled her hands back. “Now I definitely don’t want to have sex, but I do want one hundred thousand dollars for twenty years, or I’m calling the *Orthus County Post.* I can’t believe you’d bring her up.”

“I’ll do it for ten, and that’s all I got.”

“I want a down payment tonight,” she said. “I’ll have my attorney write up the rest. Plus, I need some money to get home with.”

“Let’s see if you can act right the rest of tonight, and I’ll think about it.”

The waiter showed up with the second basket of bread, and Candi smiled up at him and reached in for another piece.

“If you didn’t bring me any money,” she said, lowering her voice as the waiter walked away. “I’ll think about it for you.”

Stan pulled out the checkbook Patrick had given him and wrote a one-hundred-thousand-dollar check, and pushed it across the table. “Does that work?”

“Hmm, let’s see.” She picked up the check after wiping her hands with her napkin. “Who is Coyote Concessions, LLC? You and Paige don’t have a joint account? Shouldn’t she know?” She leaned over and put it in her bag.

"What? Why're you constantly on offense?" he asked, leaning back away from the table. "I'm going to pay you what I said, no one is going to know anything, and have your attorney include that, or I won't sign it."

"This check better not bounce," she said, tapping into his last nerve.

"It won't. I have a concessions contract at the new baseball stadium. We got early purchase orders and a bank line of credit. Now I have two full-time jobs because of you."

"Sure, Flash, because I did this all on my own." She gestured to her belly.

The waiter brought their plates, and they finished in silence as Stan thought how about lucky he was to have Gene to lean on in special circumstances like this.

"See you again soon, Mr. Thibodeaux," the concierge said as they headed out.

Stan nodded. "Yes, thanks again."

When they got to the elevator, Candi looked up into his eyes and grabbed his hand again, "Where you taking me now, Flash? You still thinking about my dress?"

Her mood swings kept him off balance, and he was nearing the limit of his brain's self-control over her advances and the smell of her perfume. "Yes, I am, but it's late." The elevator door closed behind them, and he indulged his yearning to kiss her. When the elevator door opened in the lobby, he took her hand and led her over to the registration desk.

"Mr. Thibodeaux, your room is ready. Here are the keys. Twelfth floor. Breakfast and coffee service lasts till 10:00 AM. Please ring down if you need anything. All we need is your card for registration."

He handed her small bag to her as they approached the elevator bank. "So we've got a deal?"

"Yes, Flash, we got a deal. Your son will see his father as a one-hundred-thousand-dollar check every year on his birthday."

Her words buckled his knees with the weight of ten years of resentment from a childless marriage, but then again, the annual payments he was making would protect what little there was left of it. "Good. This hotel is connected to MOTrax. It'll take you all the way to the airport tomorrow. Here's your boarding ticket."

She took the boarding ticket from him and dropped it in her bag. "I'm not riding that death trap. I'll ride-share back to the airport, unless you want to pick me up in the morning. Do you want to give the mother of your child a ride back to the airport?"

"Sorry, Candi, not this time. I have a meeting tomorrow morning in Tampa."

She reached up to kiss him, and he couldn't resist, having convinced himself it would be the last time he saw her if he had anything to do with it. "Thanks for taking care of me and the baby, Flash. It's the right thing to do, and you know it," she said.

"Thanks for coming, Candi. I won't leave you stranded with my son." He hugged her before she stepped onto the open elevator doors.

From his relaxed position on the couch, his laptop open, Officer Staton watched Stan exit the building. After he was sure Stan was gone, he took his headphones off, pulled out his phone, and texted Paige and Bill: Stan's leaving the lobby of the Summit Building, but the girl is staying here. I don't know what this means, but she's pregnant.

He read Bill's response: Thanks for the 411. We'll deal with her tomorrow morning. Tonight's the night. Head over to First and Last and post up by the MOTrax entrance. Be on the lookout for anymore duffel bags full of blow coming off the train. Stay within whispering distance. These ear pieces are older than my shoes.

Stan walked in the back door and went straight to the guest bedroom where he'd been sleeping for months. As he was pulling off his tie, he looked up to the ceiling at the sound of footsteps running down the stairs. Paige rushed into the room, tears streaming down her cheeks. "What's her phone number? What is it? Tell me, you asshole."

He slowly pulled his jacket off and avoided looking her in the eye. "What are you talking about, Paige? We don't talk for months, and now you come in demanding some person's phone number?"

"I saw the airline charge on your credit card, and I know you picked someone up from the airport. So what's her number?"

"It was someone from the Las Vegas School Board," he said, finally glancing over at her. "I came home early because the guy was tired and so was I."

"You're such a liar. Guys from Vegas don't get tired." She sounded as worn out as he felt. "I know everything. What's her number?"

He sat on the bed and put his head in his hands, almost relieved to not have to lie anymore. Hell, he didn't even need to make a decision anymore. She was making it for him. "I'm not giving you her number. This is all my fault—not hers. I'm so sorry."

"Sorry. Right. And I already have her number, jackass. You think I'd ask you for a damn thing I couldn't get myself? I just wanted to see how long you'd keep trying to lie to me. Now pack your stuff and get the hell out of my house." Before he could say anything else, she turned and walked out, slamming the door behind her, "You have ten minutes, asshole," she shouted from the other side—loud enough for the neighbors to hear. "And if you're still here, I'm calling the cops."

CHAPTER 38

Sheriff Bolek pulled into the abandoned corrugated-metal building next to Orthus Park Lake near the Orlando Downtown District, the towers and lakeside facade of the apartment complexes and shopping district shrouding the view of the far shoreline. He parked his SUV, got out, and started walking toward a group of officers in tactical gear standing around the back end of the Mobile Radio Patrol Unit, or the "Holy Roller" as they called it because they'd renovated and upgraded the van so many times they prayed it worked. Putting down his coffee for a brief moment before joining the others, he petted the two dog snouts sniffing and poking out of the cracked window of the K-9 unit parked next to him. "Hey, boys. You ready to go to work?" Their noses nuzzled in his hands. The two SUVs were parked side by side inside the old King Citrus packing house. The setting autumn sun coming through the dusty glass windowpanes provided the ultimate camouflage and was getting better by the second. Bill had staged a couple of police transport vans around the corner in a public parking deck that he confirmed were just arriving. He got to the three officers in S.W.A.T gear standing behind Officer Salermo's van. "Aright, Sal, what've you got? These guys have been telling me about it all week," he said, thumbing at Officers Lewis and Steiner.

He opened the van's barn doors slowly, smiling at Bill's expression when he unveiled three small quad-copter drones. "The FBI seized them in a drug bust down by the airport. The guy they pinched was taking them to his kids, so now we have high-tech surveillance and no one had to bother Purchasing."

"It's always good if we can circumvent Dr. No," Bill said, sipping his coffee and feigning the lack of authority to spend money, "but the FBI just gave them to you?"

"Just so happens one of Steiner's buddies from the Academy made the big time at the Bureau, felt sorry for me, and pulled some strings. The Feds get next-level quad-copters that fit in your hand, so she didn't need it."

"Yeah, I introduce Sal to my best friend," Steiner said, smiling between her strong dimples and turning up to him, "and if he screws it up, he'll have to deal with Luther."

Sal cringed. "Ouch. See what I have to deal with, Sheriff?"

"Do they work?" Bill asked, looking around at the other two officers in their uniforms puffed out by bullet-proof jackets with zip ties sticking out of their cargo pockets like frayed fiber wire. He knew it was a windfall, and was excited to see the technology in use. He'd only seen a few tested at the Florida Sheriff's Association Conference. "Can they stay up long enough to get all the way across the lake tonight, and get video of the whole tower and the surrounding streets?"

"That's why you're the sheriff, Sheriff." He reached toward the van and started placing them on the ground "Luckily we got three. These are the best ones on the market, but they can only stay up about thirty minutes, twenty if the cameras are live streaming back to my computer."

"Our search warrant doesn't include drone surveillance, but it doesn't say we can't use them as scout lookouts."

"You won't be sorry, Sheriff," he said, with the video game console in his hands. With a click, one of the drones lifted off the ground to eye level and stopped, buzzing louder than beehives. "What do you want it to do?" Sal asked, calling out over the noise.

"Catch bad guys," Bill shouted back. "What can you make it do?"

With a whirr, it disappeared out of the open end of the building and hovered at the entrance. "Lewis grab my laptop on the edge there and turn it so we can see it," Sal said, his eyes trained on the flying eye, thumbs articulating in repeated cross movements.

Like a spider snatching itself to the top of its web, the drone vanished. Bill turned to the screen to see an expanding view of Orthus Park and north past the lake to the outskirts of Orlando. "Damn, I haven't seen any video like that." Bill watched as the video zoomed down to the top of the old citrus-packing house, accompanied by the buzzing whirr as it refocused on the police vehicles and then four officers staying next to the van, finally landing on the ground in front of him.

Sal smiled, "What do think?"

"We'll see how they do in the wind, but it could be good," Bill said, folding his arms over his vest. "I know I briefed everyone earlier, but Officer Staton is headed to the target and will be our eyes and ears on the inside. He witnessed a first drop occurring this afternoon."

"Just in time for the Florida-Georgia football-viewing party they've been advertising all week on the radio," Sal said.

Bill shook his head. "We'll hang out here until the sun goes down, the suspects get disoriented, and our element of surprise materializes. Steiner, are Grizz and Luther ready to go?" Black German Shepherds were trained on them, jaws clamped shut, sitting at attention, their fixed dark eyes motionless in the back of the K-9 Unit.

"They look ready," Steiner replied.

"Don't they always," Bill agreed. "Narcotics is staging a few blocks north at the Grady School Cluster with four unmarked cars full of masked narcs and an evidence van. They're leading the charge, and I'll monitor the situation from here with Sal. Steiner, you and Lewis drive your K-9 officers over to Narcotics and go in with them, but be sure to drive a couple of blocks around the bar on your way north."

"Roger. The big dogs need to eat," Steiner said, feet spread at-ease, pony tail moving slightly with the growing breeze.

"Lewis, you can put that M-16 away. Steiner's dogs, and our helmets, will probably create more personal hygiene malfunctions than hero's stands."

"Roger that, Sheriff," Lewis said.

"We don't need any collateral damage. The only reason we're doing this after dark is because First and Last doesn't get supply until late afternoon. Craig will have it bagged and ready for distribution after this long of a wait, but we're not expecting any heavy fire from a bunch of coked-up dancing machines: handguns only."

They all responded by nodding in silence to Bill's increased intensity in the face of the always-possible loss of life.

"Everyone mount up, and we'll continue to check radio gear and wait." He turned to Sal and grinned. "Keep charging those batteries. We'll be lucky if this wind isn't a full-bore blow by midnight."

"Copy that. I've been charging and practicing all week. I got the video-feed software downloaded yesterday. I've got all the batteries plugged into that charger," he said, pointing underneath the small radio and video control desk in the back of the van.

Lewis and Steiner joined the dogs in the SUV, and quietly rolled out of the building while Bill opened a folding chair with shocks for back legs, put his coffee in the cup holder, and started rocking while Sal sat on the edge of the van. Reaching up to his shoulder, he squeezed the attached radio until it clicked. "Check-one-two."

"Staton, copy."

"Narcotics, copy."

"K-9, copy. At destination in fifteen."

"Transport, copy, and in place."

"Radio comm, Copy," Bill heard Sal's audible voice next to him and the crackle in the radios.

Bill pinched the receiver. "Sun down is half an hour from now. Staton, let me know if you see anything."

Bill was enjoying the small talk with Sal, and getting more drone information than he needed, including the meticulous addition of retrofitted flashing blue LED lights, but their large size and red power-light could be a problem. His phone rang. "I need to take this. Back in a minute." Getting up and walking away from the van, he said, "Hey, babe. What're you doing?"

"Thinking about you. Are you getting excited for Monday afternoon?" Ezzy asked.

"I would've sworn mid-week was a strange time for a wedding until a guy in my small group got married on a Tuesday. Now I'm a copycat groom. Of course, I'm excited."

"Where are you?"

"Setting up shop in the old King Citrus packing house at Orthus Park."

"Be careful it doesn't fall in on you. Bob won't spend the money to tear it down and renovate the park. Says it's a historical landmark."

"We'll be alright. If Matt Pinson built it, I'd trust it another few years."

"I guess tonight is the night?"

"Yep," he said, knowing she was going to worry. "You have to hunt criminals where they feed."

"Please be careful. Is Officer Staton there with you?"

"I don't leave home without him. He's my eyes and ears on the ground. I'm not going near the place."

"Good. Please call me later to tell me you're OK."

"I love you, Mrs. Bolek."

"It's King, and I love you, too."

"Whatever. Just keep answering when I call." He hung up and shouted to Sal as he came from behind the SUV, "Alright, let's get this party started. Crank one of those whirly birds, and let's take a look around."

"Roger that!" Sal grabbed the console and flipped a switch on the drone. The red dot signified it was powered up, and with a buzz it was gone. The screen of Sal's computer was mostly dark except for the shimmering water below reflecting the city lights, and the spraying water fountain feature in the middle of the lake. The screen evolved into a view of the Orlando Downtown District Tower ahead in the distance, as the raised back deck of First and Last came into view below. The windows of the building were checkered with lights left on over the weekend, and the second floor that included the lobby, shops and First and Last. On the far side, the three-story parking deck of MOTrax was lit up like a prison, as part of the new 'Keep A Light On For Safety' program.

"Staton, we've sent one of the drones on patrol. We have about twenty minutes. What do you see?"

"Wasted people. Lots of them."

"Normal work-place hazards. What else?"

"Another duffel bag entered the building from the MOTrax train. I left after he walked in, so as not to get exposed, but I got a bunch of pictures. I'm down in the front of the main building now, parked in the roundabout. I flipped my badge to the security guard and he left."

"We're close. Narcotics, how are you?" he asked, feeling the car tracker in his pocket begin to buzz.

"On high alert. Steiner and Lewis are ready with the dogs. I suggest we wait another thirty minutes so Craig, the jolt man, can bag his dope for distribution."

"Copy that. Transport, sit tight," Bill said. "Sal, can you scan those windows on the second floor next to the bar?" With a shift of his thumbs, the drone dove down close enough so that the video screen showed the sidewalk to the back deck about fifty feet below, and four of the tower's horizontal rows of bottom-floor windows. "Jackpot. Is that Craig sitting at his desk through the window?"

The drone came a few feet closer to the window, and Bill noticed people below the drone looking up into the dark at the same time as Sal. "We've been spotted."

"That's fine. Can you get closer?"

"I'll try."

Craig's back came into view, his hands scooping white powder from a glass jar into baggies and vials, helping himself here and there. A gust of wind modulated the screen image as it recalibrated and steadied itself, at the same time the corrugated metal roof Bill was sitting in rustled and vibrated above. He heard the beeping in his jacket pocket of the car locators he'd been using for six months tracking Bob's movements, the blinking radio button on the map pulling into the MOTrax parking deck.

"Damn, that jar's as big as my protein shake mix," Sal said, thumbing the console.

"He's a high roller. Time to pay the piper." As the words left Bill's mouth, the door opened and a few girls walked in the room and began snorting lines. Craig got up and tried to slam the door shut a couple of times before it closed, and then locked it. The image continued recalibrating as the copter blades adjusted to the breezy gusts. The girls were just the first of many coming in and out of the room.

"Sheriff, over."

"Yeah, go ahead, Staton," Bill said.

"Guess who just showed up to dinner?"

"No time for jokes, Staton."

"Our visitor from Las Vegas just arrived in an after-hours rideshare van."

"Baby and all?" Bill asked, immediately suspicious.

"Negative. Baby not on board. Been here about ten minutes I'd say."

"What's she wearing?"

"A whole lot of nothing in a black mini-skirt and to-the-sky high heels."

"Time's almost up, Sheriff. I need to bring it home," Sal said, the screen shot pulling away from the window and turning to come back across the lake, taking a winding path back to the packing house, laboring against the wind. A few minutes later, the first drone dropped in front of Bill's rocking chair, and the second drone lifted and buzzed away after Sal punched a few buttons on his laptop to change the drone video feed to the one now aloft.

The spraying water fountain features came back into view as Bill's radio crackled to life. "Commissioner Drolland just arrived, too. This looks like one swell party. OK if I go inside?"

"Be my guest," Bill said. "Let us know what you see."

Once inside, and about the time the second drone had finished a periphery sweep of the tower and MOTrax parking deck to locate innocent bystanders and bad guys, Staton came through Bill's radio again "Whew. ..., full of ... New Orleans crack house...finding a seat."

"Copy that. You're in and out, but stay where you are."

"Roger,...what I see" came Staton's garbled reply.

The screen image of Craig doling out party favors came into view again as his opening and closing office door reverberated with pulsating light from the bar. A few people were walking out, as a tall girl in a black mini-skirt and hair curling down her shoulders, came walking in and turned to lock the door. “That’s got to be her,” Bill mumbled.

“Who?” Sal asked, working the drone controls and watching the screen.

“No one. Can you get any closer?”

“I’ll try, but I can’t get too near those blowing palm trees next to the window.”

The image bouncing around, but moving closer, zoomed in on the room. The girl was smiling at Craig, running her long finger across the front of his desk. Within minutes, they were railing coke lines before she stood straight up and Craig tossed her a vial. When he came around the table, she rubbed his arm. He returned the favor by letting his hand on her back drift below her waist as they walked toward the office door together. Craig cracked the door open, and it burst open with a man-sphere stumbling into the room. The girl barely avoided being knocked down by the rumbling mass. Craig nodded to her as she left the room, and brought Bob over to his desk while shaking his head. The interlude was no different than the transactions that’d been going on all night, except neither the girl, nor Bob, produced any cash for exchange. “Staton, are you seeing all this?”

“You mean...office door…wobbling commissioner?”

“Copy,” Bill responded while looking at the screen. Bob came up from a long snort and locked eyes with Bill. His wavering hand pointed through the window at the drone.

A moment before Craig could turn to see what Bob was pointing at, the screen image dropped below the window, veering dangerously toward the palm trees with a gust of wind, and then went blank. "Damn it," Sal said. "It's toast. We'll have to get it later."

"You think Craig saw it?" Bill asked, watching Sal punch buttons on the laptop again, changing the video feed to the last drone.

"I doubt it. I can't believe Bob saw it, but we can't be sure." The last drone lifted off the ground and flew out of the building. Minutes later, the screen whipped past the empty office window and started circling the perimeter again.

Bill did one final radio check. "Everyone on the ready?" After everyone replied in the affirmative, the undulating light show that could be seen through the windows of the back deck began to morph on the edges into a wave of blue and red lights.

"Sheriff, over?"

"Go ahead, Steiner."

"An ambulance just went flying past us. Looks like it's headed to First and Last."

"Copy that," Bill replied, getting out of his chair. "Sal, get that thing on the front side of the building." The ambulance was pulling into the roundabout and slammed to a stop. Bill clicked his receiver. "It's a go. No sirens. We didn't expect an emergency vehicle, but that's what we got. Start rolling. Once you breach the entries, get loud and proud: bull horns, dogs, the works. Narcotics go through the front, then straight to the back office, and then search the kitchen. Send one of your people with Steiner and Lewis to cover the back deck. Steiner, enter with Grizz and help with search and seizure. Lewis, keep Luther at the door and let him do his thing until you hear from me otherwise. Make sure no one comes out. We'll meet in the middle. Staton, don't let that girl get away. I want to talk to her."

Bill heard the response from his faulty connection. "…zoo… gurney…" The others still outside came through his radio with message-delivery confirmations.

"Sal, keep that drone up in the air and keep checking back to that office. Let me know what you see," he said as he ran toward his SUV. Within seconds, he was speeding out of the building and up the road toward the scene. "Sal, check, one-two," he said, driving north at double the speed limit with lights flashing, but no sirens.

"Loud and clear, boss. The office is still clear. I can see Lewis coming underneath me with Luther and a narcotics rookie."

"If anyone comes in that office to do more business, they'll be jacked up. Turn on those blue lights for effect."

"Roger, Sheriff," Sal said.

"Narcotics, Staton, are you in?" No reply. "Narcotics, Staton, over?" Nothing.

Bill had almost reached the intersection in front of the towers when he heard Sal's voice, and not the others. "Sheriff, the office is filling up again." Bill wheeled into the roundabout and parked behind the narcotics officers, the K-9 Unit, and the evidence van. "Transports, where are you? Get your asses up here on the double."

"Copy that, Sheriff. We're pulling in behind you now."

"Sal, how many and who?"

"Looks like the last girl that was in there, Craig, and two other females from the check-out line earlier."

"Light 'em up. I'm going in. Communications are down on the inside." Bill pulled open the door, but before running in, he noticed the reflection of blue LED lights on the glass façade of the gas station across the street.

The plug had been pulled on the music, the lights were on, and he could hear Luther singing for his dinner in the back. A guy shoved into the corner was throwing up, as Grizz's brown face appeared in the middle of the sports bar, nose down and tracking. Steiner was holding him back with all she had as he barked to notify her of more contraband, while the narcotics officers that hadn't raced to the kitchen were zip-tying the accused. Standing on a table with a bullhorn, the Narcotics lead's voice sounded like it was coming through the speakers. "Everyone, remain calm. All the doors have been locked. You aren't going anywhere for a while, so please make a lane for the paramedics. Please make a lane for the paramedics." Police transport drivers hand-walked the detained through to the door.

Like a python digesting a pig, a hospital gurney separated the crowd with Bob Drolland's heaping mound of flesh lying across the wet bed sheets coming toward Bill. One EMT struggled to push the gurney while the other was giving a CPR clinic on Bob's chest. The oxygen mask pressed his face flat, his eyes barely opened but looking at him. His raised finger touched Bill's arm as he passed.

Bill's attention snapped back to reality when Officer Staton came around to his front side. "Where you been, Staton?"

"Comms dropped out completely after I entered the bar. Craig's locked himself in the back office and he has some girls in there screaming. Says he'll shoot them."

Luther's bark was getting louder as Lewis moved the dance party patrons into the bar area, the narcotics rookie close behind with his gun drawn. Snapping and slinging drool with every bark, Luther got too close and nipped a loose shirtsleeve. The girl retrieved her arm in time to save what was left of her top, while a guy behind her bolted toward the back deck two steps before being body-slammed by the rookie supporting Lewis and Luther. Bill hoped the ferocity of the take down would be a deal-breaker for any other would-be escape artist. "Quiet, Luther! Search!" Bill bellowed above the crowd. Luther changed to search-and-siezure mode, dragging Officer Lewis through the crowd as his snout searched every human hiding place. "You're all under arrest," Bill shouted. "Sit down and shut up. Deputies, start working through the winners and losers." He hurried down the hall to the door where Staton was standing. Bill rapped on the door and yelled, "Walker, this is Sheriff Bill Bolek of the Orthus County Sheriff's Department. You've never met me, but you're about to."

On the other side of the door, a man shouted. "Don't say a word, or I'll blow you all away. You didn't have to come in here. I told you not to."

Bill called through the door again. "Craig, if you have a gun, put it down. If you have hostages, do not harm them. I know you're high on coke. That's a forgivable sin. Just settle down. Can you open this door?"

"No way, Sheriff. Your people have been harassing me for months. I'm just trying to make a living. I see your undercover cops lurking around and following me around town. Now you're using drones. I'm sick of it. I'll shoot everyone in here if you open that door."

"Craig, I'm asking you one last time to be reasonable. This is over. The place is being cleared out except for you and us. Just come on out."

"Fuck you, Sheriff," came through the door followed by screams, and two gunshots.

With a kick of his boot, Bill was standing in front of Craig's desk watching everything in slow motion, his Glock pointing at Craig. Craig's gunshots had shattered the office window glass, revealing the blue and white glowing drone hovering at the window. The girl's screaming melted into white noise as Craig turned to point his gun at Staton. With all the diaphragm Bill could muster, he yelled, "Freeze!" before the hammer dropped on Craig's revolver. He watched the bullet exit the chamber followed by Staton fading behind his right side. Bill fired at the bullseye on Craig's chest, piercing it with his truest shots, the blue and white flashing lights exploding outside the empty window frame. Gunpowder smoke filled the air as Bill lowered his gun to survey the damage, his immediate concern being for Officer Staton. The two girls were crouched nearby, both their mouths fixed open in a scream, tears flooding their mascara, while Craig lay on his back sprawled across the desk and blood pooling under him. "It's over, girls," Bill said as they kept screaming. "Girls, shut up! It's over!" He kneeled down. "Staton. You OK?"

Staton nodded, groaning as he recovered to lean against the wall. "Damn. That's going to leave a mark." He turned to one of the girls in shock. "You sure look good for a new mom."

Her head lifted with a far-away stare painted with an open gape, her eyes wide looking at Staton. "What are you talking about?"

"What's your name, young lady?" Bill snapped.

She whimpered. "Candi."

He heard boot steps coming down the hall, metal boxes filled with tools clanking around inside. "Sheriff, is it clear?"

"Clear."

The forensics team from the evidence van, with boxes, gloves, and gear bags, halted at the door and then came in carefully. Bill looked around at the investigators. "We know this is the hub," he said. "Don't touch anything with your bare hands. No one touch the body till the coroner gets here. We'll take this place apart piece by piece after we get photos of everything."

One of the officers with his gloves on began collecting evidence. He pulled open the main desk drawer and pulled out a gallon-sized glass jar of cocaine. "This is a pretty good start, huh, Sheriff?"

"I'd say so." As he walked back toward the door, he looked at Lewis standing in the hall. "Lewis, put the dogs up. Steiner, make sure Candi doesn't leave the premises." He put his hand on the doorframe and turned back. "I'm going to get someone to look after Staton, unless you can walk out on your own."

"I'm coming, Sheriff. It's nothing a couple of weeks off won't fix," he said, pushing himself off the floor.

Once outside, he spoke to a silhouette standing in front of the last transport van, loaded and about to leave. "Jim, is that you?"

"Of course, it's me. This is big, Sheriff. Want to make a comment?"

"No comment yet. Just one more Saturday night. We'll do a press conference later." His phone rang with the caller ID registering from jail. He waved Jim off and answered. "This is Sheriff Bolek."

The voice on the other end said, "Sheriff, we got a guy down here in lock-up from the first load of arrests. Name's Randall. Said he had information about the MOTrax train crash, if we'd let him go. Want to make a deal with this guy?"

"Maybe. Let me him sit in the cooler for a little while. I'll be down later, after I report to the district attorney's office."

CHAPTER 39

Ezzy answered the phone. "Are you ok?"

"Yeah, I'm fine. I promised I would call."

Yawning in his ear, she said, "I'm glad you did. I had another dream about you, and this time we were both naked."

"In two days you won't be dreaming," he said, avoiding what he had to tell her.

"How'd it go?"

"It was almost a complete success."

"What do you mean almost?" she asked, all drowsiness gone from her voice.

"You're going to see some stuff in the news. Craig Walker shot Staton."

"Oh, my God. Is he alive? Where is he?"

"He's fine. We were all wearing bullet-proof vests like I told you, but I had to shoot him."

"Who?"

"Craig." He paused, not knowing what else to say. "Craig Walker. He's dead."

After a long moment wondering which way she would go, she said softly, "I'm proud of you, Bill. I'm sorry you had to do it, but that's your job. From one of the citizens you protect, thank you."

His emotions ran up in his throat. “Thanks, Ezzy. That’s the nicest thing anyone’s ever said to me.” Out of the front windshield he could see Officer Steiner bringing Candi to his truck in zip-tied handcuffs. He wiped his eyes. “I gotta’ go, babe.”

“See you when you get home. I told them at the gate you might come out in the morning, but only if you want to.”

“I’d love to, but I have a few things I need to tend to at HQ first. I’ll be out right after that and we can ride all afternoon after I get some shut-eye by your pool. Those marble water fountains do the trick every time.”

“The horses and the pool will be here when you get here. Love you.”

“You too, babe. Like you don’t know.” After he hung up the phone, he rolled down his passenger-side window. “Steiner, did you get her statement?”

“Yes, sir. She described it as it happened.”

“Good. Put that trash in my truck and make sure you wash your hands after.”

Candi was still in shock, her face and dress splattered with Craig’s blood. “I can’t go to jail. I have a plane to catch tomorrow. Why is this happening?” She looked back and forth between Bill and Steiner.

Steiner laughed and winked at Bill. “Because this place is filled with criminal activity and you decided to join in.”

“Why do we always get that question?” Bill scoffed, turned around, and hung his right wrist over the steering wheel. “Put her in the back and follow me in one of the narcs cars. They can double up with Grizz and Luther.”

“Roger that, Sheriff.”

Officer Steiner pulled the door open and pushed Candi up into the car.

"You touch your girlfriend with those hands, lezbo?" Candi yelled.

"Don't you wish. Watch your hands and your feet," she said before slamming the door.

The SUV rumbled out onto the street, and Bill lowered the separation glass in front of her a crack. "What're you doing in town, besides ruining your life with cocaine?"

"I'm here seeing a friend."

"I don't have time for this shit," he said, beginning to close the glass. "You're going to jail."

"Please," she shouted. "Wait! I'll tell you everything. I can't go to jail. I'm a Vegas showgirl."

"How long have you known Stan Jackson?"

"Since April. How did you know I know Stan?"

"If you ask me one more question, I'm hauling your ass to the inner-city jail and booking you for prostitution. You only answer my questions!"

"We met in Vegas. Sterling Johnston made arrangements for me to meet him through that slime-ball, Gene."

"Do you know he's married?"

"Yeah. So?"

He shook his head, driving from red light to red light headed to the Summit Building where Officer Staton had seen Stan leave her. "He's married, period. Doesn't anyone understand what that means anymore? Why are you here?"

"I found out he was a pro-football player, and I needed money. Plus Gene, who hired me to introduce myself to Stan, didn't pay me, so I convinced Stan I was pregnant."

"And?"

"And I came here to make a deal instead of taking him to court for a paternity suit?"

"Did he believe you?"

"Of course, he believed me. His kind are the easiest. They only think about themselves, practically begging me to take their money. He didn't even ask for the baby's DNA test. He thought the one my friend hacked was proof the baby was his."

"You do understand blackmail is a federal crime? Especially of a public official?"

"I can't go to jail. I have to get back. I won't come back here. I swear."

"Damn right you won't." He turned into the roundabout next to her hotel, and the unmarked narcotics unit pulled up beside them. "I'm Sheriff Bill Bolek of the Orthus County Sheriff's Department. You—along with a lot of other people—have been under investigation for six months. You're in the wrong place at the wrong time, but God's time is always on time, so we had the pleasure of meeting." He placed his big arm on the seat back and looked at her through the glass. "We're going to take you upstairs to your room. If you act out, Steiner is going to handcuff you on the ground, and if that doesn't work, I'll taze you. Is all that clear?"

She nodded. "Crystal."

Inside, Bill got her room key from the front desk because Candi had managed to lose hers at the bar. "Is this the baby prosthetic you wore? And the dress?" Steiner asked as she walked over to the bed to pick up her baby bump.

"Where is the money he gave you?" Bill asked.

She walked over to the other side of the bed, pulled the check out of her overnight bag, and handed it to him. "He was going to pay me one hundred thousand dollars for ten years from some business he started."

Bill looked at the check. "Coyotes Concessions, LLC? Interesting." Then he dropped it on the bed. "Tell you what. You're going to leave here and forget you know Stan Jackson. You're never going to speak of this night again, and you'll never step foot in

Orlando again, or I'll arrest you myself within ten minutes of being inside the city limits. Got it?"

"How're you going to keep me out of Orlando?"

"Since your word is no good, and because you're so high, I'll explain nice and slow. Us cops stick together. First thing Monday morning, I'm going to call Vegas PD. Every aspect of your life is about to get monitored. You should spend your entire flight back tomorrow thinking about what you're going to do next. My suggestion would be to do the next right thing. Keep doing it every time you find yourself at a fork in the road. We'll be watching." He pointed at the check on the bed. "That is your parting gift. I wouldn't cash it. Frame it maybe, but it's no good, or at least it won't be," he offered, setting the trap to ensnare Stan if she ever cashed it.

"That son of a bitch lied to me."

"Not really, but you wouldn't understand. And given that you lied to him, I wouldn't start plotting revenge. Steiner will be outside this door all night. She'll make sure you're on that plane tomorrow." He and Steiner nodded at each other before he looked at Candi again. "Don't come back. This is your lucky break. I'm sure you've told yourself a hundred times if you could just get one. Well, this is it."

As he was closing the door behind them, he saw Candi crumple to the floor in relief, tears finally spilling over onto her cheeks. Bill put his phone away. "Make sure she's on that plane."

"It will be my pleasure, Sheriff," he heard behind him as he jogged to the open elevator door filled with people coming in from the evening.

CHAPTER 40

Paige came down the stairs not really wanting coffee, but also wanting to carry on like life was normal—like her routine mattered—because if she could get through today, she could get through tomorrow. And the next day and the next.

She sat with her usual mug and opened her tablet to the *Orthus County Post*: "No More Chances for First Chance Last Chance" and "One Dead in Orlando Drug Bust - Commissioner Drolland Leaves in Ambulance."

She'd been up until 4:00 AM fielding phone calls, so none of this was news to her. She closed her tablet and checked her phone for messages—several texts from Bill following up on their conversation from just hours earlier, and a voicemail from Judi, who'd likely read the paper herself and was checking in on her. Paige hadn't told her about Stan moving out—or about his girlfriend and her fake pregnancy and the extortion money. She wasn't prepared for any "I told you so's" or, worse, her sister's sympathy. So she deleted the message without bothering to play it.

Her phone rang as she was setting it down and wondering how bad it would really be if she just crawled back into bed after all. She took a deep breath before answering the call.

"Hey, Bill. No rest for the weary, huh?"

The sheriff chuckled. “Who needs sleep? Sleep is for the weak. Hey, I just wanted to update you real quick. In addition to all the information those three employee-turned-informants gave us plenty on the MOTrax distribution routes and in-house sales, I got some good stuff from Randall. By the time I got to the jail a couple of hours ago, he was eager to tell me everything about the crash and would’ve given me his first-born if he’d thought it would help him. He’s been released on bond.”

“All good. Thanks, Bill. And I called the hospital before grabbing a few hours of sleep. Bob was barely hanging on.”

“Yeah, Ezzy checked on him this morning. No change.”

“And our, uh, other problem?” she asked, biting her lip to keep her emotions in check.

“My officer personally escorted her to her gate and didn’t leave until her plane took off. She won’t ever come back. I’ll give Vegas PD the heads up this afternoon. She’ll probably try to cash that check, though.”

Paige nodded. They’d already talked about this. “Right. And if she does, Stan will go to jail for embezzlement and bribery. If she doesn’t, Stan will just go away. He’s not my problem anymore.” She sipped her coffee, letting the anger move her forward before she could give the forgiveness she knew must come, for her own sake. Just not yet.

“So, are your people getting collateral evidence for our press conference tomorrow?”

“We have pictures of Craig’s gun he shot Staton with in his hand, drone video, including from the one I shot, plus shell casings, operating equipment, and cash on a big stainless-steel counter. We found ten kilos in the office, a bunch of eight-ball baggies, and a false bottom cooler next to the back door. We’ve got statements from all the witnesses, and we’re already flipping the kitchen staff to pull down their supplier.”

"Did you get the information from Kirsty and Patrick?"

"Nothing yet, but I'm going into the office now. Kirsty was supposed to give it to my guy this morning."

"What about Patrick?"

"Nope, nothing yet."

"Does he think I won't follow through with an arrest?" She finished the last drop in her coffee mug, and stood to place it in the sink.

"I don't know. I can have him picked up on your authority."

"We'll see," she said. "He has until the end of the day today. Orthus Regional owes their bond payment tomorrow, and our press conference is tomorrow afternoon. If Orthus Regional defaults, we'll close the net all at once."

"I'm almost in the office. I'll call back with any info."

"OK. Thanks, Bill." She hung up and leaned back against the kitchen counter. The painting she'd brought back from the antique show Easter weekend at home in Atlanta hung at an angle on the wall across from her, and she reached out to straighten it.

"Let's have our ice cream out on the front porch, girls," Judge gripped the armrests of his favorite recliner to push himself up. Paige noticed it was a feat that was taking longer every year.

Outside, Paige plopped down onto the cozy deck chair, eating slowly so the frost of the ice cream could melt in the spring breeze. The view had changed since Paige was little and her mother would sit out here singing to her in the twilight haze. Back then, they'd looked out onto an old run-down golf course. Now professional tournaments were held there, televised all over the world thanks to the investments of local real-estate billionaires.

"I wish Stanley could've joined us, Paige," Judge said. "I need someone to play golf with over there. Joe and I hacked it up pretty good this morning, but he's busy, too."

"I know, Daddy," Paige said, wishing any mention of Stan could've held off a little longer.

Judi put her bowl down on the table hard enough for the spoon to swirl around the rim. "May as well get used to the fact that Joe's all you got, Daddy." She fell back onto the cushion in a huff. "I can't believe he went to Vegas for Easter, Paige. If Joe ever treated me like that . . ."

"It's a business conference, Judi." Paige sighed, so tired of defending a marriage she barely cared about herself anymore. "He's out there with the County Commission Chair and the Development Authority Chair."

"A conference that lasts through Easter weekend? Come on, Paige. He's out there having fun. Without you."

"What kind of conference is it, Paige?" Judge asked, always trying to keep the peace between her and Judi.

"It's an economic development conference for politicians. You know, public officials. A big national developer pays for the trips. He does it for favors when public officials issue debt."

"What kind of debt?" Judge asked, propping his feet up on the ottoman.

"They issue billions in debt for pensions and infrastructure. Lately, more pensions and less infrastructure. Stan issued a bond so the MOTrail could be built, which is probably why he got invited. Our county commissioner and his best friend, the development authority chair, issue debt through the Orthus County Development Authority, but that's just the revenue bonds."

"Hmmm. Interesting word, authority." Judge peered at her over the top of his ice cream bowl. "I read up a little bit on the subject."

"Oh?" Paige asked, settling in and hoping Judi was cooling off. "And what did you discover?"

"Well, there are two sides to every argument I suppose, but it seems to me development authority law is a double-edged sword. The milled edge of economic development begets the dulled edge of municipal responsibility."

"You *have* been doing your research." Paige set her bowl on the table. "Anything else?"

"There seems to be a positive correlation between higher taxes and better schools in rural areas, but the correlation disintegrates in metro areas, possibly because of expansive and liberal economic development activity."

Paige nodded. "That's what most of my research leads me to believe. Furthermore, we've issued more debt than the ratings companies can keep up with for both pensions and tax abatements. Then there's the tax abatement du jour, phantom bonds, an inverted bond that doesn't show up on the balance sheet."

"Because Florida is a transaction state, you have to issue bonds for tax abatements and the development authority has to own the capital asset being built. Is that correct?"

"Exactly," she said. Judge's line of thinking didn't surprise her, because he was such a student of policy and interested in current events where she and Judi lived, "For every development, there's a different bond issue, or transaction, except our hospital and regional airport. Those were both done in the same deal, a blind pool."

"And your development authority owns all the land, and the only bonds you vote on are for parks and roads? Then you're double taxed for the services with special-option sales taxes that were supposed to be paid by property taxes, but because of all the abatements, it's not enough."

"You're nailing it, Daddy."

"A buddy at the club explained it to me." He finished up his ice cream, and Judi took the bowl from him to place it on the table. "We have similar arrangements here in Atlanta, but most developers do have hearts. Many of them are gifted visionaries with altruistic ideas. The first charter school in the city is right around the corner. You passed it on the way here."

"I wondered what that was," Judi said.

"It's a beautiful new school. You remember this place when you were kids?"

"I sure do, Daddy." Judi said. "I was lucky to get out of here."

Judge smiled over at her. "I got thank you notes from the neighbors when you left, dear. The Dean's letters from Athens were similar in sentiment."

Paige couldn't hold back her laughter as Judi scoffed, miming a drum roll, and said, "Please tip your bartenders and waitresses, folks. They'll be here all week."

Paige laughed again. "Who built the school?"

"One of our in-town developers," he said. "Part of his vision was a school. He thought the abated school taxes he used to redevelop this golf course should be replaced with something worthy of the sting. What do you think?"

"It's more beautiful than the golf course," Paige said.

"It's a beacon of hope for these kids." Judge said. "But sadly, he's in the minority along with your Esmeralda King."

Paige tilted her head. "How do you know her?"

"I don't. I have an empty nest, girls. Lots of golf and lots of research. She started King Christian Academy, right?"

Paige frowned. "Stan talks about it all the time. He's jealous."

"She's surpassed even the success of our charter school here. Maybe there's an opportunity for a friendship, Paige. You and she do seem to have a lot in common, beauty being the most obvious."

"Why thank you, but you're too much, Judge," she said. "My mother used to say I get it from my daddy."

"You're both too much. Momma used to say that, too." Paige looked over at Judi and they smiled at each other in the same way they'd done their whole lives after arguing. It was that smile that said, 'Here we are. No matter what.' Paige knew Judi loved her and wanted her to be happy. It's what Judge wanted, too.

She felt her anxiety heighten. "You're right about one thing, Daddy. You can count on one hand the developers that've built schools with the tax cuts they receive. Our local developer keeps telling Stan he'll get his money back in twenty years. What he and his friends can't seem to comprehend is that their long-term upside isn't even close to being a fair tradeoff for the risks they're taking. But it's happening all over the country."

"It would be very difficult for Stan, or any elected official, to ascertain the financial benefit of any of those projects. My research yielded no case studies with concrete conclusions of the economic benefits of—commercial centers, sports stadiums, or even apartment complexes. Only the blighted redevelopments have a chance, because the bar is so low for success. Therefore—in all fairness— it's hard to blame Stan for the proposals he receives and then takes no action."

"Well, he took two hundred million of action on the MOTrail," she said. "And they can't even pay their bills half the time."

Judi sighed. "He's still an asshole for leaving you on Easter," she said, her voice gentler this time. "I don't care what he's doing out there for work. You deserve better than that."

Damn straight, I do, Paige said to herself, and headed to her room to get ready to face the day. As she opened her closet door, her phone rang again.

"Hey, Bill. Did you forget to tell me something?"

"Nope. Just wanted to let you know I got to my office, and a big envelope from Kirsty was sitting here on my desk to greet me."

"And?"

"Hold on . . . I'm opening it up right now." She heard rustling papers and a rip. "Let's see. There're several spreadsheets here with a bunch of sticky notes attached. And a letter on the front."

"What's it say?"

"It says . . . Dunham Schauble is using the unused portion of the Orthus Blind Pool escrow accounts for business operations, the racing team, yacht maintenance, and a new sailboat in San Francisco." He paused. "Bob's condo financing is in here, too. She says it's in return for using Enzo for the blind pool. Dunham Schauble bought the second floor this past summer after the MOTrax phantom bond was issued. Some of this stuff is complicated, and you'll be able to make more sense of it than I can. But she goes on quite a bit. She, uh, . . ." He paused again. "Give me a sec. OK, she says the escrow for the Chicago blind pool and the Chicago Athletic Authority are twice as big as Progress Orthus escrows. If Orthus defaults, Dunham Schauble will fail because of all the Orthus debt they own. If Dunham Schauble fails, Chicago will default, because all their unused blind-pool escrow's been spent building out the San Francisco office. Is she talking about sports stadiums, or embezzlement?"

"Both," Paige said as she exhaled. "This is worse than I thought. Anything else?"

"Yeah. Second page is the SEC letter-of-intent-to-review. Pretty standard government stuff. Uh oh."

"Uh oh, what?"

"You're not going to like this, but a sticky note on the Coyotes Stadium memorandum says Patrick, Flash, Enzo, Sterling, and Warren are meeting today to sign the bond-issuance contracts. I guess they're working on Sunday since they heard about last night's take down."

She rubbed her forehead and sat on her bed. "I would venture to guess they're meeting on Sunday because they know something about Orthus Regional Hospital's bond payment tomorrow."

"Ah-ha. That's why you're in charge."

"I've been planning this for months. It's going to be very bad, but the bond-issuance memorandum they're signing won't see the light of day."

"Paige, the citizens of Orthus County need you. Half the stuff I just read, I don't understand. I've never been through a bankruptcy before, but I've been hearing horror stories. It sounds like a three-year shit storm, pardon my Seminole."

"It will be Orthus County's worst history. The bond markets provide liquidity until the money runs out, and then it's like a migraine that never goes away. I'll be blamed for all of the mistakes, and trust me, I'm going to need you more than you need me. You have my word the public's safety provided by the Orthus County Sheriff's and Fire Departments will be my top priority."

"We're with you one hundred percent."

She held back any overconfidence attributed to the perfect timing fate was handing her. "Can you get those documents over to my office this afternoon? If Orthus Regional defaults tomorrow, we'll stick to the plan of a late afternoon press conference. I'll call the governor this afternoon to tell him I'll need immediate emergency manager authority. Then I'll call Chicago and uncover any interest in a dual-defense strategy to hold Wall Street at bay."

"Ezzy mentioned you had classmates up there?"

"I do. There's an old saying in finance: 'If you owe the bond market a billion, they own you. If you owe the bond market ten billion, you own them.' Who knows? Maybe we're stronger together. This is a first for most of us, too. If I get the judge's arrest warrant early tomorrow, think you can pick Patrick up before noon?" she asked. "Preferably in his dealership with Jim's cameras rolling."

"On charges of defrauding Orthus County taxpayers, and theft I presume? What about Enzo?"

"Yep, embezzlement and taxpayer theft for Touchdown, LLC. I'm sure we'll find some more stuff once we get him behind bars and he starts singing. We'll let the FBI Financial Crimes Unit handle Enzo. Please notify Kirsty to skip work tomorrow."

"Good call. I'll drop these documents off on my way back out to Ezzy's."

Paige hung up, exhausted, but glad she'd had that cup of coffee after all.

CHAPTER 41

Patrick walked alongside Stan through the parking deck of the Dunham Schauble lobby, and met up with Sterling as they entered the building, the black granite floor surrounded on all sides by glass and shining in the mid-morning sun.

"Dr. Jackson, did you ride over from Orlando with Patrick?" Sterling asked.

"Yeah, I wanted to get a better perspective on some of the details of the deal and how we can help expedite the process."

Patrick was happy to drive, seeing as how Stan had apparently been shopping all morning, and his front and back seats were filled with clothes. He had the pleasure of delivering a willing student to the table. Stan had asked all the right questions on the way over about the upside potential of economic development, even though Patrick would have to split his half of the concessions contracts with him. Stan wouldn't know about the new real estate "best and highest use" option for the Johnston Limited Lofts parcel until after the Coyotes Stadium deal was inked, but that's the way it had to be done: one step at a time. Warren and Bob had already sent word they preferred a Salvatore dealership to a high school any day of the week.

"The Orthus County Administration office is on meltdown alert," Patrick said, eager to get this deal signed before anyone could ruin it. Bob's heart attack last night had been a blessing in disguise—for Patrick, anyway. "And my phone's been ringing all morning." He looked over to the revolving doors to see Enzo and a beautiful, leggy blond walking in. He wiped his palms on his pants before he reached out to Enzo. "Thanks for meeting us on such short notice, Enzo. I think you've met Dr. Jackson."

Stan stuck out his hand, causing the shirtsleeve to retreat up his arm. "Hey, Enzo."

"Hello, Flash. Did your shirt shrink at the cleaners?"

Flash lifted both his fists and twisted his arms to reveal both wrists. "No, this shirt's new. I got it for this special occasion."

"Oh, well, maybe you can get your money back," Enzo said with a smirk. He nodded to the woman beside him. "This is my Chief Information Officer, Kirsty McPhee."

"Pleasure's all mine," Stan said. The smarmy look on his face turned Patrick's stomach. Stan's "Flash" persona had a way of transfixing women at first sight.

"Why the rush to get this done today, Patrick?" Sterling asked.

"Tell me you read the news, Sterling. Bob Drolland had a heart attack last night at the scene of a major drug bust at First Chance Last Chance."

"My apologies. Yes, I read. And how is Bob?"

"He's in critical condition," Patrick answered, but he knew Sterling lacked empathy as a rule. "Orthus Regional was understaffed last night, so he had to wait in the emergency room for an hour before he was seen, and then they ran out of nitroglycerin, and could only give him aspirin until he was admitted."

Sterling pursed his lips. "Not including the additional self-prescribed medications, I imagine."

"C'mon," Patrick said after shaking hands with Kirsty. "I've been with Bob when he's been offered. He doesn't touch the stuff."

"Your naiveté is an endearing quality, Patrick. Never lose it." Sterling may as well have been patting his head, considering the amount of condescension in his tone. "Kirsty," Sterling continued. "It's nice to meet you. We've heard so much about your work."

"You're too kind. I'm really looking forward to the new stadium."

"Gentlemen, please join us in the penthouse." Enzo looked around the circle. "Warren plans to join us momentarily. He's probably landing on our helipad as we speak. Kirsty was also up at the crack of dawn to prepare some documents for your arrival." He smiled, peered down at her, his eyes almost closing, and said, "I don't know where she gets her energy, but her café con leche, using my mother's Cuban press, is supreme."

Enzo waved his arm around and started walking toward the elevator with Kirsty on his other arm. As he was leading them past the front desk, the security guard nodded, rolled the toothpick in his mouth, and said, "Good morning, Mr. Ruiz. Are all these folks with you?"

Enzo nodded back without stopping. "They sure are, as is the one on the rooftop. Thanks for keeping an eye on things. Do you recognize Flash Jackson?"

"I'm a Sharks fan, but I know who Flash is," the security guard flipped two fingers off his bald forehead and moved the toothpick from one side of his mouth to the other. "How you doing?"

Stan nodded. "Better than the Sharks," and then laughed at his own joke. "But no disrespect."

"None taken. Watch your step across the middle of the lobby." He pointed toward the elevator bank with disdain. "It gets dicey for free agents. No disrespect."

Patrick walked into the elevator behind Kirsty, concealing the amusement from the security guard's smack talk, and was barricaded in the back corner after everyone got on. They rode to the top-floor executive offices overlooking Tampa Bay, and Patrick stepped off last. He followed the group through the double doors of the glass façade that provided a view past the conference-room table with neatly placed stacks of documents, and out the other side of the building. The only thing blocking the line of sight was a narrow floor-to-ceiling stainless steel wall behind the front desk. "Who would like coffee?" Kirsty asked as she stopped in front of the receptionist's desk.

Patrick didn't want coffee. He wanted signatures on paperwork, so he held back a groan when Stan and Enzo accepted, and Sterling made a special request for tea. "Okay, gentlemen," he said. "Enzo, is it OK if we take it in the conference room?"

"Whatever you say, Patrick. Kirsty, you heard the man."

Patrick turned toward the conference room and heard Stan make an excuse for him and then offer to help. Kirsty cut him short. "It's nothing, I got it," she said.

When he got to the edge of the cubes and trading desks, Stan said from behind him, "Enzo, the upgrades look outstanding since the last time I was here. Love what you've done with the place." Patrick moaned quietly, irritated at yet another delay, and turned around to show the required interest.

"Dr. Jackson, . . ." Enzo started before Stan interrupted.

"Man, call me Flash," he said, and leaned on one of the cube entrances.

"OK. Thanks, Flash, and thanks for your kind words. One of Sterling's teams did the whole building when we went public, and then again about a year ago to spruce things up. We shouldn't wait so long to do more business together. Your potential leverage could support a lot of new economic development that's proven to support schools."

Stan blathered on a bit about the MOTrail deal signed here two years ago forging his constituents' commitment, which was stifling for Patrick because he saw how easily other officials had caught on to his secret sauce of deal making.

No sooner had they pulled their chairs in around the grand wooden conference table than Warren walked in the room with Kirsty on his arm. "Gentlemen," Warren said, "who was foolish enough to let this girl make coffee for us?" He turned to her. "Please, Kirsty, take a seat. I've got to introduce you to my son. He makes his own coffee."

As she smiled up at Warren, Patrick felt like an idiot yet again for not having enough sense to know how to play a room like the rest of them. He caught Stan's thousand-watt smile lighting up and a fixed stare on Enzo's face. Kirsty smiled back at Stan, and then shifted her eyes to Enzo's before coming around and sitting down between them.

"I don't know why we need to meet on Sunday afternoon, but I'm here," Warren said. "When I get back from getting that coffee myself, let's finish this thing. I've got a flight to catch."

Patrick folded his arms and listened to Sterling, Stan, and Enzo discuss future sports stadium designs, the suites Stan would have access to in the Coyotes Stadium, and new ideas for Stan, such as MOTrail creek-side apartment homes. Patrick tried to silence his thoughts while he waited for Warren's return, praying income from concessions contracts and a car dealership on the Johnston Limited Lofts site instead of a high school didn't come up.

"Let's get started," Warren said as he came through the door with an eyebrow raised, frowning at Patrick, and set the tray in the middle of the table.

Patrick took a deep breath as the others reached for their drinks. "I called everyone here on such short notice because of the uncertainty surrounding the county commission. Bob is in critical condition with little chance of a full recovery, so we need to get this deal sewn up before a soon-to-be-named interim commission chair decides to take a second look."

"Any word on Orthus Regional Hospital's payment?" Enzo asked.

"Should be right on time. If not, the general fund will cover it," Patrick said.

"You know it's due tomorrow, right?" Enzo asked. "I assume you've been in discussion with them?"

"Of course, I have," Patrick lied, but to say otherwise would throw sand in the gears. "They got a bump in third-quarter revenues and should be OK."

"In that case, let's proceed," Enzo said. "These documents will have a three-pronged effect. They'll allow Progress Orthus to take ownership of the parcel commonly known as the Smithson Galleria project site, all future buildings, and the stadium. They'll allow the Orthus School Board to issue a bond via Progress Orthus for six hundred and fifty million dollars for the purchase, construction, and infrastructure investments at the new site."

Patrick had already finished signing his copy, while listening to Enzo drone on like a mortgage closing attorney, and watching the others for movement. "Progress Orthus will abate the taxes of the City of Smithson, Orthus County, and Orthus School Board for twenty years," Enzo said, "while the lessee, Smithson Coyotes Stadium, LLC, pays the thirty-two-million-dollar annual principal, and interest, on the bond. The lessee will also pay the lessor, Progress Orthus, an administrative fee of seven million dollars annually for use at the development authority's discretion." Stan finished signing his copy. "Progress Orthus will pay into a special tax-allocation district around the Grady cluster in the amount of two million dollars per year. Is that reminiscent of what everyone agreed to?" They all nodded, and Patrick prayed one last time nothing else would come up. "Then if you'll all sign where Kirsty has highlighted, I'll begin putting the issue out on the street. The municipal market has a very aggressive appetite for the tax-free high yields you're offering. Dunham Schauble will keep anything we can't sell. Thank you all for this opportunity to grow Orthus County."

Warren signed finally after reading the last page of the contract, and Patrick nearly yanked it out of his hand.

Patrick turned to Sterling, who handed him his contract as well. "We'll go ahead and get the contracts ready for Progress Orthus to buy Johnston Limited Lofts, LLC, too. That sound okay, Sterling? We need to get started on the new high school funding as quickly as possible."

"Yeah, you guys go ahead and get that started," Stan said. "I'd like to have that new high school online within two years. We're busting at the seams."

"Let's let the dust settle on this deal first, gentlemen," Sterling said, capping his pen. "We wouldn't want to seem eager to spend taxpayer dollars on an investment owned by one of the people authorizing this credit facility, would we?"

"You're probably right," Stan said. "But how long before you begin construction?"

Sterling smiled. "Dr. Jackson, we have to procure the land and design the facilities, with your input, of course. Then we need to pick a construction company. It'll take time, but your new school will stand as a monument to the benefits of urban planning."

Patrick took one last shot at the hoop, not caring what the optics were, because he wasn't doing anything illegal, but didn't want to drive back to Orlando empty-handed. "Sterling, I understand your concerns, but I'd like to expedite the sale, if that's OK with you." The dual attack of Sterling's lawyer's not-so-subtle suggestions of bankruptcy, and the Salvatore CFO's threats to take his dealership, were dominating his every thought.

"Sure, Patrick. We can schedule some time next week after I get back from Vegas. I'm sure you have some ideas for design features that might be useful to Stan's new school." Patrick's anxiety shielded him from Sterling's jab for a moment, but then his stomach knotted as he recognized Sterling's sarcasm.

"Got an extra seat?" Stan asked.

Sterling turned in his chair. "Oh, my mistake, Dr. Jackson. I'd be delighted to take you back to Vegas. Give me some times you're available in the next few months. We'll schedule a trip for just you and me."

"You bet. I'll make room on the calendar, but don't let Patrick anywhere near the designs of my new high school," he said.

Relieved that Stan knew nothing of his plans for his new Salvatore dealership at the heart of the North American headquarters, Patrick shrugged. "No problem, Stan. Sterling, I can come to your airport offices as soon as you get back, and bring you the memorandum of understanding for the parcel."

"Whatever you say, Patrick."

"Well, if that's it, I'm flying the helicopter back over to Orlando for the Ospreys game," Warren said. He stood and slipped his sport jacket on, and turned back to Kirsty as he walked toward the glass doors. "Miss McPhee, would you like to join me? My son will be there."

"Kirsty and I are heading to my yacht for another afternoon of romping around the Sun Coast," Enzo said before she could answer for herself. "But thanks for the offer."

"Oh, Jeez. Sorry guys. I, uh, I didn't know. I thought . . ." Warren smiled. "Oh, well, never mind what I thought. Everyone have a great day. I'll be in touch on the details of the Coyotes next move."

"Got room on the chopper, Warren?" Stan asked. "I was going to get Patrick to drop me off, but you're quicker, and I can get us on the sidelines."

"I can get myself on the sidelines, but I've got room if you need a lift."

Stan turned to Patrick, his hands already supporting himself on the armrests as he got ready to stand. "You don't mind do you, Patrick?"

"No," Patrick said, provided with no other option. "No problem. What're you're plans for—" But he stopped himself mid-sentence as Stan followed Sterling, Kirsty, and Enzo out of the office, and he was left with his radioactive thoughts of what he'd do if the parcel didn't get sold before he had to file.

CHAPTER 42

The Monday morning *Orthus County Post* headlines read "Orthus Regional Hospital Defaults - Orthus County Imploding."

Patrick walked past the brick wall on the sidewalk to the glass showroom doors, scanned the floor to see if anyone was buying, and saw Sheriff Bolek talking to Gloria. Two uniformed officers sat on the couch reading muscle car magazines and watching TV. When they saw him, they dropped what they were doing and stood up. Bill stepped away from Gloria's desk. "Good morning, Patrick. It's been a couple of days. How you doing?"

"Fine, Sheriff." Patrick couldn't imagine he was there for more questions. He'd assured himself Paige's arrest threat was a bluff—not that it mattered anyway, given that Patrick was twenty-four hours past a done deal. "You guys in for service? I didn't see your cars." He picked up his mail. "Good morning, Gloria."

"Morning, Patrick," Gloria said, looking a little wary.

"No need for service today, Jim. We parked next door. Officer Crowley, can you bring my SUV around?" he asked, and waved his finger above him in a circle. "Officer Bozeman, please stand by. Patrick, you're under arrest for theft, fraud, embezzlement, and violation of the RICO act. You have the right to remain silent. Probably a good idea."

"Oh, my God. Should I call someone, Patrick?" Gloria asked, and pushed away from her desk.

"Miss . . . Gloria, is it? Could you get Patrick some coffee for the ride down? I promised handcuffs, but I think he'll probably cooperate. Anything you say, Patrick, will be held against you in a court of law. You have the right to counsel. If you cannot afford counsel, your friends, the Orthus County taxpayers, will provide you with counsel. Is all of that clear?"

Patrick set his mail back on Gloria's desk and looked at Officer Bozeman. "I saw you a couple of weeks ago at the development authority meeting," Patrick said, and then turned to Bill. "Please, Sheriff, right here in the dealership? Is this necessary?"

"Yeah, it was District Attorney Jackson's idea, but I didn't argue. Having Jim film your arrest was my idea."

Patrick turned to see Jim Pinson walking through the front door with a camera outstretched in his hands. Shaking harder after being read his Miranda rights, he forced a smile and said, "Good morning, Jim. I'm not answering any of your questions."

With the camera three feet from Patrick's face, Jim asked, "How much money do you get from your airport business in return for taxpayer financing?"

"Please be professional, Jim. That's inappropriate. I told you I wouldn't answer your questions." Patrick looked at Bill, who just shrugged his shoulders.

"How much will you receive from the new Coyotes Stadium contract on behalf of Orthus County taxpayers?" Jim asked.

"No comment." Patrick reached up to grab the camera, and before he knew what was happening, Officer Bozeman had his arm behind his back and his face on the receptionist desk. Patrick winced with pain as he clicked the last couple of notches of the handcuffs on his wrist bone.

He was eye level with Gloria, who had just walked back in with two cups of coffee in her hand, and her mouth was wide open. "Here's your coffee, Sheriff. Uh, Patrick?"

"For Chissake, Gloria! I don't want any coffee!"

"I'll take it." Officer Bozeman said. "That OK, Sheriff?"

Robbed of basic respect before he'd even been removed from his dealership, Patrick looked up at Bill, hoping for at least some sign of compassion.

Bill looked down at him and raised a half smile. "Yes, Officer Bozeman. You may have the coffee since Gloria made it and Patrick doesn't want it." He shook his head still looking at Patrick, thumbed toward Bozeman, who was exerting just enough upward pressure on his wrist to keep his face buried in the desk. "Take 'em to school and they eat the books. Let's go, Patrick."

Officer Bozeman grabbed his sports jacket around the back of the collar, and motivated him by tweaking his bound wrists. In the reflection of the entrance door, Patrick could see Jim following them. Officer Bozeman shoved him forward, banging his face on the glass, and then insincerely apologized.

Once they stepped outside, Sheriff Bolek nodded toward Patrick's SUV. "Would you please search Mr. McDaniel's truck, Officer Crowley? Thanks."

Officer Bozeman opened the door of the sheriff's truck and Patrick crawled in, ducking down in the back, behind the tinted window of Bill's SUV. He curled up on the floorboard to escape the spotlight.

As he let tears escape into the floor mats, he heard Crowley's voice outside the SUV window. "Hey, Sheriff. I found this paperwork in Mr. McDaniel's car."

"Oh, good. I'll take that. See you guys back at the station." Sheriff Bolek opened the driver's side door and got in. "Hey Patrick, why are there two memorandums of understanding?

One for Smithson Coyotes Stadium, LLC, and one for Johnston Limited Lofts, LLC?"

"I'm only speaking to my attorney," he said, wiping his wet face on the seat covers.

"Think Wall Street will tape all the pages together after they get shredded in bankruptcy court?"

"Sheriff, please. What do I have to do? This is going to ruin my life. I'll do anything. Please don't take me to jail." His tears continued to flow as Bill cranked the SUV, ordered Bozeman to buckle him into the seat, and reminded him not to forget his coffee.

Before Bill pulled out of the parking lot, he said, "Nice try, but what can I say? I told you so. It's the end of the line for ole' Patrick's magical mystery money machine. Are you beginning to get that moment of clarity?" The window between the seats slowly closed, isolating him.

Enzo looked around the lobby as he walked out to the Dunham Schauble receptionist desk. "Have you seen Kirsty? We walked in together thirty minutes ago. Our stock price is getting crushed. Orthus Regional Hospital defaulted, and Patrick isn't answering his phone. We need all hands on deck."

"You don't have to tell me, boss." The receptionist pointed to the real-time chart on her screen of DSBL stock showing a one-day cliff drop finalizing a two-month decline with share volume trading at all-time highs. "All my retirement is wrapped up here in Dunham Schauble stock, and the news channels won't stop calling. Kirsty came back out five minutes after you two arrived, and said she forgot something in her car. I thought she was just going to the beach like she does every day you're not here."

"That can't be." Enzo looked back through the glass. All the office staff was sitting at computers or holding phones in their hands, but all of them were looking back at him. "She's in charge of this software upgrade."

"I need to answer these phones, sir," the receptionist said. "Dunham Schauble, how may I direct your call?" She paused for the answer and said, "I'm not sure if he's available. Let me check." She put the line on hold. "It's a lady from the credit-ratings agency. What should I tell her?"

"Forward it to my office." He walked back through the cubes filled with sweating traders, crying secretaries, and people filling boxes with their belongings. Once inside with the door closed behind him, he picked up the phone. "Enzo here."

"Mr. Ruiz, this is Donna Hernandez. I have some questions about the Orthus Regional Hospital Bonds. Do you have a minute?"

"I have the utmost confidence those payments will be made. Orthus County taxpayers will obligate themselves to pay that debt."

"Sure, I understand that ultimately they're responsible, but my concerns are related to Dunham Schauble's ability to pay the Chicago blind-pool interest payments on the funds you hold in escrow given the sudden loss of Orthus Regional Hospital's interest payments to you, and possibly more lost income should any of the Orthus County bonds on your books begin to sour."

"What? You can't be serious. Of course, we're going to make our interest payments. We're the largest bond underwriter in the country." The glass walls around his office had seemed like such a good idea when Sterling suggested them, but now the entire company watched him like he was an animal at the zoo.

"Not even close, Mr. Ruiz. Can you please provide your current financial reports up to, and including, today? I need them by this afternoon in order to assess any credit-ratings changes we'll make to Dunham Schauble's outstanding credit notes, or the other municipal bonds you hold as custodian."

"There's no reason to be so forceful." He turned away from the window so no one could read his lips. "We're attending to the SEC Inquiry at the moment. We're a little shorthanded."

"Mr. Ruiz, that information provides me with an even greater sense of urgency. I'll look for those documents this afternoon."

"We'll do what we can. Thanks for your patience." He slammed the phone down, and picked up his blinking line. "Yes? What now?"

"There're some people out here to see you."

"Jesus, Mother Mary." He hung up, and walked back out to the main entrance lobby, where three men in blue jackets with "FBI" on the back were facing him.

"Gentlemen, anything I can do for you?"

"We're from the FBI Financial Crimes Unit. We have some questions. Can you please join us downtown?"

"What?" he scoffed. "Not without my attorney present."

"That's fine," the agent continued. "You're under arrest for bribery, embezzlement, and theft by taking. You have the right to remain silent…"

Their words meaningless to him, Enzo thought about the checkered flag he'd never see until they finished. He pulled his attorney's card out of his wallet and handed it over. "This man will answer your questions." Then he turned around as they placed the cuffs on him, and saw a middle-aged woman with a loose-fitting white tank top over yoga pants, standing in the middle of the lobby with a camera. "Who are you?" he asked.

"I'm Rebecca Pinson. My husband, Jim, from the *Orthus County Post,* is so busy covering the news he asked me to get this on film. Would you like to answer some questions?"

The officers guided him toward the elevator, as he strained to keep his neck and tie straight. "Turn that damn camera off," he barked.

"How will you repay Orthus County, or Chicago taxpayers, the money you borrowed to run Dunham Schauble's racing team and your personal yacht?" she asked, her chipper voice pissing him off to the point of boiling over now.

"Go fuck yourself," he said as he stepped on the elevator in front of the three men before being turned around toward the opening, now looking into the eye of her camera.

"That's what Jim said you'd say. He had one other question," she said, and paused. "Do you think they'll let you keep your suits in prison to save money on your clothes?"

Her broad smile evaporated behind the two metal doors closing together.

Paige looked over at Judge in the passenger's seat. "You sure you're okay sitting in the car for twenty minutes."

"Absolutely. I need to tie these flies before this afternoon and download my Florida non-resident fishing license. Now get going, but leave the car running. I'm proud of you, baby. You're my fa-fa-favorite daughter."

She laughed at the ambiguous claim he'd always made to both her, and Judi, but still not understanding why she'd trusted Stan over both of their objections. In the lobby outside First and Last, she got the debriefing by the on-scene investigator, and then stepped onto the elevator going up to Stan's offices. The doors opened and she stepped into the full view of Stan's executive assistant. Walking and talking, she said, "I'm leaving some paperwork in Stan's office."

"Yes, ma'am. Whatever you say, Mrs. Jackson," the young girl said, keeping her eyes glued to her mobile phone. "But Stan's not here yet."

"I know," Paige said, and kept walking.

"I had to park down the street because of all the yellow tape. Where'd you park?" the receptionist grumbled loud enough for Paige to hear her. The young woman's open contempt was generally something Paige would've addressed, but she had bigger fish to fry this morning. The breeze she made as she hurried down the hall followed her dress around the door and into the office.

The old demons Judge had tried to exorcise her whole life were boiling around in her mind. *Why didn't I see? Weren't the signs all around me?* She leaned into the glass door leading out to the balcony, nearly delirious with self-doubt. She looked north to the Smithson Galleria site, planes from OSK ascending through dust devils spinning upward from the gravel abyss several miles north, and visible from Stan's balcony, her thoughts whirring past the stripes on the parking deck floors below, as she leaned over the railing. Familiar feelings of embarrassment wrapped her in a shrouding fog until the ringing of Stan's phone pulled her back. "Yes?" she said, after racing into the office and barely waiting for the phone to reach her ear.

"It's done. Patrick is being processed. We found bond memorandums in his truck; one signed, one not. Jim got it all on video," Bill's voice said through the receiver.

"Good. The video will help our negotiating position when I have to unwind all those bonds from years of his deal making." She sat down at Stan's desk. "The FBI picked up Enzo this morning. The municipal bond market is taking some lumps. Dunham Schauble's stock price is spontaneously combusting."

"I wouldn't know anything about that. All Patrick's salespeople were standing around like they didn't have anything else to do," Bill said. "No one was buying cars, that's for sure."

"Probably because we're in the middle of a recession. Demand for hundred-fifty-thousand-dollar cars is weak."

"One of the guys told me to come back for a test drive. Maybe I'll get one."

She laughed, and appreciated the humor Bill brought to tragedy. It offered her a sweet reprieve. "Thanks, Bill. It's all so entangled and strange, like it's right in front of our eyes but no one sees it."

"It's been that way since the dawn of man, Paige. I'm headed to your press conference. Ezzy's with me."

"Thanks again. My daddy came in town for a couple of weeks, too, so we'll see you in a little while. He's looking forward to meeting Ezzy."

"Who isn't?" Bill said, and she wondered where to find a man like that.

She hung up the phone and dropped the file on Stan's desk. "Divorce Papers" was scrawled on the front, with pictures included from his dinner at the Summit Garden rooftop deck. She opened his computer with the only password he used, #1WideOut, and sent him one of his own emails. DIVORCE PAPERS ARE ON YOUR DESK. DON'T CALL AND DON'T COME HOME.

Standing up, Paige straightened her best mid-length black dress, which fit like a glove. She took a deep breath as she swung open the office door and strolled past the receptionist. "There are troubles around corners you can't see," she said, channeling her mother. "The older you get, the wiser you'll become, but for now, be very, very careful."

Paige stepped onto the open elevator and girded herself for the mid-afternoon press conference scheduled at the Orthus County Administrative Building. As she hurried out of the Orlando Downtown District building to avoid running into Stan, she received a text: This is Kate Brown. Can you call me?

Paige slid into her car seat and glanced over at her father, who was focused on the fishing line in his lap. "Everything OK, Judge?"

"Just fine. Drive careful so I don't hook myself."

Before pulling out of the parking lot, she dialed the number the text message had come from, and put the phone on speaker mode.

"Hello, this is Kate Brown."

"Hi, Kate. Paige Jackson here. How can I help you?"

"Paige, thanks for returning my call. I spoke with Patrick McDaniel last Friday afternoon, and he mentioned there might be some cause for concern regarding my upcoming tax abatements for MOTrax. He also said I should reach out to you with any questions."

"Why would he say that?" she asked, providing as much rope as Kate needed to hang herself. Judge looked up from his fly tying, pushed his glasses up the bridge of his nose, and gazed through the windshield.

"I don't know. I guess he knew Orthus Regional Hospital was going to default today, and all his current contracts might come under review."

"That's correct, anything else?"

Kate huffed through the phone. "Who would review his contracts, and under what authority?"

"Current precedent is settled regarding internal contractual review. Only the county commission has the authority to review Progress Orthus's activity," Paige said. "But I guess if things got thin, or they began to outlive their suitability, an emergency manager might review them." Paige waited patiently, compartmentalizing the time she'd have to spend on MOTrax's legacy baggage in her new job. Ultimately, she had no expectation MOTrax real estate business acumen would ever deliver the one hundred million dollars in avoided taxes, because they were overleveraged already, and that kind of additional expense would put them in bankruptcy too. The apartment complexes already under construction would sit vacant for two or three years waiting for a buyer, while she would have to send Bill's people in to put out fires, clean out vagrants, and keep the anarchists from using the first floor concrete foundations for urban spelunking tours, while she deferred demolition for as long as possible.

"Those deals have been made," Kate said. "Construction contracts have been in place for months. We're almost through with with wood-stick framing. These developments don't work without that money, Paige. Transit-oriented developments are good for all of Orthus County." Her focus on real estate operations had left MOTrax operations rudderless—according to Randall's worthless analysis anyway—but he did provide bombshell information with regard to the crash, which made the value of his plea bargain priceless.

Paige thought about how to minimize Kate's ongoing distraction. "That's too bad, I guess," she said, as she drove through Downtown Orlando, passing citizens oblivious to what was to come. "So, what'll you do now?"

"Too bad? Mrs. Jackson, I'll go all the way up to Governor Sikes, whom I've been in weekly conversations with since the accident to increase state funding for safety measures long overdue for MOTrax trains. Don't test me." Out of the corner of her eye, Paige could see Judge raising his eyebrows.

"Kate, I'm at my meeting so I need to wrap this up," she said as she pulled into the Orthus County Administrative Building parking lot. "When you call Governor Sikes, do you plan to mention your ability to manipulate a National Transportation Safety Board's crash investigation by destroying a voice recorder and altering drug testing procedures?"

"What? How did you get that information?"

Paige put the car in park with the engine still running. "We have a signed statement from one of your current employees that was swept up Saturday night, tweaking like a chicken head on roller skates. He was a wealth of information."

"Who do you think a court will believe: a drug addict or me? I'll sue Progress Orthus for the tax abatement, and I'll win, and you know it."

"Ms. Brown, I'm sure this is coming as a shock to you, but you're delusional. Orlando and Smithson are the only cities along the MOTrax line in Orthus County that've passed Redevelopment Powers Law. The phantom bonds Enzo invented provide tax breaks where they're not allowed, as they were rejected by a voting majority in the cities other than Orlando and Smithson—in theory anyway—which is good enough for me.

"MOTrax is a transportation authority like any other in this country. We can provide tax incentives to ourselves to finance projects wherever we like."

"Enzo Ruiz has created intentional short positions on municipal bonds that don't exist. He gave it a salesy name like phantom bond, and sells them to every city council and county commission in the country. The Municipal Securities Rule-Making Board specifically prohibits any short positions on municipal bonds, so how does Progress Orthus account for a short position they owe the developer for an inverted bond? They don't. The MSRB states any interest or, in your case, tax abatements from a short position in a municipal bond aren't tax exempt. It's so convoluted you don't even understand it. Or at least I assume you didn't understand it when you accepted Bob and Patrick's deal."

"I have complete trust in Progress Orthus, and our advisor, Dunham Schauble," Kate said, though her tone suggested she wasn't so sure anymore.

"I don't guess you've turned on the TV this morning, but anyway, you have two choices. You can sell all the apartment complexes to a for-profit developer that will pay Orthus County the tax revenues we need, and then resign . . . or you can be fired. The first option is much better. The funds generated from the sale would go a long way to improving the operational disaster you call a mass transit system."

"That's absurd. You can't fire me, and we're not selling the land," Kate said, as Paige saw Ezzy and Bill walking through the parking lot. She waved at them while Kate continued offering ideological arguments for what had reached the breaking point, both figuratively and literally. "Affordable housing initiatives are a proven concept encouraged all the way from the top of our democracy and enshrined in American policy."

"Interesting perspective. All the research I've done reports affordable housing, which you're disguising as transit-oriented developments, has been an abysmal failure. It's done the opposite of everything it purported to do," she said. "And you'll love this: my research shows a bipartisan consensus agrees it's an abysmal failure. Why you wanted to add them to MOTrax developments is beyond me."

"I'm not resigning." Kate's voice shook, betraying the confidence of her words. "MOTrax will get those tax abatements. You don't have any authority to stop us."

Jim passed in front of her car as he headed through the parking lot. He and Judge pointed at one another and smiled. Paige smiled too, feeling all might be well with the world after all. "Kate," she said. "Do you really want a constitutional battle about all the TOD's along the South Line to Orlando International Airport financed with phantom bonds in Orange County? What about the phantom bonds issued around the country? You'll be persona non grata at your mass-transit meetings because your aggressive attitude brought a spotlight onto their financial statements. If you want to fall on the sword for all TODs, then you'll be responsible for your public firing. If you try suing us, I'll show the courts you owe us three hundred and fifty million dollars because Patrick and Enzo inflated the bond to provide a hundred-million-dollar tax abatement. How do you want to play this?"

"I'm calling the governor."

"Good. I'll let him know." Paige hung up before Kate got the chance.

Judge smiled at her. "I might need to come see you in court while I'm here. You're good."

Paige returned the smile already pecking on her phone. "Come on. We've got a couple more items of business before you can go fishing." She got out of the car and saw Governor Sikes, who was arriving in an under-the-radar motorcade driving into the parking lot.

Kate's phone rang, and before she could think too much about why the governor would be calling her just as she was getting ready to reach out to him, she answered. "Hello, Governor. I've been trying to contact you all summer. Can we get together on safety initiatives I'd like to begin at MOTrax? The state really should be helping out."

"Good morning, Kate. Sorry, I've been busy. Paige Jackson just called with some good news. She mentioned you two have spoken, and you'd gladly resign given the extenuating circumstances surrounding the news this morning and your involvement in the crash investigation. We'll wish you well as you seek other opportunities elsewhere."

"Governor," she said, trying to keep herself from stuttering. "I didn't say that. MOTrax has entered into legally enforceable contracts with Progress Orthus. We need a hundred million dollars to build out the infrastructure for the new MOTrax TODs on the North Line. I understand we don't see eye to eye politically, but we need the state to fund more of our operational deficits."

"Kate, you knew when you took this job it was most likely temporary. We run through mass transit directors like dirty dishes. They get dirty. We get a clean one."

"But, Governor, our projects will define walkable, livable communities. These projects must be done." She felt the fight leaving her. She'd tried to get Orlando to take the broader perspective, but it couldn't seem to move away from its backward thinking. It wasn't flexible enough to sacrifice for the future.

"Kate, take Paige's advice. You have six months to sell the MOTrax parking lots to whomever will buy them. Take the money, and build parking decks next to the entrances, get some new trains, pay off some pension debt, and clean up the place. Then resign. There're plenty of mass transit systems around the country that could use your enthusiasm."

"I wish I would've known how you felt a year ago. I could've sold the lots at the height of the real estate market," she said, ignoring his suggestion to continue plying her trade among the uninformed, cynical public. Her talent should be appreciated in higher ivory towers.

"Why would you need my advice on something so obvious? I'm headed to a press conference. Turn on your TV in thirty minutes, and take a look at your future," he said, and hung up.

Kate texted Antonio, the Transit Union representative: Hey there. Can we get coffee?

Sure. What's up?

I'm back in play.

It happens to the best of us. I should introduce you to my friends in Washington. Your understanding of phantom bonds is very valuable. A lobbyist friend of mine asked about you last week.

Thanks. The sooner the better. These small-town rubes can't get out of their own way.

I'll set it up.

CHAPTER 43

"Without further ado, ladies and gentlemen, I introduce the Governor of the great State of Florida, Julius Gordon Sikes."

Paige blinked from the flashes going off, with the glare doubled from camera lights trained on the podium. The American flag was draped behind her in one corner of the vestibule, the Florida State flag in the other as Governor Sikes came around behind them all standing on stage together. Bill was in full uniform, Ezzy standing between them on her right side in dark blue. Judge was on her left side standing next to the back step of the podium Governor Sikes was about to ascend. Jim was in the front row of the press conference, with a couple standing next to him, the man wearing a slightly worn Lochloosa State Championship jacket while the woman leaned into him holding his hand. The large Heart of Pine podium was emblazoned with the Seal of Florida. A four-post desk next to it was fitted with an inkwell.

Governor Sikes took two steps to the podium, embodying the energy and omnipotence of his position. "Thank you, everyone, for gathering on such short notice. Many of you are aware of the indictments handed down by the Orthus County Grand Jury this morning. Orthus County Commissioner, Robert Drolland, Jr., along with Progress Orthus Chair, Patrick McDaniel have been charged with theft of Orthus County taxpayers and fraud. Robert Drolland has a secondary group of indictments including bribery, but since his medical condition would make his arrest inappropriate at this time, we'll wait for his full recovery. Our prayers for his speedy recovery go out to him and his family. You'll hear more about that in a moment from Sheriff Bolek of the Orthus County Sheriff's Department. Additionally, the FBI has arrested Enzo Ruiz, CEO of Dunham Schauble, a regional municipal bond underwriter. I only mention it because of his connection to the two criminal cases we are pursuing. Other suspects in both the criminal investigations, and the financial crimes case, have been apprehended in Dallas and Chicago. Any information you request in the financial crimes case should be directed to the FBI. The Orthus County Sheriff's Department, and the FBI, have wasted no effort in the accuracy of their investigation not only because of its political sensitivity, but because the citizens of Florida expect it. It's taken many man-hours of cooperation among both law enforcement organizations, and their collective work spans months."

"Furthermore, the staff, employees, and citizens of Orthus County are under intense pressure due to the short- and long-term debts that have piled up in the last nine years. Today the Orthus County Regional Hospital missed the entirety of its debt payment on one of the largest debts the county owes. Because of the complexities of municipal finance and the dire situation Orthus County faces, it is my duty as governor to install an emergency manager until the Orthus County Board of Commissioners can go through a clear and orderly financial unwinding." Paige thought of the years it would take to detangle lender seniority, unless she caught some breaks in the early years with asset sales, a friendly state legislature, and a stock market boost wouldn't hurt either. "The Emergency Manager will continue providing operational services to Orthus County taxpayers, and will have the full and intended operational authority granted by the State of Florida by my executive order. Additionally, because of questions surrounding a recent bond memorandum signed by Orthus School Board Commissioner Stan Jackson, I have decided to pull Orthus County Charter Schools from his authority. They will be entrusted to my emergency manager until further notice. After a thorough search for a competent and qualified candidate, I've come to a conclusion. With the public and generous support from our attorney general in Tallahassee, I've selected District Attorney Paige Jackson to take the helm." She felt Ezzy squeeze her hand. "She's widely respected for her financial and legal knowledge, has defined her career with bullet points of hard work, honest and thoughtful consideration of the facts, and a fair and level-headed presentation of her opinions. The Florida Attorney General's office will assign a special prosecutor for the two criminal cases to eliminate any conflicts of interest in the matter, and allow Mrs. Jackson to throw her full, unhindered efforts into the Emergency Manager position.

"Finally, the roads here are horrible. Along with emergency manager powers, I'm signing an executive order for one hundred and fifty million dollars to fix some of the most troublesome parts of your roads and bridges. Orthus County will support the infusion from the General Fund, and any reserves, on- or off-balance sheet that may exists." Paige's heart beat faster as he leaned over the wood desk to sign the executive order, thankful for the job, but hesitant to cover for his discretionary spending he would expect for his one-hundred-and-fifty-million-dollar gift. Cameras clicked around the room. "Now, I'll turn it over to Sheriff Bolek." Governor Sikes stepped to the other side away from the microphone, his arm raised in Bill's direction, "Bill, you have the floor."

Paige crossed her arms, stood more erect, and scowled when the reporters started firing questions before he'd taken a step. "Aren't there inherent conflicts of interests because of Mrs. Jackson's marriage to Stan Jackson?" "Did you have to shoot Craig Walker?" "Was Commissioner Drolland involved in the drug bust at First and Last?" "Will Mrs. Jackson pay big Wall Street banks instead of our neighbors?"

After ambling up to the podium, Bill pulled the flexible metal microphone stand straight up, and it was only barely as high as the badge on his uniform. He looked at his watch and then waved his arm high in the air a couple of times. "Good afternoon, everyone. I'm Sheriff Bill Bolek. We'll take questions at the end," and as if a circus ringleader had waved his top hat, the noise subsided. He put his hands behind his back, looked around the room, and said, "Thanks. This morning at approximately 8:30 AM Patrick McDaniel was apprehended in his place of business. Mr. Drolland will be taken into custody upon his doctor's release from the hospital. The defendants in this investigation face charges of bribery—a felony—attempt to commit bribery, conspiracy to commit bribery—also felonies—and finally, engaging in organized criminal activity, violating the Racketeer Influenced and Corrupt Organizations Act. Mr. McDaniel has been processed, and could be released on bond this afternoon. The Orthus County Sheriff's department has amassed evidence in his case for over four months leading up to the arrest. As Governor Sikes mentioned, a special prosecutor will be assigned to try this case, and we'll fully cooperate with whoever that special prosecutor might be, just as we would with Emergency Manager Jackson. A lot of resources have been dedicated to this effort, and we've every intention of providing the residents of Orthus County the justice they expect. There'll be more to follow as the special prosecutor is selected. Many arrests have been made, but most of those people are out on bond, and have already hired attorneys. And with that, I'll turn it over to Emergency Manager Paige Jackson. I'm sure she has some things to say, and you have some questions, so let's get on with it." He turned, without leaving the podium, and inspired Paige with the commanding look of a warrior, smiled broadly at her, then said loud enough for everyone in the room to hear him, "We've got your back."

Paige walked over, put her notes on the podium top, and stepped back as she would during an arraignment before a judge, releasing another cascade of camera clicks. "Good afternoon Orthus County, members of the press, friends, colleagues, and business partners. I'm Paige Jackson. You're probably asking yourself, 'Why would anyone take the job of emergency manager?' The job requires the insight of many careers with rare opportunities for service. Yet, sadly, those opportunities seem to grow with every recession, and in most cases, emergency managers get blamed for the problems by the end of the process, so let me answer this way. The man to my left, who seems quiet and unassuming, told me from a young age 'rarely are people given significant opportunities to make a difference in this world. If God gives you that opportunity, you must embrace it.' He also encouraged me to acquire the tools to make a difference, should I ever get the chance." She turned toward Judge and said, "Thank you, Judge." His nod of approval for a lifetime of sacrifice reinforced her confidence as she grabbed the podium with both hands.

"Over the course of the next six months, or longer, my goals are simple. Bring operational efficiency to the Orthus County Administrative Offices while protecting our system from Wall Street vultures, stem the tide of tax giveaways to everyone except the Orthus County resident, and begin the long grueling road of pension reform."

"I vow to remove Orthus County from the retirement-planning business. Our public employee retirement-planning system is neither sustainable nor fair to anyone and it must be replaced. A far more mutually beneficial retirement plan for both the county employee, and county stakeholders, will be phased in over five years.

Our state pension systems, and their providers, are bringing our nation's educational and transportation systems to their knees. Any pension reform should simply shift the risks to the employee from the taxpayer while enhancing the employee service options and growth potential. Corporate America has already transitioned away from these risks, generating far higher outcomes for their employees, and Orthus County must follow suit in order to unlock value for capital investments in infrastructure and services.

"Our police officers and firefighters take an oath of office to never betray our public trust. They won't strike when they could. Therefore, because of their commitment and the county's base-responsibility of public protection and security, we'll not betray them during this next phase of Orthus County's future.

"Our educational system should be populated by the best and brightest. Higher public allocation of funds for performing schools should be the norm, not the exception. Florida's charter school program should be encouraged and should have the same tax advantages of our public schools. One of my first acts will be assigning Ezzy King as my special advisor on educational improvements at Orthus County Charter Schools, and asking the state legislature to reform the current charter school application, taxation and funding policy."

"Our county's roads, bridges, water, and sewer infrastructure aren't safe based on analysis from the Orthus Regional Commission, and you, the citizens of Orthus County. Their condition is not consistent with what you should expect, given you've already paid for it once, and then you're double taxed with special option sales taxes.

"Economic development is not an experiment, and we should stop treating it like one. We lose thousands of jobs every year because we shift allocations of time and money to mythical economic development projects, and away from our core competencies; infrastructure and schools. Our world's commerce and trade have always been supported by infrastructure and learned intelligence, not sporting events and affordable housing.

"The body politic is not suited for innovation and profitability. The municipal taxpayer isn't a private equity, white-knight financier for real estate investments requiring no financial underwriting process, no securities and exchange Registration, no financial reporting requirements, and no elected official to answer any of these questions. Orthus County taxpayers aren't responsible for government subsidized racial segregation by downtown development authorities and affordable housing initiatives. Development authorities are responsible for depleting more affordable housing than they finance. Industrial development authorities give unfair tax advantages to start-up companies competing for the same clients existing businesses already serve. Development authorities tout their role as community improvers but take the risks of investment bankers. Orthus County is no longer in the banking business. Progress Orthus will be dissolved, and we'll unwind all revenue bonds they've financed over the last ten years starting tomorrow.

"Our local municipalities are competing in a downward spiral of the lowest common denominator of tax abatements. The Orthus County taxpayers have paid for their children's educational opportunities and our area's transportation needs. They're finally going to get it without raising property taxes. That is one of the easiest and quickest solutions, and I've asked Governor Sikes, and he's agreed, to put a moratorium on tax abatements across the state of Florida. We'll no longer take the easy way out of issuing debt without asking the taxpayer first. Executive sessions will cease, except for human-resources-related meetings, and all new debt, via bond issues, will go to the ballot box."

"The Orthus County motto is Forever Dream." She looked around the audience. "And I'm a forever dreamer. We can pave our way to rising revenues from commerce and tourism. We can liberate our financial profile from real estate and counter-party risks, but change must come, and I'm going to bring that change. I'll now take any questions from the floor." She thought about Judge's best advice: *Exhale self. Inhale Jesus.*

"Are you aware of suggestions your husband, Dr. Stan Jackson, is having an extra marital affair?" a reporter from the back asked, and she saw the man with the Lochloosa state championship jacket turn to see who asked.

She rolled her shoulders down, and then inhaled on her way back up. "You'll have to ask Dr. Jackson any personal questions, but for me, you can judge me by my actions. The next six months will give you a glimpse into the changes we're going to make in Orthus County. Next question."

"How will the transfer of power from the county commission to you be enacted?"

"As far as transfer of power, I'll work diligently to keep the lights on at Orthus County. As you've heard, and witnessed, Governor Sikes has approved, and signed by executive order, special emergency manager authority. Next question."

"Who will get paid, and who won't? How will you avoid the Municipal Employee's Union strike?"

"Look, this can take a week, or it can take three years, but negotiations take time. This massive debt burden wasn't created overnight. There're going to be significant hardships on all of us. Go ahead, Jim from *Orthus County Post.*"

"Thank you for your dedication, Mrs. Jackson. Will you run for county commission in the next special election? Or higher office?"

Now sure Jim was close enough to hear at the KCA tour, she looked over at Governor Sikes and laughed. He returned the smile, waved at the audience, and said, "Don't look at me. I'm done after next year."

Paige turned back to Jim and said, "At this time, my only concern is removing the bloat of Orthus County operations. We've got a lot to do, and a short time to do it. My ideas aren't new, bold, or irrational, but they need to be implemented immediately. We need to get back to basics, and it must start here. Orthus County will be ground zero for a rebirth of financial strength driven by our own brains, creativity and ideas. When, and if, I seek higher office, you'll be the first to know." She cracked a smile as everyone in the audience chuckled. "Florida deserves a thorough review of hopeful candidates that share my compassion and commitment. I know they're out there listening, and serving their communities right now."

Jim looked around the room and said, "We'll all take that as a yes." The smattering of applause took on a full-throated approval within seconds as reporters clapped their hands, filled with pens and notepads.

"Thank you, everyone. Thank you. We'll provide updates throughout the next few weeks, and months, through your local news channels and the county's website. Thank you all for coming."

After the presentation had ended, the crowd began to pack up their equipment and shuffle out of the room. Paige looked at the group she'd gathered, introduced herself and the governor to Beth and Matt Pinson, and introduced them all to her father, as they all stood on stage and shook hands. Paige looked at Governor Sikes and asked, "When do you think the moratorium on tax abatements will go into effect?"

He pulled his glasses off, wiped them on his tie, and said, "Paige, you have my full support. Any tax-abatement moratorium you can get congress to bring me, I'll sign. I'll try and twist some arms in the January session, but that's going to be a big hill to climb."

"I was hoping you could do something sooner, Governor." She frowned, without eliciting any response from him when he put his glasses back on.

Jim filled the silent vacuum. "You ready, Judge?"

"I am."

"Where're you guys going?" Bill asked.

"Shellcracker fishing,"

"What?" Bill's jaw dropped "Without me?"

Ezzy winked at Jim and Judge, and grabbed Bill's hand. "We have a court date, remember. Today is your wedding day."

Ezzy put her arm around Beth Pinson. "Matt, Beth, will you join my adventure into education?"

Beth looked at Matt, who was holding her other hand.

"Well, Elizabeth?" he said.

"Yes, Matt," Beth said. "Let's do it."

"Oh, I'm so glad," Ezzy said. "When we get back from our Christmas honeymoon, we can have a press conference. That sound OK?"

"I'll let you ladies handle that," Matt replied. "I'll call the coaches tomorrow. We've got some recruiting to do."

"Thanks, Coach. They can't wait to hear from you."

"I hope that joy rubs off on me," Paige added. "I'm going to need all of you." Paige prayed to see God's will in all its forms as they walked out to go their separate ways into the sea of protestors and reporters. The Municipal Employee Union was buffeted by the Teacher's Union, both sides blaring indiscernible chants through bull horns for full effect, and held up bouncing posters that read, "Hands Off My Pension," "Make the Banks Pay," "Pay People-Not Banks," and "No Pension No Peace."

CHAPTER 44

Paige assumed the county commissioners must've already excused themselves to executive session of the first Tuesday evening December meeting of the Orthus County Board of Commissioners. She'd come through the Board of Commissioners auditorium filled with protestors and attorneys, having been told earlier in the day they still planned to meet. When she walked into the private chambers, three commissioners were sitting at a large conference room table with plates of food before them, and one of the men standing on the other end of the table. She walked to the end with empty chairs and said, "Hello, everyone. I hope I'm not interrupting anything. I'm Emergency Manager Paige Jackson," while slinging her purse off her shoulder and dropping it in the chair in front of her. She placed her leather binder on the table.

The man on the other end of the table, assuming he was also the commission chair pro tem, was probably arguing to be installed immediately as interim county commission chairman. "Mrs. Jackson, we're in executive session. No one is allowed in here."

"Hopefully, you didn't expect me to wait out there with the unions. I'll try to begin on a friendly note," she said as she flipped open the leather binder and pulled the top off her pen. "You have no power. I'm now the ultimate arbiter, manager, and chief of Orthus County until the governor, or a bankruptcy court, decides I'm not.

The only reason I joined you here is so your constituents won't hear how powerless you are on the local news. I'm doing you a favor."

"Now wait just a minute, Mrs. Jackson," he said.

"One more interruption and I'm walking out. I have the full support of the Governor, the Orthus County Sheriff's Department, and the Orthus County checkbook. All of your county offices are having their locks changed as we speak. Would you like to hear my plan? I don't have much time, because I'll be very busy the next two years cleaning up your mess."

"This isn't right," the Orlando commissioner said.

"No, no, ignore him, Mrs. Jackson," the lady shoveling chips into her mouth said, seemingly acquiescing to Paige's undeniable truth. "I'm Samantha Jones, Ocala Chamber of Commerce President, and I'm sure you're aware that's Thomas Stutts, Orlando commissioner, Abe Zern, Sanford hotel magnate." Paige chuckled at the description, and Samantha continued. "And Jeff McCaskill, County Commission Chair Pro tem. What's your plan? None of us have been through anything like this before."

"Nice to meet you. Of course, I wish it were under different circumstances. I have a lot of ideas about how to proceed. I've been working with the city of Chicago as our futures are tied to the same anchor, Dunham Schauble. A few other large metro-bankruptcies you've noticed in the last five or six years will also provide some guidance. Like I said on the news, depending on how the unions, Wall Street investors, and our vendors behave, this could be over in a week or three years, but there're some basic outcomes I expect."

"Can you please stop wasting our time, too," Sam said, who'd been standing, but was now sitting. "What are they?"

"First, I'm postponing all county employee paychecks for six weeks until we get the remainder of our property tax revenue. The only employees that will be spared are first responders like fire and police, and critical city services like water, sewer and trash collection. We'll true up our non-emergency employee compensation obligation on the day the property tax revenues hit the account."

"They'll all quit before then," Thomas, the Orlando commissioner, said as he took a bite of his sandwich.

Paige was both puzzled, and impressed, by his apathy about the carnage of lost jobs and incomes he was going to witness in the next two weeks. "That'd definitely help my cause," Paige said matter-of-factly, and then looked around the table at them. "Seventy-five percent of all employees are going to be given permanent vacations. Next, all retiree pensions will be drastically reduced and healthcare will be eliminated completely."

"You can't do that. They were promised that money; guaranteed," Thomas said, adding nothing but noise.

"They can deal with me now, or deal with the bankruptcy courts. My legal strategy will merely change with the playing field, and I can play it either way. Next, we'll move all revenue-generating employees onto the third floor of the Orthus Administrative Building. All the lower floors will be leased out until we can make other arrangements for office space. This building is far too expensive for our current status."

Samantha wiped potato chip grease off her fingers with an Orthus County logo'd napkin and said, "I heard you're going to allow retirees to go bankrupt just so you can pay Wall Street."

"Wall Street's not getting anything," she countered. "County employees are the first priority, but they don't know it yet, and may never know it. Second, the people you've borrowed from aren't a street in New York, it's your neighbors, American citizens, and the Orthus County pension plan that own the bonds, but we'll brand them Wall Street, like you just did to bolster the court of public opinion."

"She's right," Abe said. "My broker called me three months ago demanding we sell Orthus bonds. He said I'm not going to get my money back for years, if I get anything."

Paige nodded with her hand up in deference to the comment. "He'd be right, but nonetheless, I'll use the 'Fat Cat Wall Street Bankers' moniker to avoid their demands as long as it takes. Next, we're crafting legislation now for a State of Florida funded bailout, but any success there won't be felt until after the General Assembly votes next April. Bob's made so many enemies around the state that it's going to be difficult to get their help. Don't underestimate the irony of needing help from poor rural areas, and all you get in return is 'I told you so'."

"What about the credit-rating agencies," Jeff asked?

"I'm already in conversations with them, but they're not showing their cards yet. The coming reductions in pension, and healthcare payments, will show them I'm willing to do the hard things to keep a rating. We're getting valuations on a developing list of parks and event spaces we'll sell at auction. We won't have the rating we had, but at least we won't drop off the radar. We're going to need to float one last bond for infrastructure. It won't be a big one, but some major repairs can't be neglected any longer."

"What about the governor's executive order for one hundred and fifty million dollars for new roads?"

"That's mostly spoken for," she said. The governor's words to her had been, 'That interchange gets built, and it's got my name on it. You can do what you want with the rest.'

"Can't we raise taxes?" Samantha asked.

"Not a chance. Higher taxes will exacerbate the foreclosures we're already seeing in the recession. Residential real estate management is the last thing we need more of, but unfortunately, that'll be a growing problem."

"You're crazy if you think pension reform is going to get done. The unions will sue you before the end of the week," Thomas said.

"Lawsuits began coming the day after I became emergency manager. If unions want their pension guarantees, they'll have to petition the state. We can't afford it anymore, but you're partially correct. We can't switch everyone from the state pension to a defined-contribution plan immediately, but we can change our contributions. From now on, Orthus County will only match twenty-five percent of the remaining employee's retirement-plan contribution in the 403(b). No more pension contributions, period."

"Mrs. Jackson isn't telling you the whole story," Jeff said. "We can use the tax-anticipation-note line of credit to pay the hospital bond again, like we did in June."

"Not quite," Paige said, not feeling the need to rebuke him, because she wouldn't speak to him again unless he came to her office. "Orthus County's tax-anticipation note for this year is only a ninety-million-dollar line of credit, and you've spent it all, including the Orthus Hospital payment in June. By the way, we spend three-point-five million dollars per day in Orthus County, our bank account is bouncing checks, and we don't get our next property tax revenues for another six weeks."

"You mentioned in your press conference we'd work with Chicago. How's working with Chicago going to help us?" Abe asked from the side of the table.

"We can share co-counsel on some of the lawsuits coming in from the Orthus Regional Hospital and OSK blind-pool defaults. Ours and Chicago's blind-pool issuance originated from Dunham Schauble, so we're also asking for class-action status when we sue Dunham Schauble's new owner, or bankruptcy trustee. This morning, their emergency manager and I had a conference call with one of the mutual fund's holding our debt," Paige laughed. "When we were done with him, he didn't know whether to hang up on me or quit his job."

"The unions are going to be beside themselves." Thomas continued denying his lack of authority given the new circumstances, and getting very close to the edge of her patience.

"Wait till they find out about Governor Sikes new legislation eliminating 'fair-share fees' unions get from non-members. He's also eliminating unused sick-leave payouts statewide as a personal favor to me, to draw some of the fire."

"So when will you file for Orthus County bankruptcy?" Samantha asked.

"Maybe we won't. But if we do, I'll file down-and-dirty Chapter 9. We'll use that scenario in negotiations with the unions. They know from the Detroit bankruptcy they'd do better making a deal with me now than dragging out more legal costs for an imaginary payout. If they don't make a deal, I'll void all their contracts in bankruptcy court, and they can try their luck there."

"What about all the city development authorities? Onward Orlando's been around as long as Progress Orthus," Sam said, pointing at Samantha, Abe and Thomas. "They created Outbound Ocala and Synergy Sanford this summer, and they're abating Orthus County taxes as we speak."

Paige flipped to the page in her leather binder titled 'Abated Taxes,' scanned her finger down the page reviewing the total Orthus County revenue the cities were currently abating, and proposing to abate, and said, "They have their own charters, some with Redevelopment Powers, and some without. Abe, neither you nor Samantha have Redevelopment Powers, so all of your phantom bonds are about to get challenged in Florida Superior Court. We'll drag out the process until the developers, or the bankers, go away, and maybe we win a few, but I'm going to end the days of internecine war with tax abatements in Orthus County by outspending you in court, and leveraging the services we still provide to your cities. It'll be permanent when the governor signs the moratorium into law."

"Our state legislature isn't going to draft any moratorium legislation." Thomas from Orlando said, sounding more and more irrelevant. "It's how our nation's business is done."

"If you wouldn't have been so willfully naïve when Bob was issuing debt, we wouldn't be here. If you were this thorny when Bob was asking for your vote, you would've ridden out this recession, but now your accountability efforts are too late. Plausible deniability and cognitive dissonance were the last two nails in your coffin."

"What about the MOTrax tax abatement from this past summer?" Samantha asked, obviously shell-shocked at the first shot across her bow.

"Great question. Like yours, it's not happening. Plus, I've got a long-shot strategy to cover our legal bills from the MOTrax tax abatement. Legal costs could reach as high as one hundred and fifty million."

"What?" Thomas said, his mouth full of his sandwich.

"If MOTrax wants to stay within the good graces of Orthus County and its law enforcement agencies, they'll pay their fair share of taxes, and if they don't, I'll condemn their buildings and take them with eminent domain authority. If they want to take it to court, I'll describe to a judge, and the media, how the phantom-bond contract is designed, how it's the world's strangest financial manipulation since the credit-default swap, and how MOTrax currently owes Orthus County three hundred and fifty million dollars collateralized by five parking lots, four of them with half-built apartment complexes. Imagine the scene when I counter sue them for the administration fee they were going to pay Project Orthus, and take their developments. Worst-case scenario, we get forty million from property tax on the land, or confiscated land that we sell to developers."

"MOTrax owes us three hundred fifty million? I thought it was a hundred," Abe said. He and Samantha seemed the only two willing to understand.

"Enzo ramped up the discount value, or rate-of-return assumption, on the phantom bond, so the interest payment equaled five million per year for twenty years. At the escalated equity cost of capital Enzo selected, that's three hundred and fifty million. No one ever expects the downside of synthetic financial instruments. When they go bad, everyone gets a taste."

"I don't have any idea what you're talking about," Thomas said, "but I've had enough. Are you going to arrest any of us?"

That's one question she didn't expect. "Not unless you're involved in some other schemes I don't already know about. I need you, and you need me. You're the voice of the people. Our neighbors will be screaming, but I need you to tell me which ones are screaming the loudest."

"It's going to be hard to identify over the noise," Samantha said.

"Commissioners, all of you have insight into this county I can only hope for. When good ideas are borne from this fire, you should encourage it. Tell me. I have an open door, but rest assured, I'm in complete control serving at the pleasure of the Governor. We can do this together, but there're no easy paths, or answers. This financial storm is of your own doing. You could've stopped Patrick and Bob at any time. All you had to do was raise the alarms, but instead you sat silently. Everyone clear?"

"Expect another lawsuit on your desk in the morning," Jeff McCaskill said.

"Good luck, and thanks for the warning. I'm late for another meeting, but please let me know if you have any information or questions." She exited from a back door, and read her web browser on the way to the car. The first headline read "Dunham Schauble Collapse Triggers Avalanche of Metro Municipal Defaults."

CHAPTER 46

Dawn broke through the planted pines and the bare poles of the tractor barn, as horse handlers led Tennessee Walkers down the back ramp of the trailers onto the sandy road. Bretto stood next to the main barn pulling an oiled sock through a shotgun tube detached from the gun, the horse's flanks pulsating with excitement, while setters and pointers circled and bayed in the dog boxes on the tops of the carriages. Quail guides were standing around their last edition Salvatore SUVs, testing their dog collars and planning the morning hunt. The smell of boiling coffee floated on the morning stir of the holiday season as he finished oiling the gun and re-attached it to the stock. The Salvatore SUV Cacciatore Edition, bringing Sterling and Warren down the road from the lodge for breakfast, was on the same schedule as Governor Sikes's old hunting Ford rumbling across the creek bridge down behind the barn. They both rolled up to the gravel parking lot at the same time, and Governor Sikes was the first to get out. "Good-a' morning, Governor Gordo. You always-a early to the quail shoot. You sleep-a OK last night? Grappa always get the best of me. I only get in fifty skeet rounds this morning."

"Neither your grappa, nor Warren's bourbon, can keep me out of the North Florida piney woods. How about you?"

"I toss-a and turn all night, having nightmares about-a vanishing poker chips. You a dream stealer, Gordo."

Sterling got out of the back seat and walked toward the group. "I'm nervous enough around you gentlemen with loaded guns in your hands without talk of hangovers and poker." He brushed the dust off the front of his hunting chaps. "I was reluctant to miss the sunrise back on the porch with tea and a good book. I certainly wasn't excited to leave that scene to come out in the woods for a bird slaughter."

Bretto's best huntmaster introduced himself. "Don't worry, Mr. Johnston. You're safer here than on those jets you zip around in. We've been doing this for decades. Y'all come on in for breakfast if you're hungry." He waved them toward the main entrance of the barn, the lights on top of the poles beginning to dim with the rising sun.

"Just what my doctor ordered: more bacon. Do you have any aspirin?" Warren asked.

"Oh yeah, Mr. Sanderson. We got something for that aching memory." He opened the door for the group, winked at Bretto, and said hello to all the kitchen staff making breakfast. Bretto waited as they helped themselves to eggs and bacon frying over the stainless-steel stove, his favorite hot buttermilk biscuits filling the pan on the granite kitchen counter top, honey, jam, and butter lining the center of the long oak table. Bretto leaned against a doorframe, while the huntmaster guided the sports stadium designer, baseball team owner, and state governor around the room. The huntmaster's dog whistles clanked around his neck as he walked through the room. "Drink some more of that coffee. Our blend'll cure what ails ya'. I'll be back in a minute with your aspirin, Mr. Sanderson."

Bretto filled his plate after his three guests, sat down across from Sterling and Warren, with Gordon to his right, and began to eat. Sterling looked up from buttering his biscuit. "Bretto, who did your interiors? The table service matches the sterling silver flatware, and the SM logo in the center of the bone china is fantastic. You've outdone yourself."

"I'm glad-a you like it, Sterling. You got-a great taste."

"Here you go, Mr. Sanderson. These oughta help," the huntmaster said, walking back into the long barn-style dining room. "It's cooler this morning than it's been in weeks, so they'll fly quick. Let's get a move on when y'all are done."

"That hits the spot every time," Gordon said. "You boys want to put any money on the shoot?" Bretto waited for them to respond as the sound of clinking plates echoed off the bare pine rafters, hoping they wouldn't, because if Gordon lost, he'd have to pay his portion.

Warren popped the aspirin back and chased it with an orange juice. "Gambling on a shotgun hunt? I'm definitely in."

"Whatever gets me back to that porch and quiet, I want to encourage," Sterling said, laughing at his own joke.

With their interest confirmed, Bretto looked at Gordon. "I assume we do an over-under, like-a usual?"

"Twenty grand. You shoot with Warren, and I'll shoot with Sterling. How many?" Gordon asked.

Bretto smiled wide and leaned back from the table, having already predicted Gordon's answer, but hoping to avoid a show-down in front of his new business partners. "Since you pick-a the teams and steal-a my dreams, I pick-a the number: fifteen," gambling Warren and Sterling had never witnessed the speed of a wild quail, much less shot one.

"Whoa, you're setting the bar high, but you got a deal," Gordon said, his empty bravado and constant companionship on the farm Bretto's price to pay in return for avoided state income tax on the Salvatore Motors Sunshine Complex.

"Does someone have some earplugs?" Warren asked.

"We have hats, chaps, earplugs, and shells on the tables under the tractor barn, Mr. Sanderson," the huntmaster said. "We'll take extra special care of you, sir. All of us up here are Coyotes fans.

"That's good news," Warren looked at him and laughed. "I hope I don't fall off one of your horses." Then he dragged his biscuit through the middle of the plate, absorbing all the goodness that remained.

"You'll be alright. See you gentlemen outside. Bathrooms are down that hall and around the corner."

"How close is your farm, Gordon?" Sterling asked, as he wiped his hands with the embroidered napkin.

"The back gate of this property connects to mine. My great-grandfather started with a twenty-thousand-acre tract. Over generations of inheritance splits, all I have left is two thousand acres of the original farm. My brothers, sisters, and cousins own the rest, or used to anyway. Bretto came hunting with me a couple of times last fall when he was thinking about moving Salvatore headquarters, and loved the place."

"So, I, how you say, bought-a the farm." He smiled at his guides.

"The whole thing?" Sterling asked.

"Why not? Now Gordo and I can-a hunt whenever we please. It's almost impossible to run into one another on-a twenty thousand acres, and Gordo's family can-a retire with the money."

"Damn big farm," Warren said. "But your coffee is worth the price of admission."

"Two hundred million get-a you a lot more than coffee and hunting trips, Warren," Bretto said, drinking the last of his coffee, putting it in the saucer and standing up from the table.

"And your two hundred million gets you the best seats in the house at Salvatore Stadium," Warren replied, smiling at Bretto and laying his napkin on his plate. "Do you think we paid too much?"

"Not one centismo," he said, squaring his orange Salvatore Motors hat on his head. "We get a glass and-a steel Salvatore headquarters. You get a new baseball stadium. Salvatore Motors get-a our name on it. Sterling get-a to do his design on both, and loan Salvatore Motors fifty million to have-a some, how you say, skin in the show." Bretto smiled and winked when Warren and Gordon laughed. "What-a I say?" he asked, still smiling, and continued. "Gordo get-a spaghetti junction named after him that people can drive on every time they come buy a Salvatore or see the Coyotes play. Instead of apartment complexes, we get-a car dealership next to Smithson Station, and none of us-a pay Florida corporate income tax for fifteen years. I think-a we do OK, no?"

"My loan to Salvatore is the least you can do for ruining my urban legacy." Sterling said, getting up from the table and re-adjusting his crisp chaps.

Bretto held his palms up, smiled and said, "Sterling, Miss-a Olmstead want-a us to build a merda tubo or, how you say, sewer pipes for apartments. We not-a plumbers. We race car builders and-a baseball players," he said waving his hand up at Warren. "No new apartments. No new sewer pipes."

"I think we do OK, too, Bretto," Warren said, leading them out the door as Sterling and Gordon followed him. Bretto descended the steps out of the barn when Warren said, "Thanks for pulling this deal out of the fire, Gordon. When Paige nullified the contract between the automaker's bankruptcy trustee and Progress Orthus, we needed a glimmer of hope." The huntmaster helped Warren onto his horse, and sheathed his shotgun, as the horse trotted in place with the new load.

"My pleasure," Gordon said. Bretto noticed him putting as many shells in his bag as it would hold, and far more than he needed for one morning. "Coyotes needed a home. It's my duty to help."

"The bank, and the bankruptcy trustee, were in a pinch," Warren continued from high up on the mount. "It was a fraction of what Progress Orthus was going to pay them, but they took our lowball offer on the first try." His first offer was twice as high as Bretto's, until Bretto convinced him Smithson, Orthus County, and Gordon needed a savior. Bretto had given Warren the idea of asking for the state income tax break, to give the appearance of a shrewd partnership.

Gordon loaded onto his horse and said, "When Bretto wants to cut manufacturing costs in half, I can show you a great place to build a car plant, too."

Bretto loaded up on his personal horse, his shotgun sheathed and oiled from this morning and said, "On that-a war zone Patrice trying to sell," while trotting around the group.

"No," Gordon said, pulling the reins on the ornery horse Bretto had told the huntmaster to give him. "Further north. Closer to here."

"We'll see," Bretto said. "Italian workers built-a for speed."

"I heard they're built for two months paid vacation." The embarrassing joke making Bretto feel more and more detached from him, having already grown weary of his constant barrage of property improvement and employment recommendations at Salvatore Farms. "You know, Bretto, Florida is a right-to-work state."

"Everywhere it's-a right to work, no? Salvatore Motors Stadium be-a' plenty for now," he said, and shifted the conversation. "You think Patrice will-a be OK, Sterling?"

"I hope so." He crossed his hands calmly on the horn of the saddle while his horse ate grass. "He's under a lot of pressure with his bankruptcy filing and the criminal investigation."

"Did-a he ever get any offers for his lot next to ours?"

"Afraid not. I own it all now," Sterling said. "Coyotes Stadium is going to make the place a gold mine. If not, I'll give it back to the bank."

"That's-a too bad. Maybe he can build-a, how you say, a new charity, when he gets out of jail." He saw Warren looking at Gordon smiling and shaking his head. Gordon shrugged his shoulders and smiled back. Then Bretto planted his boots in the stallion's side, trotted out front, and said, "What-a I say?"

They trotted their horses up to the huntmaster and the dog guides, with Bretto leading the mounted group, and then they began meandering through fire-scarred Loblolly Pines planted in long rows, and surrounded by a cathedral of open air. Hawks screeched overhead peering into the dried goldenrod and swiveling toward slower birds. Dogs tracked back and forth just inside his eyesight as they rode, dismounted, shot, and hunted all morning.

"Heeere! Heeere! Jul-EE. Hunt! Heeere! Heeere! Jul-EE." The huntmaster yelled through the mist, whistle tweets echoing through the live oaks. "Whuup, whuup. She's got another one. The next two dismount and approach. Y'all see her?"

"I see her," Gordon said, with the excitement that overwhelmed him whenever Bretto had intentionally missed enough birds to keep him interested. "Bretto, this might be your last chance. We're at fourteen and only need one more."

"Gordo, you-a, how you say, by the book. We already have-a thirteen, so why you get so excited? We almost-a even."

"Bretto, we-a never even," Gordon teased him. "That's-' funny, no?"

"Yeah, whatever, Gordon. That's funny," Warren said, sounding more enthusiastic with every passing moment of the sunlit horseback ride.

Sterling shifted in his saddle. "Can you two please finish this up so we can sit in respectable chairs and eat lunch?"

Bretto dismounted, crept up on the left side of the pointer, and dropped two shells in the breech. Gordon moved up on the right with his hands in shooting position. Bretto focused on Julie's delicately hovering paw, waiting for the flush, her back table straight from her bloody nose to the tip of her tail.

The huntmaster lowered his voice to keep the dog calm. "Whoa! Whoa! Julie! Whoa! Easy. Easy." He turned back to the men. "You boys ready?" Bretto nodded. "Get em', Julie." Julie's brown head darted into the thicket, her white body driving her deeper and deeper, flushing the wild quail up like fireworks. Bretto raised his gun and fired off a shot, as Gordon fired a shot, followed by Bretto's second shot and immediately by followed by Gordon's second.

"Good shot, Bretto! Good shot!" The huntmaster said. "Dead. Dead bird, Julie. Bring 'em here. Good girl. That's a good girl." Bretto silently appreciated the vision of the setters collecting the dead birds, and the other dogs pouncing around after being worked up by the gunshots, instinctively sensing dead birds usually followed.

"Damn it, Bretto," Gordon said, interjecting himself into Bretto's solitude. "You shot my bird."

"Hey, Gordo." He winked at the huntmaster. "I shoot-a two birds and you missed-a' two. Neither had-a names on them. Now me and Warren one up on you and Sterling. That's-a funny, no?"

"That's funny as hell, Bretto," Warren said. "I'll definitely drink to that. Somebody owes me ten grand."

"I'll send you a check next week, Warren," Sterling said. "Bretto should look to Gordon for his split."

"That's bullshit, Bretto," Gordon thundered, as usual.

"C'mon, Gordo," he said with all the mockery he could muster. "You sound-a like those politicians on TV. You want-a to slice-a the pie, but I just want to-a, how you say, make-a the pie bigger. Warren and I have a bigger pie now."

Warren laughed so hard his foot slipped out of his stirrup, activating one of the handlers who leapt to catch him, and then pushed him back up. "Got ahead of myself and damn near broke my hip.

Let's get back to that lodge, gentlemen." Their laughter fell across the pine-needle shadows of high noon as the hunt ended at the loop where it began. A large trailered BBQ grill with lots of men and women Bretto had invited were milling around in hunting caps. "Are all these people here for the fundraiser?"

"It's what-a Gordo like. Big-a fundraisers." After they all dismounted and shook hands, the horses ambled up into the horse trailers. The panting dogs were placed in the boxes with drinking water, and they stood around in a circle reliving a hunt most would never experience. "Please-a join me, fratelli," he said as he led them to the rear of his SUV, opened the tailgate, looked at Gordon, and said, "This place like-a wildlife paradise, Gordo. Buying Salvatore Farms was-a the best idea you ever had. I brought-a you gentlemen something from Salvatore Lodge." He pulled three original Benelli semi-automatic shotguns from the back. "These a little, how you say, tokens of my apprehension." He winked, wondering if they'd know he meant it. "They're hand engraved. What-a you think?"

"They're beautiful, Bretto," Warren said, looking at him inquisitively. "The coyotes are so close it looks like two heads on one dog?"

"You never heard of Tobias Orthus, Warren?" Gordon asked.

"Who?" Bretto said looking at him, "I thought-a you named your county for-a Greek myth."

"You neither?" Gordon asked, looking back at them in their shared confusion.

"Should I put-a picture of Tobias Orthus on-a Benelli?"

"No, no, Bretto. The guns are magnificent." Gordon said. "Tobias Orthus founded Orthus County, but lots of people have made the Greek connection just like you."

"I like the coyotes. It's pure art," Sterling said.

"I put-a two-headed dog on the gun because our-a new stadium is in Orthus County. You know that-a story. Right, Gordo?"

"I know it, Bretto, but most don't," he replied.

"This-a going to be good. Greek myth say-a Orthus is a two-headed dog. He-a guard cattle like a defender, or-a, how we say, savior, or salvatore. Me and-a Warren, we help Gordo save-a the deal. Coyotes and Salvatore like-a Orthus the dog. No?"

"That's beautiful, Bretto. Can we go back to the picnic now?" Sterling said. "I hope you two don't devour each other." Bretto laughed, hoping Sterling's prophecy never came true, but didn't trust any of them enough to count on it. They all thanked him, hugged him, and went back over to engage with his invitees with their guns sheathed.

Gordon tried to get away from the betting tab he owed, wondering how he would ever pay ten grand for a quail shoot, when one of the politicians from a nearby county cornered him on his way to his truck. "Governor, do you know how many people were counting on that one hundred and fifty million you just gave Orthus County? We need a new bridge and an airport. Now you're just giving it to Orthus County so you can get your name on an off-ramp?"

"Don't worry, buddy. I've got something bigger in mind."

"Like what?"

"An Italian car manufacturing plant located in your hometown."

CHAPTER 47

Paige hustled past the protestors roaring chants when anyone neared the entrance of the Orthus County Administrative Building. She walked toward the elevator, through the first floor, now inhabited by a used appliance store she found to sublease it, while filling the second floor with the Water and Sewer Department, and the third floor with her legal team, two people at every desk. She got off the elevator on the fourth floor and walked into her office that still reeked from Bill's nine-year occupancy. Her lean organizational structure enjoyed freedom from the bureaucratic past, while new ideas were put in place wherever there was merit, and failing strategy was removed before the procedural concrete dried. The mass firings hadn't gone well, but she had no choice because the unions wouldn't accept one iota of compromise. Her executive assistant, Anisha, one of the two that served Bob that didn't get fired, got up and followed Paige into her office.

Paige put her purse down while her assistant began. "Good morning. Whew, that smell is going to be hard to get rid of."

"Don't I know it? I'm still finding Bob's liquor bottles."

"Speaking of Bob, he's put in for his pension. His lawyer said his family needs it terribly and he deserves it because he's past the ten-year mark."

"That's fine. His family shouldn't suffer for his mistakes. It's legally his, but he gets the same deal as everyone else. Twenty-five percent cut on projected retirement and no healthcare. What a shame. His hospital bills must be through the roof."

"OK," she said. "Jonathan had some questions about the special prosecutor position. He's enjoying it and appreciates your recommendation."

"That's good. I'll call him later today to tell him cases don't get much easier than this. 'Don't screw it up' inspirational message, y'know?" Anisha chuckled at her joke, and Paige asked, "Have they set court dates yet for Bob and Patrick?"

"No. The arraignments are next week."

"How is the new Sheriff's precinct construction coming along at Orlando Downtown District?"

"Sheriff Bolek said it's coming along fine. Except for one problem."

"What's that?"

"The deputies are asking for keg refills at the bar."

"Very funny. I'll tell the sheriff he'll need a liquor license for that. Any more fallout from the Dunham Schauble bankruptcy?"

"All of their lenders and creditors are suing MOTrax for the three-hundred-million-dollar phantom bond on Dunham Schauble's books, because like you said, it doesn't exist, but they claim transit-oriented developments don't count as collateral, and they're trying to make MOTrax issue a bond to cover it."

"And?"

"They're going to court."

"Of course, they are. They beat us to it. I'll have Jonathan go ahead and sue MOTrax for the money, too. At least we can get a piece from the settlement."

"Speaking of court, we got a subpoena this morning for all the Water and Sewer expenditures for the last ten years. We received a class action lawsuit this morning by the neighbors around the lake downtown. The EPD was notified of the sewer spills, and now we're expecting fines. They're using the strategy that sewer improvement taxes were wasted."

"They're right, but they're going to have to fight for it. The fines will be a lot cheaper than actual repairs. Anything else?"

"The Municipal Securities Rulemaking Board called. They want to discuss your phantom bond theory being an intentional municipal bond short. The gentlemen I talked to said you should write a book."

Paige looked down at the stack of lawsuits that came in this morning and said, "All I'll be writing the next year are checks to bankruptcy lawyers and employee dismissal forms. By the way, Ezzy called me on the way here. She and I are meeting with Orthus Regional Hospital's administration, and their legal team this afternoon. She's going to make them an offer, I won't let them refuse."

The executive assistant smiled, pulled the last note from her stack and said, "One more thing. Someone in Las Vegas is trying to cash a check on the Progress Orthus account from a Coyotes Concessions, LLC. What should I do with that?"

"Send it over to Jonathan. He'll know what to do."

The bright red tow truck was backing into the open glass doors of McDaniel Salvatore Motors. When it stopped, the cab door opened, the driver stepped out and said, "Morning, Gloria. How's l-l-life?"

"Hey, Ronnie. Not too good obviously. Patrick called, and said he'll be here shortly."

The tow truck driver unwound the cable by hand-pulling it off the winch, and toward the front bumper of the Salvatore sports-sedan. "We'll load the last of these cars in the showroom, and be out of your hair." After he yanked on the hook to check its connection, he looked up at her. "You going to be ok?"

"I don't know. I worked here for fifteen years. I need to get one more kid out of the house, but I'll be alright."

"Did you find another job, yet?"

"Not yet. No one's hiring."

"Look. You've been good to me," Ronnie said. "The towing business is crazy busy. Sheriff Bill's people call all the time from the downtown districts with cars left overnight in the neighborhood no-parking-zones. Call this number at my office. Tell them I said get you something to do."

"Ronnie, you're just a big ole' dream boat. What would I do without you?"

"I guess you'd still be l-l-looking for a job, but I take care of my friends. Want to learn how to drive a tow truck? I can't do this forever." He laughed, stuck his arm through the driver's side window of the race car prototype, and twisted the steering wheel.

"I'll do whatever it takes."

"Can you work nights at my call center," walking back to the side controls mounted on the truck bed, behind the cab.

"Your call-center? You mean that run down man-cave you guys call an office out at the Industrial Park?"

"Yeah," Ronnie said, winching the front of the car off the ground. "What's wrong with that? It's cheap, and guess what else? It's where you all's boss, Bretto, is storing these cars until the new dealership gets built up in Smithson."

"And it's near my house. It's perfect. Like I said, I need a job."

Ronnie looked at the ground, shaking his head, knowing how hard he and his friends had fought Bob in the early days, but then lost interest because of the grueling hours required for advocacy. "All this going down is dirty business, and it smells a dirty rat, Gloria. Patrick and Bob got in way over their heads. Now we get to c-c-clean up the mess," he stuttered. "Just call that number. We'll keep you busy. You'll love us after a while."

"I love you now. Thanks, Ronnie."

The side door opened and Patrick walked through it. "Morning, Ronnie."

"Morning, Patrick. We're almost done. I'll get these last three out of here, and sign off."

"Thanks," he said quietly walking through the showroom.

"What're you going to do now," he asked, while not agreeing with any of Patrick's deals, but having the understanding of what real pain felt like? "I got a bunch of lawyer buddies if you need a referral."

"No. That's ok," Patrick mumbled. "You want anything out of this place before I close it down next week? Most of this stuff is going to auction. The recession has all the other car dealers scrambling, too, so no one needs more dealership inventory."

"You got any tires and r-r-rims laying around?"

"Sure. What do you need those for?"

"The MOTrax gangs steal the tires off the cars in the MOTrax parking lots, while circling getaway-trucks wait on the call, and then make a clean getaway. The only way I can haul the cars back to the dealerships is by slapping a couple of used tires on."

"Take all you want. There's a bunch around back in the service bays."

"Thanks, Patrick. You sure you're ok."

"Yea, I'll be fine." Patrick walked by Gloria's reception desk in the center of the empty showroom and said. "Morning, Gloria."

"Hey, Patrick. Do you want any coffee?"

"No, thanks. I'll be back in my office finishing up some files."

"Ok."

Ronnie hopped in the truck, cranked it and pulled forward far enough for the back tires of the silver Salvatore to roll over the threshold. When it stopped, Ronnie hopped back out, and began to slide the double-wide glass doors back together just as the crack of a gunshot rang out from the back office.

GLOSSARY

403(b)—Defined contribution plan designed with government employees, hospitals, and non-profits in mind. Employee contributions are deducted from employee salaries with possible employer matches. 403(b)s are virtually identical to 401(k)s.

ABT—Florida Division of Alcoholic Beverage and Tobacco. The regulating body that provides liquor licenses.

Blind Pool—A type of municipal revenue-bond financing that has no stated purpose. It can be spent at the discretion of the issuing development authority.

Defined Benefit, or *Pension, Plan*—A plan whereby an employee's retirement is defined, or guaranteed, by the employer. Remnants of these plans remain almost exclusively in the governmental sector, as corporate America has been ridding themselves of the unsustainable promise for decades.

Development Authority—A politically appointed, non-elected, non-governmental conduit with the ability to issue revenue bonds without need for the taxpayer vote at the discretion of elected commissioners or council. Their singular role is to provide a conduit, or portal, for municipal investors to invest in municipal-service-centric revenue sources in consolidated real-estate parcels via purchase or eminent domain.

DROP—Deferred Retirement Option Program allowing teachers to work an additional five years, building a third pool of retirement resources in addition to pension assets, paid sick leave, and vacation time.

Fixed-Base Operator (FBO—An organization granted the right by an airport to operate at the airport and provide aeronautical services such as fueling, hangaring, tie-down and parking, aircraft rental, aircraft maintenance, flight instruction, and so on.

Florida State Attorney General—Florida's highest-level executive overseeing the state's law-enforcement agency tasked with investigations, indictments, and prosecution of criminal activity. Headquartered in Tallahassee, with a large regional office in Orlando.

FOIA—Freedom of Information Act: Financial authorities including but not limited to Port, Transportation, Development, Industrial, Downtown Development, or Sewer, have no requirement to honor, produce, or provide information when petitioned for information, aka "FOIA request," with authority referenced by the Freedom of Information Act.

Immigration and Naturalization Service (INS)—The US administration that provides pathways for the legal process of US citizenship.

General Obligation Bonds—A general obligation bond is a common type of municipal bond in the United States that is secured by a state or local government's pledge to use legally available resources, including tax revenues, to repay bond holders, usually following a vote taken via a ballot referendum with a project list attached.

Non-recourse Loan—A secured loan (debt) that is secured by a pledge of collateral, typically real property, but for which the borrower is not personally liable. If the borrower defaults, the lender can seize and sell the collateral, but if the collateral sells for less than the debt, the lender cannot seek that deficiency balance from the borrower—its recovery is limited only to the value of the collateral.

Pension Board—A body of appointed commissioners that selects investments and directs payment transfers from the general fund into the pension in years when returns underperformed the stated guaranteed rate.

Phantom Bond—A private-placement, equity-ownership transaction between a development authority and a developer's LLC. The transaction allows for developer tax incentives via the dilution of equity control relinquished to the development authority. It is used to circumvent a voter base's rejection of redevelopment powers. The circumvention is called a synthetic tax-allocation district.

Redevelopment Powers Law – Redevelopment powers can only be given to a municipality through a direct ballot referendum by the voters. It allows the municipality to create tax-allocation districts that have special tax incentives and bond issuance privileges.

Revenue Bonds—Revenue bonds are municipal bonds that finance income-producing projects and are secured by a specified revenue source. Typically, revenue bonds can be issued by any government agency or development authority.

Tax-Allocation District (TAD)—Area encompassed by a border outlining "blighted" areas.

Transit-Oriented Development (TOD)—Centrally planned urban design consisting of high-density residential apartment complexes around mass-transit stations, that form their own development authority. Their main purpose is to transfer automobile traffic to heavy-rail mass-transit systems. Multi-family apartment complex tax-allocation districts have the highest default rate in the municipal bond universe.